PETTY'S CRIME

Satan's Devils MC - Las Vegas Chapter #3

COPYRIGHT

PRODUCTION ACKNOWLEDGMENTS

Cover Design by Wicked Smart Designs

Edited and formatted by Maggie Kern @ Ms.K Edits

Proof reading by Darlene Tallman

Photographer: Golden Czermak of Furious Fotog

Model: Gus Smyrnios

DEDICATION

*Petty's Crime is dedicated to May (Queenie) Gazley.
Queenie, I love that you enjoy my books so much, and hope Petty joins
your list of favourite characters.*

SATAN'S DEVILS MC

SATAN'S DEVILS MC

———

PROLOGUE

———

"**C**lark!"

Uh-uh. Even at four years old, I know only too well what it means when my father snaps in that tone. I sniffle and brush a hand under my snotty nose, knowing I've disappointed him.

"Clark?" Daddy leans over the top of the couch. "Ah. There you are. What are you doing hiding behind there?"

I want to say *duh, hiding,* but keep that thought in my head as he uses his body to shove the couch forward a few inches, then folds his tall frame in half and manages to slide in next to me. He glances around as if to assess the suitability of my sanctuary.

My daddy. My hero. I sniffle again. I'm not frightened of him hitting me. He'd never do that. But somehow his disapproval hurts more than the smacks my friends are given to their backsides.

I know an apology is warranted, so sniffing once more, I say the words, "I-I-I'm s-s-sorry."

"Oh, Clark," he murmurs quietly. "You've got some adaptations to make, huh?"

I don't completely understand what he means, though the sentiment isn't lost. Mommy and Daddy had warned me for

1

ages that one day they were going to bring a new sister home. I watched Mommy's tummy growing bigger and bigger, and even felt excitement when I felt Leila kick inside her. Now I know I'd had no idea what the reality would be. I'd thought she'd just be there, much like the old dog we had before he got too old and disappeared from our lives. I didn't think she'd make many changes to my well-ordered life.

But as soon as Mommy had brought Leila home, the house had felt different. I got a perfunctory cuddle, but Leila took up all her time. One cry from the baby and Mommy would leave me and go deal with her. I'd missed my mommy when she'd been in the hospital, and expected she'd missed me as well. But now she's back, she seems to keep all her attention on the ugly little thing that she'd brought home.

It doesn't even look like a girl, and no one would have known had they not dressed her in pink. She doesn't do anything other than sleep or cry. I've tried, but I can't get her to smile, even when I showed her my favourite toy car. Her lip had trembled and then she'd been screaming again.

"Come here, son." Daddy's not able to fit all the way behind the couch, so I have to wriggle to get into his arms. His chuckle shows he's not completely angry with me, and his squeeze reminds me I still have at least one person on my side. "Your nose has been put all out of joint since Leila's come home, hasn't it, buddy?"

Screwing my face up, I touch my nose, but to me it feels just like it always has. My action makes Daddy's body vibrate once more.

"Listen to me. Mommy doesn't love Leila more than you, Clark, but Leila's so little, she needs more of her time. I know it's hard for you to understand."

Now it's my bottom lip that trembles. I hadn't expected Leila to be so helpless. But Leila can't feed or dress herself, or even use the potty like I can.

With his hand on my chin, Daddy turns my head so I have to

look into his eyes. "You're a big boy, Clark, and you've got a very important job to do."

I have? I turn my big watering eyes up to meet Daddy's.

"My job is to look after Mommy, and yours is to look out for your sister. You know why, buddy?" When my head moves side to side, Daddy's fingers take hold of my chin, and keep my face turned to him. "Because we're men. We're stronger than they are. Ladies need our protection."

"Even Mommy?"

He chuckles softly. "Especially Mommy."

But Mommy's so tough. Mommy rules the house when Daddy is gone. She keeps me safe, so how could she need protecting?

Daddy takes my hand and puts it on his arm. I feel his muscles bulge as he flexes them. "You'll grow up and have muscles too, buddy. And when a man uses those muscles, he can do a lot of harm."

"I didn't mean it, Daddy," I cry out, hiccupping on another sob. Even at four years old, I knew it hadn't been my finest hour when I'd shouted at Leila and tried to push her out of Mommy's arms.

"Buddy, you're a big boy now. And boys never, ever hit girls, okay? Women—girls—are there to be cherished, loved and cared for." He breaks off and gives a little laugh. "However annoying they are. You're bigger than Leila now, and you will be all your life. You'll grow up to be stronger as you're a man. It will never be right for you to push, shove, hit or hurt a girl, okay? You got that, little buddy?"

My thumb goes into my mouth as I solemnly nod my head.

He stares at me for a moment, as though trying to see into my mind. What he sees must satisfy him as he gives a rise and dip of his chin. "When I'm gone, you'll be the man of the house, and I'm trusting you to take care of both my girls."

I fling my little arms around him at the reminder of how short my time with him is. "I don't want you to go, Daddy."

He kisses the top of my head. "I don't want to leave you either." He goes still for a moment, then he shrugs. "But I've got to go." Again, he raises my head so he can look into my eyes. "I don't want to have to worry while I'm away, so I'm asking you to promise me you'll never, ever, hurt your little sister, even if she yanks your chain at times."

I try to look as intense as a four-year-old can. "I won't. Because she's a girl."

"And boys never, ever, hurt girls." He searches my face and then smiles when he's reassured I've taken that message to heart.

"I'll miss you when I go," he says, softly. "But I know I won't have to worry about my girls. Because you'll be looking out for them, won't you, little buddy?"

I give him the most earnest expression I can. "I will, Daddy. But…" my lip trembles again, "Will you hurry home?"

He sighs, and gives a small, sad, shake of his head, the gesture warning me Daddy is leaving, and he'll be gone for what seems to a little boy, to be a very long time. He's always away more than he's home.

Daddy takes my hand, pulls me out from behind the couch, takes a handkerchief out of his pocket and dries my tears. Then he leads me back to Mommy and Leila. Mommy reaches out her arm and makes room for me alongside the baby, while Daddy looks on proudly, and makes a comment about his perfect family. Softly, in a tone meant not for my ears, he tells Mommy he wishes to fuck he didn't have to go.

The next morning, Daddy puts on his uniform, grabs his duffle and says his goodbyes. Before he leaves, he crouches down, shakes my hand, and admonishes me to remember the promises I'd made. Then he hugs me tightly to him, holding on for a few seconds. "Make me proud, buddy," he says before pulling away.

When he stands and opens the door, I think he's reluctant to go.

I don't want him to leave, but something warns me I need to

be strong. None of my wishes would magically make him able to stay. So I stand, holding Mommy's hand and try hard not to cry. In his absence, I would be the man of the house.

But Daddy didn't hurry home. He never came back at all. As far as my child's mind could understand, he was killed by a baddie in a faraway war, and as a hero, fighting for his country.

Time passed, and our depleted family settled into a routine. Mommy gradually stopped being so sad, and Daddy was no longer part of every conversation. Eventually, the day came when I had difficulty remembering his features anymore, and had to rely on photographs rather than my memory. Leila grew up and was annoying as fuck, always pushing her boundaries, but while my recollections of him had faded, one thing I never forgot. I stayed true to the last promise I'd shared with my daddy. However much my sister annoyed me, I always turned the other cheek. She grew to take advantage, pushing her luck, taunting me, safe in the knowledge I'd never fight back.

I couldn't. Daddy had asked one thing of me, and that I never could forget. *Ladies are to be loved, cherished and protected.*

I was determined to live my life honouring the promise I made. I wanted to make my daddy proud.

CHAPTER ONE

RoseLyn

"**M**isogynistic, chauvinistic, arrogant, obnoxious dick." Throwing myself down on the couch in my dressing room, I feel my hands clenching into fists. "Honestly, I could swing for that man."

Snorting, my stylist, Kylie, grins widely. "Why not say what you really mean?"

In a totally adult gesture, I stick out my tongue, causing her to shake her head and laugh. "If you feel that strongly, why don't you tell Bart that you don't get on with your bodyguard?"

It's a sensible suggestion, but raising a hand, I wave it off. "I don't have to like him, Ky."

Theatrically sighing, she makes a gimme gesture with her hands. "Tell me what he's done now."

I exhale air in an equally dramatic fashion. "He treats me as if I'm stupid." I lean forward. "I'm not even sure he likes women."

"He's gay?" Her eyes widen.

"Fuck no." I scoff. "He's a man's man. And not in that way," I add hastily, seeing the beginnings of her grin. "It's like he doesn't think I can think for myself." Shaking my head, I continue, "It's me who's at risk. Me, who my ex wants to hurt. I don't need him dotting the i's and crossing the t's all the time. I know the danger is very real." I pause. "Honestly, his attitude makes me want to show him the finger and walk off just to spite him."

She rolls her eyes. "That would be plain stupid." She doesn't need to see my nod, confirming that I'm very well aware. "I think you should talk to Bart. You could grow careless if you don't trust your bodyguard."

But while sometimes I wonder whether Petty really believes there's a crazed man who's got it in for me, I can't fault the way he does his job. I doubt anyone could get past him, and that's the kind of security that I need. I shrug. "Though in his mind the jury's still out on whether the threat is real, he's certainly acting as if it is. What more can I ask?"

"He clearly winds you up." She studies me for a moment after making her observation, but when my shoulders rise and lower dismissively, she goes to the wardrobe and pulls out a dress from the rack. "This is what we're going with tonight, isn't it?"

Nodding at her selection, I tell her, "I don't have to get along with my bodyguard. I'm no Whitney." I chuckle at the comparison. "As long as he does what he's paid to do, what he thinks or his character shouldn't matter to me." Sitting forward, I sigh. "And I'm bringing enough trouble to Bart. He's gone out of his way to organise protection for me. Seems pretty *petty*," I huff a laugh at the irony, "of me to complain."

Brushing out imaginary creases, Kylie shakes her head. "You're his bread and butter, RoseLyn. Bart's got a vested interest in you staying happy and healthy." She gives me a serious stare. "*I* know you're in danger, and so does Bart."

As if the mention of his name has summoned the devil, a rap-pitty-tap knock comes at the door. Kylie and I exchange grins when the familiar sound is followed up with, "Are you decent in there?"

Kylie hangs up the dress again and goes over to open the door. "Why don't you come in, Bart?"

Preceded by his middle-age paunch, my fifty-something and unashamedly gay manager steps inside the room. Approaching with an assessing look, he crouches in front of me. "You holding up okay, RoseLyn?"

Kylie's narrowing eyes find mine and her hands go to her hips. "Is there something you should have told me, babe?"

I grimace. "Just more of the same." Strangely enough, I'd have been more upset if my bodyguard hadn't riled me up. My horror at yet another intrusion into my life had been put on the back burner with the comments Petty had made.

My stylist stares at me accusingly. "Why am I just hearing about this? And what was it this time? Heavy-breathing phone call? Mysterious flower delivery—"

I butt in before she can list everything that's ever happened to me. "An 'in deepest sympathy' card left on my windshield."

"They're going to have to swap out your rental again." Bart, as usual, focuses on the practicalities.

Sitting back on the couch, I fold my arms. "Again being the operative word. Whatever I do, Bart, he's one step in front of me." It's annoying how clever my ex has become, though my view is that he made some contacts in jail.

He's totally mad, of course. His gifts range from things expressing how much he still loves me, to threats about how I'm going to feel when he catches up with me again.

I know it's my ex's access to information that draws Petty to think I'm making it all up. When I hire a new car, within days, or even hours in some cases, he seems to know exactly what make and model I'm driving. Same with my house. When I moved to evade him, a letter turned up in my new mailbox the very next day. I don't know how he's finding everything out. I'm just worried that he does.

"Petty said you looked shaken," Bart continues, eyeing me carefully.

Petty should mind his own fucking business. "I'm fine," I lie. Getting a death threat, which I interpret the card as, is never pleasant. I know the blood had drained from my face when I'd opened the envelope—carefully, of course, always conscious for fingerprints that my ex has so far been too clever to leave. It could only be him, but as far as the police are concerned, they need proof to proceed.

I huff to myself, noting Bart's phrasing. Petty had said I'd *looked* shaken, not that I actually was. Does he think I'm that good of an actor?

Mine is the sad, typical story of women who can't see what's in front of their faces. I got into a relationship with a man who seemed so perfect for me, so caring and loving. I jumped in with both feet. Then I discovered his controlling side and his jealousy. I wasn't buying what he was selling, and the first time he hit me, I called it a day.

But women don't walk out on Saul Ranger, as I found to my cost. He followed me, caught me, and beat me up so badly, I was in the hospital for a week. It didn't have the desired effect of making me go back to him. Instead, I brought charges, and he ended up in jail.

And now he's free, he's coming after me for revenge.

I'm a no-name singer who's been lucky enough to score a residency at a fancy casino in Las Vegas, an opening act for the major stars who the customers really come in to see. But from the day I first started two months ago, I've had someone stalking me.

At first, I just brushed it off, thinking it was probably a fan who had an unhealthy obsession. I'd even been flattered that I was apparently worth so much attention. But then the threats became more pointed and personal. That it coincided with Saul being released was what had alerted me, and I know the type of mental games that he plays. He's taunting me like a cat playing with a mouse, and one day soon, he'll jump in for the kill.

It was when I'd only just managed to jump out of the way of a truck heading straight for me that Bart decided we had to take things seriously.

The cops would do nothing. They couldn't find evidence that Saul had entered the state. I got the impression that the bored lieutenant who'd interviewed me wasn't convinced that I wasn't making everything up for attention.

I was torn. I didn't want Saul to have more influence on my life, but neither was I going to give him another opportunity to hurt me. So I'd agreed with Bart we needed to do something about it until he could be caught and again sent away.

It had been my lucky day when Bart had approached me with an offer to manage my career. In him, I'd found someone who believed in me. It was down to him that I was given this chance. He believes in me, and that this is only a steppingstone to my making it in the big time. Wanting to protect the investment of his time and unwilling to lose the money that comes along with managing me, Bart had decided the threats were serious enough to employ someone to provide protection.

Did I mention I'm not one of the major stars? Well, I'm certainly not someone used to having security wherever they go. Being very far from famous, until now, I could get away with living off the strip, and doing most of my everyday stuff without anyone recognising or bothering me. I do, or did, my own grocery shopping, without fear of being stopped and asked for my autograph. I still could, were it not for the fear that Saul could leap out and confront me.

My bank account, and Bart's, thanks to me, is reasonably healthy, but I attract nothing like the dollars that major stars make. Hence, we couldn't afford to go to a reputable company. Bart used his contacts with the various casinos and found an outfit that would provide their services relatively cheaply.

He'd come up with an organisation that had been in the security business for some time, and who had recently landed a good contract with one of the casinos. But what they hadn't done before was provide personal protection services. It seemed it was something they wanted to get into, and so this was an opportunity which benefitted us both. This was a good opening for them, and, as it gave them experience and hopefully a good reputation—as long as I'm alive at the end of it—it came at a relatively low cost for me.

That's how come I'm now guarded by a rotation of men from the Las Vegas chapter of the Satan's Devils MC.

Blend into the background they certainly don't, nor do they wear the kind of uniform of bodyguards you've come to expect to see in movies. No, they don't come complete with black suits, and dour but clean-shaven faces with earpieces in their ears. Oh no, not at all. My bodyguards? Well, they're tattooed leather-wearing bikers, whose adornments might run to studs and earrings and chains which attach wallets to their belts.

At the very least, their presence should dissuade Saul from messing with me.

I've three members assigned, all of whom are vets, and each taking eight-hour shifts. Their names are Petty, Sarge and Roller. Each of these men shadow me everywhere I go, and even stay in my house while I sleep. As well as having someone with me at all times, back at the Satan's Devils' base, other members are trying to solve the problem that has so far stumped the police—that being where the hell is Saul?

Saul wants to hurt me. There's no more mystery than that. I got away from him and he doesn't like it. While I acknowledge the suggestion it could be someone else, I don't give any weight to it. I live comfortably but have no savings. If I died, no one would benefit from my death. To my knowledge, I haven't upset anyone. It has to be Saul. There is no one else.

Up until two weeks ago, I'd been trying to deal with it myself, but my growing fear and nervousness was affecting how I was performing on stage. I started forgetting lyrics and musical cues. When Bart and Kylie had found me crying in the dressing room, scared to go home, Bart was determined something had to change.

Over the past week, I've had to get used to always having someone with me. It's done wonders for my peace of mind.

While it's not nice knowing my ex is out there and is fixated on me, having now worked with the Devils for a while, I know he wouldn't get past them. The feeling of safety has helped me get my head back into the game. I also have more confidence that the Devils will eventually track him down than I have in the police.

Sarge is great. When Petty takes me home after my performance, he's already waiting in my modest house, having made sure there are no nasty surprises waiting for me. He's been quite open about the fact he suffers from PTSD, and has difficulty sleeping in the dark, so volunteers for all night-time shifts. He's a perfect houseguest—clean, tidies up after himself, and never bothers me.

Roller takes over at eight am and is my companion for most of the day. I worry about how boring it must be. I don't have a very interesting life. I attend rehearsals, shop and keep my house clean, just like any normal person, but he never complains, just follows me around stoically. He's ever vigilant, his eyes scanning everywhere, and even at home, he takes regular turns around my yard.

Then, there's Petty.

If I've any complaints, they are all about him. Unlike Sarge and Roller, he voices his opinions and quite loudly. He has no patience with anyone, including me. He's pretty to look at, there's no denying that, but what's between his ears is twisted and dark. Earlier today, my gay hairdresser was trying to be friendly to him and Petty called him a pervert. Sure, he'd yanked his chain by suggesting they'd look good together, but there was no reason for Petty to respond as curtly as he had. It hadn't surprised me. Around Bart, he acts as if my manager has something that could be catching, keeping his distance and any interaction to a minimum.

Bart clears his throat, the sound putting a stop to my mind's ramblings. "If you're really okay, RoseLyn, I'd better go and let you get ready. Petty's right outside." I'm not sure if he mentions the bodyguard's presence to warn or to comfort me.

Shaking myself out of my reverie, I push myself up straight. "I'm fine, Bart. You go, and Kylie will work her magic and get me ready for the stage."

After one last assessing look at me, as if to reassure himself that I'm really going to be fine to go out and earn us both some money tonight, with a mock salute, he goes to the door. Even with it closed, I can hear him issuing instructions to my bodyguard.

"Anyone standing outside will be able to hear anything we talk about," Kylie reminds me with a smirk.

I shrug, knowing she's alluding to my outburst when I'd entered the room. But Petty probably didn't need to hear the opinion I spat out about him as I've left him in no ignorance to my views. I doubt he'll be bothered, as he doesn't seem to have any respect for me either.

I can't, however, criticise his professionalism at his job. As long as he keeps me safe from Saul getting close enough to throw acid in my face, knife me or shoot me, then I won't complain. And yes, those are some of the threats which Saul has so tactfully made. All preventable though, were I stupid enough to return to him. Yeah, right. If I did that, my week's stint in the hospital would probably end up feeling like a short vacation once he got me in his clutches again.

A part of me feels sorry for Petty as he's drawn the short straw, or perhaps it could be the long one if his preference is to be in with the greater chance of seeing some action. I'm most exposed during the times I'm between my dressing room and stage, when I'm performing, and at the end of my show when I stop to greet the few fans who are waiting for autographs.

I let Kylie dress me as though she's clothing a dress-up doll, squeezing me into a spandex glittery gold sheath, and making sure my tits are securely taped and positioned to make the most of my cleavage. Standing stoically, I let her make sure everything's secure, so when I shimmy and prance on the stage, I'll have no wardrobe malfunction.

Kylie's great, and since we've been together, I've had no slips of my boobs or anything else. As usual, I watch transfixed at my reflection in the mirror as the girl next door gradually transforms into someone I don't recognise. When she applies my makeup and sweeps back my hair into yet another impressive style, I have to blink my eyes to make sure I am indeed still looking at myself.

"Don't you ever go work for someone else, you hear me, Ky?"

"Aw, you love me." She mock blows a kiss at my reflection.

"I mean it." I do. Not in a girl crush way, but she's got a magical touch in how she prepares me for the stage. As a result, I go out knowing I look the part of a star even when I may not be feeling it.

Kylie shakes her head. "Feeling's mutual girl. Where else would I find someone so open to my ideas? I've worked for divas before, RoseLyn, and I much prefer working for someone like yourself."

She's my stylist, I trust her. Why would I try to override her opinions when I pay her to make me look good?

With makeup and hair done, my dress smoothed down and checked with Kylie's expert eye, I slip my feet into the five-inch heels, which I know will make my feet ache later tonight.

"You'll do," she pronounces finally, then shoos me in the direction of the door. "Now go knock 'em dead. Oh, and try not to kill your bodyguard."

Grinning, I toss her a look that says I don't promise anything, then step out into the corridor where Petty is waiting for me. His eyes take me in from head to toe, then he sneeringly looks away with a shake of his head.

I'm a confident woman. I don't need approval from him. I content myself by smiling sweetly while gritting my teeth.

Petty's right at my back as we walk through the hallways.

When we approach backstage, he indicates I should stay back so he can check the area out first. Then he beckons me forward to where I greet my band. The instruments are all set up, ready but hidden from the audience by the glittery curtain.

"Ready?" the stage manager asks.

The band goes to their instruments while I position myself. I take my normal deep steadying breaths, then raise my chin and respond, "Ready."

As the curtains start to part, a loud voice thunders over the speakers. "Ladies and gentlemen, may I present our very own RoseLyn."

The announcement is my starting pistol. Despite the height of my shoes, I run out onto the stage, waving at the unseen crowd behind the spotlights. I go to the microphone and sweep it off its stand.

"Good evening, Vegas."

I give them a moment as the greeting is returned to me. The number of voices raised suggests it's going to be a good night, and I turn to see Bart looking out from the wings and giving a double thumbs-up. Then, I turn slightly and see Petty with a blank look of boredom on his face.

Fuck him.

As the first beats of the drum get my blood coursing through my veins and the rift of the guitar intro counts me in, I place my lips close to the microphone and let myself go.

CHAPTER TWO

Petty

Christ, *that woman can sing.* I didn't anticipate being impressed the first time I heard her. I'd expected a sound like the sweet girl next door, or maybe the twang of a country singer. I wasn't prepared for the raw, husky voice that's worthy of Janis Joplin. It always surprises me where that comes from, as she doesn't smoke from what I've seen.

Unfortunately, I'm not paid to watch her. My focus has to be on the audience, and in the wings, though, while I'll never admit it to her face, I actually love it when my surveillance takes in the stage for a moment.

It's the only time I allow myself to look at her, and for those few seconds, I'm as much in a trance as everyone else while she's strutting her stuff, bellowing out those songs with so much emotion, and moving that body so smoothly and sexily to the beat.

Off the stage, she's the type of woman who doesn't appeal to me. I prefer women to be small and curvy. I stand six foot two, and in those killer heels, RoseLyn is almost as tall as me. The whole reason we're here is that she didn't give a man a second chance and left him, or tried to, the very first time he hit her. That's one thing to admire about her.

Despite how she comes across in those dresses, she's not a feminine woman at all. She knows her own mind and isn't afraid to say what she means.

Nah, the word feminine can better be applied to that ass of a manager she has. Still, he's obviously got her best interest at heart, and it didn't take me long to dismiss him as the one being in league with her ex. Somebody has to be. It's worrying how her stalker always seems to be one step ahead. Unless it's an inside job, in that RoseLyn's planting everything herself, presumably as a cry for attention.

Still, I'm the only hangout who harbours suspicion the stalker might not exist, and not wanting to be caught napping on the job, do my duties as though he's very real.

On meeting her, RoseLyn definitely doesn't seem the victim type, and you have to wonder at the balls of the man who'd tried to break her. She works out daily in the gym and has muscles that could put many a man's to shame—another reason I don't find her attractive. I like soft whereas she's all hard. Sometimes I've wondered how she was persuaded she needs protection. I've seen her hitting a punch bag and have to admire her form.

She's brash, direct and doesn't take shit from anyone, including from me—though I wouldn't tell her, I find that amusing.

If the story about her ex hadn't checked out, I'd have been disbelieving that RoseLyn had been a victim of abuse. I just know I'm hoping he does exist and tries something on my shift. I wouldn't be able to keep my hands off him. No man ever hits a woman, whatever the provocation. Even if living with someone like RoseLyn had led him to distraction, he shouldn't have tried to bring her to heel by using his fists.

My eyes scan the auditorium once more, then I allow them a moment to settle on the stage. I swallow a couple of times at how magnificent she is. It's lucky that once that makeup's been removed and she's transformed back into something else, I can easily forget this weird attraction she holds for me.

Fortunately, I don't have to like her as I'm not here by choice. I'm only here as my club picked up the contract for providing her with bodyguard services, and oh lucky me, I raised my hand and got picked for the job.

The job I'm supposed to be doing. Dragging my eyes away from the stage, I survey the audience instead. My personal feelings toward her aren't a consideration. I'm here to keep her safe, and to make sure no one who shouldn't gets near her.

I've voiced my question about whether we're really looking for her ex or just a run-of-the-mill stalker, or anyone at all, to Prez and my brothers when we've discussed this assignment in church. I'm apparently out on the limb for doubting there's a real threat. But, as Prez said, even if I'm right, we're making bank while protecting her, and as long as she doesn't end up dead, it's all credit to us.

I'm not letting my doubts influence how I protect her, even if it's against an imaginary danger. If I think I'm wasting my time, I'll keep that to myself.

If her stalker is her ex, as she's convinced, I have to wonder why we haven't found a trace of him. The cops have fuck all, and despite Keys using all his abilities and even leaning on the tech experts at the Utah chapter, we, ourselves, are no further forward. It's like Saul's dropped off the face of the earth. I think we'd all be happier if we found him living it up in Alaska or some other distance state.

In the meantime, I'm not certain everything adds up, and there's still that possibility that RoseLyn is making the whole stalker thing up. Take that card I found on her windshield earlier —she'd only got that rental yesterday. She could have easily put that there herself. Why? Now if I had a concrete answer, maybe it would confirm my doubts. But the only reason I can think of is that it makes her appear more important and exciting than she is. Maybe she gets a kick out of having strong men around her? Perhaps it's a ploy to get her more noticed in the business. Huh. What do I know about up-and-coming singers? My knowledge could probably be written on the back of a postage stamp. But why should I care? My club gets paid whether the stalker is real or not.

Maybe some people would see the Satan's Devils getting into security more as a case of the fox knowing how best to guard the hen house, and there's probably some truth in that. Whatever. When asked whether the club wanted to expand its security business to provide personal protection services, it had seemed a no-brainer. In recent years, our skills in the security arena have been recognised and we're getting more business as a result. Which means whatever lies at the bottom of RoseLyn's problems, Prez is convinced this is our steppingstone into getting more close protection work, and therefore, I need to ensure nothing, real or imagined, gets close to her.

Of course, our security business, our previous money winner, is now only secondary to the new main business of the club, having recently become partners in the Lucky Fortunes Casino. But instead of sitting back and relying on one source of income, we've agreed diversification is our strength and we're not going to give up on any of our other endeavours.

Needing to pull my weight, to regain some of the respect I'd lost recently, including having my ass handed to me by Prez in the ring, I'd volunteered to take part in our first foray into bodyguarding, knowing there was no option other than for it to be a success. I also accepted that while there didn't have to be mutual respect between guard and guardee, it came as a surprise to find I actually disliked the woman I've been asked to protect.

A test for certain. A close protection officer should be prepared to step in front of a bullet to save their mark, and while I'd lay down my life for any of my brothers, I'd be hard pressed to want to do it for her. After some soul searching, I'd decided saving her would be an extension of saving my club, and if my life ended up on the line, I'd go easy, knowing it was for them. Our new business venture wouldn't go far if our first customer ended up dead.

Yeah, I really don't like her.

But that voice. Listening to her makes me forget her other shortcomings.

Despite my efforts, my eyes are drawn back to the woman who comes to life on the stage. She fucking owns it. She gives every ounce of her energy during her performance, and for that, even I have to admire her. Having escorted her every night back to her dressing room, I know she returns exhausted and drained.

I can't understand why she's only a support act, and not the headline of the day, but maybe she's not everyone's taste. Some of the fuckers in the audience aren't even looking her way. It makes me want to shake them and tell them to pay attention. Instead, it's my own head I shake as I remind myself, I don't care either way.

Time to do my rounds. Catching his eye, I indicate to one of the casino's security guards that I'm going to take a stroll and check things out from the ground. He nods back, showing he'll watch the stage area while I'm away. We've been doing this dance for two weeks now, and have it well choreographed.

Angling my way around the tables, I surreptitiously let my eyes rest on the patrons in turn. Some I recognise as having been in before, others are obviously visitors to Vegas, in for some entertainment that doesn't require losing money at the tables. There are a few guys who seem to be paying RoseLyn particular interest, but if her performance gets me to overlook her short-comings in all other ways, how can I blame them for enjoying the show she's putting on? If she wasn't able to command such attention, she wouldn't have a job.

I've studied pictures of her ex and can tell he's nowhere around. But I have to stay vigilant just in case it's not him, but someone else. Not for the first time, I think how identifying a stalker is like looking for a needle in a haystack without having any clues to go on. If he even exists, that is.

Having done my walk around and not having noticed someone carrying a gun or something labelled "bomb", I return to the stage, show security I've got it from here, and then lean back, folding my arms, more convinced than ever she's created this fiction herself.

I suppose it's a plus I enjoy watching her move and hearing her sing. At least it makes my role less boring. I don't mind the hours standing sentry outside her door. I'm a vet. I've had boring duties before. It's the babysitting parts that I hate. The times when I'm forced into close proximity to her and have to bite my tongue, sometimes not very successfully. She's under no illusion that there's anything about her of which I approve, and I hadn't needed to overhear her outburst to her stylist earlier to know she can say the same about me. My lips curve slightly. At least we've one thing in common—our mutual feelings about each other.

Another night passes, another dollar earned. She finishes her set, then under my eagle eyes, signs autographs for those who want them. When that's done, she goes back to her dressing room and transforms herself from superstar to girl next door. I drive her home in complete silence, and when we arrive, as expected, Sarge is waiting.

Sarge has PTSD and I know he sometimes struggles with his limitations to what he can give back to the MC. He can't cope with loud noises or the dark. When he needs rest, he naps during the day. But these drawbacks make him the ideal candidate for the graveyard shift as there's no danger of him falling asleep. It makes this an excellent opportunity for him. He wouldn't be able to swap shifts with me. There's no way he'd be able to cope with being with her while she's on stage, not with the noise levels in the auditorium.

On my part, I'd find watching her while she was sleeping boring. Give me the chance of some action any day.

Having successfully passed off my responsibilities, I swap the SUV for my bike and enjoy the ride through the darkened streets back to the clubhouse. Near the strip, Sin City never sleeps, but here on the outskirts, there's a distinct difference between night and day, and for part of the time, mine's the only vehicle on the road.

Wind in my hair, pavement under my wheels, and I can forget all my worries as the engine rumbles between my thighs. Riding is a balm to the senses, and a chance to put everything else in the rearview. As I ride, I leave all thoughts about RoseLyn behind, locked up neatly until the next day when I'll need to turn the key and pick them up again.

I have a couple of drinks, share a few jokes and exaggerated tales with Hammer and Cobra, then go to bed.

When I go to sleep, I dream of a nightingale with a rasping voice, singing songs in my head. It's certainly not the lingering remnants of that vision that makes me wake with a hard-on. Not at all. No, that's just morning wood.

The sun shining straight onto my face rouses me earlier than I wanted, and I open my eyes, wishing I'd remembered to close the fucking blind before I laid my head down. I turn over, but now awake, can't settle again.

So I start my day earlier than expected, and that's just the start of everything going wrong. I've eaten my breakfast and returned to my room, pondering whether as I'm not due back on bodyguard duties until four pm, whether to make the most of my unexpected free hours and go lose myself on the road, when my phone rings.

It's an unknown caller, but my second mistake is to ignore that and answer. My whole body tenses when I accept the call from the penitentiary.

"Hey, Clark." The use of my government name doesn't help me relax, nor does the voice I never expected to hear again.

"Britney," I respond, cautiously, pronouncing it how she always preferred me to do with the 'e' sounding like an 'a'.

"I got an early release. They're letting me out on parole."

And she's calling me, why? I couldn't give a fuck whether she's being let out or not. My silence prompts her to continue speaking.

"Can you come pick me up tomorrow at ten?"

My hand starts to shake and I have to grip hard to keep hold of the phone. My ass hits the bed as my legs give way while my brain tries to process what the fuck is going on. *She wants me to pick her up? Demanding it, in fact, as if it's her right?* The shock makes me stammer. "Y-y-you didn't let me visit. I-I-I haven't s-s-seen or h-h-heard from you in s-s-seven years." *Hell, could I sound any weaker?*

Her voice takes on that what I'd hoped was a long forgotten familiar whine. "Clark. I didn't want you to visit me inside. I couldn't stand you seeing me that way. But I didn't sign the divorce papers you sent in, so that means I'm still your wife."

My palms sweat, and my head feels dizzy. That's the little fact I've tried to overlook over the years, thinking it was an omission and not an ulterior motive.

Out of sight, out of mind. While she's been locked up, I've been living and enjoying life as a single man. I tried to set things straight, had the divorce papers sent to her, but as she's just reminded me, while I'd done my part, I'd kind of overlooked that she hadn't done hers. That important document remains unsigned. Technically, we are still married, whether I want to be or not. As the realisation sinks in, I know if anyone was around to take my blood pressure, it would be off the fucking charts.

This can't be happening, can it?

As the phone threatens to slip out of my hand, I realise my palms are sweating, and there's a tremble in my grip. Just her voice sends me back to the man I was seven years ago. But just as she's apparently done her time, so have I. The difference being is that I've moved on, and I'm no longer the man I once was. Or I've tried very hard to become someone else.

I'm a biker, a member of a one-percenter MC. I'm feared and respected in equal measures and answer to no one except my club and my prez. Yet just hearing her voice is threatening every-thing I've built.

My jaw clenches. I swallow hard and speak slowly and deliberately so I don't stammer over any more words. "I don't think it's a good idea." That's putting it mildly. It's a fucking terrible idea.

In return, her voice drips with emotion. "Honey, I've changed. I promise you. I've worked hard inside. That was part of the reason I didn't want to see you. I wanted to wait until I got myself sorted out. I… I never stopped loving you, Clark, and I'm still your wife."

I'm still your wife. How can four simple words have such an effect? My hands fist, my phone in danger of being crushed.

For seven years I'd thought I was free. My chest feels like a weight's been dropped on it and for a moment, I can't breathe. I don't know how to deal with it. I want to tell her to go fuck herself, but she's right, she's still my wife. And as such, much as I want to deny them, I have obligations.

I'd rather deal with a bullet to my brain.

A hell of a lot has happened in the time she's been gone. She was the one who refused my visits, letters and calls, so it's her fault there are things she doesn't know. It probably won't come as a surprise that I'm no longer in the Army, but not what I've done since I've been out. Not least, I'm no longer in the same state that she is.

"I can't come and pick you up."

"Why not?" she snaps. The hardening of her tone makes my jaw tighten.

"Because I'm too fuckin' far away," I spit back, then swallow hard, trying to cool my temper.

She digests that for a moment, then asks, "You are still in North Carolina, aren't you?"

"Nah." When I served, I was based at Fort Bragg. I left that in my rearview years ago. "I got out. I'm in Vegas now." And a member of the Satan's Devils MC.

"Vegas?" A swift mood change, as now I hear the smile in her tone. "That sounds exciting. But, honey, that means you won't be able to collect me. I'll need some money if I'm going to join you there."

My eyes flick around my room, assessing the life I've built for myself. The life that Britney might well be about to destroy if I let her into it. But what choice have I got? While I'd cut off my right arm to have the strength to tell her to get lost and that she's getting nothing from me, I just can't do it. She's still my wife, however much I don't want her to be.

Still, I try to dissuade her. "You sure that's what you want to do? You'll know no one here—"

"After seven years, I have no friends here either," she's quick to respond. "So Vegas sounds good. A fresh start. I'll have to sweet talk them here and get them to change my parole officer, but I'll be joining my husband, so there's not much they can object to."

Isn't there? I don't think an ex-felon's parole is best served if she's living with an outlaw MC. It's on the tip of my tongue to tell her that my circumstances have changed, and that the law would probably regard me as a criminal, maybe an easy out for me. But I lose my chance when she interrupts my thoughts.

"Honey, I can't talk any longer. I've got to go. Just send me the money and I'll let you know when my flight is due to land. Love you, Clark."

Then she's gone. I end the call, feeling sweat bead on my brow, totally unable to process that in twenty-four hours, I'll be back with *my wife*. I feel the sentence she was given is ending as mine is about to start. But how can I turn my back on her when she still wears my ring?

Love you, Clark. Her parting words echo in my mind.

I loved her once. I loved her even when she went inside, unable to process she'd been taken away. I would have stood by her, but she broke off contact. That had given me time and space to escape the thrall she'd held me in, and eventually come to realise that fate, or her felony, had done me a good turn. I sure as fuck don't love her today, nor can I see myself doing so again.

As for her declaration, I'm not sure if there was ever any truth in it, and that she does so still holds no ring of truth. It was her who, by omission, had signalled our relationship was in the past.

Why the fuck didn't I pursue the papers not being signed? The answer's easy. Because I assumed she'd never want to come back.

Realising I'm still holding the phone, I place it down and put my head into my hands. The truth hits me. I doubt she wants to return to me now, but probably needs a place to land, somewhere to serve out her parole and get her life back on course.

That must be it. We were only ever together for eight months, and that kind of whirlwind romance doesn't withstand an absence of years. She's saying words that she probably thinks I need to hear without any emotion behind them.

That makes more sense, and, thanks to her, I'm used to being used. Maybe it won't be too terrible to help get her feet back onto solid ground and then get that well-deserved divorce.

This doesn't have to be a life sentence.

I stand, breathing a little easier, feeling I've got myself back into some semblance of control.

Though it's not sufficient to stop my fist rising, seemingly of its own volition, and putting a hole in the drywall. As I watch the particles of loosened plaster flutter down, I realise my state of calm was only fleeting.

Fuck, fuck and fuck again.

Why Britney?

And why, now?

CHAPTER THREE

Petty

The pain in my fist brings me to my senses as it dawns on me, even if I accept that fate without putting up a fight about it, Britney can't just waltz into my life. One look around my bedroom which doesn't even have the luxury of a private bathroom, reminds me it's really not the place to bring my wife. And cooped up in close proximity would drive us both mad. After seven years, she's little more than a stranger. And far more important, her new address would not be considered appropriate by her parole officer.

It might seem weird, but I'm not looking forward to the intimacy or sex on tap. When I'd first met her, Britney got my engine revving, there's no denying that, but that was in the past, years back. Would I even still find her attractive? And what about me? I'm hardly the clean-cut soldier she married. My hair's grown out and I've allowed scruff to grow on my face. I have tattoos. I wear a cut and my most prized possession is my motorbike.

She's not going to think I've made much of my life. No, the riches I have would not appeal to her. She'd think nothing of the family and brotherhood which mean the world to me.

If she was meeting me for the first time, I doubt she'd give me a second glance.

If I've changed so much, I expect she has too. What does she look like now? Have the years been kind? Back then, she'd been every man's wet dream, and it so happened I was the lucky fucker who took her home. Unwilling to lose her, I'd put a ring on her finger fast.

It hadn't been long before everything soured. What's the saying? Marry in haste, repent in leisure? It couldn't be truer in my case.

But thinking over the mistakes of the past aren't helping with anything practical now. Fuck it. In twenty-four hours, Britney will be back by my side, and she'll be expecting her husband to provide. I haven't thought of myself as a married man in a very long time.

Therein lies my first fucking problem. Neither does anyone else.

Fuck, shit and damnation.

Tangling my hands in my hair, I tighten my grip and pull hard as though another bite of pain is going to knock more sense into me. I can't see beyond panicking right now. Blood's rushing through my veins so fast it's causing a buzzing in my ears.

Could I run? Start a new life somewhere where no one, let alone Britney, will ever find me?

Chances of that are fucking slim. The MC wouldn't look kindly on one of their own taking off without explanation, and if they caught up with me, a wife would be the last of my worries. Leaving my brothers in the lurch would not be rewarded with a pat on the back. Red still views me with suspicion after the crap that went down with his kid, and I'm still not on solid ground. Christ. Is he going to see my omission as a lie to the club? I shudder as chills go down my spine.

I can't lose the club. I can't let Britney chase me away from the best thing that's ever happened to me. This MC has done more for me than anyone I've ever known. It's not just a club, it's a brotherhood. I earned my way in with toil, sweat and blood and I'm not going to give it all up without a fight. I'm loyal to my club as, hopefully, overlooking my sometimes questionable behaviour, they are to me.

Except... I wince. I've kept a big fucking secret from everyone and now it's all going to come out.

I don't see it as a lie. I didn't hold back the fact deliberately. Maybe it had been wishful thinking, but I'd never dreamed I'd hear from Britney again. I never thought for a moment she'd ever want to come back. I'd taken the message I'd thought she'd given to me and left her in my rearview. I'd lived the life of a single man because that's who I believed I was.

It's her who went incommunicado for seven fucking years.

Jesus. All I'm doing is standing here, literally pulling my hair out. *Think, man, think.* Giving myself a mental slap, I know where I've got to start. I've got to bite the bullet and go straight to the top. I've got to come clean to Prez.

Decision made, before I can have second thoughts and seriously start googling whether people run away to join the circus anymore, I stomp to my door, throw it open and walk out. My feet clang down the metal staircase, catching the attention of the prospect, Owl, who glances up, his eyes sharpening in case I need anything. I give him a dismissive wave and force my feet in the direction of Prez's office.

So wound up and refusing to let myself think of any excuse to delay this moment, I throw open his office door after a perfunctory knock, *then* beat a hasty retreat. The vision I see for a split second seared on my eyeballs, of Red on his knees in front of his old lady.

"Get your ass in here," Red's voice thunders.

Gingerly, I turn the doorknob again and glance through the crack, peering cautiously between my fingers, having no desire to see my prez's naked ass. I note that Red hasn't moved, but I also see what I hadn't noticed before, that both are fully clothed. Red gives a glance behind him, grins widely, then turns back.

After placing a kiss to his wife's rounded stomach, he slowly gets to his feet.

He lays his hand against Cher's cheek and gazes into her eyes with such love that although I might not be interrupting an intimate sexual moment, I feel as great an intruder at the emotional connection between them.

Rising on tiptoe, she kisses his lips. "I'll let you know if he starts moving again."

"Do that," Red says softly. "This time, I want to be here for everything."

I shouldn't be witnessing an example of a happy family unit when I've none of my own and don't expect to. The blessing for Britney and me was that we never had kids. Red, though, already has one he didn't know about until the kid was fifteen, through no fault of his or Cher's, and now another's on the way and, if my recollection is right, should be here in about four months. No wonder he's determined to be involved for the birth of this child.

Even while I'm wondering if I can use their moment as an excuse to delay this meeting, my brain glues my feet to the floor. I have no alternative. I'm racing against time and much as I want it to, ignoring my problem is not going to make it disappear.

Red's eyes are soft as they follow his woman out of the door, but harden when they land on me, swapping from loving husband to MC prez in an instant.

"Whatcha need?" He waves me to a seat in front of his desk and takes his chair behind it.

I sit, then clasp my hands between my knees, thinking perhaps I should have taken a moment to decide on the story that puts me in the best light without just diving in. I'm already on shaky ground with Red for my past behaviour.

Red sits back, linking his hands behind his head. He gives me a moment, then getting impatient, he narrows his eyes and prompts, "Everything okay with RoseLyn?"

For a second, I don't know what he's talking about. Since

speaking to Britney, everything else has been wiped from my mind. Quickly, I pull myself together and shrug. I haven't hidden that I don't one hundred percent believe her, and don't want him thinking I've rocked the boat.

"All's fine on that front." For a second, I wonder whether she's made a complaint about me. But apart from not mollycoddling her, I've done my job well enough. Thinking about the prima donna makes my mouth twist.

He snorts. "You can't hide your fuckin' dislike for her." Giving a chuckle, he adds, "But at least it means I don't have to worry about you tapping that."

I widen my eyes in disgust. He must be fucking joking if he thinks I'd ever go near someone like her. And right now, women are the last thing on my mind. Apart from Britney, that is.

Red twists the top off a bottle of water and swallows a few gulps. He wipes his mouth on the back of his hand, then tries another prod to get me talking. "So what is it?"

Grimacing, I prepare to spill the tawdry secrets of my life, wishing it showed me in a better light. I take a deep breath and start. "Eight years ago, I was on leave from the Army. While I was stateside, I met a woman. We seemed to click. I married her."

Red's bottle slams down and his brow creases as he seems to run back over my out-of-the-blue statement through his mind. His eyes first widen, then sharpen. "You're married?" Then he shakes his head. "Divorced, I presume?"

My lips press together. Up to an hour ago, I wouldn't be having this conversation at all. But now I have to admit to the truth. "No."

"No?" Now he leans forward, his face furrowed, his eyes blazing with suspicion. "Never fuckin' knew you had a wife, Petty." His fingers rap on the desk, and his expression screams the unspoken question, *what else have you been hiding?*

Before he gets onto Keys, our computer expert, and complains that he hasn't done a thorough enough background check, I quickly give him more. "Not many people did, not even Roller." Again I grimace as I realise my friend is going to have lots of questions for me. "I didn't alter my service records and didn't add her to my insurance." It had been one of those things that I'd been putting off, always thinking there was plenty of time. But as it turned out, there hadn't been.

He seems genuinely surprised and intrigued. "Can I ask why?"

I breathe deep, then let out the air on a sigh. "Because..." Because, even blinded with love, something warned me she wasn't my happily ever after. Because I quickly discovered she wasn't who I thought she was. But I don't tell him that. Instead, I give him the truth that can't be questioned or disputed. "She was arrested on a felony charge of aggravated assault."

He sits back, his mouth dropping open. A couple of minutes pass while he digests that. "Well, fuck. She guilty?"

I'm not surprised it's the first thing he asks. Being in an MC, we tend to know too many people who the police have stitched up, so it's easier to ask if there had even been a crime.

Raising and lowering my shoulders, I give him the answer she'd told me. "She went into a convenience store. The owner was there on his own. He ended up smashed into the glass door of an upright freezer."

Red's brow creases as he obviously thinks through what I haven't said. "Because?"

"She said he came on to her, wouldn't take no for an answer. But his story was that she got angry when he thought she was shoplifting and accused her."

He's looking at me curiously. "Her word against his, eh? Surveillance recordings?"

"Fuzzy," I tell him with another shrug. "Could support either story. But the jury believed him and not her."

"So she, what? Pushed him and he fell into a glass cabinet? And that was a felony?" Prez is shaking his head.

I feel a tic at the side of my mouth. "She got in a punch first and then shoved him. Hard."

"But if he'd been feeling her up, then she was quite within her rights to defend herself." Prez has firm views on women and consent, as do I.

Nodding, I agree. "Yes. But unfortunately the glass went through an artery in his leg. She left the scene…" though he doesn't know I use her own words, "in shock. If another customer hadn't come along, he'd have bled out." And the charge would have been murder or manslaughter. Or maybe, if he hadn't been around to present an alternate view, she might have gotten away with the story she was a woman protecting herself.

Red wipes his hand over his face. "I can see how she didn't garner much sympathy, but can also understand why she fled. Must have been distressing for a woman not used to violence and blood."

Nodding I agree. Yeah. It probably would have been if Britney had been someone else. Sucking in air, I puff out my cheeks. "She got sent down for ten years. Served seven of them. Got a call just now to say she's getting out. She's coming back to me." *She's coming back to me.* Oh hell. I'd been on autopilot explaining the bare bones to my prez. Suddenly, the implications hit me fast. *Britney's coming back.* I look around, trying to spot where the garbage can is in case I need to vomit.

I realise Red's looking at me oddly, so I try to disguise the shaking of my hands as I raise it to indicate upstairs, and tell him the reason that would make sense. "I don't know what to do, Prez. I've only got a fuckin' room. That won't be enough for her, and that's even if you'd let a strange woman you don't know live in the club."

He leans forward and clasps his hands. His expression would make a weaker man shudder. "Hold up a minute. What exactly are you telling me, Petty? You got married, your wife got locked up. You forget about her for seven years, act like you're single, now she's getting out, you're what? Going to play happy families?" His head moves side to side as if he's having trouble getting this new information to sink in. There's a tic in his jaw as though what he's hearing isn't pleasant. "Never had you down for a one-woman man. You've always been all about the pussy. Couldn't give a damn about that. But you having a wife? Shit."

While MCs aren't necessarily known for treating women properly, in the Satan's Devils MC, most taken men tend to stand by their women and practise monogamy. That said, Red might frown on, but never criticises if a man wanted to do things differently, as long as it didn't bring trouble to the club.

But I don't want him thinking the worst of me. Her coming back is the last thing I want. And while he might now think I'm a cheating, selfish ass, the truth is, I didn't consider myself married since long before I joined the club.

As his brows draw down, I try to explain so he doesn't think too badly of me. "We hadn't been married long when she went inside. When I tried to visit, she refused to see me. I wrote letters, but she never returned them. I was fucking faithful to her until I got out of the Army. She'd been gone three years by then, with never a word. She couldn't have sent a clearer message to me, so I sent her divorce papers. She didn't sign them." I don't know how much more anyone could want of me. "As far as I was concerned, I was a free man. Maybe not legally, but who could blame me for finding comfort elsewhere?"

I think I can see a softening in Red's stance. "She never responded to you? Or called you?"

I shake my head. "Last time I saw her was when she was being led away to start her sentence. Last time I spoke to her was the morning before that."

Shrewd eyes stare at my face. "Are you seriously telling me, you haven't heard from her for seven years until she rang you today?"

I breathe in and blow air out. "That about sums it up."

He, too, inhales deeply. "And now she wants to pick up where you left off?"

That's what I got from the phone call. "Seems that way." Then I add my thoughts. "Or maybe her having a husband to go to helped her to get paroled."

He gives another little shake of his head at that, then his green eyes pierce me. "You love her?"

If Red hadn't met the love of his life for a second time only a few months back, I doubt it's a question I expected my prez would have asked. But he had, and he knows better than anyone that it is possible to reconnect after a long time apart. In my case, though, his question is easy to answer. Whatever feelings I had for Britney were killed years ago, and I doubt they could ever be rekindled.

"I did," I tell him. "But it's not an emotion I've considered for a very long time." Love kind of dies when there's a lack of communication to reinforce it, and when you've had more than enough time to do some thinking.

"Shit, Petty." For once, Red looks lost for words. "I don't know what to say." His hands brush back his hair. He looks down at his desk as though he might find some answers there, and then back at me. While still looking sympathetic, his eyes have hardened a little. "We don't know your wife, and," he huffs a short laugh, "from the sound of it, neither do you. Seven years is a fuck of a long time."

I could remind him he hadn't seen Cher for longer than that, and it hadn't taken them long to reconnect, but I keep quiet. I'm not sure Britney and I had had the same connection from the start.

Why did I marry her? Well, she was beautiful, soft, petite, had a sharp wit and was funny and affectionate—everything I wanted in a woman. That she wanted me too was something that had taken me by surprise. I'd fallen in love fast, and putting a ring on her finger had been as much to mark her as mine, than me thinking things through, or doing the sensible thing and waiting until I'd really gotten to know her.

Of course, I'd been close to being shipped back overseas. If I hadn't tied her to me, she might have strayed, and for some reason, having her legally tied to me gave me a sense of security.

Then events caught up with us. She was arrested, and I got her out on bail. She insisted it was all a mistake, that she was going to be cleared. But she was sentenced instead. I was posted back overseas and I'd never seen her again.

So, no, Red's right. Maybe I don't know my wife at all.

He's clearly thinking. "For you, this might turn up to be a blessing in disguise." A quick half-smile and I know he's comparing my situation to his and Cher's. "It could be a chance you didn't know you were seeking. But old ladies have to be voted in, and that's after the brothers have had the chance to see who they'll be inviting into their home." He pauses and rubs his jaw. "Then again, we have strays staying. Don't see why she shouldn't share your room, on a temporary basis, while we see how she fits in." He's being magnanimous.

"Yeah, Prez, my room." As far as I can remember, Britney liked her creature comforts. "I can't see she's going to be happy with that. I haven't even got a bathroom." Then I remember how she's lived without those conveniences for years, and it makes me wince. Whatever my feelings for Britney are now, I feel like a failure as a husband if I can't offer her better than what I have. "And there's the fact her parole officer wouldn't be happy with her staying here."

He grimaces as he acknowledges my statement. Suddenly, his hand slaps down on the desk. "Angel Hair." I crease my eyes as he mentions the hairdressers we provide security for. He half-smiles when he sees my confusion. "This could work out. Only yesterday, Angie asked for some leeway on her payments as her tenant in the upstairs apartment just vacated. Don't know what it's like, but it's got to be better than a single room, and you'd be doing the club a favour."

It takes me a moment to realise what I could be doing for the club, but then I catch up. Me paying Angie rent would mean she wouldn't have to leave us short.

Part of the attraction of living at the club is that I don't have to pay for accommodation. But hell, I'm an adult. I'll just have to suck it up. It's not like any of us are particularly hurting for cash.

It's a good idea, and better than bringing Britney back to the club. Not only would a proper address satisfy her parole officer, I have a strong feeling that it's best to keep her separate from the club. I don't want her fucking shit up for me. "You think it's still available?" Suddenly I feel more positive.

Red grins. "Way Angie put it was it would be a fuckin' miracle to get someone fast, so yeah, I think it probably is. I reckon you should get your ass around there and see it. When's your woman arriving?"

"Tomorrow if she can get a flight." Which reminds me, I'll have to get the money to her.

Again he sighs. "Look, I'll get Cobra to cover your shift with RoseLyn for a couple of days."

I open my mouth to say he doesn't have to do that, then I realise how much I've got to get organised. I don't know if the apartment's furnished or not, and even if it is, I'll have to move my shit over. I feel I should make some token protest. "I can still work."

Red's eyes become slits. "Your job is making sure you're aware of everything and anything going on around RoseLyn. Any other time, for that I'd say you were one of my best people. But now? Fuck, man, you've got too many distractions. Like your wife," he pauses to snort, "unexpectedly coming back, and all the changes you're going to have to make to accommodate her in your life." He levels me with the prez stare he's perfected over the years. "Can't risk something happening on your watch, so I'd rather we have you covered."

"As soon as Britney's settled, Prez, I'll take over again." Under other circumstances, I might be pleased to not have

RoseLyn as my responsibility anymore, but I don't want to be seen as a man who walks away from a commitment.

"I'm sure Cobra will appreciate that." Red grins, then points to the door. "And you better get out of here if you're going to get everything squared away before," he pauses, and huffs, "Brit*nay* arrives."

CHAPTER FOUR

RoseLyn

I've just gotten out of the shower, having come back from the gym when I hear the sound of male voices downstairs. Nothing unusual in that, it just tells me the time. It's four in the afternoon and must be the shift change.

There is a difference today, though. One of the voices I don't recognise.

It's not unusual for me to eavesdrop at this time. I've noticed how Petty, taking over for his evening rotation from Roller, is so different when greeting his friend than greeting me. First, I'd hear the loud slaps as they beat each other's backs, then, often chuckles and laughter. I first started listening to see if they were joking about me, but no, it was always something or other that one of their brothers had done. Then they'd holler to each other as Roller walked out the door.

When I appear, Petty would be completely different. He'd no longer be relaxed. He'd be tense. There'd be no joking with me. Instead, there was sarcasm and sometimes direct rudeness, and that's if and when he deigned to speak with me. Usually he'd settle for a disdainful look, and wouldn't bother with conversation if he could get away with using a few grunts.

But today's voice greets Roller in a very different way. There are a few back slaps, sure, but that's followed by a whispered conversation, a *what the fuck* exclamation, and absolutely no laughter at all. When footsteps approach the front door, there's a "keep the shiny side up" salutation which seems a cursory afterthought.

Intrigued, I get dressed, rough dry my hair and pull it back into a ponytail—leaving it for Kylie to properly style it later—then descend the stairs to find a stranger making himself at home in my kitchen.

Petty and Roller aren't on duty all the time. They do Wednesday to Sunday with the other two days being covered by Hammer and Shadow. Sarge, however, is always here during the night. He says if he can't sleep anywhere, he may as well stay awake at mine. This man, though, I've never seen him before. But he's wearing the Satan's Devils cut and Roller let him inside so I'm not at all worried.

"Hey," I greet him politely.

He swings around. He glances at me for a moment then gives a warm smile. "You look different on stage."

I roll my eyes. What does he expect, for me to wear spandex and heavy makeup all the time? I ignore his comment. "You obviously know who I am. You are?"

"Cobra, ma'am. At your service." He makes an exaggerated bow. "Hope you don't mind, but I'm grabbing a coffee. You want one?"

This is so totally different to what I've become used to over the last two weeks. Normally after Roller's gone, at best, Petty ignores me. He'll do his rounds of the house, inside and out, clearly taking his work seriously. But there's been no attempt at friendliness.

"I'll take a cup." Well, why not? It's not often in my own house that I have someone to serve me. "It's good you can multi-task. Like making beverages and protecting me."

My slight criticism doesn't faze him at all. "Oh, I assure you, I'm quite skilled." He winks at me as if inviting me to take that anyway that I want. "Roller told me it's all been quiet."

Just as it is most days, thankfully, with only the occasional reminder that my ex is still out there to keep me on my toes.

When he sent the first note, I was terrified to go out of the house, but as time passed, I realised hiding away was giving him a satisfaction he didn't deserve.

It's a fine balance between not letting him think he's winning, and me being able to stay out of danger. Hence my bodyguards give me the space to live as normally as possible while keeping me safe.

It could be that the threats are serving their purpose, keeping me off balance and afraid, but I can't take the risk that if I let down my guard, he might strike for real. I've been at Saul's not so tender mercies one too many times already.

He knows my address. He knows where I work. I've had shit left on my car at the parking lot of the stores I frequent. Until the Satan's Devils security team had come on board, I was scared wherever I went.

I like my privacy which I certainly don't have now, but I'd rather sacrifice that than my life or my freedom. I just wish Saul would come out of the woodwork so we could put an end to this once and for all.

Not for the first time, I wonder whether my success has riled Saul, or whether he'd have chased me if I'd still been the girl that he'd known. I had an ordinary childhood, an ordinary life. Nothing much remarkable had happened to me until after Saul and I had parted. Then, determined never to be under the thumb of a man like him again, I sought to be independent. I joined a gym, got fit, and plucked up the courage to sing on stage. It wasn't long until I was picked up by a talent scout and my career had taken off.

It was no secret in my hometown that I'd come to Vegas, but I was surprised Saul would follow me here.

It's like he's become obsessed with me.

As we sip our coffee, I notice, while he's still paying me attention, Cobra keeps one eye on the window, and that his holster is visible under his cut. As he's staying alert, I start to relax.

The question why Petty isn't here enters my head. For the last couple of weeks, he's been here on all the days he's supposed to work. I've only just about tolerated him, and it should be a pleasant change to have someone different. Someone who seems far more approachable—Petty had never made coffee for me.

I should be happy I don't have to put up with his scowling face, and glad that Cobra seems eager to please. But perversely, I miss the man I've gotten used to.

By the time I've swallowed the last of my coffee, my curiosity gets the better of me.

Rinsing my cup, I place it in the drainer. "So, why isn't Petty here today?"

"Miss him?" Turning, I catch Cobra's expression. He's wearing yet another one of his grins. I'm beginning to suspect they're his customary look. "I thought you might be relieved." He chuckles. "He's not the easiest person to get on with."

I have tried to keep my thoughts on the man to myself. So either I've been unsuccessful and I've let too much slip about how obnoxious I find him, or his behaviour isn't limited to me.

"Just curious is all." I shrug. "No matter. I'm sure you all take time off, occasionally."

Cobra takes out his gun, checks it, then puts it back in his holster again. "I'm just going to take a check around outside. As for Petty, apparently, he's got some personal shit to deal with."

Personal shit that's none of my business from the closed-off look in Cobra's eye. And why should it be?

I put the missing bodyguard out of my mind as I go about my normal routine. I don't give much thought to either him or his replacement, other than to notice he's just as competent and vigilant as Petty as he drives me to the casino. There's nothing different until I walk into my dressing room where Kylie is waiting.

"You're not swearing," is her greeting, her brow creasing. She walks to the door I've just closed, opens it, glances out into the corridor, and then comes back in beaming. "You've upgraded, I notice."

For a second, I wonder what she's talking about, then chuckle as I realise. "Looks like I have." Personally, I still think Petty's got him beat for looks, but Cobra's personality is a huge improvement.

Unabashed, Kylie opens the door and takes another peek out. She nods with approval as she again closes it. "Is it permanent? Has Petty been sacked for being an asshole?"

I don't know much about motorcycle clubs, but I doubt they're something you get booted from, or not for personality traits at least. "According to Cobra, he's dealing with a personal situation."

She fist pumps the air. "Long may it continue."

For some inexplicable reason, my feelings are mixed. "That's not fair, Ky. He's good at his job." I justify myself with the thought as yet, Cobra's untried. Maybe he won't turn out to be so vigilant. Something about Petty had made me feel safe.

Giving an unapologetic shrug, she imparts her views, "And as unpleasant as shit to deal with."

Not understanding my strange desire to defend him, I let the subject drop. Why should it matter to me which of the Satan's Devils are providing protection? As long as my stalker doesn't get close, it shouldn't matter one iota. They can swap them around to their hearts' content.

Having put Petty to the back of my mind, the night proceeds exactly the same as numerous others before. Kylie gets me ready, I go on stage and perform my set, talk with a couple of fans and sign my autograph, then return to my dressing room and change from singer to normal girl once again. With the last traces of makeup removed, and the hairspray brushed out of my hair, I open the door and Cobra gets into step beside me as he escorts me to the parking lot.

"Seemed to be a good night," he comments.

"Pretty standard," I agree. I notice him looking at me oddly. "What?"

He chuckles. "Just can't get over how different you seem. Up on the stage, you're someone else, unattainable. Here, walking along next to me, you're as down to earth as anyone could be."

I presume it's a compliment so I grin and take it that way. I know my stage persona is different. I'm another person when I'm in front of an audience. It allows me to be freer than I otherwise would be, as I can pretend to be someone other than my usual boring self. Performing has allowed me to have an identify far removed from the victim Saul had made me.

As performing takes it out of me both mentally and physically, when we reach the SUV, I yawn widely as I get inside. Taking the hint, Cobra lets me rest my eyes and doesn't initiate small talk. When we arrive back at my house, Sarge is already there, having let himself in with a key.

Cobra and he exchange a few words, a couple of grunts and nods of their heads, presumably confirming Sarge has already checked the place out, and then the changeover is complete. Cobra leaves, his duties performed to my satisfaction. He might not be Petty, but he still gives the assurance he knows what he's about.

I'm left in the care of the man who when I'd first met him, thought to be taciturn and reserved, but over the weeks, I've come to learn more about Sarge. I'd go so far as to say we've become friends. He's quite open about his PTSD and the effects that it has on him, not asking for sympathy, but just sharing the facts so that people can understand.

"How d'you find Cobra?" Sarge asks as I place my jacket on the hook.

"A bit different to Petty." I chuckle as I respond. I'm tired but I could do with a nightcap before bed. As I walk through to the kitchen, I continue to speak. "I've kind of got used to Petty not talking to me."

Sarge follows me in, shakes his head to a beer, and watches as I top off a glass of wine. "Don't take it personally. Petty's an acquired taste."

"Did someone say something?" I'm worried that Petty might have been kicked off the job because of me.

Sarge creases his eyes. "What do you mean?"

I shrug. "As you say, Petty's not the easiest to get along with, but I don't need someone to be friendly if they're going to protect me. I just wondered whether he was off the job permanently."

Sarge rubs his hand over his short hair. "Not as far as I know. Not that I know much. Petty's wife's unexpectedly came back into town, and he's getting her settled. Shouldn't affect the work he does for the club." Having shared the information, he gives a small frown.

"*He's married?*" I swing around. My jaw drops and I quickly pick it up off the floor. "I'm so sorry, that was rude." I just can't imagine any woman tying their wagon to his. How would you begin to handle such a misogynistic brute?

Sarge chuckles and gives one of his easy grins. "No matter. I was surprised myself. None of us knew he had a woman."

I know these men like to play their cards close to their chests and I'm honestly surprised he's said that much. As I sip my wine, I wonder if he'll gossip more. My innocent questions are more normally curtailed with just two words, *club business*. But I decide to push as the reason for Petty's absence has sparked my interest. Not that I have any designs on the man myself, Sarge's wording just sounds odd.

Casually I reach for the bottle and top off my glass. "What do you mean, you didn't know?"

"We didn't know," he repeats. "She's been…." His eyes flick to mine, then he shakes his head and lamely completes his sentence with one word. "Away."

Away? Now my interest is really piqued. Over the weeks I've discovered that to become a full member of the Satan's Devils you have to prospect for a year, and so Petty must have been with them far longer than that. If they didn't know he was married, then where the hell has she been?

I try to sound nonchalant as if it doesn't bother me at all as I pry for more details. "How long's Petty been with the Devils?"

"Three, four years?" Sarge states, then narrows his eyes. "Why are you asking?" He sits back, putting his thumbs through his belt loops and his lips quirk. "You worried Petty's off the market?"

My eyes widen. *Absolutely not.* "Just making conversation."

He grins as if I'm transparent. "Well, I've said all I'm going to say. Petty's ol' lady's come back to him, and he's having to take time to get things squared away." He makes a show of zipping his lips.

I finish my wine, knowing there's no point in asking more. The men of the Satan's Devils MC are tight. If I want to dig for more dirt, I'll have to wait to get it from the source. If Petty ever comes back to work for me, that is.

Maybe he won't. Maybe he'll be languishing in marital bliss. But after at least three years, I can't help but wonder where she's been. Had she got fed up with his boorish ways and they'd split up? Had he strayed or had she, and they'd agreed to separate? Why is she back, is it to stay?

Telling myself I'm far too nosy about a man who does nothing more than annoy me, I wish Sarge a good night and then take myself upstairs to get some much-needed sleep.

CHAPTER FIVE

Petty

Will I even recognise her after seven years? As I stare out at the travellers exiting the arrivals area, it wouldn't be too much of a stretch of the imagination to think she could have already walked past me.

Fuck knows, I've changed. The last time she'd seen me, I was a soldier in uniform. Now I have a preference for a t-shirt and jeans and, of course, my cut, which I've worn so proudly for the past three years.

While I don't think that time has treated me too badly, I definitely look older, a few creases here, and a few lines there. When I stare at my reflection, I see a maturity that was lacking when I was in my twenties. More than years have transformed me. The things that I've seen, things that I've done, have added a hardness to my features. Yeah, there's a good chance she won't recognise me.

Maybe it would be for the best. If I don't notice her and she doesn't see me, maybe I could just leave, go back to the club, and forget, like I've done so successfully over the past seven years, that she even exists.

"Clark?"

Well fuck me. While I've been examining the travellers approaching, she's come up from behind. I'd know that voice anywhere.

Sucking in air, I turn. "Britney."

For a moment, as if by mutual agreement, we take a few seconds to examine what time has done to each of us. *Is her face looking harder?* If so, it's probably not surprising, considering where she's been. There are lines on her forehead that weren't there before, and she's put on weight, not much, just enough to emphasise her curves. The softness of her body being part of what had originally attracted me, perversely, does nothing for me now. Seems I might have gotten a little too used to a lithe, slim singer. *Fuck it. Why the hell am I thinking of RoseLyn now?*

Bringing my mind back to the woman in front of me, I notice her hair, once long, is now cut in a short bob, but it frames her pretty face nicely. Despite the wrinkles under her eyes and the tautness of her mouth, it seems the intervening years haven't treated her too cruelly.

She's first to speak. Tugging at my leather she scrunches her eyes. "What's this?"

"I… er… I." Fuck, this stumbling ass isn't me. Or hasn't been for a fuck of a long time. I clear my throat and start again. "Let's find somewhere to talk. We've got a lot to catch up on."

We're standing in the middle of the concourse with travellers having to move around us. It's not a good place to have a discussion about the twist and turns my life has taken, ending up with me becoming a member of the Satan's Devils MC. Her story, I suspect, would be far shorter. She's been stuck in the same place for seven years.

Glancing around, she spies a coffee shop, and inclines her head in that direction. When I raise and dip mine in acquiescence, she leads the way and takes a seat. I pause before heading for the counter.

"Cappuccino?" It was what she used to drink.

"Americano. Black," she responds. I suppose in prison she had to give up some luxuries.

It emphasises how much we've both changed. *I'll have to learn about her all over again*, I muse, as I join the line and make my own selection. She's probably no longer the woman I knew during our whirlwind romance which had been followed by the short marriage before the law had stepped in and parted us.

I return to the table, setting down the two cups, then take the seat opposite her. Having managed to pull myself together, I state the thought foremost on my mind. "I'm shocked as fuck that you contacted me." Raising my eyes, I see her nonchalant shrug.

"Why?" She picks up her drink, blows on it, then takes a sip. "You're my husband. I love you. Where else would I go?"

I'd happily taken responsibility for her the day I'd made her mine, but how the hell does she think that still applies after we've had no contact over the intervening years? It's been a long time since I've considered her my wife. Again, I have to wonder whether she's only come back to me now as she's nowhere else to go. As for her professions of love? Well, I don't believe those for a moment.

Ours was never the love story of the century. It was more like infatuation. Looking back with hindsight, I can see lust played a bigger part than affection and I can't believe what she felt for me was enduring. My blind emotions for her slowly died as the months and years during which we had no communication passed. I'd slowly come to my senses to the extent that now I doubt any prior feelings could ever be resurrected.

I'm no longer the soldier home on leave, desperate for some female attention. I'm a member of an MC, more likely to have to fight women off rather than work hard to attract them. I have female admiration wherever I go, even if it's just something about the bad boy Harley I ride that gets their motors revving.

If I was meeting her for the first time, would I be attracted to her?

Grimacing to myself, I really don't know how to answer. What I know now, I hadn't known then, and that's what would sway me from taking the same decision. Attracted, maybe. Would I marry her again? I shudder.

"Clark?" she prompts when I've been lost in my thoughts.

There's so much I need to tell her. Hopefully, she might not want to be with me once I've told her what I've been doing all these years. I swallow a mouthful of my beverage, then start to fill in the gaps in her knowledge.

"I served a couple of tours after you..." I pause, wondering whether I should try to phrase it delicately or state the blatant truth. I settle for, "After you went away." She smirks as if she recognises my difficulty. I continue, "Didn't re-enlist after that. Had enough of dancing to other people's tunes. There was this guy, Roller, I met him when I joined his team. We became solid buddies. Turned out we were going to get out at the same time. He knew this guy..." I stop, that part's not important. "We jumped ship together and joined the Satan's Devils MC as prospects. Served our time and got patched in." I indicate my cut. "That's what I am now, a member of the MC."

"A motorcycle gang." She says it without any inflection.

"Club," I correct her. "But yeah."

She lets that soak in for a moment, then the corners of her mouth draw down as she realises the implications. Her cheeks glow as she spits out, "You're a fuckin' down and out. Not a solid member of society." She leans forward, a tick in her jaw, glancing around as though hoping no one else hears her. "Clark, you're a fucking criminal. If my parole officer finds out, I'll be straight back inside."

My skin heats at her criticism. "Hold up." I raise my hand. "First, I'm no fuckin' criminal. The club earns its money legitimately. Hell, Brit, we part own a casino and have our own security business. And," thanks to Keys and some of the preparations I put in place yesterday such as getting all the paperwork submitted legally, "I'm a gainfully employed employee of SD Security Services if your parole officer checks up on me."

Again I pause, thinking of all the things I've put in place for her. Everything I've done since getting that phone call yesterday, busting my ass to cover all bases. I wish I could say that she's worth it, and I've not done it all from a sense of obligation, but I can't. I can't keep the sadness from my voice as I tell her, "I've moved out of the clubhouse, rented an apartment for us."

"Well that's good I suppose," she sneers. "At least I won't be living in a club full of rowdy bikers."

I bite my tongue. Fucking good? Does she not realise how my life's been upended? Before I say something I may later regret, I turn the tables on her. "You came to me, Brit. You're hardly in a position to complain. I've not heard from you in seven fuckin' years. You refused to see me, didn't respond to my letters. You led me to believe I didn't have a fuckin' wife."

Shrugging, she sips her coffee again, a wide-eyed expression of innocence on her face. "But I am still your wife. I didn't sign the divorce papers."

And that's probably because she'd been keeping her options open so she had somewhere to go when she was finally free, only to use me if she had no better opportunities. I don't bother asking for confirmation. She'd probably lie. Brit would say anything if it suited her purpose.

My view's corroborated when she smiles at me and emphasises, "You are still my husband."

I tense. "What if I'd moved on, Brit? What if I have another woman? What if I have a family?"

Her eyes narrow and for a moment, she looks uncertain. "You don't, do you?" She does that huff again. "And you couldn't have made it legal. You're married to me."

Despite that I could get some kind of pleasure stringing her along, I put her out of her misery. "I've no permanent woman in my life."

Her hand moves across the table and rests on mine. Although I feel like a hot iron is burning into my skin, I force myself to leave my fingers under hers. "You've been waiting for me." She flutters her eyelids. "Just like I was waiting for you."

Grimacing, I wonder whether I should disillusion her, but here's not the place to make a scene.

Her turning up out of the blue has my mind all over the place. I never expected to see her again. While I've told myself it was because of her I've never wanted to make a commitment to another woman, my mind wonders could it really be, that deep down, I was waiting for her to come back to me?

Fuck it. If someone asked me whether the sky was blue, at the moment, I wouldn't have an answer. Britney's always had that way of confusing me.

My head's whirling with memories of the past, visions of a possible future, worries about how she'll fit into my life. Although people quite rightly think I'm an asshole and would have predicted that instead of pandering to her, I'd have told her to get lost, I can't turn her away. I'd made a promise when I said my vows. It's impossible anyway because it's *her*.

"What do you want, Britney?" I ask her straight. "Are you just using me because being married made getting parole easier?"

Her face loses its harshness as she deigns not to answer that. "I want to pick up where we left off." Even her tone has gentled. "I still love you, Clark. I always have."

Her words shock me. I sit back and examine her. She's still the woman I was originally attracted to. She's still the woman I cared enough about to put a ring on her finger. She might say she still loves me, but I have no such feelings for her. But now she's sitting here in front of me, I realise it looks like she truly wants to pick up where we left off, wipe away the past seven years and act as a married couple again.

I can't believe that's her desire. It's far from mine. But maybe

I'd accepted that was my future when I'd moved into the apartment. Had I stayed at the club, there's no way her parole officer would have allowed her to come back. But I'd pandered to her, jumped to accede to her request. Just like I'd done so often in the past. Whatever else, that hasn't changed in our relationship.

I press her. "That's really how you see us? Playing happy families once more?"

She gives another soft smile. "We were happy once, Clark." She waggles that fucking ring on her finger, making me realise I have no idea where mine is. Lost somewhere in the past, just as I'd thought our relationship was. "You married me for better or worse. We've had the worse, now let's make our better."

Poetic words, but better for who?

But she's here, and I've made the adjustments that means we can give it a shot. What choice have I got? It seems Britney and I are going to try to make a go of it.

I've never been able to say no to her.

It's like the clock has been turned back, seven years wiped out, back to the time when I had little say in matters. What Britney wanted, Britney got. And as much as I'd like to say otherwise, seeing her today has put me back under her spell.

Finishing the dregs of her coffee, she picks up her purse. "Let's go see this apartment we're going to be living in."

Feeling more like I'm heading for my execution, I stand, take the handle of her suitcase and pull it along.

We're more like two strangers than a married couple as we walk silently through the airport, exiting into the hot Vegas air, and then going to the parking lot. I unlock the SUV and lift her case into the back, while she opens the passenger door.

"Nice car."

Well, something impresses her. Shame it's not mine. "It's the club's," I explain as I slide out of my cut, fold it carefully and place it on the back seat. I don't know if this is the right time to tell her I only have my bike. You wouldn't find me in a cage by preference. I only ride in one for occasions like this or for doing my job.

Still, the air-conditioning is welcome as it starts to work. Exiting the airport, I set out on the shortest route to take me to the place which has so quickly become my home, mentally cataloguing the things I'm missing out on by not living at the club. The beer that Owl would have had waiting, the conversations with my brothers, and, of course, the services offered by Pixie, Jinx and Angel. *Do I even fancy Britney anymore?*

Casting a sideways glance at her, I don't think so. If she expects intimacy, I'm not sure I'll be able to rise to the occasion. Or not until we know what footing this renewed relationship is on.

She leans forward as if to get a better view of the area. "Are we going to drive down the strip?" She casts an excited look my way.

I wasn't going to. As a Vegas resident, I do everything to avoid the tourist trap. But for so many visitors, it's the highlight of Sin City, so I make the detour to give her what she wants.

As we make our way slowly past the famous hotels and casinos, her mouth drops open and her eyes sparkle. "It's even more impressive in real life," she states, while I just harrumph in response.

"I was wondering why you moved, but now I can see the attraction. I can't wait to explore. Can we come here tonight and see the lights?"

My hands grasp the steering wheel so tightly my hands turn white. There's no less way I'd like to spend my evening. A tour guide I am not.

"Came here as that's where the club is based. Didn't come here for this," I say gruffly.

"But it's a plus. Oh, look..." Her eyes have been caught by something, I don't even bother to glance that way. The strip no longer holds anything to interest me. She says something, gushing about whatever she's seen.

Nowadays, when I reluctantly visit the strip, rather than the glamour, I see the whores touting for business and those for whom the casinos didn't work out begging for handouts. Like anywhere in the world, there's a not-so-hidden underworld that most people try to ignore.

Vegas? Visitors just get to see a veneer. Residents know all that glitters is not gold.

CHAPTER SIX

Petty

Having completed the detour, I finally pull up in the small parking lot behind the hairdressers. As I reach for the doorhandle, Britney puts her hand on my arm to stop me.

When I glance at her, her face looks pinched as she asks, "Why have we stopped here?"

I point to the apartment on the second floor. "That's your new home."

"Home?" If anyone's ever managed to put more disgust into the utterance of one word, I've never heard it.

It's strange how a tone of voice can send you back in time and just like muscle memory, you react in the way you'd always done. Instead of righteously getting annoyed and pointing out since her phone call yesterday I've moved heaven and earth to find her a place to stay, I try to placate her.

"It's not much, but it's what I could get in the time I had. I was living in the club until yesterday, Brit. I had twenty-four hours to find something." I sigh as I offer, "Now you're here, we can look for something better together."

She cranes her head to look out of the window again. She sighs. "I suppose it will have to do."

I suspect it's far better than the accommodation she's had over the past seven years, but of that, I don't dare remind her. Instead, I get out of the car, then take the suitcase out of the back. Bouncing the keys in my hand, I wait for her to come join me.

I don't miss how she scans the environment, but she'll not find anything to object to. This is one of the businesses that the Satan's Devils keep an eye on. There are security cameras all around, and we ensure nothing like drug dealing takes place in the parking lot after hours so there'll be no paraphernalia on the ground.

While it's not in the most prestigious area, I have no qualms about bringing any woman here.

Finding nothing to immediately criticise, she instructs, "Well, let's see inside."

I bite my tongue to keep back the comment there's no other immediate option if she doesn't like it, and follow her up the external stairs that lead to the front door. Taking the right key, I slide it into the lock and turn it.

"Oh." Again one word which carries so much weight with it.

I defend myself, reminding her, "I only got this place yesterday," as she goes through the door. Apart from the usual appliances in the kitchen, there's little more. The boys and I had moved my bed in from the clubhouse, and I brought my desk and chest of drawers along. But basically, that's all the furniture I've got. "I thought you'd prefer to furnish it yourself, rather than me getting stuff that you didn't like." In truth, I hadn't thought that far, but as I speak the words, I think they work.

"Can you afford it?" Turning, she waves her hand at the cut I'd put back on as soon as I'd gotten out of the SUV. "I mean, you hardly have a proper job."

My jaw clenches but I manage to retort, "I can afford it."

The apartment is small, but there's a separate bedroom. It's that she walks into, sneering at the bed. "This isn't new. I'm not sleeping on someone else's mattress."

"It's not that old," I contradict her. "It's mine. I bought it for my room at the clubhouse." Not having much need for anything else, I'd spent cash on a decent mattress and frame.

She puts her hands on her hips. "So how many other women have been sleeping on it?"

I tell her the truth. "None." And there are certainly no notches etched on the bed post to disprove it. I might have brought quite a few to my room for sex, but none have ever stayed the night. What I don't add is that it's seen plenty of action.

Which makes me belatedly realise that presumably tonight, I will be sleeping beside the only woman I have ever spent the whole night with. With no other choice, Britney and I will be sharing the same bed. The thought causes my dick to shrink instead of doing the opposite.

She looks into the built-in closet, noticing my clothes already hanging there, but most of the space has been left for hers. Then she checks the drawers and nods approvingly when I've only taken up one and left her the rest.

Next, she returns to the kitchen and examines that. If she finds anything there to complain about at least she keeps it to herself.

She leans her hands on the kitchen countertop, and huffs out a breath. Then she straightens and looks around with mock enthusiasm. "Right then. Looks like we've got some purchases to make."

We do indeed. We need a sofa and television at the very least to make this place habitable. Not to mention groceries if we want to eat.

With nothing in the apartment to delay us, we spend the next couple of hours trawling around stores, me flashing my card and her buying the shit that she likes. Obviously, she didn't believe me about who I'd had in my bed, as a new duvet, pillows, sheets and covers are added to the pile we've accumulated.

The furniture will be delivered in the next day or so. The small stuff we can take home. But mindful that the only place to currently sit is the bed, I suggest we eat out and after I'll take her to spend the evening at the club.

Dinner is the second time we've sat at a table together today, but small talk doesn't come any easier. It seems she's not much interested in what I've been up to while she's been away, and I don't ask her about her interment, as I expect she did more or less the same thing every day.

I try to get a conversation started by talking about her intentions. "You need to get a job to satisfy your parole officer?"

"I'm supposed to, yes. But there's no hurry, is there? Not with you to support me." She leans over the table. "I liked how you were splashing the cash, honey. You sure I didn't put you in the red?"

Nowhere close to it, but I'm not telling her that. It's one thing having a wife again, but now I'm having to get my head around she means for me to support her as well. And as I've so recently been reminded, her tastes are expensive.

I rack my brains for some suggestions. "The club part owns a casino, I told you that. Maybe there's something there for you to do." I'm thinking of asking Red.

She snorts a laugh then points to herself. "Felon here, remember. Doubt if any casino would take me on."

There's a restaurant which we also provide security for, and I know Erika, the owner, had recently complained one of her best waitresses was moving on. That could be an idea. But when I suggest it to her, she looks insulted.

"Me? A waitstaff? Oh, I'm worth much more than that."

A frown comes to my face. "Well, what are you thinking of doing?"

She laughs again and shakes her head. "I've got plenty of time to think about it. I'd like to learn more about Vegas first. Let me get my feet under the table, and then we can talk about me finding a job." Her eyes narrow as she spies the expression on my face. Her voice softens and hitches as she adds, "I was only just released, Clark. At the moment, I don't know which way is up. Let me acclimate to the outside world before making any decisions." I swear the way her bottom lip quivers makes me feel like an ass.

Reaching my hand over the table, I rest it on hers. Although it's an intimate gesture, I feel no connection between us, and raise it again just as fast. "I'm sorry. I was just trying to help." Despite my misgivings about her reappearance in my life, I have to spare a thought for how terrible it must have been having spent so much time locked up. As a freedom-loving biker, I can't begin to imagine being confined to just four walls, and I've known brothers literally go stir-crazy because of it.

Her hmm and tilt of her head away from me doesn't really show me whether she's accepted my apology.

We finish the meal much like we began, in awkward silence. Once again, I hand over my card, and exiting the restaurant parking lot point the SUV in the direction of the clubhouse. Immediately I begin regretting my decision to take her there tonight, but what else are we going to do in a mostly unfurnished apartment? In some ways, it's like ripping a band-aid off. My brothers will have to meet her sooner or later, might as well get it over with now. I'm just anxious how my brothers will take to the woman who bears the title of my wife.

They'd been pretty shell-shocked to find I'd ever been married, and even more so that no divorce had been made final. Roller's reaction was hurt and anger that I'd kept something so important from him. He'd had my back so often while we'd fought beside each other, he'd thought he'd known everything about me.

When I replied I'd thought that chapter of my life was done and over, there had been some debate about whether I actually owed her anything as it was her who'd stayed out of touch. If she'd been an old lady rather than a legal wife, I'd have had nothing to tie us together and would have been free to move on.

Some, I know, think that piece of paper wasn't enough, and that I'm stupid for turning my life around to accommodate her, and they could well be right. But the ring she wears tells me I'm still responsible for her, and the vows I took said I'd care for her until death.

Now I'm worried as to what they'll make of the woman I'm giving up so much for. They might hold their tongues in front of her, but their feelings will surely be communicated by creased or raised brows and eye rolls, and their thoughts will rebound on me when she's not around.

If they thought me a fool, they couldn't be more right.

It's perverse, while no man wants another to be swayed by his woman's attractions, neither does he want them to ask why they'd tied themselves to *that*. On looks, I know Britney won't disappoint, and some will think I'm a lucky motherfucker. But sometimes when she opens her mouth… I cast a sly look at her, remembering all the times I've cringed in the past. Yet how can I tell her to be on her best behaviour without sounding like an ass?

If she disrespects my club, it won't be her that catches the flack.

As I drive through the gates of the compound, my eyes drift to the row of bikes, mine standing proud but forlorn. Oh how I wish I was riding it, unencumbered by the woman beside me.

I hadn't had a motorcycle when I'd met Britney, and since I have, I've never had the urge to take a bitch pillion. I'm certainly not enamoured by the idea of taking her on my bike, even though her status will be viewed as my old lady. My gut roils at just the thought of her arms around me, holding me tight. But I feel lost without it and I can't see myself being able to ride it back to the apartment unless she can drive the SUV.

But is her driver's licence still valid? Fuck, there's so much I need to find out.

I park the SUV, slide out, shut the door, put my cut back on, then, as I pass by it, satisfy myself by resting my hand on my bike for a second.

"Why do you do that?" She points at my cut, and adds, "Take your vest off when you're in the car?"

She knows fuck all about bikers. I need to rectify that. "It's a cut, not a vest. And it's big disrespect to my colours to wear them in a cage." Patiently, I try to explain, "I'll be fined if I'm caught doing it."

She rolls her eyes, and mutters under her breath, "Boys."

I grit my teeth. This is my lifestyle, not some childish game. Again, I'm worried as to how she'll behave with my brothers, and what standing I'll be in if she upsets the club. I might be legally tied to Britney, but my heart's with my MC. If it comes to a tossup, she's not going to win it. But the time for abandoning her has passed. I should have turned her away as soon as I heard from her. I've made my bed, whether or not I like lying in it.

As we approach the door, I envision the interior, trying to see it through the eyes of a stranger. It's an MC clubhouse in a converted warehouse. Nothing will disguise that. The bar takes up the whole of one wall, and there are tables, chairs, couches, pool table, games machines and everything we'd need for our entertainment. Thanks to Rosa, the ex-prez's old lady who's still very much a feature of our club, the prospects keep it fairly spotless. But there's no hiding the underlying smell of beer and smoke, nor the taint of sex that lingers in the air.

Bracing myself for whatever reaction she might have, I push open the door, then stand aside to let her enter.

Fuck me, I groan inwardly. It looks like every fucker is here. I suppose they all want to see the old lady they knew nothing about. Curious buggers, the lot of them. Feeling much like I'm a teenager bringing a new girlfriend around to meet my parents, my nerves are on edge as I follow her in.

Red, Crash, Hammer and Fox are at the bar. They turn and lean their backs against it, not trying to hide their interest in any shape or form. Indian and Twister stop their game of pool. Cuff slings his arm over Rope's shoulders and raises a challenging eyebrow. Keys, Shadow and Titch cease their conversation. Cobra is missing, but I already know he's covering for me with RoseLyn.

It's Roller who I focus on. His eyes are narrowed and I know he's got a way to go to forgive me for keeping Britney a secret. Hopefully in time, he'll realise it wasn't deliberate, but more an effort on my part to wipe her from my life and forget her. But it's him who approaches us first, giving Britney an assessing glance.

"So, you're the one who owns this fucker." His words deliberately taunt me. He stops in front of us, and without showing any of the bad feelings I know he's holding onto, he stretches out his hand. "Welcome to Vegas. I'm Roller."

Britney, who'd been tense by my side, relaxes and gushes, "I'm so pleased to meet you." She surveys him, then turns her attention to the room. "It's an amazing place you've got here."

Maybe that's going a bit far, but at least she's not being outwardly judgmental. I let out some of the breath I'd been holding.

"I'll get you a drink and introduce you," I suggest, pleading to Roller with my eyes that he keeps our differences between us, and doesn't include her.

"Yeah, it's this way." Needlessly, he stands back and indicates the bar that a blind man would be unlikely to miss. "So, how are you finding Vegas?"

As she steps in the right direction, he glares at me behind her back. I know what he's doing. It's what any brother would—checking her out but not in an acquisitive way, rather assessing the effect she'll have on the dynamic in the club, and more importantly, between us.

"Vegas seems so much fun," Britney answers, her voice full of enthusiasm. "I'm so glad Clark moved here."

"Clark?" Roller snorts.

"Brit." I pull her back and tell her quickly, "Here, I'm Petty."

Her eyes roll and she pats my arm condescendingly. "Then buy me a drink, *Petty*."

Our club dues fund the bar so no purchase is required. Ignoring Roller, I place my hand to the small of her back and encourage her over to where Owl is waiting, poised with my normal beer in his hand.

"What do you want?" I ask her.

I'm actually impressed when she quickly scans the limited selection on offer, and then grins. "A beer will be fine."

"Welcome to the clubhouse," Red growls as he steps up behind us, reminding me I haven't yet introduced her to my prez.

I rectify that immediately. "Prez, this is… my *wife*… Britney." Again, I pronounce it as *Brit-nay*, just as she'd want me to. "Brit, this is my prez, Red." I then go on to introduce the brothers alongside him, and Shadow and Titch who have wandered over.

After she's exchanged a few pleasantries, she leans into me and whispers, "No women? That's not what I was expecting."

Red overhears. "Cher!" he calls out.

His old lady comes out from the kitchen, brushing something off her hands. "Whatcha want?" But any annoyance at being summoned disappears as she locks lips with her old man. I notice Red's hand goes automatically to rest on her swelling belly.

When they finally part, Red nods his head toward the woman standing beside me. "This is Britney. Petty's wife."

She's not surprised, so Red must have warned her. Instead, she reaches out her hand. "It's good to meet you. This one's mine if you haven't gathered." She grins. "It will be good to have more old ladies swelling the ranks. So far, there's only me, Tiffany and Rosa."

Britney takes her hand and shakes it warmly. "Good to know I'm not alone."

"Mom?"

And here comes Zeke, Red and Cher's sixteen-year-old kid.

As usual, they're dressed flamboyantly, in some flowery harem pants and a pink shirt.

As Red and Cher's attention turns to them, Brit whispers in my ear, "What the fuck is *that?*"

Now I've had my own difficulties getting my head around Red's nonbinary child, but once I got to know the person inside, while I don't understand, I can accept how they are different. I find myself bristling at her tone of voice, while telling myself it was only a few months back that my reaction was similar.

"Red and Cher's kid," I whisper back tersely. "And they're nonbinary. Don't show any disrespect, Brit, nothing else will have you out of here faster."

She harrumphs but keeps her mouth shut. While Red's focused on whatever Zeke has to say to him, she looks around the room once again, then pulls my head down to hers. Once more, she speaks directly into my ear. "What about them? Are they gay?"

I notice where she's looking. Rope and Cuff are still standing close, and Cuff hasn't yet removed his arm from his brother's shoulder.

"Unless my gaydar's fucked, then no," I reply to her with a chuckle. They might be kinky fuckers, but I've only ever seen them fuck women and not each other.

It's awkward as fuck introducing her around, but to give her credit, she's polite, respectful, and if someone makes a joke, laughs in the right places. As the evening goes on, I see my brothers are being charmed. Even when the sweet butts make an entrance and leave no one in any doubt what they're there for, Britney restricts herself to a small frown and an assessing look my way with a promise that we'll be visiting the topic later. But in front of my brothers, she keeps her mouth shut.

While she's practicing her rusty pool skills with Twister, Roller comes up to my side.

His elbow goes into my ribs hard enough to make me catch my breath. "Don't know why you kept her secret. She's a great catch, Brother. Pretty, knock-out body, and look how she fits in. Don't think you could have done any better."

Words that should make me proud, instead awakens something inside. Feelings that I'd thought I'd moved past.

Fear and dread at what I've brought back into my life.

CHAPTER SEVEN

RoseLyn

Cobra's fun. He's also polite and considerate. So why the fuck do I miss Petty?

Strangely, though, for some reason, I do. I miss his snide comments and the looks he gives me when he doesn't approve of the costume I'm wearing, while all Cobra says is that I look nice. Kylie thinks his replacement is a huge improvement, and says I'm far more relaxed. But I feel less energised when he's not around, as if something about him makes me come alive. Even if it's only the desire to give him a piece of my mind.

I can't even say I regard him as a friend, so it's crazy that, without him, there seems to be a gap in my life.

I can't fault Cobra for the way he does his job. He's just as diligent as the others, and I doubt anyone would be able to get through him. I have no justification for any complaint, or to demand that another man takes his place.

I must have lost my mind for missing the challenge and the spark Petty brought.

Cobra's now taken his shift for two nights so I'm wondering if it's now become permanent. That wouldn't surprise me at all. What newly returned wife would want to lose her man to another woman—even if only to provide protection—during the evening hours? Surely that's when they should be reconnecting, picking up their threads of their life, going to dinner, seeing friends, taking in shows and having fun?

It's not normally within me to be jealous. Previously, if a man showed his preference for somebody else, I'd just move on rather than put off the inevitable. But while Petty's nothing more to me than a bodyguard, for some unknown reason, I feel envious that he's spending his time with her and not with me.

It can only be because he's such a good bodyguard. Of course, I have no other designs on him. Even before I knew he was hitched, I hadn't harboured such thoughts of him. The very idea makes me laugh. We're as different as water and oil. We'd never mix and would always butt heads.

So, I come back around to my original question again. Why the hell do I miss him?

"Roller's here. I'm off," Sarge yells out.

"See you tonight," I call back, while continuing to brush my hair and catalogue what I need to do today.

A couple of hours in the gym, a practice session with the band to go over some new material to keep my set fresh, and a shopping trip with Kylie to get new costumes. Roller, though, has become used to my day, and never complains. But I suppose for the money I'm paying his club, he'll put up with anything.

It's only Petty who makes his disgust known.

Huffing, I wonder whether that just proves he's genuine.

I finish putting on my minimal day makeup—just a touch of face powder to take the shine off my skin—a far cry from how I doll myself up in the evenings, and then descend the stairs.

Roller stands to greet me. "Hey, RoseLyn. So what are your plans for today?"

Before I tell him, I wave him to retake his seat. "Nothing that can't wait." I sit opposite him. "I was, er, wondering about Petty, and whether he'll be taking over from Cobra again?"

Sitting forward, Roller's mouth twists as though he's got bad news for me. Bracing myself, I prepare for the disappointment to hear I won't be seeing the taciturn man again. But Roller surprises me.

"I'm sorry, but Prez has told him the club comes first. He's giving Petty one more day, then he'll have to return to duty." He gives me a look of sympathy.

I know Roller and Petty are great friends, but also that Roller's not blind to the offhand way in which Petty treats me, and expects his news to be disappointing.

His words, though, take the wind out of my sails, as bracing myself for never seeing Petty again was all for nothing. But now I'm getting my desire, I realise it could be the old adage, be careful what you wish for. I frown. Petty's hardly likely to want to be apart from his wife when he's only just reconnected with her. He'll probably be twice as obnoxious as he normally is.

I frown. "Won't he mind? I wouldn't object to Cobra continuing."

Roller chuckles. "I'm sure you wouldn't, but Cobra's needed elsewhere."

While Petty doesn't talk much, his brothers do. As a way to while away the time, I've gotten to know a little bit about Roller. Though I should leave the subject of Petty's mysterious woman reappearing, something makes me ask, "You served with him, didn't you? Did you know he was married?"

Again his face twists as if I've touched a nerve. "No, I fuckin' didn't."

Hmm. His snapped response shows me it's a sore subject. It also raises more questions as I know Roller and Petty are tight. Why did Petty keep something so important from his friend? I get a bad taste in my mouth as I think of a reason. Petty's probably been fooling around with other women, and kept the knowledge of his wedded status to himself so he wouldn't be criticised for being unfaithful.

Then again, I can't see bikers being worried about marital loyalty. In their masculine world, a man can do whatever he wants to.

Though I try to bite my tongue, I can't still my curiosity. "So where's Petty's wife been? Did she walk out on him?" That might explain why no one knows anything about her. He might be embarrassed that she left. In which case, why's he having her back? I didn't take him as the type to forgive easily.

"She's been in jail." Roller's eyes widen, then he clamps his mouth shut, only opening it a few seconds later to warn with creases lining his brow, "And you didn't hear that from me."

But of course, as my mouth opens in an O at his surprising answer, I've even more questions now. "What was she in for?"

He shakes his head. "Nope. You'll get nothing else from me."

At least that explains why she's been out of the picture. Sitting back, I do some calculations. I know Petty and Roller have been with the Satan's Devils for about four years, and before that they served together in the Army. So it must have been years that she's been locked away, if that's truly where she's been for all that time. What the hell was she in for?

And still I pry into something that's none of my business. But knowing outside influences forced Petty and his wife apart, I feel sorry for them both. "It must be hard for them to reconnect after so long. I would have thought Petty would have liked more time together, instead of coming back to babysit me."

Roller snorts. "What Petty wants has nothing to do with it. You think any of us were pleased to find he's kept such a huge fuckin' secret from us? Prez making him work is part of his penance."

Now that I don't understand. "Why should it affect the club?"

He sighs. "Fuck, woman. You can't leave it alone, can you?" He settles back again. "You already know we prospect a year to make sure we're a good fit, are loyal to the club and have the trust of the brothers?" He knows I do, he told me himself. "Ain't much different for an old lady, except for the prospecting bit." He glances at me, and I nod to encourage him. "We vote old ladies in. Sure, there are times we might take on a married man, but we'll vet any woman who comes along with him. Can't risk bringing in trouble."

"And what happens if you don't approve of a woman someone has chosen?"

"Then she doesn't get voted in, and doesn't get access to the club." His mouth twists. "I know it's hard for a citizen to understand, but the club is a family, and the clubhouse is our home. We need to trust and get on with anyone who's brought in, and know, in turn, they'll have loyalty to us."

Put that way, I can comprehend what he's saying.

"And does she? Petty's wife. Does she fit in?" It sounds like Petty's being punished for not being open about this important woman in his life. I'm starting to become concerned about how he'll feel if his club doesn't accept her. Would he have to leave the Satan's Devils? I might not know him well, but like the rest of the men I've met, they live for their club. They work so hard to get in, it must mean everything to them. What would that do for his relationship?

When I glance at Roller, I don't expect to see him grinning. "Yeah, she's going to fit in just right. I admit I had doubts before I met her, since Petty had kept her quiet, but she's nice. Respectful." He winks at me. "Quite a stunner too, all soft and curvy… mmm mmm. I can see why Petty was attracted to her. She's just the kind of woman he likes."

Well that puts me out of the game if I had harboured notions of Petty and I getting together in an intimate way—which of course, I don't. I could hardly be described as soft. Though my body's shaped right, I work out in the gym to keep my muscles tight and firm. There's nothing about me that jiggles, except for my tits when I go without a bra.

I like to keep fit. That's how I can give my all on stage, and I happen to like the shape of a muscular body much better than a curvy one. I'm also blessed with a metabolism that means as long as I keep active, I don't have to watch what I eat.

Nah, if Petty likes women with more meat on them, no

wonder he's never looked twice at me. I grin at the thought, knowing it doesn't matter a damn to me.

"So what's today's plan?" Roller asks brightly, though his eyes are narrowed, warning me the conversation about Petty is over.

I update Roller then we leave to go to the gym. This Roller enjoys as he normally ends up working out beside me. Then after I've come back home to shower and change—I hate using the gym's facilities—we go out again. I meet the guys in the band and go over the new songs we intend to add to the set. It goes so well we finish early, and I know Kylie won't be ready to go shopping with me.

Roller drives me back to the house, regaling me on the way with some of his thoughts about an idiot we come across who could use some education about what his indicators are for. I'm belly laughing at the way Roller's describing how said lessons could occur.

I'm still chuckling when he parks the car and I wait while he walks to the house. Like has become normal, I'll wait outside in the car while he checks the place out. While whoever's on shift always insists on doing this, to date, there's been no intruder lurking.

"All clear?" I call out, already getting out of the car, planning to go straight to the kitchen and mentally going through what I can get out to snack on.

"Stop!" Roller's voice seems higher than it has before.

But my momentum keeps me moving and I'm halfway up the path before my brain registers his instruction. I'm stopped by Roller's hands on my biceps.

"You can't go inside," he tells me.

Which perversely means immediately I want to. I try to move past him. "What's going on?" The door seems secure and doesn't look like it's been broken into. There's been no alert from the alarm.

But Roller's stopping my progress. "RoseLyn, let me get you out of here."

"It's my house, Roller." If there's a danger then I'll be guided by him, but he's not acting as though there's someone inside armed with a gun.

He rolls his eyes. "I'm aware of that but—"

"What is it?" I'm getting impatient.

"For fuck's sake. Don't say I didn't warn you." He steps aside and puts his hand on the door. "Just look, but don't enter."

Mystified and feeling his warmth at my side, suggesting he's staying close enough so he can pull me back if I disobey him, I, admittedly now, slightly reluctantly, wait for him to push the door open.

I actually hear it before anything comes into sight. When it does, I step smartly back with my hand over my mouth.

"Snakes?" I cry out at the same time as I give a whole-body shudder. I'm a complete wimp when it comes to them, especially the rattling kind. He doesn't need to nod to confirm it, but he does anyway. "How the hell did they get inside?" I don't know how many there are, but the house seems to be crawling with them.

Roller's looking around. He takes my arm as though he doesn't want me to stray from his side, and his gun appears in his free hand. He starts to move, looking cautiously at the ground.

I tiptoe along with him, carefully looking where I step. The hairs on the back of my neck have risen and goosebumps cover my arms. Snakes are my freaking nightmare.

"Fuck!" Roller comes to a sudden stop. He stares at where one of the vent covers is lying on the ground and rolls his head back on his neck. For a few seconds, his eyes are focused on the sky. "Jeez, RoseLyn. We fuckin' made sure the house was secure from any human entering. But fuck..." He points to an empty sack on the ground, lying as if the person who deposited untold numbers of venomous snakes in my house wanted it to be found.

I glance at his face to see he's gone pale, and it's not hard to imagine the reason why. If he hadn't been entering cautiously to check the house out, we might both have walked in completely oblivious there were unwelcome guests in the house. I might have sat on the couch, or my bed, or… Sweat covers my body as implications go through my mind.

I know that if treatment is received quickly enough, rattlesnake bites aren't normally fatal, but they can be very unpleasant. Apart from that, the idea of being so close to those slithery creatures has my skin crawling.

Saul's upped the stakes now. He freaking knows how much I am afraid of them.

Suddenly I lurch away from Roller, bending double, I vomit the contents of my stomach up onto the ground.

Then he's there, scooping up my hair and holding it back. "I'm so damn sorry. I did try to warn you." His words though sound like they're as much for himself as for me.

He had. I could have gone back to the car and waited for him and wouldn't have been confronted with them. But he'd still have to have told me that snakes had invaded my house. And imagining that would have been equally as bad as seeing.

Roller's comforting hand is moving up and down my back. With his free one, he hands me a wad of tissue to wipe my mouth.

"Better?"

While I still feel nauseous, I don't feel like I'm going to hurl anymore. I straighten, and avoid looking behind me. "What am I going to do about them?" I ask in a shaky, needy voice, so unlike my own. Right now, I want to burn my house to the ground. Then I think of all the mementos I've got inside, and don't want to take such drastic action. But snakes…

He grimaces. "I'll get some of the brothers here. We'll search the house and make sure we get rid of them."

But what if one's left? What if it comes slithering out in the middle of the night? What if it gets into my bed…

"I can't stay here," I sob, hating that I've turned into such a pathetic woman, but snakes really are my Achilles' heel.

He looks at me, then back at the house, then wipes a hand over his face. "Don't fuckin' blame you," he says quietly as if to himself. Then louder, he says, "I'm gonna call Red. Tell him what we're dealing with. You wait in the car, okay?"

CHAPTER EIGHT

Petty

I have mixed feelings about how Britney got on with my brothers in the club last night. They'd all seemed to have taken to her and she appeared to fit in well. But it bothered me that she portrayed the persona that had originally drawn me in. I'd caught glimpses of the woman I'd first met, and the behaviour that made me want to marry her.

It had taken time and distance to realise I'd been sucked in with an image that wasn't real. Even when she'd shown her true self, I couldn't accept that I'd been so deceived, and looked for reasons within myself, and not within her. No man wants to admit to being a fool.

I'd made so many excuses for her.

My older self recognises that I proposed in haste because I knew I was going to be posted back overseas and didn't want anyone else to have her. Seeing her around my brothers last night had reminded me how I'd been conned into thinking she was someone she wasn't.

When we'd left, she'd made a show of saying her goodbyes, blowing air kisses to Cher and promising to meet up with her. She was smiling, laughing, looking like she had no cares in the world. But when we exited the door, it was like a switch being thrown.

As we got into the SUV, I'd braced myself for sarcastic comments about the club and my way of life, but whether it was because she remembered which side her bread was buttered, any such thoughts she'd kept to herself, though her stiff posture and the look of disdain she threw back as we drove through the gates spoke volumes.

When we arrived at the apartment, it was as awkward as fuck. There was only one bed and unless I wanted to sleep on the floor, I was going to have to share it with her.

On the pretext of making a call, I went outside while giving her time to do her nightly routine and get under the covers, then returned and took my turn in the bathroom. I told myself I've sometimes shared a bed with Roller when we visited other clubs, and hadn't even felt odd about the necessity. It shouldn't be much different with the stranger who was once my wife. As with my friend, I took off my tee, but stayed in my jeans.

But when I got into bed, she made sure to let me see she was wearing next to nothing, and it seemed like she had certain expectations. Even though she'd made so much effort, she was out of luck. My dick didn't so much as twitch.

Then her hand started to wander and reached my groin. "I can help you with that," she murmured seductively as she'd felt my limp cock, rubbing it through the denim.

My stomach actually roiled at the thought of getting intimate, and I lifted her hand off. "Not tonight."

"Oh, come on, for old times' sake if nothing else." She'd tried to snuggle closer. "It's been a long seven years for me."

My ungenerous thought was she might have lacked for cock, but I'm sure she'd seen some dyke action while she was inside. Not that she'd have been anyone's bitch, but I'm sure she'd have had someone do favours for her.

"No," I repeated, firmly.

But she didn't get the message. Her hand started to explore

again and tried to pull down the zipper of my jeans. Instead of arguing further, I'd rolled out of the bed, slipped my tee back on and left to go sleep on the floor I'd rejected before.

It was hard, unyielding, but far more relaxing than lying beside her. But not, I admit, conducive to sleep. I'd not gotten much rest but doubt I would wherever I was. My mind refused to stop going over and over how Britney had re-entered my life and just exactly what I was going to do about it.

I'd risen before she'd woken, for a moment going to the bedroom door and staring at her, resenting how comfortable she looked in *my* bed, as if I were the interloper and not her.

The shit we ordered yesterday started arriving soon after I'd had my first coffee. I'd paid extortionately to have delivery expedited.

Now, as I bring my mind back from revisiting the past night, I note the couch, which was cheap as it had previously been on display in the store, looks good enough in the apartment. I've also managed to successfully hook up and get the new television working.

I've assembled the flat-packed table, resorting to the instructions when the parts supplied didn't make sense, and standing back admiring my handiwork. I admit the place now looks more homey. The kitchen cupboards are stocked with the necessities, and the fridge is full to bursting.

Whether by accident or design, Britney hadn't woken before I'd mostly finished the jobs, but after making coffee, busies herself washing the new pots and pans and putting them away, while moaning about the lack of space.

I stay quiet. There's more room, more furniture, than I've been used to in the clubhouse. Personally, I don't think we've done too badly in getting it kitted out. However, her sneering expression betrays there's nothing about this place that seems to please her.

Again, I recall the different face she wore around my brothers yesterday. They probably wouldn't believe the person she's portraying today.

It had been easy to see they'd liked her, and I hadn't missed some of the admiring glances they'd sent her way nor the envious looks in my direction. I know, though, they might look but they won't touch. It's our code. No one puts their hands on a woman belonging to another.

If only they knew. I'd happily step aside if someone wanted to try their luck with her. They're welcome to steal her away. Though caveat emptor would very much apply. Would I warn them if that were the case? *No one warned me,* I remember.

"Clark?" I jump as her voice breaks into my reverie.

"Yeah?"

"Can you help me here?"

Stopping what I'm doing immediately, I walk to where she's pointing to a cupboard door that's aligned badly. Remembering she can show signs of OCD, I go back to where I'd left my tools and promptly return with a screwdriver.

Standing back, she watches me critically and then asks, "We going to the strip today?"

"No," I tell her, gritting my teeth as I try to keep the door straight while adjusting the screw.

As I check whether any of the other doors need to be realigned, I notice her hands go to her hips and her mouth forms a pout. "Why not?"

With my ass propped against the countertop, I fold my arms and look at her. "Because while I could afford the spending spree yesterday, I don't have much else. Certainly not money to burn if you're thinking of visiting the casinos." What I spent yesterday didn't really touch the money I've got in the bank, but I'm not sharing those details with her. And even if I were the richest man in the world, gambling it away is a loser's game.

"We could just look."

Yeah, there's plenty to look at in Vegas, and fuck knows I'll probably have to take her there one day, but I really don't fancy standing among the crowds, watching the fountains at the Bellagio or the pirate ship at Treasure Island, let alone the volcano or any of the other tourist traps to be found in Vegas.

"Brit, I'm really not in the mood today, okay?" I'm tired from lack of sleep and putting together all the shit that I have.

Her eyes narrow. "Well when will you be in the mood? Hmm? Tomorrow you'll be back to work which means we won't get another chance for a few days."

The word 'work' is clipped. When I told her I was currently providing bodyguard services for a singer, she seemed surprisingly alright with me spending time with a woman who wasn't her, asking me lots of questions and wondering whether she could get free tickets to the show. Taken aback, magnanimously, I'd offered to ask for her. I'd been suspicious at the time that she wasn't as okay as she was making out.

"I'm back to work in the evenings, but in the days I'm free. And I get Sundays and Mondays off." She raises an eyebrow. *Fuck.* "Alright, we'll go on my next night off." As her smile suggests she's won this fight, I inwardly swear. What am I getting myself into? For a moment, I wonder whether taking her out to see the lights could be palmed off onto a prospect. Then I remind myself this is my *wife* I'm talking about. I should not be okay with another man taking her anywhere. It speaks volumes that I couldn't give a damn.

"That okay now?" I jerk my head toward the cupboard door.

She squints as though trying to find fault, then nods. "It's fine."

Pushing away from the countertop, I go to walk past her when my phone buzzes in my pocket. I take it out.

Red: Need you at RoseLyn's

Me: Roller's there.

Red: Need you there too. Something's happened.

Me: What?

Red: Roller will update you once you get there

Me: Is this urgent?

Red: Urgent and fucking important.
Shit.

What the fuck's happened? My first thoughts are about Rose-Lyn. Not that I have any particular interest in her, but she's my mark and I'm supposed to be keeping her safe. With the club's expansion of its security business, if we lose a client who we're protecting, I can't see a glowing recommendation coming our way.

I'm still frowning down at my phone as I tell Britney, "Hey, I've got to go out."

"What?"

Engrossed in my thoughts about what could have happened and hoping I'm not going to arrive to find RoseLyn injured or dead, I'm distracted and not giving her my full attention.

"It's work. Sorry, Brit, but I've got to leave now." I pat my pocket to make sure I've got the key to the SUV and start to walk to the door where my cut is hanging. My arm is yanked back and my face suddenly stings with a resounding slap.

"You told me you have tonight off," she shouts at me. "You're going to that bitch instead?"

I've told her about my work, that I'll be out five evenings a week. I explained all about the job I was doing. Ruefully, I rub my cheek. "What the fuck, Brit?"

"That's right. You walk away when we've not even gotten settled. You go back to the woman you replaced me with. Drop everything when she texts, why don't you?"

I hold out my hands palms up, trying to keep calm. "First, it wasn't her who texted me. It was my fuckin' prez. I can't ignore him. I've got to go. And I've no time to argue with you."

Her eyes blaze. "I don't care who texted you. It could have been the president of the United States, but you've got shit to do here. I need you."

For fuck's sake. "I can't do this now, Brit. I've got to go." I complete the few steps it takes to cross the small apartment and grab my cut off the hook. "I'll see you later." Without waiting for a response, I open the door, close it, then wince as I hear something thud against the wood.

Taking a second I can't really spare, I rest my face in my hands. Then after taking a deep breath, straighten my back, and take the stairs at a run to get down to the SUV, wishing like fuck it was my bike.

Trying to push Britney out of my mind, I try to concentrate on what could have happened to RoseLyn instead. I might not like the woman I'm paid to protect, but in this moment, I care about her more than I do my wife I just left.

Having been anticipating the worst, I'm relieved when I pull up outside RoseLyn's house to find no red and blue flashing lights. I do, however, see a fuckload of bikes and realise I wasn't the only one called in. Despite the hot sun beating down, for some reason, my brothers are wearing full leathers and gloves.

RoseLyn's rental is parked on the drive and as I park alongside, I see the woman herself sitting in the front seat, engine running and windows shut tight.

Wondering what the fuck's going on and preferring to hear it from a brother rather than being forced into conversation with her, I get out and wave my hand as I see Roller step out of the house.

Like the others, he's wearing a full-face helmet with the visor firmly down, and is carrying a sack held away from his body.

Still no clearer on what's going on, I watch as he goes to a truck and throws the sack into it. I intercept him before he returns to the house.

"What the fuck, Brother?"

Acknowledging my presence, Roller removes his helmet and shakes his hair out. I notice he's looking decidedly pale. "You okay?" My concern is genuine.

He shakes his head, then inclines it toward the truck. Mystified, I follow him over. There are half a dozen firmly tied sacks which for the moment make me no wiser until I realise they're moving, and there's an odd rattling sound coming from them.

Once my brain computes what the noise might be, I automatically leap back. "What the fuck?" I repeat and waggle an unsteady hand toward the live cargo. "Are those snakes?"

"Someone put them through the vent in her house," Roller says tersely. "I don't like them, but she's fuckin' terrified, Petty."

Snakes?

He stares pointedly at me. "Saul knows she has a phobia."

I know he's making a dig at me for suggesting it could be someone else who's after her, or that she could have been making this all up, but I have to agree, this definitely points to her ex.

I eye several brothers who are coming in and out of the house. "You clearing them?"

"Trying to," Roller agrees. "Fuck knows how many there are or where they could be hiding. RoseLyn won't go back inside, and I don't fuckin' blame her."

"Shit." I find it hard to blame her myself. I might not be scared of snakes but I have a healthy respect for them, and would make a point of avoiding the venomous type. I do take it that as RoseLyn's sitting in her car that she wasn't bitten, else she'd have been in the emergency room. Thank fuck for small mercies.

Being in the SUV, I don't have my helmet and gloves nor a jacket with me. My t-shirt only has short sleeves. I shudder as I notice my brothers are all better prepared, but still I offer, "You want me to come in and help?"

Roller shakes his head. "No." He grimaces. "Red doesn't want to take the chance we might miss one of the fuckers, and to be honest, RoseLyn might shit herself if we ask her to go back into the house. He wants you to take RoseLyn to a hotel and get her settled, then go to the casino with her. Sarge will take over at midnight as normal."

I narrow my eyes, remembering how angry Britney was that I had to leave her. "And no one else can do that?"

Roller shrugs. "Cobra's helping to find the slippery fuckers, and," his mouth quirks, "maybe Red thinks your lack of compassion will somehow steady her."

Well fuck. I am sympathetic, who wouldn't be for someone who returned to find their house occupied by these no-legged beasts. But the relationship I have with Britney means I wouldn't show it to her. Maybe Red's right and it's a way to stop her from freaking out.

Half-turning, I notice RoseLyn still seated in the car. She's wiping her eyes and looks like she's maybe crying. "She took it badly, I take it?"

Roller half snorts. "What do you think? She's fuckin' devastated, Brother. If the snakes hadn't decided to explore the living room, she might not have known until one bit her."

Grimacing, I turn back to the truck. "What's going to happen to these fuckers?"

"Some are dead, but the live ones we're going to let free in the desert."

I could do that for them. "I'll stay and take care of that for you. You comfort our singing diva."

But Roller again shakes his head. "Red was specific that you take care of her."

I think I'm the last person she needs now, but there's no point arguing. Seems like the next few hours I can't avoid being in close quarters with a bitch. But then, if it wasn't RoseLyn, it would be Britney. In comparison, perhaps RoseLyn would be better.

"I'll get her out of here." My reflexes are fast as Roller tosses me the car keys and I catch them without fumbling. I start to turn away, then look back. "We got the asshole who brought them on camera?" We have, of course, installed security cameras around her property.

"Keys has been checking it out, but the fucker kept his hood up and his face turned away."

"But we think it's Saul?"

He shrugs. "Her fear of snakes isn't in her bio, and he definitely knows how much they frighten her. This isn't the work of a crazed fan who wants to get close to her. This is someone who wants to scare her, hurt her, and doesn't care if she ends up dead."

One of my suspicions has been crossed off the list. RoseLyn's certainly not behind this and doing her own stalking to get attention. Even though I know, better than most, how well a woman can act, thinking she'd filled her own house with snakes would be stretching it past the limit.

As Roller gives a shudder, replaces his helmet and walks back into the house, I place a call and get details of the hotel that's been booked for her. Having gotten the details, I stand, tapping my phone against my palm for a moment. Whether it's her ex or not, and yeah, the current situation suggests it's Saul and not some unknown assailant, he's getting closer and more dangerous. There's a twitch of excitement within me, hoping the bastard responsible for hounding her will make an appearance tonight. I'm in the fucking mood to take out my anger on something.

"We think we've got them all." Considering the task he's just completed, Cobra sounds surprisingly cheerful when he updates me. "Her bedroom's been cleared so she can come back in and pack a bag now."

"I'll tell her." I nod at him.

As I approach the car, I don't miss RoseLyn's guarded glance toward her front door, nor how the blood fades from her face when I'm close enough to speak to her and suggest she come inside. I get the feeling that Red is right and that I spark something within her, as instead of giving in to her fear, she straightens her back and steps out of the car. Her steps falter as she approaches her house, and I chide her.

"Scared?" My dismissive tone is meant to rile her, and has that effect. With a disdainful look toward me, she walks forward again.

While I admit to being ambivalent toward the woman I'm

protecting, today I have genuine sympathy for her. Especially when we walk into her house and find it in such a mess. The couch has been overturned and cushions removed, and there's blood on the floor suggesting one of the reptiles was apparently too difficult to catch. I place my hand on her arm to steady her as she rises on tiptoes, and feel the goosebumps on her skin.

"Just one bag of the necessities," I remind her softly.

She coughs to clear her throat, but her words still come out as a squeak. "I need to get a cleaning service in."

"We can handle that." Her fear is palpable, her bravery evident as she walks toward her bedroom where I can see that the bed has been stripped.

Her closet and drawers have been emptied, but neatly so there are piles of clothes on the bare mattress. Noticing she's keeping her feet well away from the void under the bed, I open the suitcase that someone had obviously gotten out for her and open it myself, running my hands around the lining to reassure her.

The courage with which she had entered seems to have deserted her, and she stands still as a stone. She's completely white, shivering, with her hands wrapped around herself. Knowing she's nearing panic mode, I take over.

I wave my hand toward the contents of one of the drawers. "What do you want from here?"

She tells me, then I indicate the wardrobe. Likewise, I follow her called-out instructions as I go into the bathroom. Soon, the suitcase is full, and I can get her out of there.

Although she's anxious to get out, RoseLyn takes each step cautiously, freezing after each. She's hyperventilating, her eyes going everywhere. It's slow progress and takes a lot of encouragement and my repeated assurances my brothers have cleared the house for her, but eventually, we step outside into the bright sunlight.

Once there, I place my hand to the small of her back and she jumps into the air, then swings around, her face now coloured with embarrassment.

"My skin is crawling," she explains, rubbing her hands up and down her arms.

I can understand that. The hairs on the back of my neck had risen the entire time we'd been in the house. "Come, I'll take you to the hotel." I walk her to the car and get her settled inside. Once I've closed the door, I notice Cobra beckoning me to one side.

"You're taking her?"

I nod, noticing the set to his jaw. "You got something to say about that?" I raise a brow.

He scowls. "I like her, Brother. And I don't know that you're the best man…"

"For what?" Now both brows reach my hairline.

Cobra clenches his teeth. "She needs support and you won't give her that."

"And you will?"

Cobra sighs. "She doesn't like you—"

I slash my hand through the air. "I don't give a damn whether she likes me or not. I'm here to do a job. And yeah, she's just had a shock, but she's a grownup and doesn't need to be handled with kid gloves."

Cobra throws up his hands. "You better be prepared to answer to Red if you push her too far and lose the job for us."

"And we'll fuckin' lose this job and all others after it if anything happens to her." I try not to let my impatience show. RoseLyn seems to have all my brothers wrapped around her little finger. Luckily, I'm immune to her.

With a shake of his head and a glance which clearly says, *on your head, be it*, Cobra stalks off.

I go to the car, start the engine and head into Vegas. A sideways glance shows while her eyes are still red, she's got a little more colour in her face.

"You going to sing tonight?" I ask, brusquely.

Her eyes come to mine. If she's looking for me to show my sympathy, she won't see it. I'm validated it's the best approach when she draws back her shoulders. "Of course. I can't take a night off." She pauses, then adds, "And however I feel, I'm not letting him win."

Good girl, I think quietly. "You think you not going on stage is what he wants?"

She shrugs as she considers my question. "I don't know what the fuck he wants. But it's likely, isn't it?"

I hate myself as soon as the words leave my mouth, but somehow can't stop them coming out. "What the fuck did you do to make him hate you so much?"

CHAPTER NINE

RoseLyn

What?

I try to remind myself that I'd missed Petty while he'd been gone, but for the life of me, I can't think of the reason. It must be a form of self-flagellation as now he's sitting beside me, he's riling me up all over again.

It's not that there's anything inherently wrong with the question he's just thrown at me, but it's the way that he's asked it, as if I'm truly in the wrong.

And to be honest, I have no answer. When Saul hit me the first time, he was taking his anger out on me for something that wasn't my fault—a bad day at the office and an argument with his boss. Maybe that was why it had been easier for me to say once was enough and to walk away. I hadn't had any excuses to make for myself and could find none for him.

When he'd come crawling to me with apologies, I wasn't going to give him another chance. If he'd done it once, he could do it again. Any desire I'd had for him had become tainted by distrust. My parents had brought me up to know my own worth, and my value was higher than being a punching bag for any man.

I'd put it politely, set out why our relationship wouldn't

work. That's when Saul had turned nasty and had beaten the hell out of me.

But despite me knowing nothing I'd done had justified him turning on me, part of me wondered what it was about me that had made him violent. Had he thought I was weak? A pushover? A convenient outlet to vent his frustrations on? Was there a sign over my head that screamed victim?

That's part of the reason I started working out. No man would ever see me as weak again.

Before Petty had started speaking, I'd been wallowing in self-pity, wondering whether I'd ever dare go back to my house. But his question had fired me up. Now I glare as I respond, "Of course that would be what you think. That I'd done something to deserve Saul's treatment of me. What do you think, Petty? What could I have done to make the man fill my house with poisonous snakes?"

"Venomous," he corrects me. While I'm not a violent person, his comment makes me want to slap him around the face.

"Instead of thinking there's something wrong with him, you think the fault lies with me. Fucking typical," I spit out. As he sucks in air, I lean forward, my sadness and shock disappearing, being replaced by indignation. "Don't you fucking think I've gone over this a million times in my head? Don't you think it keeps me awake at night? Not so much that it happened in the first place but that Saul is intent on ruining my life. Why don't you think on what kind of man it takes to do that? Perhaps if you tried to think the way he does, you'd have more luck finding him."

He rears back, surprised at my vehemence. For once, I've got him off balance, but he quickly recovers. "I can't think the way he does," he rasps. "I know you don't think much of me, RoseLyn, but I've no time for a man who can hurt a woman." Obviously recalling how he started this conversation he emphasises, "Whatever the provocation, nothing can justify what he did, or what he's doing to you. And, in asking what you did, I was trying to find out how he thinks. So help me out here. How did you get involved with him in the first place?"

The glance he gives me appears both genuine and contrite, so, relenting a little, I tell him, "He moved to my hometown while I was in college. It's not an unusual story. We met in a bar when I was out with friends. He bought me a drink and we started talking, I thought he was nice. Having things in common, we began dating, and that progressed to him asking me to move in with him." I break off, and run over that time in my mind, but I'm still unable to see that I'd missed any red flags. "He said he loved me. So, I did."

"You were living with your parents at the time?"

I nod, then realising he's focusing on the road, explain, "I'm an only child, and they have always been overprotective. But they were also aware of the danger of smothering me, so as I would be staying close by, they didn't make an issue when I moved out. They liked Saul." I break off, biting my lip as I remember how he had us all fooled. "He was a lawyer working for a local firm, prospect of becoming a partner, and he treated me as a good man should do."

"You say he loved you. You love him?"

I turn and look at him sharply, and for a moment watch him drive, noticing how he's constantly looking in the mirrors as well as the road in front. He's being vigilant and I know he's making sure we're not followed. Despite that I think he's an ass, his competence helps me to relax.

I gaze out the windshield and give him a truthful response. "I thought I did, but I was young. Now, looking back, I think it was as much the excitement of something new. My friends were finding partners and shacking up with them, and now I had my chance. I was happy enough and committed to him, and I thought we were getting on well." That's why what Saul had done had come as such a shock.

"Until he turned."

"Until he turned," I agree, and shiver. "I couldn't put up with that."

Petty visibly tenses and it annoys me so much I give an exasperated huff. Does he expect I should have stayed with Saul after he'd shown me who he really was? I don't understand how that would agree with his statement he abhors violence to women. Surely he'd be on my side?

"Where is he?" The question's asked under his voice so it makes me wonder whether he's even talking to me. "What does he want from you? Is it money?"

The final part is definitely addressed to me. "Money?" I snort. "He's barking up the wrong tree if that's it. I don't have money."

"Even with what you're earning?" As he glances at me, I see his eyes widen.

Huffing a laugh, I enlighten him. "I've a residency at a minor hotel in Vegas. I've no recording contract. I make enough to live comfortably on, but not enough to have an extravagant lifestyle."

His brow creases. "But you've got opportunities. Bart said you were going places."

My shoulders rise then fall. "Maybe. There have been a few talent scouts, but I'm not getting my hopes up. There's so much competition. Even if I was ambitious, I'm not sure I'd want to step into that cutthroat world."

"So you're happy doing what you're doing?"

Why shouldn't I be? I give a slight up and down move of my head. While the thought of producing records and getting myself a name that's known nationally is enticing, I thrive on the relationship between me and my audience. I love performing live. If a contract comes up, I wouldn't turn it down, but I'm not going out of my way to chase it.

We get to the hotel and Petty, after cautiously circling once more around the neighbourhood, parks out of sight around the back. It's not one of the big names and off the strip, but when we go inside, it's clean and comfortable looking. Petty takes care of getting the key cards and escorting me up to my room. Once there, he opens the door to the adjoining suite and nods in satisfaction.

"Sarge will be staying in there," he informs me.

I'm relieved I won't be here on my own. Saul's antics are escalating. Warning letters, notes left on my car and flowers delivered are one thing, but leaving snakes in my house? If I'd entered alone, I think the shock by itself would have killed me.

It's wearing me down. As I timidly unpack my bag, worried that I might find a lurking snake they've missed, I allow myself the luxury of anger directed toward the motherfucker who thinks he's got a right to make my life a misery. *How dare he?*

I won't give him the satisfaction of thinking he's reduced me to a nervous wreck, and I'm determined to go on stage tonight and sing.

Petty's loquaciousness seems to end as he takes a seat on the chair and starts scrolling through his phone. I'm quite happy to continue without a conversation that leaves me on edge, not quite certain what he's getting at, or how he thinks.

I shower and get into the swing of my normal routine. I'm on time when Petty escorts me down to the car and we drive to the club.

Petty surveys the surroundings before allowing me out of the car, then walks close alongside as we approach the rear entrance. More than ever I realise how vulnerable I am, and I breathe a heavy sigh of relief when I step over the threshold and the security door snicks shut behind.

"You've been crying." Kylie greets me with her accusation as soon as I open the dressing room door. She eyes Petty pointedly. "Well, I suppose your peace didn't last long and I can see you have something to cry about."

I snort back a laugh while Petty ignores her. Instead, he pushes in and starts checking around, going into the attached bathroom and sliding the shower curtain back.

"I already checked it," Kylie calls out with an exaggerated roll of her eyes.

But I'm just pleased, knowing now Petty's not just checking for a lurking assailant, but for anything one might have left behind.

When he's satisfied and has stepped out to position himself outside the door, Kylie waves her hand at my eyes.

"So what's got you upset? Is it Petty?" The last she says in a loud stage whisper.

Her accusatory pointed glare at the closed door puts me in a better humour and I chuckle as I take my seat in front of the mirror. As she starts applying my makeup, I give her the shortened version. "Saul escalated matters. He came to my house and left snakes inside."

Her hands stop in midair. "You're fucking kidding me."

"Nope." When she goes to speak, I wave into the mirror to get her attention.

Her mouth works and she swallows a couple of times, as though she's lost for words. Eventually she finds some. "Snakes? Alive?"

I wish they'd been dead. "Alive, yeah. Rattlesnakes. My living room was covered in them."

"Oh my," she squeaks, then shakes her head. "You call the cops?"

I shrug. "No point. Even if they believe Saul's behind it, they won't be able to find him. No one can."

"So that's why dark, handsome and obnoxious is back? Because your ex has again raised his head? I thought he was taking some personal time to reconnect with his wife?"

Inwardly I grimace. I feel guilty about that. I've presumably taken Petty away from what should be his happy reconciliation time. But it's Red, their president, who decides who to send. If Petty needs to blame anyone, that's the direction his finger should point.

"I presume Red called him back in," I reply. "Because the other bikers were tied up removing reptiles from my house."

Pausing, holding a handful of my hair, Kylie looks thoughtfully at my reflection. Her mouth quirks. "And he hasn't any other hotties to assign?"

I snort. "When I see him next, I'll ask if he can put all of them on rotation." I grin at her in the mirror. "But I get first dibs, remember?"

She pouts. "I'm always the fucking bridesmaid."

"Look, how about I put them through their paces, then I can give you the rundown of who's worth going for?"

We both know casual sex is something I don't do, but Kylie plays along, sighing dramatically.

"You would be saving me a heap of trouble. I mean, who wants to go to bed with someone who can't bring his A game?" She pauses, then asks with a gleam in her eyes, "Did you put Cobra through his paces?"

Our heads turn in unison at the growl coming from the other side of the door.

Grinning widely, I respond, "I certainly did." The growl turns to a bark.

"And?" Kylie prompts, smothering her laughter.

As the door handle starts to turn, I give her the details. "He can make really good coffee."

She snorts. Both of us eye the handle which has moved back into position.

"Fuckin' bitches," we hear and both crack up.

Once she's got herself under control, Kylie stares toward the door, standing with her hands on her hips. She lowers her voice. "Well, now. That convo certainly got to Petty." She raises her eyebrows.

I shrug. "Red probably forbids them from fucking clients."

"What a waste." She sighs. Then grins cheekily. "What about their stylists?"

There's more than one reason why I'm glad Kylie works for

me. Apart from the magic she works with my makeup and hair, she always manages to raise my spirits, and usually, whatever mood I'm in, I end up smiling.

After I've been transformed into a superstar, or the closest to it I'll probably ever come, I walk out to the stage door flanked by Petty.

As always, I take a few deep breaths steadying myself and try to put everything other than the coming performance out of my mind. Then, as ready as I'll ever be, I plaster a big smile on my face and walk out to a round of applause as soon as I'm announced.

For the next couple of hours I'm transported away to the world where nothing exists except the band behind me playing their music and the words coming out of my mouth. I move automatically to the beat, and bask in the adulation of the crowd.

It's a good night. Two encores are requested and supplied.

When the curtain comes down, I'm drained, having given my all on the stage. But when Bart indicates there are fans waiting for my autograph, I go over to them, plaster the smile back onto my face, and stay as long as it takes.

I'm surprised when I'm finally escorted back to the dressing room that Cobra is there waiting for me, leaning nonchalantly against the wall with his hands in his pockets.

"What are you doing here?"

He exchanges a look with Petty over my head before looking back down to me. "Just want to make sure no one follows you to the hotel." Then his eyes raise again. "Sarge has checked it all out and given the all clear."

"No one followed us," Petty says sharply, as if he's been accused.

Cobra shrugs, while I just feel relieved they're taking my safety seriously. At least I won't have to worry about finding a snake in my hotel bed.

Leaving them waiting in the corridor, I enter my dressing room. Kylie helps get me ready for my performance, but when

I've finished, I'm on my own. There I quickly down two full glasses of water and remove my heavy stage makeup. It takes little time to reverse the process from star to girl next door, and having changed back into a t-shirt and jeans, and brushed out my hair, I grab my purse and am ready to go.

Cobra and Petty flank me, but also talk over my head.

"I need this, Brother," Petty states.

I hear Cobra's sigh. "You fuckin' take care."

"As I would my own, Bro."

When we reach the parking lot, all becomes clear. Cobra escorts me to the car, after he's handed off the keys to what is presumably his bike.

"You're letting Petty ride yours?" The question comes to the fore as Cobra doesn't look happy as he watches Petty get astride the big machine.

"He needs it. He's going stir-crazy in cages," he says, as if that's explanation enough.

At first, I watch Petty in the side mirror as he follows the SUV, then at one point, he comes in front to escort us. Unfortunately, that gives me a grandstand view of the way he competently handles his brother's bike. Under the streetlights, I can see his body flexing as he leans to take a corner, righting the machine with expertise as he completes the turn. He does it so effortlessly in a fluid motion, he appears to be one with the huge motorcycle he rides. It makes me wonder if he shows that much skill in everything that he does. *My, that man is fine.* Then I remember the two important things I seem to have forgotten. One, he's everything I dislike in a man, and two, he's married.

It makes me blurt out a question that I know I shouldn't ask.

"Have you met Petty's wife?"

Cobra snorts, and looks my way. "No, she visited the clubhouse while I was with you." I shrug as if it's of no interest, as it shouldn't matter a damn to me. But as I turn to look out of the side window to take my eyes off the man riding in front, he adds, "But Hammer reckons she's a hot piece of ass."

As did Roller, so it shouldn't surprise me. A woman who can catch the attention of someone like Petty would have to be. And, I suspect, it doesn't take the machinations of her stylist to get her looking that way. For her, it probably comes naturally.

Me? I'm just ordinary when I'm not wearing makeup with my hair fancied up.

I shouldn't have asked, and there's definitely no reason to feel this burst of jealousy.

I don't even like the man for fuck's sake.

CHAPTER TEN

Petty

To be honest, I preferred exercising my mind, trying to think of how to catch RoseLyn's ex and being in my bodyguard role to spending time with my wife. I'd welcomed the valid and credible excuse to leave Britney alone in the apartment where we'd lived little more than twenty-four hours.

Having handed RoseLyn's security over to Sarge, it's just after midnight by the time I reluctantly give Cobra back his bike and again, trapped in a cage, which seems a euphemism for my life at the moment, drive to what has become my home. Though my ride had been too short to clear my head, it was good to feel an engine throbbing under my thighs once again.

Neither wanting to face Britney's anger for leaving her alone, nor wanting to risk her trying to push for a more intimate relationship that I'm in no mood for, seeing the lights off, I creep quietly in. I head straight for the new couch, thankful that while it's really too small, I'll at least have something other than the floor to lie on tonight. Unfortunately, as I'm still not familiar with this new place, or which of the floorboards make the least sound, I tread on one that makes a noise like a pistol discharging and disturb her.

"You're late." She exits from the bedroom, rubbing her bleary eyes.

I draw in a deep breath, knowing she's not used to my routine. "I'm normally back at this time. I work four to twelve, then it takes me half an hour to drive home."

Dressed only in a flimsy negligee which hides nothing from my eyes, Britney walks into the room and takes a cigarette out of the pack on the counter. I'd given up smoking years ago, shortly after she'd gone inside, and now am firmly on the side of those who find the smell obnoxious.

But I don't ask her to go outside. Instead, I open a window.

She cackles as though I've made a joke. "You're unbelievable, you know that, Clark? Does this singer know what a wimp she has protecting her? I doubt she does, else she'd have requested someone else instead. Or has she fallen for your pretty face, hmm? Does she not care as long as you satisfy her in bed?" She pauses, shakes her head, then adds, "Hopefully it doesn't take much to please her."

My hands fist but I keep them by my sides. "I'm her body-guard. The relationship between us is purely professional."

Her hands wave dismissively. "I wouldn't expect you to tell your wife if it wasn't."

I didn't know I still had a fucking wife until the day before yesterday.

Oh, sometimes a niggling thought at the back of my mind had reared its head, reminding me that she'd not signed the divorce papers, but I hadn't dwelled on it. I'd tried to contact her enough times to remind her about it. When she hadn't replied, I thought she'd washed her hands of me and, as much as she could while inside, had got on with her life. If I'd known what I do now, I'd have made more waves at the time. Goddamn it that I hadn't.

I go to the kitchen and take a bottle of whisky out of the cupboard and pour myself a generous shot. I swig it back in a couple of mouthfuls, then wipe my lips with the back of my hand. Placing my palms on the counter, I lean forward and look down. *Christ, give me strength.*

Until Britney contacted me, I felt I was a free man. I have zero designs on RoseLyn, a woman who might be attractive had she more meat on her bones, though she does have nice tits and ass, but her character turns me off completely. She's far too sure of herself. But while I wouldn't want to go there, I'd had no restrictions on whether I could or could not. It's hard to get my head around that I'm now considered a married man, and because of that, should be faithful to Britney.

"You coming to bed?" asks the woman whom I have absolutely no desire to get intimate with, and who I don't even like. I'm stuck in the trap made by my younger more gullible self.

"I'll stay on the couch," I respond, without turning around.

Tensing, I feel her come up behind me. "Then there is someone else. A man like you would never go through a dry spell. You never turned me down before, Clark."

Before was many years ago. What once got my cock excited now causes not so much as a twitch. Without turning, leaving her looking at my back, I firmly voice my denial. "There's no one else. Not RoseLyn, not anyone." There have been hookups and one-night stands over the years, but no relationships. I was never going to put myself through that again.

Her hand rests between my shoulder blades. Like a switch being thrown, her voice goes from hard to soft. "I want everything, Clark. I want what we always planned. To be at your side, to have your children. Life got in the way and tore us apart, but now I'm back and we can have a fresh start."

The whisky I've just drunk sours in my stomach and threatens to make its way back up. It's not that I'm against kids. Britney's right, when we first got together, we had our whole life planned. I couldn't wait to get started on having a family with her until I saw the parts of her I didn't like and which I wouldn't want in my children's DNA.

"Life didn't get in the fuckin' way," I growl, my voice low. "You got yourself arrested and banged up."

"It wasn't my fault." The lie falls easily from her mouth. Even now she's done the time, it seems she's still sticking to her story. "Come to bed, Clark. We can't make babies—"

I swing around, catching her off guard, but not wanting her to fall to the ground, stabilising her with my hands. I remove them as soon as she's got her balance back. "There won't be any making babies, Britney."

"You always wanted kids." Her eyes open wide.

"Some of my wants are well in the past." I can't tell her I still wouldn't mind having a rug rat or two running around, but not hers. It's unlikely to happen. To procreate, I'd have to have a relationship with a woman, and she's soured me for that.

She's watching me intently, creases appearing on her brow. "You already got a kid?"

"I haven't been in any other relationship," I start. "I'm not going to lie to you and say I've been faithful, 'cause I haven't." I'm not going to hide anything from her. "What was I supposed to do? You didn't want to see me, sent quite a sign you didn't consider yourself married. I moved on, Brit. I moved on. But no, there's no little Pettys running around."

"You moved on," she repeats with a sneer. "And you never questioned why I didn't want my husband to see me inside? You never thought how much it might hurt me to speak or read letters from you saying what was happening in your life. You never gave a fucking thought to me being locked up."

Anger bubbles up and I slash my hand through the air. "Don't tell me what I did or didn't do. I wasn't the one who left. That was you."

"You would never have left me," she chucks in my face. "You hadn't the guts, soldier boy, and you're not going to walk away from me now."

I try to summon up the backbone she'd always accused me of never having before. "Let's get this straight, Brit. I'm here with you while you get yourself sorted. Once you're in a job and your parole officer's happy, then I'll move back to the club. I'll support you financially—"

It's her turn for her hand to sweep through the air. "Money from you isn't what I want. I want you, Clark. And that's exactly what I'm going to have. If your little singer thinks she can have any part of you, then she'll have to think again. You're mine, and no one else is ever going to have you." She gets an ugly look on her face, one I remember only too well. "I hope you enjoyed yourself while I was away, because mine is the only pussy you're ever going to have."

She moves as if she's going to get in closer, maybe try to steal a kiss from my mouth, or press herself up against me. Deftly, I slide to the side and evade her. I might not have the hots for her anymore, but hell, I'm a man, and as weak as any male. Although my cock's at defcon five right now, the right attention from any female is likely to have it at defcon one. To give in would only complicate matters and we seem to have a lot to sort out. For a start, we've got very different views of what our marriage now looks like.

"It's late," I remind her. "I'm going to sleep on the couch." Deliberately, I turn my back and remove my cut, folding it carefully and gently placing it over the back of a chair. I go to the closet and get one of the new blankets, shake it out, place it on the seat cushions, then, sitting down, remove my boots and my socks.

Barefooted, I stand. Ignoring her, I head for the bathroom have a piss, wash my hands and clean my teeth. When I emerge, she's still where I left her.

I wait for her to have the last word, but instead of trying to argue me into her—well, it's actually my—bed, she huffs. When I walk past her, she lashes out and her fist makes contact with my kidney.

Sucking in air, my hands go to the small of my back. *Fuck, that hurt.* But by the time I'm able to breathe again, she's disappeared into the bedroom and closed the door.

My body crumbles down onto the sofa. I place my head in my hands, rubbing at eyes which feel watery while reminding myself that big boys don't cry. She's been back in my life for less than forty-eight hours, and already she's reduced me to the man I was before my lucky escape.

Why is she always like this?

Britney is beautiful, I fell for her looks. Then, believe it or not, for her engaging ways. What does the nursery rhyme say? *When she's nice, she's very very nice, but when she's bad…* Britney can be utterly horrid.

Our marriage was like walking on eggshells, I never knew what to say or how to judge her mood. A casual comment might make her smile one day, then the next, the same words might send her over the top.

I never realised how on edge I'd gotten until she was locked up. I resented freedom at first. They'd stolen my wife, the love of my life. Then with tentative steps a different me began to emerge, one who was no longer afraid to speak or who kept their thoughts to themselves.

I'd vowed no one would ever see me as weak again, and my self-promise had worked.

Until forty-eight hours ago.

I can't do this again.

What choice have I got? I married the woman for better or worse, though the latter is all I really ever got. When I said my vows, I'd meant them. I wouldn't have walked away if we hadn't been driven apart. Fuck knows what would have happened to me, but something about Britney would have made me stay by her side.

The distance, the lack of communication, had eventually lifted the veil from my eyes, letting me see how bad she'd been for me. Believing she'd wanted nothing more to do with me enabled me to petition for divorce. That she hadn't responded

I'd thought was just another of her cruel ways to prevent me moving on with someone else. Which hadn't been an issue. I was never going to risk putting my head in the noose again.

Where do I go from here? A relationship between me and Brit isn't going to work in a million years. But wouldn't I be a complete asshole to turn her away when she needs the stability of a husband and home to fulfil the requirements of her parole? And God help me, I haven't the guts to turn her out on the street.

Maybe we can pretend. She can stay here in the apartment that's rented in my name and I'll go back to the room at the clubhouse. I'll have to buy another bed, but other than that, it will work.

Surely my brothers would understand that so much time has passed it's impossible to pick up where we left off. Or would they expect me to man up and give her a chance? I frown in the darkness. After her performance in the clubhouse, her success at getting them on her side, I doubt if they'd believe my side, even if I wanted to come clean about it. *Little Brit? No way. Petty's yanking our chain.*

Lying back, I try to get comfortable on the couch which wasn't made with someone like me sleeping on it in mind. My feet hang over the edge, and the arms are in the wrong place. Even if my mind weren't racing a mile a minute, I doubt I'd get any sleep.

How could my life have changed in such a short time? I feel like I've been picked up by a whirlwind, and though I know I'm not in Kansas anymore, I've no idea where I'll land—or if I'll survive.

The thought that I'm trying to evade enters my mind. *Rose-Lyn's ex only had to hit her one time.* She had the sense to walk away, while I stayed, making excuses for Britney's behaviour every time, being the wimp Britney accused me to be. I can't let it be the same this time around.

There's a parallel with the singer's situation. Like her ex, Britney isn't going to let me go easily. She's made that clear. And if I don't let her have her way, she'll find some way to fuck up my life.

How can I extricate myself from this marriage?

I practice telling Britney to get out and leave me alone, of telling her there's no place for her by my side. I think about kicking her to the kerb both verbally and physically. I clench my fists, knowing I'm only being brave in the middle of the night. Brit drew me under her spell years ago, and now I'm back there again. My mind's not my own. It's under her control.

I don't understand how she has this effect on me.

RoseLyn had been strong. She'd walked out. But she hadn't gotten away scot-free. And therein lies my problem. Neither would I. Britney would not let me go easily.

I berate myself, put forward arguments and counter them, wondering why I'm unable to get over this blind spot in my mind, regretting I didn't change my phone number, and trying to come up with something that would rid Brit from my life. In the dark it's easy to be strong, but when daylight comes and I'm faced with her, any plans I've come up with will be smashed into dust. She just has that effect on me.

Eventually my tired mind blanks out, and at some point when I close my eyes, they stay shut.

But I'm still not free. Visions haunt me. Memories of the past merge with the present. A nightmare where my brothers all laugh as Britney regales them with a list of my deficiencies. Then Red's there, stripping my cut, disgust in his eyes, knowing I'm so weak.

Then, as if to punish me further, I get a fucking dream that seems only too real. Hands lower my zipper and start caressing my balls, slowly massaging my dick into wanting some action. A wet warm mouth engulfs me. While I know this is all in my head, my hips thrust, a swallowing action almost making me lose my load.

Just when I'm nearing the point of no return, the mouth pulls away, turning my dream sour. *Even in sleep I'm left unsatisfied.* But before I can groan in frustration, there's the sensation of lips surrounding my dick again. But this time it's different, and it's a pussy bearing down, enveloping my cock so snugly, it makes me gasp, and my hands grip the blanket.

RoseLyn. The name comes unbidden to my mind. *Fuck, this feels good.* I've not had a wet dream since I was a teen, but I'm happy to go with the flow right now. *RoseLyn.* I picture her in my head, bouncing on my dick, and in my sleep, I know that I smile. Seems I don't need to like her to get aroused.

I can't believe the strength of my imagination. My hands are nowhere near my dick, yet it feels like it's being squeezed. This time I do groan aloud, from pleasure.

The sound from my mouth wakes me up, but the feelings continue and the dream doesn't end. *Something's not right.* My eyes open to enough light to allow me to see Britney, naked, on top of me.

This is no fucking dream. It's a nightmare.

I want to stop, but my hips buck of their own volition, muscle memory ignoring the sanity signals from my brain. This isn't what I want, but she's got me so far gone, so close, I can't fucking help my response.

While my body responds on reflex, my brain continues to whirr. "Brit, stop." Even I admit my voice sounds weak.

Britney grinds against me, murmuring seductively, "I'm your wife. No need to stop, not when this feels so good. And it feels good, doesn't it, lover?"

Good, fucking fantastic. But I don't want this. I don't want her. Sex will just complicate everything. But as she rides me like she's riding a fucking bronco, her body misinterprets my attempts to buck her off.

"Brit. No," I plead.

This feels so wrong. Nothing about this is right. She's got me aroused in a moment of weakness, in that state between waking and being asleep. Now I'm fully awake and know the last thing I want to do is ejaculate into her cunt.

But my cock's got other ideas. While my brain is screaming *no*, blood is making my dick swell, and I'm unable to stop the betraying tingle in my balls and the resultant explosion as I would be able to halt the eruption of a volcano.

Her fingers are furiously working her clit, successfully as she clamps down around me and I'm completely lost. With a roar that's part relief and part disgust, I thrust up inside her, holding myself there as the inevitable happens and semen bursts out of me.

For a moment, we're lost in our individual ecstasies. Wanted or not, the draining result is the same. I come to my senses as I open my eyes and see her smiling down at me.

I push her off then roll myself from underneath her and stumble to the bathroom, only making it just in time before my stomach heaves and the bowl gets filled with vomit. I lean over until there's no more to bring up.

I flush, wipe my mouth with a paper towel and splash my face. My hands are shaking and my legs feel weak.

As I zip my jeans and look at my reflection, I see a stranger staring back at me. Someone so pale it looks like all the blood has drained from their face, their eyes blank and haunted.

I've had sex when I didn't want to.

I had sex with the last woman I should have allowed near my dick.

If she hadn't have gotten me to the point of no return before I fully woke up, I'd have thrown her off me. I hadn't given my consent.

I'd said no. She ignored me.

I feel like something's been stolen from me.

We didn't use a condom.

What if I just made her pregnant?

CHAPTER ELEVEN

Petty

'm so ashamed of myself and harbouring such ambivalent feelings toward her, I can't face Britney. Instead, I turn on the shower, step under the water and let the flow beat down on my head. Even multiple passes with the soap doesn't wash away the filth that I feel from her unwanted touch.

Why couldn't I control my body? My fist hits the wall, and then again and again, moving to some rhythmic beat as I mentally berate myself for being so weak.

She'd taken advantage. She'd gotten me to the point when although my mind said no, my body was unable to stop. *Christ!*

I feel so dirty. It doesn't matter that I continue to scrub until the water flows cold, I can't get clean. I'll be forever stained by the knowledge of what we've just done. I can't even consider the implications which might tie me tighter to her.

When I turn the water off, I sink to the floor, put my head in my hands, and only just manage to swallow a sob.

How have I come to this?

I'd upset my friend when I never mentioned I was married to Roller after we'd shared almost everything else. He and I had clicked when we were put on the same team and forged a strong bond on those long boring nights when we weren't quite sure whether either of us would still be alive in the morning. He'd told me about his life, and I'd told him about mine. Except for the fact I had a wife.

Britney had been like an addiction to the most addictive drug there is. One hit and I just kept going back for more. At the start, I'd have done anything to keep her by my side. Looking back, I can't be proud of the man who I'd become. Whether I'd ever have broken the habit if she hadn't been arrested, I haven't a clue. Maybe going out on another tour would have given me that welcome time apart. But whatever, when she'd been sent down, I'd initially been lost, adrift without my rudder.

I'd been desperate to make contact with her, but every message, every call, every attempt to visit, was ignored. At first, it fuelled my dependency on her, and I could barely function for myself.

I'd been a different man when I was with her. Free of her, the ties that bound me gradually began to drop off, and I started rediscovering the man I truly was. When I'd realised the damage she'd done to me, I didn't want to think, let alone talk about her. So I kept her a secret and put the entire episode behind me.

Now she's back. And... fuck. Now I've made a colossal mistake. I should have stopped us having sex. But I'd slipped back under her thrall just as I'd done so many times before, as if no time at all had gone past.

The cool droplets of water on my body make my skin form goosebumps, and I start to shiver, but still I stay put. For some reason, maybe just as a meal ticket, Britney clearly wants me and she's got no intention of letting me go. And when she wants something badly enough, she can be devious about getting it. Believe me, I know. She tried to trap me.

She might have my kid.

It would be hard enough to walk away from her. But from a child? There's no way I could leave it with her.

If, fuck it, if my seed bears fruit, I'm imprisoned worse than she's ever been.

I don't know how long I stay ruminating in the shower, but it's long enough that when I eventually turn the water off, I can hear her in the kitchen. The clattering of plates suggests she might be getting breakfast. My stomach threatens to rebel again and I'm uncertain I could eat anything she could dish up.

I grab a towel and wrap it tightly around my waist, wincing as it comes into contact with the bruise Britney left on my back, then step into the bedroom which I at least know is vacated to get my clothes, feeling like I'm putting on armour.

The pair of jeans I was wearing earlier I discard into the laundry basket. They smell of her, and the scent makes my nose wrinkle in disgust. The feeling of being used just won't leave me.

I can't stay here like a coward, hiding from her all day. I grab a t-shirt, put it on, then pulling back my shoulders I go into the living room and pick up my cut. Wearing it will hopefully remind me I'm a tough biker.

Yeah. Right.

"I've made breakfast." Britney looks over and smiles, the very epitome of the perfect wife.

I look at the plate of over easy eggs and strips of bacon on the side and have to turn away fast. I don't want to talk to her. Don't want her to crow about what she'd stolen from me in the night, and certainly don't want to discuss the implications.

"Red wants me at the clubhouse." I tap the phone in the pocket of my cut as if to suggest I've had a call from him.

Her eyes narrow. "I've got an appointment with my parole officer."

"Let me know the time, and I'll get a prospect to take you." While it's not fair to get Meat and Owl to ferry her around, the benefits of being a full member means they have to do what I want, and the less time I spend in her presence, the better.

Her eyes now become slits as she realises I'm palming her off onto someone else. I brace for the blast of anger, but instead, she asks, "You working tonight?"

Unlike myself, Britney seems to have worked up quite an

appetite. She sits down and soon is shovelling eggs into her mouth. She makes a little hum of appreciation, probably as they're better than prison food, but the sound she makes turns me right off.

"Yeah, I'm working." Belatedly, I answer her.

Her fork pauses halfway to her mouth. "Guarding your singer?" she sneers. "She does know you'd probably run away from an assailant, doesn't she?" She stares at me for a moment, then her mouth quirks. "Hmm, perhaps I should meet her and tell her who you really are."

I decide there and then that she's never coming anywhere close to RoseLyn. Fuck knows what garbage would come out of her mouth. And I'd lose any respect RoseLyn might hold me in. *She* cut loose from her abuser. I stayed and kept going back for more.

Fuck. *I am a wimp.*

Instead of defending myself, I turn on my heels and pick up the keys from where I'd left them on the side. I pause only to tell her, "Text me the time of your appointment and I'll make sure a prospect is here to take you."

Ignoring whatever words she throws after me, I close the door hard. I take the metal stairs down, breathing in a deep lungful of fresh air. At the bottom I stand, sweeping my hands back through my hair at the realisation I'm running away.

I would face down any man. Someone disrespects me or mine and they'd be feeling my fists pretty fast, but against a woman, I'm defenceless. My only weapons are words, and mine opposed to hers are like someone bringing a Glock .22 up against a Howitzer.

I stare at the SUV waiting for me in the parking lot, an emphasis of how I've been emasculated today. If I had my bike, the roar and vibration would comfort me and remind me who I am.

People would turn and stare and my cut would ensure everyone knew that while I might be riding alone, I've got my brothers and the reputation of the MC behind me. On my bike, I'm a fuckin' man in my own right. A mother may pull her child away, a man give me a chin lift of respect, and a boy might stare after me with envious wide eyes. I would raise my middle finger up to the world just because, and ride on.

I wouldn't feel like Britney's husband.

In the SUV, I lay my cut on the seat beside me, and pause before starting the engine. Banging my fist on the steering wheel, I wish to fuck I had nothing in my life to regret or that my past hasn't caught up with me.

Ladies are to be loved, cherished and protected. It was my fault all along that I'd failed. I'd never been able to stand up to Britney. I just hadn't been brought up that way.

As I near the clubhouse, I practice putting a smile on my face. My brothers are nosy fuckers and if they notice anything about my behaviour is odd, they'll want to know why. None of them would see a problem in being woken by a blow job. If I admit I was forced to have sex, they'd laugh their asses off. As would I if anyone tried to sell me that story about anyone else.

Thinking of their reaction makes me scoff at myself, but I can't suppress the feeling I've been used, nor change that I feel dirty as a result. The shudder shaking my body keeps me in the vehicle even when the engine is turned off until a rapping at the window makes me jump.

"Petty?"

Lost in my head, it takes me a second to open the door, get out and respond to Red. "Prez."

"Glad you're here. Wanted a word." He steps back and waves inside. Feeling relieved that as it turns out I hadn't lied to Britney about having a meeting, it's one less thing for her to berate me about, I follow him in. I raise my hand or chin to the brothers milling around, as we make our way to his office.

Once there, I take the seat in front of the desk while he sits behind it. He rests his chin on his hands and stares at me for a moment.

"You look like shit."

I add to his observation by wincing as I shift in my seat to get comfortable, and offer the explanation he'll be able to accept. "Sleeping on the couch isn't great."

I only realise after the truthful words have left my mouth that I've apparently said a fuck more than I meant to. Red's not stupid. I watch his brow crease as he processes my statement and the implications. I prepare myself for an inquisition, but instead he sits back, folds his arms over his chest, and makes a statement.

"I'm still trying to get my head around the fact that you've got a wife."

"Welcome to the club." I shrug, then, because he's my prez, he deserves to know where my head's at. "You know the story. I thought it was over and that I'd never see her again."

"Have to admit on last night's showing, she seems a good fit for the club." He chuckles softly. "Cher was quite taken with her and wanted to know if she'd be sticking around. So what do you think? You going to make a go of it? Or is sleeping on the couch signs of things to come?"

How the fuck do I answer that? Once I'd vowed to love her until death, but time and circumstances have changed my view. The few hours together that we've had showed I've no desire to set the match to the flame of any old passion, even if I could. *But I did*, I remind myself, trying to keep the scowl from my face, though my response was forced from me. Any answer I give Red would probably be different depending on whether she's pregnant or not. *Hope to fuck she's not.*

With that possibility, I leave my options open. "So much water has flowed under the bridge, Prez." Again I raise and lower my shoulders. "Honestly, I'm not certain where we go from here, or whether there's any future in it. You were shocked? Huh. I had the wind knocked out of me."

He grins. "I feel you there. It sounds a bit like me and Cher. I never expected to see her again, yet here we are." His eyes soften as they land on a photo on the corner of his desk.

Yup. There they are—happily married and expecting another kid. Inwardly grimacing, I hope he's not comparing my situation to his. Cher and Red rekindled their love, but there's no chance of that for me with Britney. A baby? A cold feeling seeps through me. I fucking hope not. One thing I'll be buying before going back to the apartment is the male equivalent of a chastity belt. Yeah, that's it. I'll stop off and buy a cock cage, and throw the key away. Let's see Britney find her way around that.

Red leans back, linking his hands behind his head, watching my face which I hope isn't betraying my thoughts. "What I need to know is how is your new situation going to affect you protecting RoseLyn? I'm sorry for pulling you away to deal with the situation yesterday."

It had been a welcome interlude, a chance to put space between me and Britney. I'm certainly not going to complain about that or put forward a case for spending more time to reconnect with my estranged wife.

I sit up straight and raise my chin. "Britney coming back is not going to affect any work I do for the club, Prez. I took the protection job on. I'm not going to step away from my commitments."

His eyes narrow. "You certain about that? There's no conflict with your obligations to the woman you married?"

"Britney knows the score. I've told her what I'm doing." I don't add that a fool could see she doesn't like it, but something on my face must give me away.

He seems to consider my answer carefully. His brow creases. Then, using his seemingly mind-reading prez ability, waggles his fingers. "Give it to me straight, Petty." When I don't respond immediately, he encourages, "You and me, we've had our differences. I don't mind admitting I had you in my sights for a while. But when push came to shove, you came through for Zeke, and that means a lot in my eyes. You might not see me as a natural confidant, but I am your prez. Don't tell me what you think I want to hear, tell me what's going on."

I think for a moment. Prez handed me my ass when he could have taken my cut. And while I'm probably far from his favourite brother, since we've had it out, he's not treated me different. I don't feel like confiding in anyone else, so while I may keep some things to myself, I'll give him an inkling of what I'm thinking.

I grimace. "Fuck knows what I'm doing, Prez. But Brit and I can't immediately jump into playing happy families." *And God help me, I hope I never have to.* "Getting out working? Well, time apart will give us a chance to learn about each other again without being smothering."

He smirks. "The apartment a bit small?"

I nod. Yea, and there's no handy bar where I can go blow off steam with my friends.

His head dips and rises. "Okay. Well, it's for you to handle on that side. Just let me know if it becomes too much. I, for one, hope it works out. Britney made a good impression." I suppress a snort. He doesn't know her like I do. Again, though, as if he's read my mind, he continues, "Like no one should step between a man and his wife, no one should interfere either way in a personal relationship. Just wanted you to know if it came to a vote, the brothers wouldn't have much objection about her. It's up to you whether you want to take that step or not. Whatever you decide, we'll be behind you."

When I give a grateful nod, he changes tack. "Tell me, what are your thoughts on the latest with RoseLyn?"

"The snakes?" The raise of his chin confirms that's what he's talking about. I rub my temples, then begin, "I'm worried, Prez. Her ex knows all about her snake phobia. If she'd gone back to that house alone, she would have freaked. She could have had a panic attack—"

"And possibly been bitten." Red looks grim.

I nod and wince.

He taps his fingers against the desk. "I take it you've no longer got doubts it was the ex?"

As I move my head from one side to the other, I confirm, "I was an ass." I admit I'd been playing devil's advocate for the sake of it.

"You're always a fuckin' ass." The statement's without any mirth accompanying it. I shrug. I've given Red more than one reason to believe that I am. "While it's good to have an open mind, everything, in my view, has always pointed to him. What I hate is that we're no closer to finding the fucker."

"And he always finds her." My mouth twists.

Red steeples his hands and looks at me carefully. "You've got a look that suggests you've been thinking of something?"

I have. "He seems to know too much about her. Her address, the cars that she drives. With his track record, it probably won't be long before he discovers her hotel unless we keep moving her."

"I hear you, but how the fuck is he doing it?"

"Thought about that too, Prez." I lean back, and cross my legs. "He was a lawyer, and I wondered if he had a friend in the cops."

Red stiffens. "Helping him stay under the radar which is why they can't find him—"

"Or even seem like they want to," I interrupt.

"And that's how he's getting his info about her." He looks interested. "I think you might have something there. I'll get Keys and the Utah brothers seeing if they can come up with some connection."

I hadn't lied when I said I thought he'd be able to find where we've hidden her. He seems to only be one step behind the whole time. What worries me is if he gets the jump on us, on her. While I don't worry about our ability to protect her, there's always a risk. I wouldn't want RoseLyn getting caught in any crossfire. "I'm not happy with RoseLyn staying in Vegas," I tell him.

Red lifts his chin. "I concur. This bastard is always too close." He rubs at his temples. "Crash and I have been thinking about laying a false trail for Saul to see if we can draw him out." His hands move down to scratch at his beard. "It would be useful if we could sneak her out of town, and replace her with a decoy. In a pinch, Angel could pass like RoseLyn from a distance."

Taking the offensive is what I'd prefer. "Her parents are in Texas. Perhaps she could go there." I've no idea what footing she's on with them. It's not like she and I have friendly chats. She's a job, nothing more than that. I've picked up that much from overhearing her speaking with her manager and that defi-nitely-not-one-of-my-fans, Kylie.

"That could be far enough away." He thinks for a moment. "Get her out and swap her with Angel. The more I think on it, the more I like that idea. As long as Angel doesn't have to sing." We both share a chuckle. Angel's got a voice like a drowning cat. He rubs the side of his nose and grimaces. "We can't afford to fuck this up. No plan is ever watertight. Though we're stretched thin as it is, we can't have anything happen to RoseLyn so someone has to go with her if she agrees to go to Texas. Won't do our rep any good if RoseLyn ends up dead."

I raise my chin acknowledging his very good point.

"To that end, I want both you and Cobra with RoseLyn tonight."

Again I make a positive gesture with my head.

"Oh, and if you get a chance, have a word with RoseLyn about getting out of Vegas. See if she can make a short-notice visit to her parents."

Again I dip then raise my head.

His body language suggests this interview is over. I leave his office but pause outside taking a second to think. I'm pleased Red listened to me about RoseLyn, and pleased they've come up with a plan. Idly I wonder whether it will be Cobra they'll be sending with her to Texas, and clench my hands. *Kylie and RoseLyn were surely joking about hitting up my brothers, weren't they?* I snort to myself. Even if they weren't, it's none of my business.

Though that dream… when I thought it was RoseLyn, I hadn't been complaining.

Fuck it. I'm a married man, possibly a soon-to-be father. Heaven help me.

I slap the side of my head and try to get my mind back into the game. I'm hoping to be a part of the sting that takes Saul down. While I might not be able to do anything about an abusive woman, just let me get my hands on an abusive man. He'll be begging for death long before the final blow is delivered. But then, I might not get the chance. I'm just a grunt. I'll go where my club instructs me.

Luckily, nothing's compelling me to go home.

I instruct Owl to take Britney wherever she wants to go, and make sure he has her number and vice versa. Then I take my bike and just ride, wanting nothing more than the freedom of the road.

I head out into the desert and for a while the wind blows my worries away. I feel the cleanest I've felt since early this morning. But the downside is that I have to go back. With each mile taking me in the direction of Vegas, my concerns flood back, my problems descending in full force when I reach the city limits.

For the next eight hours, I'll be with RoseLyn and working.

After that, I'll have to return to face Britney. And maybe, due to the time I've left her alone, for once, I'll deserve any punishment she metes out.

CHAPTER TWELVE

RoseLyn

I'm bored out of my mind.

Roller took over from Sarge as normal this morning, but he didn't want me to go out of the hotel. Luckily there's a gym here, but apart from that, I've been stuck in this room. While I normally would appreciate time to do nothing except catch up on a book I wanted to read, as I'm forced to, I resent it and can't settle.

I want to return to my house, the home that I made mine. But even thinking of going back makes chills run down my spine. I hate snakes with a vengeance. It's more than that, it's true ophidiophobia. Even a picture can trigger a flight response, the actual creature a full-blown panic attack.

While the Devils have assured me they've caught and removed every one, my mind can't accept it, and I have no idea if I'll ever be able to go back.

I had a nightmare last night. I dreamed I was lying in my bed and it felt all too real as I woke to a rattling sound and the feeling of something slithering over me. I'd woken Sarge with my screaming. Luckily for me, unfortunately for him, Sarge knows about nightmares only too well. He'd calmed me by talking to me, and not trying to dismiss my fears, instead trying to help me work through them.

While I hate staying in this hotel, hate that Saul has pushed me out of my home, I'm far from ready to return.

Most of all, I hate Saul. Hate that he's doing this to me. I hate myself for ever getting involved with him. I wish the police or the Devils could find him and lock him away. Mind you, if the Devils got a hold of him, I'm not sure he'd be left alive. Surprisingly, that thought doesn't bother me.

It's not hard to rationalise why. If a snake had bitten me, there's a chance I might have died. I'm not sure my phobia would have allowed me to cope rationally, or whether I'd have been able to seek help in time. Of course, with my protectors with me day and night, the chances are I'd have been saved. But alone? I think I would have frozen into a curled-up ball and died.

Saul knew how the venomous creatures scared me. Putting them in my house was not the action of a sane man, nor one who had my comfort and health in mind.

Picking up my e-reader again, I try to concentrate on the story, but it's hard to keep my mind on the words. Instead I watch the clock, ticking off the minutes until I can get ready to go for my show tonight, my slice of normality where I become someone else, if only for a while. On stage, my musical persona takes me over, the beat stirs my heart, the words flow automatically out of my mouth. The music energises me and while my performance leaves me exhausted, I also feel refreshed and cleansed. That's what I need to get out of my head. To put Saul and all he's putting me through out of my mind.

At four, there's the normal shift change. I don't know whether Petty will be back, or whether it will again be Cobra, but when Roller opens the door, it's to them both. A few words explain that with the risk of me being followed, both will be escorting me again.

Petty seems quieter than normal when he and Cobra arrive.

Well, perhaps that's a bit of a stretch seeing as, apart from yesterday, he's usually not talkative. Even so, he normally manages to get quite a lot across, with a roll of his eyes, a grunt, or a sarcastic shake of his head, showing his disproval of just about everything.

Today though, he's zombie-like, as if he's given up caring. When I drop a folder of music I'm carrying, he comes across, bends, collects the sheets up, then hands them back without saying a word, nor giving the sneering look that conveys women can't do anything.

A closer look at his face shows his forehead is lined and his eyes are slightly reddened, and an unsuppressed yawn shows that he's tired.

Hmm. I suspect his wife's been keeping him busy, but if she's been gone as long as I've been told, they've got a hell of a lot to make up for. No wonder he looks like he can't keep awake, they probably fucked all night.

I suppress the disappointment I've no business nor sense to be feeling, and as I've still got time to go before leaving for the casino, I ask, "Want a coffee?"

Cobra answers immediately. I have to ask Petty a second time before I get his attention. He seems so distracted that I'm glad they've doubled up on the protection tonight. I bristle. If his head's with his wife and not on the job, maybe he shouldn't be working.

"Coffee? Yeah."

I get the answer eventually, and line a third cup along with the others. I make them just as the guys like to take them.

"Usual plans?" Cobra checks in professionally, his mind, unlike Petty's, obviously on the job in hand.

"Uh-huh." I blow on my hot drink while answering. To the casino and then home, nothing different to that.

Cobra's drunk his coffee much quicker than I can, and checks the time on his phone. "I'm just going outside to make a phone call."

Dismissively I wave my hand toward Cobra. When he leaves all I seem able to think about is the distress my ex put me through yesterday, as well as the financial impact he's having on my life. I'm having to fork out for this hotel for one thing. Already I'm not in the best of moods so I'm not pleased to see Petty staring out the window, as if his mind is somewhere else.

Anger gets the better of me as I snap, "Why didn't you stay with your wife if you don't want to be here today?"

That, he certainly heard. He swings around and looms close, almost threateningly over me. "What do you fuckin' know about my wife? Who the fuck told you anything about her?"

I refuse to let him intimidate me. Instead, I broaden my shoulders. "I didn't know it was a secret." I can't understand why he's so upset and justify why I asked. "Since you've arrived, you've been distracted. How can you do your job if your mind isn't on it?"

"My mind is on my job, and my business is just that. My fuckin' business."

"And it's my life we're talking about." His response has done nothing to calm me down. "Cobra will be sufficient to protect me today. Why don't you go back to *her*."

"My job is here—"

I slice my hand through the air. "I won't tell if you don't, and if your mind's not here, then you could be a liability more than a help. Go back to your wife, Petty. I'm sure you've got plenty of things to sort out and time to make up for." I turn my back in dismissal.

His fingers clutch my shoulder and turn me to face him. Doing so, I see his free hand clench and his face darken. "And what do you fuckin' know about things I've got to sort out?"

He's not going to let me get away without answering him, so I shrug. "All I've heard, Petty, is that she's been gone for a very long time. You must be elated now she's back."

"You know fuck all," he snarls.

"Hey! What's going on?" Cobra runs between us, his hand

landing on Petty's chest and pushing him back. "What the fuck's gotten into you, Brother?"

Petty slaps Cobra's hand away. "You been spilling my business, *Brother*?"

Cobra's eyes open wide. "The fuck you talking about?"

Petty has an inch or two over Cobra and he uses them now, looming threateningly over his brother. "My private life is exactly that and not something to be gossiped about. Our client doesn't need to know anything about me."

Cobra raises his hands defensively. "Hey. You talking about your wife returning?" As Petty glowers, Cobra takes a step back. "Brother, I wasn't the one who told her."

I don't think Petty believes him. Worried I'm going to have bloodstains on the floor if I don't do anything to stop it, bravely I step in between the two men who tower over me, putting one hand on each and fruitlessly trying to push them apart. Although I can't physically move them, they do break their stares at each other, and I'm the immediate attention of two pairs of glaring eyes.

"I can't remember who originally said it." I keep my voice steady as I look from one to the other, then settle my gaze on Petty. "It wasn't Cobra, I know that. But I'd simply asked why you weren't on duty, and was told you were reconciling with your wife. I'm sure no one realised it was such a big secret and thought there was no harm in telling me the reason why."

The tension doesn't completely leave Petty, but he does back down. He doesn't apologise that he'd accused his friend, but at least it no longer looks like they're going to beat the hell out of each other.

He might not have said anything, but his reaction to me knowing his wife has turned up speaks volumes. If he'd have been happy about it, I'm sure he wouldn't have acted like that.

Of course, it could just be that he's a biker used to being able to do what he wants, and people now knowing he has a ball and chain will prove a cockblock. What do I know about the faithfulness of bikers, or how they treat their women?

While standing my ground, making sure they've both backed down and that I'm not going to have to mop up blood, I consider Petty for a moment. In all my dealings with him, he might not be the pleasantest person to be around, but he's been professional. He's not flirted with myself or Kylie, nor any of the other females I've witnessed him coming across. There are plenty of skimpily clad dancers at the casino where I work, and I can't remember his eyes lingering on any longer than they should. And that was before his wife was on the scene.

So if it's not that she's cramping his style, I wonder why he's not over the moon to have her back.

But as he said, it's none of my business. I've enough problems of my own.

No longer required to play referee, I pick up the coffee I'd made a short while ago, and grimace when I realise it's gone stone cold. Collecting the three full cups, I put them on the side for room service to clear up. Cobra says he's going to check the SUV for trackers and *snakes* he adds with a wink which makes me shudder and roll my eyes. Then he'll wait for us outside.

I hear footsteps behind me. Turning my head, I watch Petty approach.

It's only been a few minutes since I experienced his violent side, yet I don't feel I have anything to fear from him. Nevertheless, I'm wary as I meet his eyes. I needn't have worried.

He stands in front of me, pinching the brow of his nose. "I'm sorry."

As though he hadn't gone toe to toe with another man just now, I shrug. "No matter."

Dropping his hand he shakes his head. "I lost my temper and I shouldn't have."

If I'd have realised it was a sensitive subject, I'd have kept my mouth shut. I had been guilty of listening to gossip. If I'm honest, I'd love to know why no one seemed to know Petty was married, and what had made them decide to reconcile after obviously quite a lot of time had gone by. But I can also understand being a private person. Who am I to object? As he'd remarked, I'm just a client. It's none of my business. I don't need to know anything about the men who are paid to protect me, unless it affects them doing their jobs.

"I should apologise." When I'm in the wrong, I admit to it. "I shouldn't have said anything."

He walks to the window and stares out. I don't think he's going to say anything more, so it surprises me when he does.

"It's complicated."

"I get complicated," I reply honestly. And I do. Here I am hiding out in a hotel room because I'm being hounded by my ex.

"I suppose you do," he murmurs. He stares out the window for a time, then he gives a visible shake and his back straightens. When he turns around, he gives me his full attention. It's like a switch being thrown. My bodyguard's back once more. "We think you need to get out of Vegas."

My mouth drops open. "And go where? For how long?"

"Not long, but we want to lay a trap. Try to get Saul to walk into it. It's time to stop this once and for all."

I'm not going to argue with that. "Any suggestions for where I should go?"

He shrugs. "We thought, your parents."

I waggle my finger at him. Like that's going to happen. "Uh-uh, no way." At his raised eyebrow I continue, "My parents have no idea Saul's after me, and I'm not going to enlighten them. They'd be worried sick about me."

"But—"

"No." I put emphasis on the one word to show there will be no further discussion. My parents worry enough about me being so far away and already think Vegas is a den of iniquity. If they knew Saul had reappeared with evil intentions, they wouldn't be able to sleep at night.

He inhales a deep breath. "RoseLyn, Saul, at the very least, is trying to frighten you, and at the worst wants to cause you serious harm. Now we're not going to turn work away, so it's no skin off our nose how long you pay us to protect you. But apart from the cost, there's always a chance that however good we are, that he might be able to get to you. It's not enough just to provide you with protection. We've got to stop him before he slips by us."

I round on him. "Don't you think I know that?"

While I've spat the words at him, conversely he's remained calm. "Which is exactly the reason we need you out of town."

"Not with my parents." I move my attention back to the task in hand and return to making coffee. "They had me later in life when they thought they'd never have a child. While they've tried not to smother me, they hate that I've moved away from home. If they thought I was in danger, it would just about kill them. Dad's already got a weak heart." Another thought occurs to me, making me gasp. "What if he suspects I've gone home and follows me? They could be in danger."

"You won't be in danger. You'll have one of us with you."

I huff. "And what part of 'I don't want to worry them' did you not understand? Me walking in with a bodyguard?" I make a gesture with my hand to show how ridiculous it all is.

"We'll just have to be diplomatic about what we tell them." His brow creases. "Leave it to me. I'll try to think of something."

Petty and diplomacy were words I hadn't expected would go together. I thought he'd have insisted on charging in like the proverbial bull in a china shop, having no consideration for the feelings of anyone who got in the way of his job being done.

"Petty." I narrow my eyes. "Don't go around my back. I'm not having them brought into this. If they knew, they'd never let me come back to Vegas."

He meets my eyes and raises his chin. "Leave it with me. I'll sort something out."

It's the most I can hope for, and more than I expect from him.

I start to wonder whether with the return of his wife, his personality is changing.

But then he's true to form when he takes his and Cobra's remade drinks and I overhear his words to his friend.

"She's a fuckin' woman. She'll do what she's told."

Misogynistic dick, I think to myself, and spare a moment's thought for his wife.

Is that why she stayed away so long?

CHAPTER THIRTEEN

Petty

I'd love RoseLyn's fucking ex to appear just so I have something to vent my rage on, but like all the other evenings I've been her bodyguard, he's not put in an appearance. After an uneventful evening, I drive the SUV while Cobra provides an escort and take her back to the hotel.

Sarge is already waiting in the adjacent suite, and Hammer's already in the parking lot. Although Cobra and I are pretty certain we weren't followed, Hammer's going to be hanging around for a while to make sure.

On the homeward journey, I follow Cobra for a short distance before he heads off in one direction and me in another. I envy him like hell, for the fact he's on his bike and not in a cage, and that unlike me, he's returning to the club and to the company of our brothers. If it were my choice, I'd rather sleep on the floor in my old room than go back to the apartment I now share with my wife.

Why the fuck didn't I try and divorce her without her agreement? Why did I let it ride? Why did she have to come back into my life? Hadn't she done enough damage previously? And why am I letting it start all over again?

Because I'm just as she delights in telling me, weak as fuck. Hell, if my brothers knew who I really am, I wouldn't be a Satan's Devil very long.

Disgusted at the man Britney turns me into, I put off the inevitable, stopping off at a local bar to get a drink, needing to fortify myself before facing her.

RoseLyn had very rightly pulled me up on my distracted state of mind, and with that sharp reminder and how I'd definitely lose my patch if I let something happen to her, I'd put Britney out of my head and concentrated on what I should be doing. As the evening had gone on, I'd more or less successfully put my troubles to the back of my mind. Now, knowing I'll be facing the woman I no longer love and have started to actively hate, they come full frontal once more.

I've been unable to forget that this morning Britney had taken advantage of me.

I finish my first drink and ask the bartender for one more.

What if I made her pregnant, and she's tied us together? Could life be so cruel as to punish me for just one mistake? Why hadn't I stopped? Why had I allowed my body to come inside her?

And why the fuck should fate look favourably on me now? It sent her back to me. With my luck, she's probably already with my child. And fuck knows that means I could never leave her. Or leave a child with someone like her.

On the chance that the gods aren't all against me, I can't let myself get into that position again. Two drinks are all I allow myself. I need to sleep lightly so any attempt by Britney to touch me will wake me. As I stare into the bottom of my glass, I wonder whether I can attach a bell to my belt or padlock my zipper. I regret not stopping off to get a cock cage.

The thought that we might have made a baby makes me sick to my stomach. The thought of Britney as a mom, impossible to consider.

Exiting the bar, I go to the SUV and reluctantly turn it in the direction of the apartment. I coast in through the entrance to try to keep the noise down, then on my tiptoes walk up the steps. I take it as a good sign that the lights are off. Not wanting to risk waking her up, I use the flashlight on my phone and remove my boots.

I'd pissed at the bar so all I need do is brush my teeth. I go into the bathroom and do that as quietly as I can, then I pause by the door to the bedroom, holding my breath. But from within comes no sound.

In my socks, I step back into the main room and go to the couch, seeing immediately the fucking bitch has removed the blanket and pillow. She's trying to force me into her bed, but she's not going to be successful.

Laying myself down, I rest my head on the arm, and fully clothed, close my eyes and try to sleep.

It's hard to relax when I'm expecting someone to come in and start molesting me.

While I've always been disgusted to hear of any child that's been assaulted by an adult they should be able to trust, or a woman who's been ignored when she's said no, I've never been in the position of actually being able to feel empathy with them before. Now, lying here, unable to sleep with my ears on high alert for any sound that might indicate her approach, my eyes unable to shut in case she creeps up on me unawares, I under-stand only too well how horrific such situations are. I'm actually scared in ways I've never been before, even when patrolling areas in foreign territory peppered with insurgent snipers.

I'm a fucking man. This shouldn't be me. In the dark, I clench my jaw, unable to believe that everything I thought was behind me is catching up with me. I thought I'd escaped my past, thought serendipity had taken my nightmare away. Now, due to my own stupidity and a case of letting sleeping dogs lie, it's caught up to me.

Eventually I must fall into an exhausted sleep, as I wake with a start when I hear the curtains being ripped back. Opening my eyes just a crack, I inwardly sigh with relief when I see Britney's fully clothed and not dressed to seduce.

"You going to lie there all fucking day?"

I reach into the pocket of my jeans and extract my phone. It's six in the morning, and I've only been sleeping a couple of hours.

"Give me a break, Brit. I was working last night."

She places her hands on her hips. "Oh yeah, your *body-guarding* duties. You get up close and personal with this singer then?"

I sling my arm over my forehead and breathe a heavy sigh. "Cobra was there as well. Why don't you fuckin' ask him what went down? This is my job, Brit, not a chance to get my rocks off. And one of us needs to take working seriously."

Her eyes widen. "I can't help that no one wants to employ a felon."

Knowing I'm not going to be able to go back to sleep, I swing my legs over the sofa and sit up. "You haven't even fuckin' tried."

Sparks now fly from her eyes. "How do you know? You're not here half the time."

And she wasn't there for seven years. But sensibly I keep quiet. Instead, I get to my feet and go into the kitchen. The coffee maker isn't even switched on, so I do that myself and proceed to make a drink.

As she hadn't tried to molest me today and I'm grateful for that, I make her a cup too, then look into the fridge for the makings of breakfast, only to find she must have used every-thing from our initial grocery run the day before yesterday. There's a box of cereal in the cupboard so I pour myself a bowl of that, offering one to her politely, not surprised when she lifts her nose in the air and declines.

"What are you doing today?" She takes her coffee and leans back against the counter.

Glancing to make sure it's a genuine enquiry rather than a trick question, I wipe the milk off my mouth with the back of my hand. "I need to check in with Prez, then this afternoon and evening I'll be working again."

"You work too damn hard." Her criticism, though, is voiced with confusion rather than ire. "You're in a fucking outlaw motorcycle club. Shouldn't you be riding around causing mayhem?" She shakes her head as though I'm a disappointment to her, which I probably am.

"Nothing's handed to you in this world for nothing," I remind her, while thinking how the state has housed and fed her for the last seven years.

Do I bother telling her that all the Devils work for themselves? We own the businesses and take a cut of the money coming in. A decent cut if I'm honest. It's not the same as working for the man, and a damn sight better than taking the risks that drug dealing and gun running can bring. Pulling my weight in our security business is just a different way of having my brothers' backs. But loyalty was never one of Britney's strong points.

She's looking at me as if she can't comprehend the man I've become. In the end, she seems to give up trying to puzzle it out. Shrugging, she just asks, "What the fuck am I supposed to do when you're out most of the day and most of the night?"

I bite back the response she could do what any wife or partner would—either try to get herself a job, or busy herself here, tidying up. Looking around, it's clear she did fuck all yesterday. If she's looking to me to bring in the money, then she should play her part.

I force myself to see it from her side. She's moved to a city where she's never lived before, and doesn't know anyone. Opening my wallet, I take out some cash. "Get the prospect to take you to a mall and buy yourself some new clothes." Isn't that something any woman would like?

Her face doesn't show much pleasure in my suggestion, but she's quick enough to grab the bills from my hand.

"And what about this evening? You're leaving me all alone again?" She's pouting now.

It's been too long since I've had to think about the comfort of someone else. Again I try to put myself in her position. I'd probably get myself out and go to see what's around, but without a driver's licence, it's hard for her to do that.

Despite my misgivings I offer a suggestion. "I'll talk to Prez, see if you can go to the club for the evening. But," I focus my more serious stare on her, "no fuckin' messing around, Brit. They won't put up with snide remarks or your brand of humour."

"Oh I can behave so I don't upset your friends' fragile egos," she tells me. The grin she's sporting shows she's got exactly what she wanted.

It's not fragile egos I'm worried about. If Britney shows her true self around them, I'm probably more likely to come home to a corpse. *Or,* I frown, *it's me her behaviour will reflect on, and I'll be the one getting a beatdown.*

Although part of me wants to receive an answer in the negative, as it turns out, when I ask Red, I find Britney made enough of a positive impression the first time I took her to the club for him to be totally okay with her going back without me by her side. Cher, his old lady, had taken to her enough to feel sorry that she was being left on her own after only just moving to a new town, and would welcome the company of a new old lady.

Shaking my head, wondering why the world can't see Britney as I can, then remembering I wouldn't be in this situation if she hadn't fooled me in the same way, I arrange for a prospect to ferry Britney around, and then bring her to the club.

Part of my day is spent in a meeting while we brainstorm trying to find Saul. With him putting the snakes in RoseLyn's house, it's not that we're taking things more seriously, it's that finding him quickly has become more vital. Fuck knows what the asshole will do next. A phone conversation with Utah shows they're embarrassed and annoyed that they haven't been able to do more to help find him. Though, apparently, they have suspicions about a cop who could be helping him and feeding him information.

As soon as they've firmed up on it, they'll let us know who and we can take over the investigation.

I sneak in a ride on my bike to clear my head, and at three thirty, reluctantly swap two wheels for four, and head to the hotel where RoseLyn is hiding out.

Being forced out of her home is taking its toll on her. Instead of the happy, carefree woman I'm usually met with, she's downbeat and looks tired, as though she's been unable to get a good rest. She's also fidgety and eager to leave for the casino, and seems restless until it's time to go.

Once she's at the casino though, she's more back to her usual self, which probably is down to Kylie. As I lean against the wall outside the dressing room, I hear their voices from inside, the insults sliding off me like water from a duck's back and making me smile. *Seems I'm still fooling someone, projecting the kind of man I want the world to see. Someone who's strong and so fucking sure of himself, he'll take no shit from anyone.*

She exits the dressing room transformed into someone else, and goes on stage at the allotted time. As always, I can't help the gasp of shock when she opens her mouth and that astonishing voice comes out.

I force my eyes away, and scan the audience, mentally comparing every face to the image of her ex I hold in my head. After walking around, he's not here, I'm certain of that.

While I make sure to keep her in sight, I find a quieter spot at the rear of the auditorium and take out my phone. I call Roller.

"Bro. What's up?"

"All good here," I reassure him, then ask the question that's been playing on my mind. "How's Britney doing?"

I grit my teeth as I hear the admiring smile in his voice. "Yeah. She's fine. She's close if you want to talk to her."

"Nah, Brother." I shut that down fast. "I'm good. Just wanted to make sure she was alright." *And wasn't causing any damage.*

"Tiff's not in—she's got the flu or some shit. Cher and Britney seem tight. Think Cher likes the female company."

"Zeke there?"

"Was." I hold my breath. *Please don't say Britney insulted them.* "Your woman's great, Petty. Zeke seemed to get on well with her."

There's a pause as if he's moved a distance away, maybe outside the clubhouse as the noise level drops from his end. "Don't know why the fuck you kept her secret. She's one to keep hold of, Bro. Respectful as shit, doing her best to fit in. Shy though." He snorts. "The brothers are tiptoeing around her. They're trying not to make her run for the hills."

Brit shy? That's a part of my wife that I've never seen.

I mumble something to Roller to end the call, then rest my head back against the wall, the sound of RoseLyn's performance reaching my ears. *What game is Britney playing?* I'm certain she's up to something, I just don't know what. She's trying to inveigle her way into my life, a life where I don't want her.

Not that I'll have any choice if she's pregnant.

Though I'm itching for a fight, the night passes without incident. No flowers delivered, no suspicious notes left and no sign of Saul. Cobra arrives just before the end of her set, and we again escort her back to the hotel while checking we've got no tail. I hand her over into Sarge's gentle care, feeling like we're in the eye of the storm and that there's something coming.

Her ex wouldn't be content with chasing her out of her house. He's getting closer, I can feel it.

On my own time now, I go straight back to the dreaded apartment. Owl has already confirmed he'd delivered Brit safely home. On tenterhooks I enter the door, but the lights are off, and hopefully she's already asleep. I grimace as I see that uncomfortable couch again, but know it's better than the alternative, sleeping with Britney and sharing the same bed. Still dressed, I settle down for another night where I'll rest with one eye open.

But I can't sleep. My mind's whirring. I'm in a mess that I see no way of getting out of. I can't even go to my brothers for understanding as they all seem to like Brit. She's portraying the perfect persona of an old lady, and only I know it's an act. The only way I could extract myself from this situation is to tell the truth, and that would mean me losing my patch. My brothers wouldn't want me riding beside them if they knew who I really was.

I'm not sure if I get any sleep at all. Morning comes eventually and my eyes are open when Britney emerges from the bedroom. My breath catches when I see her in her negligee, and bile rises in my throat as I get an instant recall of her hovering over my dick.

I try to rationalise it, tell myself it can't be that bad. I've had hookups in the past that I've definitely reconsidered the next morning, normally after having downed too many beers and the woman I saw in my drunken haze bore no resemblance to the one I'd seen in sober hindsight. Those encounters, I'd managed to laugh off. But my brain can't seem to get past the thought that Britney had taken something that I hadn't wanted to give.

Worse, I can't look at her without wondering about the implications of her actions, and am too scared to ask if there's any likelihood of her being pregnant. I'm not ready to hear the answer.

She fucking approaches me with her lips puckered for a kiss.

Turning my head away, I snarl out, "There's nothing like that between us."

She snort chuckles. "You didn't complain the other morning."

I'd said no quite clearly, but she carried on. "I don't want that, this, with you, Britney."

She regards me for a moment. "Oh come on, Clark. I know you, remember. You can't go too long without sex." Her brow furrows, "Unless you're getting it from the bitch—"

"I've told you before, I'm not getting anything from RoseLyn or anyone else."

A grin appears. "Then if you intend to be faithful, and Clark, dearest, I wouldn't recommend you be anything else, you'll have to get what you want from me." She attempts a seductive smile, her fingers drawing attention to her lips. "You already know I can satisfy you."

In the past, sex between us was one thing that was not a mistake. But now the idea leaves me flaccid.

Rather than telling her the thought of sex with her turns me the fuck off, I blurt out, "Could you be pregnant?"

Oh, the look on her face is so smug, I know I've played into her hands and she's got me exactly where she wants me. She puts her finger to her lips for a second, then grins. "Well, I don't know, Clark. You tell me. Your cock was in my pussy, and… do I really have to tell you how babies are made?"

I stand, brush my hands through my hair and spit out angrily, "I know the fuckin' mechanics, Brit. Are you on anything?"

"My, my, temper, temper. And what do you think? I've only just got out of prison and there was no likelihood of getting pregnant there."

So she's not. And while I know she's not in the middle of her period, she could be anywhere in the other three weeks, so what are the odds?

Fuck! I feel like screaming and pulling my hair out.

"It's not the end of the world, is it, Clark? We're married and you always wanted kids."

I don't anymore. Or not with her. Or not with anyone as how could I ever trust another bitch?

Christ, but I want to wipe that smirk off her face. She's standing there, an eyebrow raised in challenge. Then she chuckles. "You just don't have the balls, do you?" She turns away.

Seems like she did do something useful yesterday. She must have gotten the prospect to take her to a grocery store as the cupboards are again stocked. But when she offers me breakfast the thought of food makes my stomach curdle.

I make my coffee myself.

She cooks bacon and eggs that I've no appetite for. I use the time to go to the bathroom and put on fresh clothes. When I return, it's to find her eyes on me.

"How the hell did you ever get into that gang, Clark?"

"We're not a fuckin' gang—"

"Yeah, yeah," she says dismissively. "Your *club*. I mean, the men I've met there are real men if you get what I'm saying. You're a fraud, Clark. How don't they see it?"

I prospected with them. I've fought alongside them. I've proved I'm their equal time and time again in the ring. They see the man I want to portray…

Not the man I am with Britney.

She doesn't wait for an answer, just goes back to digging into her breakfast. I notice how at home she appears to be in the apartment, and that it's me who seems to be the interloper. Having said her piece, she stays quiet, but satisfies herself with snide glances which end with an upturn to her lips as though she's planning something.

The thought of what it might be makes me shudder.

I don't stay longer than necessary. I get out of there and away from the woman who calls herself my wife, and only feel I can breathe properly when I arrive at the clubhouse. I park the SUV, walk past my bike, stopping for a moment to let the sight soak in, then carry on inside.

Red's standing at the bar, drinking a cup of coffee as I enter.

"Got a moment, Petty?"

When I raise my chin, he waves me into his office and then to the chair in front of his desk. His eyes fix on me for a moment, and then he chuckles. "I wasn't sure what to expect when you asked for Brit to come here without you, but your ol' lady's a good fit. Behaved herself well yesterday evening. Haven't heard anyone say anything bad about her."

Which just proves how little they know her. Grimacing, I correct him. "She ain't my old lady."

Red looks at me from underneath the eyelashes that I've

heard the sweetbutts say women go crazy for. "That ring on her finger says otherwise."

Even if there was a small part of me that thought Britney might have returned changed, and we might have been able to make a go of it. I now know the truth, nothing's any different to how it was before. Except, I'm no longer willing to fake it. Red's probably judging me by his own relationship with Cher, and I need to let him in on the truth of it.

"There's a piece of paper that says she's my wife. I've no intention of patching her or putting her on the back of my bike." His mouth opens, but before he can speak, I continue, "We'd have been divorced long ago if she hadn't have gotten locked up. We've nothing in common, Prez." *I don't even like her.*

His eyebrows form a V. "She seems to think you're both giving this relationship a chance. Have to say, Petty, she thinks very highly of you."

If she does, she hasn't said shit about it to me. As I stay silent, he continues, "I told you before, if it came to a vote, I don't think anyone would object to patching her in, and after last night, I've no doubts about it."

No. It would just be me who's the holdout. I can't help wondering what her game is, and why only I can see that she's playing one.

Red even seems to have sympathy for her. "Cher's been speaking to me. Britney having the label of ex-felon doesn't make it easy to find work. Hope you don't mind me stepping in, Petty, but I had a word with Erika, and she said if we vouch for her, she's willing to give her a try as a waitress."

We'd taken on the contract to provide Erika's restaurant with security and protection while I was still a prospect. I respect the woman and like her.

Red raises his chin. "All Erika wants is for you to say that she's trustworthy." He raises his eyebrow.

For a second my mouth gapes open like a landed fish as I try to think of how to answer. I'm in an awkward position. My natural inclination would be to palm her off on someone I don't like, not someone who's basically a friend to the club.

Can Brit be trusted? Well, she's never actually stolen anything, that was the whole point. But has she the temperament to make a good waitress? She certainly doesn't like the idea, I'd raised that suggestion before. But now, maybe, she'll have had second thoughts as she knows how hard it is to get a job as a felon. Maybe she'd be on her best behaviour and wouldn't let me, or the club, down.

Britney needs a job, and if Erika has a place for her, how could I deny her the chance? Maybe getting out of the apartment will sweeten her temper.

I finally settle for mumbling, "She'll do okay. I'll tell her about the position."

"Erika will want to interview her," Red warns.

"Of course." There are positives to the idea. It means she'd probably be working the evenings while I'm doing the same, and hopefully it will stop her complaining about me being out so much. And Britney won't be left to her own devices, nor able to spend so much time without me in the clubhouse.

"Was that it, Prez?"

"Fuckin' wish catching up about your marital bliss was all it was." He smooths his hand over his beard. "Nah, I got a job for you, Petty."

I'm all ears, leaning forward. "Anything you want."

"I'll keep you to that, Petty." He leans back, linking his hands behind his head. "We're putting our plan into action to catch this Saul motherfucker once and for all." His mouth forms a line. "The feeling is Saul got her out of her house for a reason. We've upped the security there, but now she's been forced to move out. All she's got to protect her are keeping her location secret and always having one of us around. Escorts, as you know, can be distracted or removed, and finding her location is, for him, probably only a matter of time. We need to force his hand before he forces ours."

I'd like to say he's wrong, but I've been thinking along the same lines. Though we try to make sure she hasn't got a tail, and the room she's in is in a fake name, if Saul's got a contact helping him, she might not be able to stay underground. I raise my chin to show I agree with him.

"RoseLyn's off for the next couple of days, yeah?"

Her residency is five nights a week, so yes, she is. Again I dip and lift my head before returning it to the neutral position.

"We want her to go visit her folks. Stay there the night so we can put shit in motion."

"RoseLyn doesn't want to worry her folks and admit there's anything up."

He's got an answer for that. "She doesn't need to tell them. Surely she goes home to visit them from time to time? Especially when she has time off?"

She must do. She hasn't said, but I believe that they're close, else why would she worry so much about upsetting them? "What about her protection?" My brow furrows. "I thought we were sending someone with her. We can't guarantee that the fucker will stay in Vegas and not follow her home. And if she turns up with a bodyguard, her family will get suspicious for sure."

Red's lips curve. "Won't be a bodyguard we send with her. Wouldn't be strange for a girl to take a new love interest home."

I have no fucking interest in bitches, and least of all RoseLyn. So why should I feel on edge hearing she's got a boyfriend in the wings? He must have been out of town as I've never met him, and she's never mentioned him which is strange. The thought shouldn't unsettle me. I tamp that reaction down hard. "Have we checked him out, Prez?" I hope my voice doesn't sound as brittle as it feels.

He chuckles loudly. "Don't need to check him out. We already know all there is to know about him."

So that's that. RoseLyn will be flying off to Texas while we make Vegas safe for her to return. "What's the plan, Red? Where do you want me?" Hopefully I'll have a chance to teach Saul what happens to abusive men.

He snorts. "On a plane to Texas."

My mouth opens and shuts. "But you said you weren't sending a bodyguard—"

"I'm sending a pretend boyfriend who can play both roles."

As his meaning sinks in, my head starts moving side to side as my mouth states the word, "No," and then I repeat it again, "No."

"No? You refusing a direct order from your prez?" His eyebrows meet his hairline.

"Send Cobra," I say in desperation. "He gets along with her. He—"

"He's got tats for miles and is enough to scare any potential in-laws off. Nah, you're the much better proposition."

"Me?" My voice squeaks and I cough to clear it. "What the fuck, Prez? You think I'm boyfriend material?" Grasping at straws, I add, "I've also got tats."

"Not on your face and neck," he retorts.

I'm too busy continuing to shake my head to formulate much of a response. All that comes out of my mouth is, "You must be fuckin' joking." I scramble for an excuse.

The idea of being with RoseLyn, of pretending to be someone special to her for even a few hours is both exhilarating and frightening at the same time, and I don't understand why. All I know is I can't do it.

"No, Prez. I'm not right. There must be someone else."

Red barks a laugh. "I'm trying to think who's got experience of anything other than fucking and am coming up short. You're married, Petty. You must have dated and wooed Britney before you put a ring on her finger. I'm sure you must remember how that shit works."

And look how well that worked out. But I can't deny he's right. I was the perfect suitor when it came to Britney, and she pulled me in hook, line and sinker. Enough so I was never going to show a vulnerable side to any woman ever again.

Now I fuck 'em and leave 'em. Far less complicated. But he's reminded me of another excuse, the one I actually should have started with. "I'm married. Britney wouldn't like it."

"I'm not a fool, Petty." Red's laser eyes focus on me. "Britney might have convinced us she's the perfect woman, but you've made it clear you're holding yourself back. You're off kilter with Britney back in your life, and have admitted you sleep on the couch and feel trapped in that apartment." He pauses and his mouth twists. "Can understand it. You had no time to get your head around the idea of her coming back. Maybe some distance for a couple of days might help you get your head straight and decide what you really want."

I'm all for a time-out, but not in this circumstance. "And you think Brit would be okay with me pretending to be another woman's boyfriend?" I can just imagine how that conversation would go with her.

Red slams his fist on the table. "She doesn't have to know what you're doing. Club fuckin' business and none of hers. And I'm not asking you to get your dick wet. Just telling you to act friendly in front of RoseLyn's parents." He continues to stare me down. "Your woman got a problem with the club and the work you do for it?"

She's got a problem when it comes to RoseLyn, but he's right, I needn't tell her that's where I'm going. All I need to tell Britney is this is club business.

But I don't even *like* RoseLyn. How can I pretend to be in love with her? She's not my type. *She's got a great ass, and that voice when she sings…* Pity she won't be singing her way to Texas, then we might have a chance.

I'll be away from Britney.

"I don't know if RoseLyn will accept the suggestion." I'm weakening and Red knows it.

"She will if you do your job right and persuade her."

I look down at my hands. How can I convince RoseLyn to go home to her parents and take me along with her as a pretend suitor? How could we possibly make it work?

"You gonna let me down, or you gonna do this?"

I won't let my prez down. I can't. After inwardly grimacing at Britney's probable reaction if she ever finds out the truth about where I'm disappearing to, I raise my chin toward my prez. "I'll do it."

But how to persuade RoseLyn?

I decide to enlist help.

CHAPTER FOURTEEN

RoseLyn

A very unladylike snort laugh makes me reach for a tissue and blot my nose. "You've got to be kidding me." I chuckle again waiting for Bart to join in, but my manager just watches me quietly. A kernel of warning settles inside me. "You can't be serious." I feel my eyes opening wide.

Bart grimaces. "I don't know what else to do, RoseLyn. It's costing us a fortune to keep all this security going. Something's got to give, and it doesn't seem likely it's going to be your ex. If there's anything that can help, then we've got to do it." He breaks off and rubs his forehead.

"By getting me out of the way and using a decoy to catch him." That's the first thing I have to process, and perhaps the easiest part to understand. "I don't like it, Bart. It's putting another woman in danger—"

"She's one of their kind. She knows the risk in that life." My jaw drops, as Bart shrugs. "The Devils are hardly choir boys."

"You thought their contract was a good one."

"It was cheap," he cries. "You needed protection, and it seemed to work out. But we can't ignore their reputation."

"I don't like the thought of a woman putting her life on the line."

"Better her than you," he snarls. He visibly calms himself down, and his tone grows more reasonable. "They think by controlling the situation they'll keep her safe, and they'll catch Saul and end this thing once and for all."

Or Saul might be enraged if he finds he's being toyed with by a girl wearing a wig and pretending she's me.

Breathing in deeply, I offer an alternative. "If you've got so much confidence in them being able to control the narrative, then why use a decoy? Why not use me?"

"I can't risk you, RoseLyn."

"I can't risk an unknown woman. I know what Saul's capable of."

"The Devils won't go for it." He states that as if there's no point having this discussion. "You're heading out of town on those days off, and when you come back, the situation will be resolved. You've got a part to play, and I need you to step into that role."

"But—"

"What's the point of paying for protection and then going against their advice?" he challenges me. "Do you think I want to put anyone in danger? Of course, I don't. But Saul's fucking dangerous, and he needs to be caught."

As he said, the Satan's Devils aren't choir boys. "If they catch him, he won't be going back to prison this time. They'll kill him."

Bart doesn't flinch. "He's a rabid dog that needs to be put down."

Not for the first time, when I analyse my feelings, I realise I'm less concerned about that outcome than another woman getting hurt. Saul's lost any sympathy I might ever have had for him. It's either him or me, and I'd prefer to stay alive.

Can I trust the Devils to ensure that only Saul gets hurt? I don't want it on my conscience that Saul gets to another woman instead. I stand, pace, and think on it for a while. Bart gives me the space to come to terms with the idea. I think what I know of the men and that they'll be using one of their own. I have to trust that they know what they're doing, and won't take unnecessary risks. If, as he said, they're in control of the situation, it's more likely Saul will be going down.

If I accept that, I also agree it's best for me to be out of town, so I'm not a distraction to whatever they've got planned. Which brings me to the part that I'm finding harder to digest.

My parents would be delighted to have a visit, and it's past time to make the trip home. They've been at me for weeks about when they're next going to see me. They won't find it alarming or unusual for me to decide to go to Texas out of the blue.

I can also accept that just in case Saul doesn't fall for whatever the Devils have planned, that one of them comes with me, but that's where the plan starts to fail. To ensure my parents aren't alerted or worried that something is wrong, said Devil will pretend to be a boyfriend that I'm wanting to bring home.

Such a visit would suggest there's something serious between us, or at least the prospect, else I wouldn't be taking him with me.

My parents were devastated when Saul first showed his true colours. They'd stood by my side during the trial, but I knew they were taking the blame on themselves for accepting such a man into their lives. They felt guilty that they hadn't seen the true person underneath, as well as worried, I myself hadn't seen what I was stepping into.

They don't like that I live so far away from them, and would prefer me to be closer to home. If they knew the current situation, they would be beside themselves with worry for me. With Dad's weak heart, I'm not going to do anything to concern them.

While taking a man home on false pretexts would be something akin to a lie, in balance to protect them from the truth, it's something I'm not too concerned to have on my conscience. An excuse offered later as to why it didn't work out would easily explain why he was no longer a fixture in my life.

That part I can get my head around. The bit that I can't is that they are proposing that one of the Devils will be by my side. Men with muscles and tattoos and definitely not the kind you take home to meet Mom.

"No." I shake my head adamantly. If I don't pull this off and my parents suspect the real reason I have someone with me—as a bodyguard—they'll panic for certain. I'll probably end up with them wanting to come to Vegas and stay with me. Or, I'll have to move back home to placate them.

As Bart raises an eyebrow, I raise my head to the sky, then look back down again.

"You're going to take one of Red's men home to meet your parents. He'll pretend to be your boyfriend." He breaks off to grin. "You can spend the time letting them share all the embarrassing details from your past." Then he sobers quickly. "Or we can do it without all this rigmarole and tell them the truth about the situation."

"I've already said no." Standing, I walk to the window and look out unseeing as I wrap my arms around myself. I don't seem to have much option. I want Saul caught more than anyone else and want to be able to live without constantly checking over my shoulder. I'll have to fabricate a relationship with one of my biker protectors. "Who drew the short straw?" I ask without turning back.

Bart hesitates only an instant before saying, "Petty."

I'm glad I'm not eating or drinking as something would have shot out of my mouth. As it is, I choke. Waggling my finger into my ear. I think something must be wrong with my hearing, then I turn and give my manager my attention. "I'm sorry, for a moment I thought you said Petty?"

Bart has the grace to look sheepish. "I did."

My mouth opens and shuts for a couple of times before I can get words out. "Why the hell does Red think Petty and I would be able to convince anyone that we're in a relationship? And he's married for God's sake."

Bart raises an eyebrow. "Maybe that's why he's been chosen. So he won't act inappropriately toward you."

My parents wouldn't be expecting any boyfriend I brought home to ravish me on the couch, but they'd expect little touches and kisses here and there. Which starts me wondering what Petty's kisses would be like and that, in turn, makes me wonder if I've lost my goddamn mind.

The whole suggestion is preposterous. "And if I refuse?"

Bart wipes his hand over his head. "I love you, girl, you know that. But we can't keep bleeding money to keep you safe. Either you accept this as a way to be on top of the situation and get Saul out of the way, or maybe it's time to leave Vegas."

I go rigid. "You what?"

Bart holds up his hands. "Both you and I know that while the Devils are relatively cheap, we're bleeding money that we don't have. It's taking almost all that you earn just to keep you alive, RoseLyn. And I, for one, don't want to see you end up dead."

"I agree I should get out of town, but maybe I can go somewhere else?"

"You're due a visit with your parents. I thought you'd want to go home. And the Devils have checked out their security, and are happy you'd be secure enough at their house."

"If they get a sniff that something's wrong, they'll want me to move to Texas." And with Dad's health, it would be hard for me to deny them.

"You're a twenty-five-year-old woman, not a fucking child." Bart's eyes flash with rare annoyance.

But he doesn't understand. As far as offspring go, I'm all they've got. I was the late baby, the one they didn't expect to have. And while he's right, they have no control over me, they'll worry themselves into an early grave if they even suspected I was in danger. I couldn't have that on my conscience.

Biting my lip, I wonder how to proceed. Surely Petty must have cracked up with laughter when he'd heard the proposal or at least raised his snooty nose in the air. There can't be any way he would have agreed.

That gives me an idea. I should talk to Petty who probably thinks as little of the idea as I do myself, and maybe the two of us can convince everyone the plan won't work. Though who would make a good substitute, I'm not sure. Sarge is a nice guy, but his problems probably rule him out, seeing as he sleeps during the day and paces at night.

"You going to agree?" Bart picks up his jacket and stands. "It's only for two days, RoseLyn."

I shrug. Until I speak to Petty, I'll make it look like I'm going along with their plan. Inwardly I grin. I'm absolutely certain he'll have plenty to say about the suggestion and none of it in support.

Bart calls Roller back into the room and tells him I've agreed. I try to read the expression on Roller's face, but clearly he's following instructions given by his prez, and his personal thoughts remain hidden.

Bart leaves and I'm given no time to process what's going to happen, as almost immediately he closes the door behind him, Petty arrives.

I'm not surprised he scowls when he sees me, though he greets his brother pleasantly enough, with back slaps and a laugh. Then Roller waves to me and leaves us together.

No. This will never work out. Even if I'm a good enough actor, I doubt Petty will be able to slide into the boyfriend role. From the expression on his face, he's hating the idea as much as I do myself, and I doubt I'll have much trouble persuading him there's no way this will work.

As, for once, he and I will be on the same side, I summon a small smile as he approaches. But when I open my mouth to voice the cons, he pre-empts me.

"Flights are booked," he growls, suggesting he's getting no pleasure from this. "Are your bags packed?"

For the second time this morning, my mouth gapes like a fish dragged onto land. "Hold on a moment. Bart's only just raised the idea with me. I haven't even spoken to my parents to see whether a visit is convenient to them." Thoughts about getting Petty on my side are quickly abandoned.

Petty frowns. "Well you better get onto it."

Bristling, I straighten my back. "I don't think this is a good idea."

"Fine." He shrugs. "Our objective is getting you out of Vegas so we can keep you safe while we bring Saul down. I'll call your parents myself and explain the situation to them. They'll want you home as they'll be worried about you, and I'll go as your bodyguard."

"You can't call them," I cry out.

In response, he raises an eyebrow and leans his arm against the doorframe. He gives me a moment, then announces, "Our flight leaves in two hours and a half. You going to get a move on, or am I going to make that call?"

For a moment I'm frozen, as my brain calculates what I can do. With no doubt that he'd carry out his threat and knowing that a stranger ringing with news I should have relayed to my parents myself would send them straight off the deep end, I quickly consider that if I at least pretend to go along with him for now, that I may still have a chance to dissuade him.

Petty has no good side, so it's no use appealing to it. Try as I might, I can't find any option but to put aside my misgivings and capitulate. "I'll pack."

To his credit, he just lifts his chin, and doesn't smirk like he's put one over on me.

The first thing I do is place a call to my parents, hoping they've got plans. But of course, Mom says they'll be delighted to see me. And when I said I wasn't coming alone, I knew she could hear wedding bells ringing. I try to explain that my 'boyfriend' just had a hankering to visit Austin but know that didn't take root. Fortunately it's not the first time I've made a spur-of-the-moment decision to visit them, so no alarm bells were raised. However it is the first time I'll be bringing a male companion with me, and so now I'll have to work out how to manage their expectations. *Maybe arrange a falling out in front of them?* I'm sure that won't be hard. A fool would be able to see Petty and I aren't compatible, and Mom and Dad certainly aren't fools.

It only takes me a few moments to throw some bits into a carry-on which will tide me over for spending the night with my parents—which begs the question, will Petty expect to sleep with me? My parents aren't religious. If I bring home a boyfriend, they'd expect him to be in the same room.

It's not that I don't trust Petty, he's got a wife for goodness' sake. It's the thought of having to be in close proximity with a man that I really don't like. I remind myself it's good that he's got an awful personality, else otherwise I could be in trouble. He's so damn good looking and appeals to my lady parts, but he's obnoxious and married, and just one of those facts should be enough for me to cool my jets.

When he takes my bag from me and wheels it to the car, somehow he makes it appear that he's doing a poor weak female a favour rather than acting gentlemanly. Rolling my eyes, I get into the passenger seat and fasten the seat belt as he gets into the driver's side and starts the car without saying a word.

While I'm trying to think how to begin a conversation about how this is the worst idea that anyone living, or dead for that matter, has ever come up with, Petty flicks the indicator and turns into a gas station.

"Tank's empty."

At least he bothered with an explanation though I could have guessed anyway. I idly watch as he tops off the gas then disappears to pay. When he comes out, I flinch as a woman carrying a coffee and not looking where she's going crashes into him. He steps back, hands held up, shirt completely dripping.

When he's steadied and righted her, I wince, expecting him to go off on the woman, but strangely, though I'm too far away to hear what they're saying, it looks more like he's asking her if she's okay. She's clearly apologising profusely, but Petty waves his hands dismissively and walks away.

When he reaches the car, he pulls open the back, reaches into his pack and extracts a clean shirt. I don't know why my eyes are still glued to him, but I can't look away when he strips his dirty one off.

"Oh!" I gasp, my hand going to cover my mouth. Petty's got a huge ugly bruise on his back, about right where his right kidney is. It must have been a hell of a punch to mark him so much. Starting to yellow, it looks a couple of days old.

He turns fast at my exclamation and pulls his clean shirt on fast, his frown showing he's disgruntled at what I've seen.

Not wanting for the awkward moment to pass without comment, I can only come up with inanely saying, "I hope the other person looks worse."

Petty starts, and his back goes ramrod straight. "I didn't hit back." Then his mouth clamps shut.

It seems a very odd thing to say for a biker. I've seen them around for a couple of weeks now, and often caught them play-fighting with each other. Sarge has even told me of their fighting bouts to keep them fit. I doubt Petty's any stranger to violence, so why has he allowed someone to hit him without fighting back?

On the personal front, having a pacifist for a bodyguard may not be much help.

Now I understand why, when he retakes the driver's seat, he gently eases himself back, a slight grimace on his face as he does. But I say nothing else as we wind our way through Vegas.

As we draw near to the airport, I make one final attempt. "This isn't going to work."

Petty just spares me one sideways glance. "It will." Then he concentrates on driving again, the subject clearly closed.

The next period of time is taken up with parking, checking in, and then being called to our flight. We have seats together and Petty just assumes I'll want the window seat as he takes the aisle.

I'm not keen on flying, so squeeze my eyes shut while the plane takes off. Once we level out, I begin to breathe again, and grit my teeth for the just-under three-hour flight.

"Nervous flier?" Petty sounds curious.

I respond with a look that just says *duh*. I think that's quite easy to see and having Petty as my companion doesn't make it easier. When I fly with Bart, we can at least talk over performance schedules and discuss the venues where I'm going to play, but I can't imagine making small talk with the taciturn biker.

He, however, seems to have different ideas. "Tell me something about you."

I'm surprised that he's even speaking to me. "Like what?"

He shrugs. "Like things a boyfriend should know." He thinks for a moment. "If your boyfriend was going to send you flowers, which kind would you like?"

Despite my nervousness, the idea of Petty sending flowers to anyone makes me snort. "What, you, send flowers?"

He shoots me a glance. "You'd be surprised at some of the things I'd do. But this is all hypothetical and shit I need to know to convince your parents that I'm stepping out with you."

Having great difficulty imagining this man anywhere near a bunch of flowers, I turn the tables on him. "What type would you send?"

Instead of being annoyed, he creases his eyes and considers me for a moment. "Roses would be too cliché for you. I reckon you'd like something that appeals to your senses. Freesias perhaps, or lilies maybe. Something pretty and full of perfume."

My own eyes widen as he's hit the nail on the head. The inclination of my chin shows him he's right, as I ask my own question.

"If I was going to send something to you, what would you like?"

"Not flowers," he replies fast, with a slight quirk to his mouth. Then lines appear on his forehead as he gives it some thought. "I'm not much of a drinker, but I do appreciate a good whisky. Something like a nice imported Scottish malt."

"You'll get on well with my dad then. He loves his whisky, but he tends to stick to the American brands."

He gives me a chin lift. "That's a thought. Should we get anything at the airport to take to them? Flowers, chocolates?"

Wow. Didn't expect him to think of the niceties. I shake my head. "They won't expect anything, Petty. They'll just be glad to see me, and intrigued as to who I've brought with me." Again my eyes find his face. "I really can't introduce you as Petty—"

"Clark," he provides quickly and helpfully.

"Clark." I try it on for size.

"Just think of Superman." His lips quirk again.

My eyes widen. *Has Petty just made a joke?* "Superman, eh? Well you've got a lot to live up to then."

Now he actually grins at me, then snaps. "Favourite colour?"

"Red. You?"

"Blue. Food?"

"Tacos."

"Steak."

CHAPTER FIFTEEN

RoseLyn

We continue back and forth, learning each other's likes and dislikes. But by the end of it, while I think I know the basics about him, I need to know more than I do, like how he's supposed to demonstrate he's my boyfriend rather than a stranger I picked up off the street. Is he into holding hands, or will he flinch away if I try to hold his?

My parents know I'm an affectionate person, and it would be hard to keep my hands to myself. Of course things wouldn't go far in front of them, but a chaste kiss to the cheek or even the lips would likely be expected. Would Petty be receptive of that?

"What are you worrying about?" Turning, I see Petty staring at my hands twisting in my lap. "Are you worried about the landing?"

Well, there is that, but also, "My parents will expect to see some kind of affection between us."

His brow furrows. "Of course. We'll be able to manage that."

Biting my lip, I state my objection. "But you're married," I hiss. "You might be able to forget you have a wife, but I can't. Does she know you're here and what you're doing? If she doesn't, what would she say if she found out?"

His personable tone is absent as he snarls, "You just leave me to worry about my… wife."

A growl actually sounds from my throat. "How the hell can I pretend you mean something to me when there's another woman waiting for you at home?" I glare at him. "I'm not that woman."

"You're right. It's pretend."

"Damn it, Petty." I swallow and make an effort to lower my voice. "I can't touch you, kiss you, or anything that I'd do to an unattached man. I won't come between you and your wife."

"So come clean. Admit I'm your bodyguard—"

"I can't do that! Dad's got a weak heart and the worry might kill him."

Petty turns his head and stares at the back of the seat in front. I have no idea what's going through his mind, but he seems to have decided this conversation is over. A few minutes pass during which I feel a change in the plane's motion which suggests we're preparing to lower altitude and come into land. When I've about given up on any further discussion, and worrying myself sick about how quickly my parents are going to see through our charade, Petty, at last, opens his mouth.

"I don't consider myself as having a wife." After this statement, he glances at me out of the side of his eye, then shakes his head. "You know she reappeared after seven years away?"

"I didn't know it was that long. Did she leave you?" *Or did you leave her?*

He snorts. "She had no choice. She was in a penitentiary."

I swallow my gasp. That was unexpected and I certainly didn't know that. "But you stuck by her?"

"Hell no." He snorts. "I filed for divorce. She didn't sign the fuckin' papers, but I thought we'd separated for good." He pauses, and his head hangs low. "Surprised the fuck out of me when she turned up. I truly never expected to hear from her or see her again." Once more his head moves side to side. "Last thing I expected was that she'd want to play fuckin' happy families."

"But she wants to start back up with you?"

"Fuck knows what she wants," he growls.

I hesitate before asking, "And what do you feel about her? Are you pleased she's back?"

"Fuck no." He spits out the denial. "She and I were doomed from the start. You want the fuckin' truth? I was saved when she was locked up."

I inhale sharply, thinking that sounds a bit harsh, and also a very strange thing to say. "What was her crime?"

"Assault."

I look at him quickly. "You?"

"No. Some innocent fucker."

There seems to be an unspoken *this time* that he hasn't voiced. Suddenly things start to gel in my mind, like the bruise on his back and his admission he didn't fight back. Is his wife violent or was her crime just a one-off?

"Petty…" I pause, then use his real name. "Clark. Was it she who hit you?"

"It was an accident," he says fast, facing me fully with his eyebrows raised in challenge. "A fuckin' accident, okay?"

I stare at him. Yeah, I'd been tempted to pass Saul's first attack on me off as that until I realised I couldn't risk there being a second time.

The tense moment is interrupted by an announcement informing us the plane is indeed landing, and the flight attendants coming around to make sure we're all buckled in safely.

As I shrink back into myself, my nails starting to dig into my skin, he reaches over and clasps my hand firmly. I don't pull away. Instead, I squeeze tight and don't let go until the wheels touch down, the brakes are successfully applied and the plane begins to slow. When the plane comes to a halt, I wince as I see the prints of my fingernails on his hand, but Petty says nothing about it.

Instead he stands and reaches into the overhead bins, pulling down our carry-ons. Then, as I move from my seat to stand beside him, he leans down.

"I don't consider myself married, okay? It's no hardship for me to play boyfriend."

Is that a suggestion I should think of him as available? Or just an endorsement that in my acting role in front of my parents, I can do anything I feel it's necessary to do?

Along with the other passengers we shuffle forward and eventually get off the plane. Bypassing baggage claim we go direct to the arrivals hall, where I easily spot Mom and Dad waiting for me.

As I start walking faster, Petty catches on fast. He's wheeling my suitcase and has his own duffle bag over his shoulder. He places his free hand in the small of my back. The move makes me falter for a split second before realising he's slipping into the role we agreed.

My steps speed up as I approach my parents, throwing myself first into my father's outstretched arms. After a quick hug, he hands me to Mom, who puts me at arm's length and gives me the once-over, checking that I'm the picture of health which, luckily, I am.

"Clark." I hear Petty's deep voice as he introduces himself to my father.

Remembering my manners I turn, linking my arm with his, the action feeling surprisingly natural.

"Mom, this is Clark. Clark, my dad, Rufus, and my mom, Martina."

There follows the obligatory shaking of hands and, as we walk toward the parking lot, the conversation revolves around their hopes that we had a good journey, and our assurances that we had. Dad tries to take my suitcase from Petty who refuses to give it up, hefting it into the trunk of my parents' car when we reach it in the parking lot.

I notice Dad eyeing the duffle that Petty has placed beside it.

"Army?" he challenges.

"Yes, sir," Petty replies. "Did my eight years."

"Thank you for your service."

Petty looks embarrassed, so I try to move my dad along. "We going straight home?"

"Yes, unless you're hungry and want to stop on the way?" Mom asks. "I've got your favourite dinner for later."

Petty grins down at me and stage whispers into my ear, "What's your favourite?"

"Her mom's lasagne," Dad replies with a chuckle.

I loved it in the past. As I've grown older, my tastes have changed but I'm not going to turn down anything cooked with love. Mom's cooking always reminds me of when life was so much simpler than it is now. Of times when I yearned to become an adult without realising what all that entails. And certainly before I had something necessitating me to have security to keep me safe.

"Just so happens I love lasagne." Petty grins at my mom, an expression that's almost boyish in its enthusiasm. She actually preens as the full force of his attention lands on her and for a second I almost feel jealous.

What the fuck?

Reminding myself that Petty's legally married whether he wants to be or not, I slide into the back seat. Politely, Petty closes the door and then walks around to the other side to get in. Dad gets into the driving seat and once Mom has settled herself beside him, we're off.

And hell, we're taking the long way home. Mom excitedly points out the school I attended, and goes into the story of my prom, how I tripped and the high heels I was unaccustomed to wearing had ripped my gown and her ensuing quick trip with a sewing kit to save the day.

Dad idly comments how he waited with a shotgun at the ready until I was safely home.

Glancing sideways I see Petty's grin widen. From how his body is shaking, I suspect he's suppressing his laughter, while I want to shrink and disappear, wondering if mortification can be fatal.

I'm even more surprised when he takes my hand and winks at me. But I suppose this is exactly how he's supposed to be behaving and I'm just surprised he's so easily slipped into the adoring boyfriend role.

The rest of the relatively short journey is taken up with updates from my parents as to the local gossip, and me telling them that my shows are doing well. Soon we're turning into the driveway that takes us to the house where I grew up. I notice Petty looking at it, as if assessing it in some way.

That's confirmed when he whispers quietly, "Your dad has good security." He raises his chin approvingly.

His comment brings me back down to earth. I hadn't thought too much about my trouble following me. Could I have brought problems to my parents' door?

"You think I'm at risk here?" I whisper back, now worried on their behalf.

His face tightens and he purses his lips. "I don't think so, but we can't let down our guard."

"What are you two love birds discussing?"

Looking up, I see Dad glancing in his mirror.

"Leave them alone, Rufus," Mom chides him. "Come on, let's get them settled in and then we can have a good catch-up." I don't miss the knowing look she gives him and can easily translate such catch-up turning into an interrogation, knowing Mom will want to find out everything there is to know about my new supposed man right down to his shoe size.

Inwardly I grin, wondering how Petty is going to cope with the interrogation to come. I've often wondered why the CIA never recruited her.

But a few hours later I decide that Petty must have had a

personality transplant during the flight. Maybe I'd dozed and aliens had invaded our plane and replaced him. Something must have happened. He's a completely different man to the one that I've known for the last few weeks.

Instead of taciturn, he's friendly. Instead of being dour, he's been laughing and joking with my dad, and courteous around me and my mom. As if he's the perfect boyfriend, there's been little affectionate touches, and chaste kisses—of the type acceptable in front of parents—delivered to my cheek. If I had doubts how he'd be able to pretend a devotion to me, I have none now. I'd be feeling more guilty had he not explained his true relationship with his wife, though my conscience isn't eased entirely, thinking her view of their marriage must be different. She did return to him.

It puts me in a bit of a quandary. If she loves him, is what I'm doing encouraging him to be unfaithful? Although he's crossing no line, I doubt she'd be comfortable with how he's acting.

But she hit him.

And, from what I've surmised, has hit him in the past. While Petty's listening to my father regaling him with some story or other, I wonder about him. Why didn't he leave when she first showed her true colours? I'd left Saul after only one time.

But maybe fate had stepped in and parted them anyway. I can't imagine Petty putting up with behaviour like abuse.

As the day draws on, Petty stays firmly in character. While I'm helping Mom finish dinner, he assists my dad secure some guttering which had come loose, all without complaint and taking pains to take most of the more arduous burdens from the man who I'm pained to say is showing his age now.

Mom's one hundred percent team Petty, going so far as to tell me he was a keeper for life. I think she's already hearing those wedding bells. Being completely bemused by the change in him, I don't have it in me to contradict her plans. There's part of me thinking if this was real I wouldn't object to them.

What the hell has happened to the Petty I know and dislike?

I've never seen him so relaxed. The only explanation I can come up with is that he's either an excellent actor wearing a mask, or has dropped the one he normally puts on. While previously I'd wondered how on earth he'd gotten anyone to marry him, now I'm no longer surprised she wants him back.

He's attentive to me without being stifling, respectful of both my mom and my dad. When, after dinner, he jokes that he'd like to know more about me, Mom doesn't hesitate getting the old photo albums out.

I roll my eyes but settle in to be embarrassed. I'm sitting on the couch next to him, and when his arm comes around me pulling me close, it's all too easy to relax into his side. I don't even have to pretend I'm enjoying this close contact with him. To my shock, I find myself breathing him in. It wouldn't be difficult for me to fancy him, probably like most women he comes across. He's sex on two legs. But like this? Gentle, turning what could be interpreted as laughing glances toward me, pretending an interest in my life, and getting on so well with my parents? Well, I have to force myself to remember he is married, as otherwise I suspect he'd be on his way to capturing my heart.

That is, if I knew, which was the real Petty.

Mom's in her element as he examines page after page of photos, and he shows interest in my childhood, my friends, and the cousins that came to play. He grins and laughs at some of the related antics we got up to.

After he closes the final album, he smooths his hand over the cover before handing it back. His brow is creased as though he's thoughtful, and he watches as Mom returns the albums to their home in the cupboard.

"What was your childhood like, Clark?" Mom asks.

Clark's arm is still around my shoulders and I feel his hand clench slightly. I start wondering about the wisdom of Mom asking that question and whether I should deflect her onto something else when he starts to speak.

"My dad died when I was four. He was in the Army and,

well, an IED took him out. It was shortly after my sister, Leila, was born."

Mom's eyes glisten in sympathy. "That must have been hard."

Petty shrugs. "I grew up being the man of the house. I always had the memory of my dad as a hero, so I signed up when I was eighteen and followed his footsteps. Then I saw too many good men die for a cause we didn't really believe in, so I did my time and got out."

"Your mom and sister still around?" I ask, suddenly curious about the people who made Petty into whoever the fuck he is. I'm still trying to work out if the real man is sitting beside me, or whether the true version is the one I knew in Vegas.

"Mom got hit by a car when I was overseas, a few years into my stint."

"Oh, I'm so sorry." Mom looks like she wants to give him a hug herself. "What about your sister? I suppose you were close."

"Close?" Petty raises and lowers his shoulders again. Then he grins. "She was a pain in my fuckin' ass. Always pushing boundaries and getting away with things as she was a sweet little girl. She's doing fine by all accounts, married a good man. But I haven't seen or had contact with her for a few years now."

I nudge him. "So what were you like as a big brother?"

His eyes meet mine. "Protective and watching out for her, whether she wanted me to or not. And believe me, there were a good few times she wished I'd stayed out of her business. But I was the man of the house, and my dad had told me I had to watch out for her." He chuckles softly. "Not an easy job when she tried to run with the wrong crowd, but she's moved on now, thank God."

Protective and interfering. Yes, I can imagine that.

"I'm sorry you lost your parents," Mom says, giving a pointed look toward Dad. "But we'd be happy to adopt you."

"Mom!" I sit forward sharply, worried that this is a step too far and that they're taking our pretend relationship far too seriously. I'm also concerned that when I announce Petty and I have broken up that they'll be devastated at losing him as a potential son-in-law. But there's a part of me that's impressed he's made such an impression on them.

As for the man himself, what does he do? Well, he sits back and barks a hearty laugh.

CHAPTER SIXTEEN

Petty

They want to adopt me? Both her words and the serious manner of Martina's delivery startle stunned laughter out of me.

I like this family of RoseLyn's. I like them a lot. They're unpretentious and accepting. I'd given them the Cliff's notes version of my family history, and left out the bits that wouldn't impress them quite so much, such as how Leila had become a spoiled brat once my dad was gone. Both Mom and I had doted on her, and she'd ended up getting everything she wanted. Of course, what she wanted didn't include a big brother who was always watching out for her, interfering, as she put it, in her life. She'd pushed at the boundaries I felt quite right to set, being as I was older. Oh, the fights we'd had, with her always pushing me to the limits. But never once had I forgotten what my daddy had said, *boys don't hit girls.*

That she'd turned out okay in the end I'd taken some credit for, though she hadn't seen it that way. Mom had been the glue that had held the family together, and once she'd gone, Leila and I had only made perfunctory efforts to stay in touch.

"I'm sorry about your mom and your dad," RoseLyn says

softly. When I glance at her, eyes full of compassion are staring into mine.

"Dad died so long ago I barely remember him," I tell her. At times I think I only recall the promise I made him, and my vow never to break it. "And likewise, Mom went many years back."

"Still, it must be hard to lose them."

Petty, the hardened biker, would shrug her concern off, but the man I've allowed myself to be in Texas squeezes her hand instead.

Her mom seems to realise the conversation has turned maudlin, so breezily changes the subject. She waves her hand toward the cupboard that now houses the photograph albums she'd so recently put away. "I enjoyed that trip down memory lane." She reaches forward and touches her daughter's knee briefly. "But I'm pleased I've got the real live version here in front of me. It's so good to see you, RoseLyn."

Rufus snorts. "You get those albums out at a drop of a hat, Martina. You showed them to the new pastor a couple of months back."

Roselyn laughs. "A new pastor wanted to see all the old photos? What made you torture him, Mom?"

Martina looks abashed. "He was very interested in you, Rose."

The hairs on the back of my neck prick up at the mention of someone being interested in her. It couldn't have been Saul himself, they'd have recognised him. But it's possible it's his accomplice, the hypothetical help he's getting from someone in the police. Maybe it wasn't just information they'd been providing.

"Whisky?"

"Please," I answer Rufus, then wait while he pours us both a generous portion of amber nectar, which as RoseLyn had indicated was pure and not the blended stuff. He then produces two wines for the ladies.

After rolling the liquid around in the glass, breathing in to appreciate the strong aroma, then finally taking a sip and showing my appreciation with a small sigh, I lean forward and place my glass on the table. I try to get them back on track. "So what's this new pastor like?" I ask, as casually as possible.

Martina smiles, and her eyes lose focus as she travels back in her mind. "Lovely fella. He's new to the area and wanted to get to know the residents on his patch. Very talkative and friendly. When I said I had a daughter, he wanted to know all about her, and one thing led to another, and we were looking through all the old photographs."

Photographs which include many pictures of her growing up, and ending with some of her earlier performances. I wonder what other secrets Martina had innocently spilled when discussing the daughter she so obviously loves.

Rufus is shaking his head and chuckling. "Martina doesn't get out much. I feel sorry for the man. We don't even attend church, yet she kept him trapped all afternoon."

"Well, he was nice." Martina glares at her husband as she defends herself. "And you were out playing golf."

As I'm wondering how I can probe further without showing my hand, RoseLyn, showing she's far from an airhead says, "He must have been nice if you chatted with him so long. What was he like?"

Martina winks at her daughter. "Quite young, mid-twenties at most. Really cute. His hair was dark, neatly cut, and he had these twinkling blue eyes."

"Your mom was trying to flirt with a man of the cloth," Rufus puts in, chortling.

RoseLyn rolls her eyes, then asks, "What church was he from?"

Martina shifts her eyes and looks a little contrite. "I didn't catch that."

Rufus laughs again. "She was too busy ogling him to ask."

Dutifully I chuckle at Rufus's remark, but something smells

off to me. Why should a pastor visit a potential parishioner without canvassing for the church he's a member of?

"Oh." Martina suddenly jumps up. "But he did leave this for me." She goes to a shelf piled with papers and magazines and pulls off a leaflet.

When she passes it over, I clearly see it's a flyer for a local evangelical church. My nose ceases to twitch quite so hard, but I do make a mental note to follow up the lead and dig into the pastor a little further.

"What was his name?" Again RoseLyn saves me from having to ask.

Martina scratches her head. "Johnson, I think? Pastor Johnson. He offered his first name as Walt."

Discreetly taking out my phone, I tap out a message to Keys, asking him to look up the name of the man and the church that I've sent to him. While looking at the photographs is indeed a coincidence, if Johnson was who he said, then I can't see how a man of the cloth has anything to do with the shit that's been happening to RoseLyn.

Nevertheless, I don't let it lie. "Apart from enjoying the trip down memory lane, did this pastor ask anything else about RoseLyn?"

Martina gives me a sharp look as if wondering why I should ask. Then she brushes it off with a laugh. "He didn't have to ask. I'm so proud of what my girl has done, I think I might have bored him to death telling him all about her." She sends a slightly guilty look to the woman I'm supposed to protect with my life. "He did ask whether you carried the Lord in your heart."

RoseLyn snorts. "I hope you answered him correctly, Mother."

"I told him we brought you up right," Martina says, defensively.

Rufus reaches over and puts his hand on her arm. "We did,

love. But the child's got to find her own way in life, and her own spiritual guidance."

Martina gives me a considering look. "If you hadn't already got a boyfriend, I'd have liked Johnson for you, RoseLyn. He was very attractive and had this way about him."

It's time I stepped into the role I'm supposed to play. Letting a touch of possessiveness invade my voice, I pull RoseLyn into my side. "It's lucky I got in first then. If you see this pastor again, please be sure to tell him RoseLyn is taken."

I cement my words by turning her face to mine, and placing a kiss on her lips. Her gasp shows I've taken her by surprise, but she responds to the warning in my eyes with a hint of laughter. Without words she's letting me know that she's happy to be saved from her mother's matchmaking.

Although the evening is getting on, Rufus and Martina want to make the most of this visit from their daughter. They get out a board game which initially makes me groan inside, but my competitive streak soon wins out and I'm quickly engrossed and enjoying myself. When Rufus cleans up, we then watch a romantic sitcom, which even has me chuckling.

All the time RoseLyn sits close, snuggling under my arm. For some reason, I feel at ease, and find I'm forgetting the problems that I left at home and I'm in no hurry to get back to them. I stretch out my legs, feeling totally relaxed, pushing the wife waiting for me to the back of my mind.

Though I hoped to hear from the club that Saul has been caught and it's safe to go back, my phone remains silent in my pocket. But it's early still, and I have my hopes up that soon I'll receive good news via message.

When the movie finishes, Rufus and Martina make sure we have everything we need, then take themselves off to bed. As soon as they leave the room, RoseLyn disentangles herself from me, and smooths her hands down her arms.

She looks up at me through her eyelashes. "I'm sorry for making you sit through that."

I'm taken aback by her apology. To be honest, with all that I've got going on with Britney, this has been a pleasant interlude, an oasis of peace in an otherwise tumultuous situation. It's given me some breathing space, and time to think with clarity.

"No worries," I tell her, meaning it.

"What did you think about the pastor?" She hesitates. "I must admit it made me uneasy. I've been so fixated that Saul's behind everything..." Shaking her head, she shivers. "Could I have been wrong? Or is it coincidence someone's been asking about me?"

In situations like this is, it's all too easy to see demons hiding in every corner. It too had made my sixth sense twitch. I'd long been on the bandwagon that her stalker wasn't her ex, but recently, particularly after the snakes, I'd been convinced.

"I doubt it," I respond, after giving her suggestion serious consideration. "Johnson was probably trying to get on your mom's good side, and realised you were her Achilles heel. But we can't dismiss anything at this point, so I've already texted Keys." I brush back my hair. "We can't ignore it. Anyone asking questions about you raises a red flag."

"I wasn't too happy about how easy it was to get information from my mom. Sometimes there's a downside to her being so proud of me." Her eyes cast a look in the direction her parents had disappeared, but she doesn't seem critical, just accepting of what they've possibly done with the best of intentions. Back at me she suggests, "I suppose we better get some sleep."

It's been a long day, and that coupled with the previous two relatively sleepless nights, I'm completely down for that. When I raise my chin, she leaves the room and I follow her.

The guestroom we've been assigned has an en suite, so I let RoseLyn go through her bedtime routine first, and then complete mine after her. It's a king-size bed so we can leave plenty of space between us. It seems strange when I recall so is mine, but I didn't want to be anywhere near Britney. RoseLyn, though, is a different matter entirely. Probably because I know there's no way she'd want to take advantage of me.

When I lay my head on the pillow and close my eyes, I feel nothing but relaxed. I'm drowsy and soon on the verge of drifting off.

I'm disturbed by her soft voice. "You're so different to how I thought you'd be."

My eyes blink open again. "How so?"

She chuckles softly. "I never thought you'd be able to convince them that we were together."

I could continue to be an ass, tell her it's an act I've perfected, but instead, I find myself giving a truthful reply. "Your parents are lovely people. It's easy to relax around them."

I hear a shuffling and turn my head to see that she's situated herself on her side facing me, her head propped on her hand. "So who are you, really? The obnoxious Petty in Vegas, or Clark, the man who's here with me?"

Copying her motion, I turn over as well. This places my back toward her. Half under my breath, I grumble, "I'm the same fucking man."

It's not something I want to discuss with her. The problem being, I'm not sure which I am. Clark is the man who was taken in by Britney, and who she rightly identifies as a wimp, the man my brothers wouldn't want to ride beside and who'd be embarrassed to have in their ranks. Petty, though, well, he's the rough, hardened biker who won't take shit from anyone.

For some reason, it's been all too easy to become Clark these past few hours. And he and RoseLyn haven't butted heads in the same way that Petty and she would do. To avoid further questions, I stay quiet and allow my breathing to even out. Obviously getting the hint, she switches off the light.

Again I close my eyes. My mind ponders a while on how comfortable I've felt slipping back into the persona of Clark, but I must be overtired as my thoughts don't keep me awake. If she speaks to me again, I don't hear.

I feel hands fumbling at me. I try to push them away. I'm naked. My cock's in her hands... I twist, trying to evade her touch.

Not again! She's looming over me. I'm helpless... I can't move. Feeling like I'm fighting against gravity, my limbs leaden, I struggle to raise my hands in an effort to fend her off... No, no, no, no, no. I'm trying to scream but I'm mute. My mouth opens but no sound comes out. My terror finally breaks through my paralysis and I shove and push my attacker away then roll, managing to get out from under her and...

And come awake as I land on the floor with a thump. When the light snaps on, I hold out my palms, warding my attacker off. I scramble away, half blinded.

"Hey, hey! It's me." A panicked face looks down from the mattress. "Petty, are you alright? You were having a nightmare."

I... What? I shake my head, trying to clear it, still in the grasp of the vestiges of what I quickly realise was a bad dream, leaving me fumbling for the knowledge of where I am.

Fuck, I'm in RoseLyn's parents' house. I'm in, or was in, RoseLyn's bed.

Recognising it's RoseLyn's face staring at me, I remember trying to fight someone off in my dream. "Did I hurt you?" I demand.

"I wasn't the one who fell on the floor."

I brush that off. "I'm fine. Let me check you—"

"Petty, you pushed me away, that's all. I'm sorry, it was me shaking you that made you fall off the bed." She bites her bottom lip and looks contrite. "I was trying to wake you. You seemed so distressed."

Knowing I'm wallowing like a stranded turtle on my back on the floor, I roll over and pull myself onto my knees. Wiping a hand over my face, I again shake my head, trying to rid the person who seems to have hold of my mind. The memories that nightmare brought back make my stomach roil, and I need a moment to swallow down the bile. *It had seemed so real.*

RoseLyn moves across the bed, swinging her legs over the

side. "Do you need help?" She reaches her hand out as if to help me.

And fuck it, but I reel away from that innocent touch.

"Petty?" Understandably, her face creases in lack of comprehension.

"It's not you," I refute, fast. "Oh, fuck, I'm sorry. It's just a dream that's got me all twisted up."

Though it's not a dream's paralysis this time, I feel frozen to the spot. The past, the present, all seems mixed up and right now I don't want to be close to any woman again.

As she can see I'm not about to move from my position on the floor, RoseLyn settles back onto the bed, plumping the pillows to rest her head but remains half sitting up. "Is it PTSD? Like Sarge? Something from when you served?"

Hell, I wish that it was. I snort at the ridiculousness of it, but it was a personal fight and far from any of the world's known war zones. Though she could be right, that nightmare and after-effects aren't a million miles from Sarge's PTSD.

"Do you want to talk about it?"

When most women suggest that you talk, they expect you to concur. If you remain silent, they pick at the scab. But RoseLyn doesn't say more, just leaves the decision completely to me.

After a few moments, she asks softly, "Do you want a glass of water or anything?"

There's a wealth of concern in her tone, a desire to help, even though she has no idea what's wrong. That must be the reason the truth blurts from my mouth. "I was dreaming about Britney."

"Your wife?" I've surprised her. She rolls over on her stomach and again looks down at me. "You were freaking terrified." She regards me cautiously, a slight quirk to her lips. "Is she really that scary?"

I shudder. Even if the details of my nightmare are growing sketchy now, I fully recall exactly how I felt the morning after the event that triggered my dream. Huffing, I respond, "You'd be fuckin' surprised."

She gives me her full attention for a moment, before inviting, "Come back to bed."

But I can't. Maybe it was lying in such close proximity to another woman, breathing in her feminine perfume, that had triggered the memory. Instead, I eye the room and indicate the chair. "I'll sleep on that."

"What?" She looks at it herself and scoffs. "Hell, Petty, there's no way you'll be comfortable over there." Then her eyes crease, and worry lines appear. "Is it something I did? Did I touch you? Oh my God, if I did, I'm so sorry Petty—"

"It was nothing you did." I interrupt her fast, though I suppose she could have inadvertently let her hand stray and it had generated a chain reaction in me. When she speaks next, it's clear I haven't sufficiently assuaged her fears that it hadn't been her fault.

"You have the bed, Petty. I'll go downstairs and sleep on the couch." Looking away from me, she adds, "I knew my parents would put us in the same room. I just didn't think you'd have a problem with that. I'm so sorry to put you in this position. Of course you don't want to be unfaithful."

Now I feel like a total ass. "It's not your fault." As she moves to leave the bed, I shoot out my hand and grab hers. "Stay, please."

"It's not fair—"

Before I can think better of it, the truth escapes. "Britney forced herself on me the other night."

She stills, her head slowly turns as though on a swivel. "Forced. You?"

It sounds so stupid putting it into words. "I was sleeping. I woke up..." I wipe my free hand over my face, unwilling for some reason to lose the connection to her. "She was naked, on top of me, and I was..." How do I explain? "I thought I'd been dreaming."

Her eyes narrow. "She touched you when you were sleeping?"

It sounds so stupid put like that. Maybe this is what I need, to talk it out, make myself understand my overreaction.

"I tried to stop her. Our relationship isn't like that. I didn't want sex with her. But she had her mouth on me. I told her no, but my dick was hard. She positioned herself over me..." I feel so sick that I couldn't control myself.

She wrenches her hand away. For one fleeting moment I think she's disgusted at my revelation, but she throws herself off the bed and comes down to her knees beside me.

Her hand raises my chin, forcing me to face her. "Let me get this straight. You didn't want sex with Britney, but she took it anyway?"

I wrench my head away. "I didn't even want to sleep in the same bed. She came to me while I was on the couch. But I... I couldn't stop. Didn't stop. I must have wanted it." My mind didn't, but that didn't prevent my cock from doing the job.

"Oh no, Petty. Your body just had a normal reaction. If you didn't want her, she took something without your consent. Petty, she—"

I cover her mouth with one of my hands, guessing what she's going to say, but not wanting to hear it. It doesn't happen to men. It doesn't happen to me. Even half-awake I should have been able to stop. Giving it a name would exonerate me when I don't deserve it. "Don't say it."

But she twists her face away and says it anyway. "She raped you."

Taking hold of both her hands I squeeze them tightly and look at her angrily. My face has reddened and my voice is harsh. "Men can't be raped."

"Of course they can."

"Not me." I extricate myself and get to my feet, walking to the wall and putting my forehead against it. "Not me," I repeat.

CHAPTER SEVENTEEN

RoseLyn

I sit up straight, completely stunned. Whatever I expected Petty to say, it wasn't what he'd just said. He'd had a nightmare about something so bad it triggered an episode of PTSD. It could have had any number of root causes, a bomb while he was serving, bullets flying in some battle or other. But the real reason had shocked me. His wife forcing him to have sex when he neither wanted nor consented to it? When he'd said no, she hadn't stopped.

What kind of woman does that?

I feel my forehead creasing as I contemplate further. Under other circumstances it could be a reason for laughter, a fully grown male woken up for sex. But I'd just witnessed his reaction to his nightmare. He'd been thrashing, fighting an unseen enemy, whimpering as though in pain, which shows that, for him, this situation is very far from a joke. While he's denying the label I put on it, it can't be described as anything other than rape. And like anyone, to be a victim of that, it's truly devastating. It lessens it none that he's a man not a woman.

I force myself to speak calmly. "If something was taken from you that you didn't consent to, then yes, Petty, you were raped."

He suddenly swings around, his eyes blazing. "I came, Rose-Lyn. I fuckin' came. So how the fuck was that rape?"

Although I'm lucky enough never to have been in that position, I know enough about the subject to tell him, "Some women do as well. It's the body's automatic reaction. Doesn't mean you wanted to, or that you enjoyed it."

There's something about Petty's stance which makes me think he's trying to understand, both what his wife had done, and his extreme reaction to it. It gives me the confidence to continue to talk it out. I want him to say it again. "Did you tell her no?"

His breath leaves him on a sigh. "I tried. She ignored me."

So why didn't he push her off? He's not a small man. He's over six foot and muscular. Unless she's some kind of female bodybuilder, I've no doubt he could overpower her.

There are so many questions I want to ask. Like why, when he so obviously doesn't like her, is he still with her, or more accurately, why he let her come back? How did he get with her in the first place?

Getting up from the floor, I sit on the bed, and pat the comforter beside me. "Come talk to me, Petty."

"It's the middle of the fuckin' night."

I shrug. "I doubt you're in the mood for sleep right now, and I'm certainly not." It's not like we've got a long drive in the morning, just a plane ride then a short journey home. Petty's shown me a different side of him during this visit, and I still don't know which is the mask. Tonight he seems vulnerable, but is that the real him?

I wouldn't have dared initiate a personal conversation with him as he was before, but now? If this is my chance to help him, then I'll take it. Once we return to Vegas, I suspect his shields will go back up.

He's wavering, looking at the bed, then at me. To lighten the mood I raise my arms. "I promise I'll be hands off."

He snorts. "You're not her."

That gives me an opening. As he weakens and comes across, sitting, but with a few feet between us, I take advantage. "How not? Tell me about her, Petty."

At first he shakes his head as if he's not going to say a word. He even looks at the door as if wondering if he can escape out of it. Then he tenses and meets my eyes.

"You promise you won't tell anyone what I'm about to tell you?"

"I promise," I earnestly respond.

He stares at me for a moment, then lowers his head into his hands. After rubbing at his temples, he raises his face and stares unseeingly at the wall.

"I was a grunt in the Army. Enjoyed what I did. I was good at taking orders, didn't want to give any myself." He pauses to gather his thoughts. "Saw some shit though, can't deny that. The kind that messes with your fuckin' mind." Thinking it's not time to thank him for his service, I stay quiet.

"Fuck did I need those times on leave. Space to get my head back on straight. It was worse after the first tours, knowing what I was going back to." He glances at me as if to check I'm listening. "Met Britney when I was on leave." I notice his eyes glaze slightly, and there's a slight upturn to his lips. "She was all I ever wanted in a woman—pretty, good figure, funny, loving. I fell hard. Knew it was fast, but knew I wanted to keep her. So I put a ring on her finger. I only had a couple of weeks with her."

He shrugs. "I was sent on a mission. I was away for two months. When I returned, at first, Britney was the girl I'd married. She settled into my apartment—I'd planned on getting married quarters organised—but the space seemed to suit us for now. Then," he shrugs, "then I began to experience the side of her that she hadn't shown before."

I wait for him to tell me, but the silence continues so I prompt, "In what way?"

He jerks as though I've startled him out of a memory. "She had a temper. A violent one. And the violence wasn't just restricted to words. When I first left the toilet seat up, she threw a jar at me." Idly he rubs at a slight scar by his brow. As I'm thinking of something to say and repress the *no woman likes a toilet seat left up* that wants to escape, he resumes, "If I was late home, I got her fist. And there were many times she'd hit just because she felt like it. I was a fuckin' punching bag." He winces. "I walked on eggshells, trying to do everything to placate her—"

"You never hit back?" My eyes widen.

He spins to face me. "Of course not. She was one hundred and ten dripping wet. I'm a man. Men do not hit women."

"Why didn't you leave her?"

Petty moves his head side to side. "I married for better or worse, and while I may not have done enough due diligence before, I thought maybe things would get better and… I loved her. Each time she hurt me, it upset her as much as me, and she'd tell me she loved me, and that it would never happen again. But of course, it did. Until I went back on tour."

"Did you tell anyone what was happening?"

He gives a mirthless chuckle. "No. Oh, it was noticed that I had become very accident prone, always had a cut or a bruise, or was limping or favouring my arm, but they'd never have believed me. Britney was a charmer and projected the image of a vulnerable woman. No one would have imagined she'd been the cause of my injuries. She didn't look like she could hurt a fly, and had perfected that look of innocence." I honestly don't know what to say. But I don't need to say anything. He hasn't finished. "That's what drew me in, a woman who needed a man to look after her. I thought I could step up and be him."

He shakes his head again. "I loved her, Rose. I fuckin' loved her. She wasn't violent all the time, and in between, she was the sweetest woman you could wish for. After one of her rages, she'd calm right down and be as kind as anyone could be. Until something made her fly off the handle again. Or," he grimaces, "I looked at her oddly." Another pause. "I took my vows seriously. Of course, going on tour meant I was out of the way and you know what they say, absence makes the heart fonder. It was easy to forget, or minimise, what she could be like while there was distance between us."

"Then I got injured again. Took a bullet in my leg and it damaged the muscles. For a while they weren't sure whether it would come right again. Got sent stateside to get treatment." He huffs a laugh. "Britney was actually a good nurse in her way. Did what she could to help me. Then…" A sigh almost of disbelief, "She went to the store and got accused of assaulting one of the employees."

I notice his phrasing. "You say she got accused? You don't think she was guilty?"

A slight snort now. "Oh, she pleaded her innocence. Told her story, putting a different slant on the evidence on the tapes. But the jury saw it the store employee's way. He was quite badly injured." He gives me a quick glance then looks away. "You want to know what I think? I think she was holding back on me as I was laid up and recovering. Even she couldn't hit a man when he was down. But all that pent-up rage had to go somewhere." Another sideways movement of his head. "Let's just say, I wasn't surprised when the police came to arrest her."

"And you put it behind you and moved on."

"No." He pauses, again seeming to gather his thoughts. "I was embarrassed as fuck. What kind of man was I to be cowed by my own wife? To be pleased when she was removed from my life? Oh, at first I was devastated, missed her every day. But as time passed, absence didn't make my heart fonder, it made me think straight. I realised I'd been infatuated with her. It couldn't have been love. How could I love a woman who treated me that way?" It's a rhetorical question so I don't answer. "From the start, Britney refused to see me, or have any contact with me. I tried to visit, but I wasn't on her list of approved visitors. I wondered if she blamed me, but," again he shrugs, "I took it as a sign that in her eyes, our marriage was over. Anyway, my leg recovered so I had full use of it, and I was sent back to the sandpit again. This time to a new team—that was when I met Roller. Britney was going to be gone for years, and I knew by then I was going to divorce her. So I saw myself as a single man and never admitted the embarrassment of my marriage or my wife to anyone. Even to Roller, who quickly became my best friend."

I realise he's ashamed. "What Britney did wasn't your fault, Petty. You didn't ask to be treated that way."

"You don't think?" he refutes fast. "RoseLyn, Britney saw a weakness and grabbed her chance to exploit it. I didn't walk out. I stayed." He gives me an intense look and I know he's thinking of that particular difference between us. He barks a laugh. "I've learned my fuckin' lesson. I'll never be weak ever again. I'm a fuckin' man, and how I live now proves it."

"Does it?" I raise my eyebrow. "She's already hit you since she's returned, and she raped you. She's got you back under her spell."

In front of my eyes, Petty changes, a new mask descending over his features. His jaw tightens and his eyes harden. "This time she's picked on the wrong man. I'm not going to take it lying down. I'm not going to play the victim again. Britney might have come back into my life, but she's not going to stay. I'm never going to hand over the reins of my life to a woman ever again."

Despite everything else he's said, for some unknown reason, that last statement pains me.

This evening I've been treated exactly the way I'd want a boyfriend to treat me. Petty fits in with my family like he was meant to be there. I already knew I was attracted to him, but thought that was just because he was a pretty bad boy, and maybe okay for a fling, but not as any permanent fixture. But while I've been trying to ignore it, a feeling's been growing that I wouldn't object if this situation were for real.

But he's been damaged, and now I know how badly. I don't know if it's even possible for him to ever love again.

Suddenly he turns those now hard cold eyes on me and striking as fast as a snake, his hand comes out and grips me by the throat. Not hard enough to bruise, but firm enough to be a warning. "Never, ever, tell anyone what I've told you. I'm not the man I was then." He holds me until I nod slightly, then he releases me.

Even though the air around me is warm, I shiver. In front of my eyes, Clark has transformed back into Petty. The warning glint in his eyes threatens retribution if I leak any details of our discussion.

I understand his secrets and his reasons for wanting to keep them. I hadn't needed the threat.

It's easy to make the promise. "You can trust me. I won't say a word."

CHAPTER EIGHTEEN

Petty

*C*an I trust her?

I stare at her, trying to read her mind, trying to tele-graph it would be in her best interest to keep quiet about the secrets I'd spilled so carelessly. Even now I have no idea what made me open my mouth.

I'd never hurt her. I've never hit a woman in my life, or not since I was four years old and shoved my baby sister.

I've never spoken to anyone as I had to her. Even in the honeymoon days with Britney, I hadn't spilled much about myself. For the moment it had been cathartic, as was knowing there was someone taking my side. But now I've come to my senses, I know I've said too much. I've revealed too much of the man that I am deep inside. I've painted myself as someone my brothers would laugh at, and not trust to have at their backs.

She doesn't seem that bothered by my threat as, with a slight huff, RoseLyn lies down, turns away from me and goes back to sleep, or pretends to. After a moment, I rest my own head and close my eyes, but I stay awake, unable to relax.

My loose words can only be down to that fucking nightmare, and the belief I owed her some explanation for waking her in the middle of the night. Truthfully, reliving what Britney had done to me, had fucked with my mind. The problem is, I've now given a woman I barely know the weapon that could destroy me.

I worked so fucking hard after Britney was arrested to become a man not a mouse. Men don't cower and allow themselves to be controlled. With her out of the way, I was able to take a good look in the mirror, and what I saw, I didn't like. Britney had known a victim when she'd seen one, and I swore no one else would ever take advantage of me in that way again. Without her around berating me, I saw how weak I really was, and what I needed to do to rectify it. Since then, I've lived up to my ideal of masculinity—strong, decisive, taking no shit from anyone. I'm in an outlaw MC for fuck's sake. You can't get much harder than that.

A by-product of me becoming a man's man has been to hate weakness in anyone who has a dick, and I give them shit if they don't live up to the ideal I strive to. Like who can be a proper man if they're attracted by the same sex? I've nothing but disdain for them.

Though Joker and Lady are good men to have at your back. Yeah, but they fuck each other. In the dark, I sneer in disgust.

Rope and Cuff? Thinking of the pair I shudder. I like them well enough, would hate to find out they share a bed and each other as well as the women they take there. I'd need to re-evaluate my feelings about them. *Don't ask, don't tell.* Better all around.

It's surprising how, despite my initial reaction, I've come to like Red's child, Zeke. Zeke's got a dick, but they're nonbinary. I suppose in my twisted mind they're not pretending to be a man, so they can be weak.

Men's men don't get abused by women. I'd become a laughingstock if that ever got out.

I'd been pleased with the new improved Petty who wouldn't take shit from anyone and could have continued this way forever. A pep talk each morning, and I was fit to go.

But then Britney came back.

Like a switch being thrown, she'd undone all the reparation I'd managed to the damage she'd left.

I can't go through this again.

Fuck knows why she came back to me, but I can't let her stay. I have to finally get that divorce.

Unless she's pregnant. Fuck, fuck. Fuck, fuck, fuck!

My hands bunch into fists. If she is, I'll be trapped forever.

I loved her once, but not anymore. I'd been in her thrall, but am no longer. Surely she can't love me, or she'd show it in more reasonable ways. Together, we're a fucking disaster.

Was RoseLyn right? Had she raped me? I'd responded. I'd come. While I hadn't initially been a willing participant, my body had enjoyed it enough, though my brain thought my dick had betrayed me.

Why can't I see Britney in the same vein as the women I've fucked and moved on from, never thinking anymore about it? A convenient hole to get my release. There's been no emotional connection with any of them, but nonetheless, a pleasant enough physical enjoyment, and zero regrets.

Why do I feel so dirty and used, as if I've been taken advantage of? I came. I was satisfied. For all I know, Britney's protected and we didn't need a condom anyway. Though she hinted otherwise, that could have been to fuck with me.

But it wasn't consensual.

RoseLyn said it was rape.

Balling my fists, I press them into my eye sockets, trying to escape the thoughts in my head, but it's impossible. My mind continues churning, not allowing me any rest. I lie awake as the sky lightens and the room goes from dark to dim.

When eventually there are sounds of life in the house around me, I give up any pretence at sleep. I take a quick shower, then return and pack my duffle with the few things I'd emptied from it.

The sound of me moving around awakens RoseLyn.

I frown when it looks like she wants to start a conversation, and turn away. It was bad enough that I spilled my guts to her in the night. Now I need things to get back to the way it's always been between us—me showing her my masculine side, one where I don't tolerate frailty, where I expect men to be men, and women to stay in their place.

Her narrowing eyes, pursed lips and the little shake of her head suggest she knows only too well what I'm doing and is placating me.

Christ, I can't wait for this gig to be over, and for her to get out of my life. Why, of all people was it her I confided in? Sure, she's got nice enough tits and a great ass, but normally I'd tap that, not talk to it.

As I wait for her to make herself ready for the day, I send a quick message to Keys to see whether he's gotten any further with the information I'd sent. His lack of response doesn't worry me. He'll get back when he's anything to say.

When I came to Texas, I'd known I'd need to step outside of the role I'd carved out for myself if I was going to come over convincingly as boyfriend material. I'd reverted to the man I'd been when I'd first met my wife when meeting RoseLyn's parents. It had been surprisingly easy to slip back into the familiar routine, like putting on a pair of worn but comfortable shoes. Last night, I'd relaxed and had enjoyed myself. Last night, I sat with a woman, held her, laughed with her, and with no ulterior motive about getting her into my bed.

Today, for the sake of my sanity, I have to get back to the man Britney had made me become.

But I've given RoseLyn the keys to destroy me, and I can't forget it.

Red calls me while she's still in the shower. Eagerly I answer, hoping it's the news I've been waiting for.

"Safe to come home, Brother."

"You got him? You got Saul?" A wave of relief floods over me. For the first time since I woke, I feel I can relax. There's no need for delay and this protection gig with RoseLyn is over. We can go our separate ways.

And I'll be going home to Britney. I straighten my back. *Only to get her out of my life.* I'll just have to find my balls and do it.

"Yeah, we got him." Quickly I bring my mind back to what Red is saying. "Got him in the basement all trussed up. Rose-Lyn's in the clear. He's been softened up to admit it was him who was after her."

"And Angel?"

"Played her part well. Reeled him in like a fuckin' fish and got away without a scratch." Thank fuck for that. My only concern about the operation had been putting a woman on the front line.

Prez ends the call saying he'll see me soon as I hear the shower turn off. It's good news all around. So why do I feel deflated?

RoseLyn appears, her hair wrapped up in a turban. She's dressed though, in denim shorts and a t-shirt. She has a freshness about her that draws me in. I catch myself staring at her, then force myself to turn away.

With my back toward her, I tell her in clipped tones, "Red rang. Saul's been caught. It's safe for you to go home."

"It's over?"

The disbelieving tremble in her voice leads me to confirm, "It's over."

I hear the sigh that leaves her. A quick glance over my shoulder shows she's standing with her eyes closed. Her hands fist then gradually relax as she comes to terms with the pronouncement I've made.

"Thank fuck," she states eventually, and a smile appears on her face. As if forgetting the mood I was in, she approaches me, making me fully turn around. Her hands land on my biceps. "Thank you, Petty. Thank you and your club." Her head moves side to side. "I can't quite believe this is all over."

"It's over," I confirm again. "He'll never get near you again."

"That man, the pastor—"

"Saul's already confirmed he was your stalker."

And you'll no longer need protection, from me or my club. I should feel pleased, but instead sadness settles within me.

I may not have spoken aloud, but it seems our minds are aligned. Her hand moves to rest on my chest, and she stares at where it touches my shirt.

Without meeting my eyes she speaks softly. "If you weren't married, if you were the man who I got to know during the night, I'd feel something for you… Clark."

Fuck. Why did she have to go there? I try to remind myself quickly that RoseLyn is not my type. I like soft while she's hard. I like meek while she's not. I like… Fuck knows what I like. Right now, I want her.

I can't help myself. I raise her face and lower my lips, then take hers with a growl. I kiss her like I mean it, demanding entry with my tongue. She clutches at me rather than pushing me away and gives back the same as I'm giving her. Our tongues fight for dominance. Our mouths devour each other. She smells delicious, her shampoo or whatever she uses, not overpowering but fruity and her. She tastes of peppermint from the toothpaste, making me want to find out the brand so I can use it myself to remind me of her. The moans in my ears are like music sent from the heavens above.

I lose myself in that kiss. My dick swells, my lungs heave, until finally I come to my senses and pull myself up to get air and push her at arm's length. *That was the biggest fucking mistake I've ever made.* I'd been swept away in the moment because this woman had declared she was developing feelings for me. Feelings that, fuck, I have to acknowledge I reciprocate.

Feelings I'd act on if I ever wanted to put myself at the mercy of a woman again. And once, believe you me, was more than enough. As it is, I've given her too much ammunition to use against me.

I can't let this go further. I have to shut this down fast. I slip back into the man I became once I was freed from Britney.

"You wanna quick fuck, darlin'?" I thrust my hips against her. "I'm down for that." I raise an eyebrow in question. "One for the road, what do you say?"

Her eyes narrow as they meet mine, and while I try to ignore it, I fucking love the way her face is flushed and her lips swollen and that it's down to me. I'd love to love her in the way she'd want to be loved, but a quick fuck is more in character. I have to step back before I fall any deeper.

"You're still married," she reminds me, her mouth twisting in disgust.

"I'm married," I concur with a shrug, hoping to convey what I'm offering is a promise of nothing more than two consenting adults getting their rocks off. I know I'm safe and that she'd never accept such a proposition, though my cock jerks as if hoping I'm wrong.

Her fist hits my chest, but oh so gently as her eyes settle on my face, making me feel uncomfortable as if she can see right down to her soul. "I know what you're doing, Petty. And you're an ass." But she says it without ire.

An asshole, yeah, I'll own that. But that's who I've got to be to protect myself and the life that I've built up. Without the Devils, I'd be nothing.

As RoseLyn goes to splash water on her face, I stand, body tight, finding it harder than usual to tamp down the softer side of me and find the man I truly am. I suspect it's all RoseLyn's fault that it's harder than usual to become the façade I've so carefully cultivated.

When she returns, the yearning to kiss her once more almost blindsides me, making me even more determined to never let her see the Clark side of me again.

I can't even allow myself to relax in front of her parents. But sharp as RoseLyn is, she explains my abruptness by telling them that I wasn't looking forward to the flight ahead. They give me a few funny looks, but all in all, I think I get away with it. Especially when I force myself to put my arm around her when I lead her to the car. No, why lie to myself? I let myself enjoy that last permissible slip before I return to keeping my distance, and my hands firmly to myself.

It's her who keeps the conversation going while her parents drive us to the airport. She hugs her parents goodbye, holding on tight for a few seconds. Rufus eyes me in an assessing way when he shakes my hand, but Martina ignores the standoffish vibes I'm putting off, and envelopes me in her arms and gives me a kiss on the cheek.

"Don't be a stranger, you hear?" Martina tells me. "And you take care of my girl."

I'm saved from having to answer as RoseLyn tugs at my arm. "We've got a flight to catch, Mom. I'll give you a call when I'm home."

And then we're alone, and there's no need for me to pretend anymore. Or to be correct, even more need than ever.

The flight is a reversal of yesterday's, with RoseLyn obviously uneasy and scared. And I'm a bastard, as even though I know how nervous she is to fly, I can't bring myself to hold her hand. Staring straight ahead, I ignore her.

I get her bag down for her and carry it off the plane. I'm a man, it's expected. Then we traverse the terminal and exit to the parking lot.

It's only when we're at the SUV that RoseLyn places her hand on my arm. She waits for me to look at her, then allows me to see how earnest she is as she makes me a promise. "Your secret's safe with me. I won't let anyone know."

She sounds so compassionate and forgiving, it makes me realise what a motherfucker I am, and how lucky I am to find a woman who seems to get me. She's the one who's got the right to be angry. As she continues to stare at me, I have to drop my eyes. Turning away, I grunt, and tersely reply, "Appreciate that."

There's no further attempt on either of our sides for any more conversation.

She's taken aback when I head toward her home, but there's no need for her to hide in a hotel now. She's clearly reluctant when, after I've parked, I open the door and get out, taking her bag and carrying it for her, then waiting for her to put her in the front door.

She's nervous as hell, clearly on the lookout for snakes that might have escaped. Her pale face and slight tremble shows she's far from comfortable. But I ignore all that, and act oblivious even while I know some assurance about how my brothers will have cleared them out would be welcomed.

My desire, *need*, to put distance between us, is absolute.

Unable to say my conscience is clear, I leave her and head back to the clubhouse where I exchange the car for my bike, strapping my duffel onto the back. Then I walk inside.

I seem to enter in the midst of some kind of celebration. Men are laughing, raising glasses, and on seeing me, Roller lifts his hand in welcome.

I stand for a moment, letting the atmosphere sink in. *This is the life. This is what I can't give up.*

Red gestures toward me and pauses his conversation with Crash. "You dropped RoseLyn at the hotel?"

I scrunch my eyes. "The hotel? I took her back to her house." His expression worries me. "It is safe for her now, isn't it?"

He sighs as if in exasperation. "Safe, yeah, but with the shock she'd had, I thought it would take her a moment to ease into the idea of going back. She's so fuckin' scared of snakes, Brother."

"We cleared them all out." I shrug.

"Yeah, but up here," Red taps his forehead, "she might not accept that. You're a cold-hearted bastard, aren't you?"

"Ass," Crash says loudly, but the turn up of his mouth shows there's not much weight behind it.

But he's right. Maybe I should have paid a little more attention to her state of mind, but all I'd been thinking of at the time is how fast I could get away from her.

I raise and lower my shoulders again. "Far as I see it, our job is done." I jiggle on the spot a little as though to show my impatience. "Or will be when that fucker you picked up is dealt with. We going to have a chat with him? Or have you finished already?"

Red grins now. "We've left him to think on his crimes. We've got plenty of time to play with him. Don't think he deserves quick, Brother."

"Yeah, we're in no hurry," Crash supports Prez. "Now why don't you go home to that pretty little wife you've got waiting? Appreciate you thinking club first, but you probably can't wait to see her. We'll leave something of Saul so you can get your turn at him."

Red raises his brows, but doesn't comment, though I think he suspects I'm not quite so eager to get back to her as his VP might think.

My brain works a mile a minute, thinking of excuses and rejecting them just as fast, not wanting to show my reluctance to carry out Crash's suggestion. I'm only trying to delay because I'm scared. Scared of going back to the apartment. And I'm fucking furious at myself for having to acknowledge that—I'm a man for fuck's sake.

And a man would give a lewd wink, adjust his pants, and show the world I'm more than ready to take advantage of the situation offered.

So I mock salute the VP, wave and call out a general, "Later," to my brothers, and leave the clubhouse with rowdy comments of just how I might be going to celebrate the reunion with my wife.

Much as I welcome the feel of my bike under me, the journey's far too short for it to have any impact on my mood. I turn into the parking lot behind the hairdressers, reluctant to turn the engine off. It's only knowing that Britney will have heard my bike that overcomes my desire to turn around and keep riding.

Britney. The last twenty-four hours have been like a pleasant interlude, an oasis of calm when I could be myself, a chance to be the man I was before she came into my life. With each step up the stairs, my spirits drop and my heart becomes heavy. With every rise and fall of my feet, it becomes harder to maintain my resolve.

I don't know who I am anymore. Am I the man I relaxed into yesterday evening, the man before Britney? Or the nervous, jumpy, vulnerable man I was during our marriage? Or the strong persona I've built up around me like a protective shell when she wasn't around anymore.

Who am I now? What's Britney going to turn me into this time?

Although away from her I'd determined enough was enough, and that she and I had no future together, as each step I get closer to her, my determination fades. She must have me brainwashed as I feel like I'm being stripped of my masculinity, hunching in on myself, mentally preparing for what lies ahead.

If my brothers saw me now… They wouldn't understand how I, a man, can be fearful of a woman who's not much more than half my size, or why my hands sweat at just the thought of seeing her. Why does my heart start to beat faster in dread? How can she so easily strip me back to the man she damaged so badly?

Pausing at the top step, I take a deep breath.

I'm not afraid of pain. I'm as likely as any of my brothers to run into rather than away from danger. I can face up to the barrage of abuse from any of the people who buy security from us but don't want to pay up when the bill is presented. I've been bullied by sergeant-majors without turning a hair, and by all of my now brothers when I was a prospect. So why is it I tremble when faced with the ire of a woman I could break in two if it wasn't for her sex?

What is the power she has over me, and how can I escape from under it?

I wait so long, lost in my thoughts, that the door is pulled open before I have the chance to do it myself.

"You're back," Britney sneers, her body blocking the doorway.

"I'm back," I confirm unnecessarily, trying to assess the mood that she's in. After hearing RoseLyn's soft voice for the last day, Brit's nasal tone sounds harsh and grates. "You going to let me in?"

Part of me wants her to say no, then I can go back to the club-house with a clear conscience. I've done my duty by coming here and won't even have to feel guilty.

But she steps aside. As I pass, she even offers, "Would you like a coffee?"

"Thanks, but I'll have a beer." I go straight to the kitchenette and head for the fridge.

She leans on the countertop. "Did you have a good trip?"

I can do conversation. My brow creases as I think of the answer. It was enjoyable but I doubt that's what she wants to hear. "So, so," I eventually reply, seesawing my hand, "It achieved its objective." If, that is, the objective was for me to admit I'd become resolute about getting a divorce, and that I do harbour thoughts I shouldn't have about RoseLyn. Fuck knows what Britney would do if she could read my mind.

I raise the beer bottle to my mouth, my mind more on the conundrum I'm dealing with rather than the woman who's facing me.

I don't even notice her leaning in until she suddenly spits, "I'd say you had a very good time." Her mouth is twisted, and her eyes blaze.

Stunned by her sudden change in demeanour I take a step back and put my beer down, holding up my hands defensively. My heart rate rises. "What the fuck you talking about?"

She rounds the counter and comes toward me, her accusing

finger pointing my way. "You dare come home stinking of the bitch you've been with?"

Do I smell of RoseLyn? I've been in close proximity to her so I suppose it's quite likely some of her perfume might have rubbed off on me. Strangely, I wasn't really aware she was wearing any. She smelled good. That's all I can remember.

I'm not quite sure how to address the accusation. "You know I'm guarding a woman, Brit. I've just sat beside her on the plane for the last three hours."

Her eyes widen. I'd told her I'd be out on club business, not that I was going away. My statement has just added fuel to the fire.

"I know what you said." If sparks flew out of her eyes, I wouldn't be surprised. "I also know that you're a man with a dick and probably not fussy what hole you put it into."

"RoseLyn's my job," I stress, my tone higher than normal. "Other than that, she means nothing to me."

"Your job?" She snorts. "I'll bet she's a fucking piece of work. No wonder you don't want to share my bed when you've been sharing hers. She's trying to take you away from me."

If she was, then it wouldn't be too hard for her. RoseLyn and Britney are so far apart in personality it's unreal. If I had a choice over the other, I know who I'd choose.

"It's not like that—"

I should have been prepared, should have been on the lookout for it and braced my muscles, but when Brit suddenly lets her fist fly into my stomach, she catches me unawares and I bend over, gasping for breath. When her knee comes up and catches me straight in the balls, I grab my crotch and fall to my knees, my eyes watering.

"Brit…" I gasp in a voice several octaves higher than normal.

"You cheating bastard." She's gone around my back and now her foot's collided hard with my kidney, still bruised from where she hit it last time. For a small person, she packs one hell of a punch. One kick isn't sufficient for her. She's kicking out again and again, as I roll away, trying to get out of range. But she follows me and I feel a rib cracking as she connects with it.

I'm gasping and trying to suck in air. *She's out of control.* Suddenly I've no doubt that she'll kill me unless I stop her. I stumble to my feet, lurching forward as I breathe through the pain and turn to face her. She's got an iron skillet in her hand and it's raised to strike me. Even in the state I am, I can appreciate the cliché.

I reach for it and try to pull it out of her hand. We grapple for possession, her unwilling to let it go, and me determined she's not going to hit me with it. With my extra hard tug, she finally releases it, but the momentum has her falling face down, hitting her head on the side of the countertop.

For a moment, she lies prone, and I'm worried she's taken a blow that's killed her. But before the thought *oh God what do I do now* can be completed, she raises her head and touches her face with her hand. Her nose looks broken and there's blood pouring from it.

I did that. Okay, so I didn't mean it, and I didn't lay a finger on her, but I'm the reason she's injured. I go cold. *I didn't hit her, Daddy. I didn't.* My head falls into my hands. *I didn't. Did I?*

For a moment, I'm a four-year-old kid all over again. Then I shake my head to clear it. She's not my newborn sister who I need to protect. She's the woman who I tried to stop from killing me, and whatever I did was in self-defence. Not even my daddy would judge me.

I didn't fight back. I stopped her.

We're both standing like combatants, our chests heaving, eyes caught in each other's. Realising I'm still holding the skillet, I place it down on the counter. As my head clears and the present and past settle in their proper boxes, I know I have to make some sort of recompense for her being hurt. But the words that I'm sorry get stuck in my throat as I can't be anything other than pleased my action brought her assault to an end. My gut roils, though, at the thought of how she might pay me back. As my adrenaline fades, my current injuries start making them-selves known to me, but I put that aside for now, as I wait for what happens next.

I wait for the ire. I wait for her to spit words at me. I wait for the tears, for her to accuse me of hurting her. I wait for the howl of pain and the remonstrations.

What I'm not expecting is the maniacal laughter that begins to spill from her mouth. She's like a madman, with spittle covering her lips as the laughter keeps roaring out.

"You… you've done it now!" she screams eventually, but in utter and total glee.

Then she launches for the skillet and while I have a split second to realise she's about to hit me, it's not enough time to take evasive action.

CHAPTER NINETEEN

Petty

I don't know how long I've been out, but I come to with every part of me hurting. My balls throb, a sharp stabbing pain gets me when I take a deep breath, and my head is a ball of agony with an egg-shaped lump on it. Cautiously I open my eyes, but Britney is nowhere in sight. Listening carefully, I can hear nothing that would suggest she's still in the apartment.

Groaning, I roll over and get to my feet. My head spins with the strength of the blow that had taken me out and I have to steady myself with a hand on the countertop as I feel so dizzy. From the soreness over my body, I suspect she'd continued kicking me while I was out.

Staggering into the bathroom, I get out some painkillers from the cabinet and throw them into my mouth. As I chase them down with water, I realise this has to stop. She's gone too fucking far this time. Bowing my head, I realise I can't go through this all again. *If only she'd signed those fucking divorce papers.*

The question I should have paid more attention to before comes into my head. Why didn't she? She's not in love with me anymore, or even pretending to be. My evidence? Unlike in the past, she's not hung around to show remorse and offer empty promises that it will never happen again.

Though maybe it's different now. Before she's had no reason to accuse me of infidelity. Not that she's any cause to now. I didn't do anything with RoseLyn, other than that kiss which I immediately regretted. *And which had made me want to go back for more.*

The agony I'm in helps me get clarity in my head. Even though I suspect Britney's come back because me being her husband is of use to her—maybe that's why she didn't sign the papers I'd sent, even then she was planning to use me again—I can't let this go on.

Man or mouse, this time was too close. She was out of control and I'm lucky she didn't kill me. What would I do if it happens again? I don't have it in me to retaliate. Everything inside me screams that I can't hurt a woman, that she needs my protection and support rather than violence. She might pack a hard punch, but mine would be far worse. No, I can't lay a hand on her, I can't risk losing control of my temper.

I'll move back to the clubhouse. Set the divorce in motion again. Get a good lawyer.

I raise my fist, but put it down gently, not wanting to add any additional pain. *To hell with any problems it might cause with her parole officer. She's broken us, not me.*

I don't want to be around Britney anymore. For the sake of my sanity, I can't be around her. Yes. Moving back and leaving her to fend for herself will be my best bet.

She might follow me to the clubhouse. She might out me to my brothers. She might…

It takes me a moment in my pain-filled haze to recognise the vibrating buzz of my phone. Taking it out, I glance down, wondering whether it's her calling to apologise for her over-the-top reaction. It's what I used to expect in the old days—her to hurt me, then offer some form of reparation.

But it's not her. It's my prez.

"Red." I clear my throat to try to strengthen my voice.

"Need you at the clubhouse now."

Grimacing, not feeling up to riding my bike, I wonder whether I can put him off. "Is it urgent, Prez?"

"What part of *now* don't you fuckin' understand?"

Christ, he sounds pissed off. So pissed, there's only one answer I can give him. "I'm on my way."

Has something happened to RoseLyn? She's safe, isn't she? God forbid there was a remaining snake in her house. Feeling guilty at the way I just left her, I check my phone but there are no other calls or texts that I missed. Fuck, I hope nothing's happened to her. Could she have made a complaint about me? Nah, Rose-Lyn's not like that.

Red's known for his redheaded temper, and once roused you don't want to be in the vicinity. Is he annoyed in general, or is it specifically me?

RoseLyn might have betrayed my secrets to him. But while I feel vulnerable having put the truth out there, I still don't think she'd out me.

But she might…

Fuck, women. Why don't I learn I can't trust them? I should have put my foot down and refused to go to Texas at all, then Britney would have had no reason to hurt me.

She doesn't need a reason, I remind myself. *And RoseLyn's not her.* I can't see any reason that RoseLyn would have betrayed me.

Fuck, I can't even think straight through this pain. Putting my hands to the small of my back and using them to help me straighten, I realise my kidneys have taken some blows, and I suspect I'll be pissing blood for a while. My balls feel tender though the pain no longer makes me want to throw up. Limping a couple of steps, feeling a sharp stabbing which has me wondering whether she stomped on my knee while I was uncon-scious, I face the mirror.

Britney hasn't lost any of her skills over the years. Apart from the paleness of my face, my red-drawn eyes, watery from that kick to my groin, my skin is unmarked. Fuck it, but I thought I was done with this seven years ago. Seems though, yet again, I've got to call on my strength, hide the hurts that she's done, and walk into the clubhouse and face my prez as if I'm the very picture of good health.

No one can know. If I feel like I've gone ten rounds with the world heavy-weight record holder, I'll have to keep that to myself.

It's not that I'm a stranger to injury. I was a soldier for fuck's sake, hurt in the line of duty. And you don't live the biker lifestyle without picking up a few scars. Apart from those who pick battles with us just because they don't like our faces, I often spar with my brothers and take part in our regular bouts in the ring. Only a couple of months ago I was out of line and said some painful things about Red's kid—my excuse that was before I got to know them. Prez rightfully took me down in the ring, and I can tell you, that man hits hard. And then I got into a car crash when I was supposed to be protecting Zeke. They left me bleeding with a broken nose, cracked ribs, and a bump on the head coincidentally in about the same place that Britney had hit me.

So yeah, I'm no stranger to pain or having to deal with it. And like most men, I've got my brave face perfected. But this is the first time in seven years that I've had to actively hide anything's happened to me. *I thought I was done with that shit.*

I'd rather curl up in bed and groan my way through my pain, but while I might not know what's got my prez riled, whatever it is, I'm not fool enough to make it worse by refusing his instruction. I can't tell him the truth. No fucking way. I'd die before I let him know how weak I am.

Eyeing the painkillers, I take another dose. Not what a doctor would order, but I need some help. I toss my bike key in my hand, take a deep breath, then exhale sharply as I regret it, and make my way out the door.

"You okay?"

Glancing down as I've descended the first step painfully and stiffly, I notice one of the hairdressers who works in the salon downstairs, putting out some trash. Breathing more carefully, I make every effort to stand straight.

"Fuckin' ace, woman," I growl.

Used to me and my rudeness, she shakes her head and that's the end of her sympathy. I wait until she's disappeared inside to complete my torturous journey down the stairs.

Oh shit, oh shit, oh shit. I force myself over to my bike, my head spinning, and my whole body in agony. *Am I safe to ride?* Doesn't matter whether I feel it or not, I'll have to be. But even when I sit my ass on the seat gingerly, my tender balls make me suck in air.

Fuck Britney and what she's done to me.

Vowing this will be the last time she'll ever lay a hand on me, then scoffing at myself because I've said that before, I start the engine, tap into gear, let out the clutch and pray I get to the clubhouse safely.

Every bump shoots daggers of pain through me. Every lifesaver turn of my head makes my skull throb, and kicking up through the gears makes my knee remind me she must have kicked me there. The vibrations through my groin make me nauseous.

I ride through the gates relieved to have gotten here shiny side up, pull to a halt and on the second attempt, get my knee to work sufficiently so as to kick down the stand. The air seems to ring with blessed silence once I've turned the engine off.

I lean over my tank, breathing lightly but fast, and send up a thankful prayer that I'm here in one piece. I add a plea that I can pull this off and leave no one any the wiser as to what's happened to me.

I swallow the pain as I dismount, then make sure I'm balanced evenly on both legs and that my back is straight as I walk toward the door, determined no one will have any reason for questions.

I'm a fucking man. I can't let them know a woman did this to me.

Even pushing the heavy door pulls on my ribs, but I grit my teeth and wipe the grimace off my face. I enter, noticing the room is as full as when I left it, but what is different, is how all conversation stops as soon as I appear. It's hard to read the expressions on all the faces, but none of them look particularly happy at my arrival.

My eyes find Roller, my partner in crime, my ride-or-die friend, but there's sadness in his eyes, and he shakes his head, then turns his back.

What the fuck?

The crowd parts as Red strides through, coming to a halt right in front of me. His jaw is clenched, and too late, I notice his fist is too. I barely have time to notice it coming at my face before it connects with my nose, and hell, now I think he's broken that too. *So much for my unmarked face.*

The blow knocks me off my feet. Coupled with all my other injuries, I'm in too much pain to stand, but then it's probably safest to stay down. Unable to do much more than pull myself to my knees, I look up into the face of my prez, tears streaming from the knock to my nose.

I try to blink the blurriness away. "Wh-wh-what was th-th-that for?" Pain makes me stammer.

Red's green eyes flare. "You've gone too fuckin' far this time."

What the hell is he talking about? Has that blow to my head made me forget something important?

"I-I don't know what you mean." My body was a mass of pain before, now it's almost unbearable to breathe let alone speak.

"Whoa. Titch."

As Twister's voice thunders out, a kerfuffle draws my attention, letting me see both Crash and the enforcer with their arms locked around the older man.

"Let me at him. Fuckin' abusive dick," the big man roars and tries to get free.

What?

I've had two blows to the head in relatively quick succession. Who can blame me if I'm not thinking straight? But I can see that all my brothers are throwing murderous looks toward me and it's not just Titch they're having to hold back.

"What the hell's going on, Prez?" I raise my eyes, hoping someone will enlighten me, or just shoot me and put me out of my misery. At the moment, I don't know which I'd prefer.

Red bends down, puts his hand on the neck of my t-shirt and ignominiously drags me to my feet. I swallow down the exclamation of pain that his action causes me. When I'm on my feet, he lets me go so violently I stagger.

"You're a fuckin' piece of shit, Petty. Never did fuckin' like you. But also never thought you'd stoop to this." While I'm still bewildered, Red calls Hammer over and says in a disgusted tone, "Take him downstairs and get him out of my sight."

Using what strength I have and ignoring the agony, I try to shrug Hammer off. In a voice that even I don't recognise, I blurt out, "What, Prez? What the fuck am I supposed to have done?"

Red's eyes widen. "You fuckin' kidding me? You want to know what you did?" He eyes me, correctly reading my confusion. "Do you truly not think you've done anything wrong?" His voice thunders louder. "In your world, Petty, it might be alright to beat on your wife, but it certainly isn't in mine."

"Not mine," Cobra echoes him, and spits in my direction.

"Nor fuckin' mine," Rope copies.

One by one, all the brothers show solidarity with the prez.

Pain forgotten in my bewilderment, my mouth gapes open. "Brit?" I ask cautiously. Then my stomach starts to churn as a memory comes back to me. *"You've done it now."* My voice hardens. "What the fuck's she been saying about me?" I glance around but she's the one person I can't see.

"She didn't have to say anything," Red sneers. "Though she

confirmed it was you when we asked her. And if you want to know where she is, Rosa and Cher have taken her to the emergency room." He stops talking to me and addresses Hammer instead. "I thought I told you to get him out of here?"

Hammer and fucking Cobra take each of my arms and roughly pull me forward. It takes everything in me to stop crying out at the pain that they cause.

I can't compute what's happening to me, how Britney got here, or how she told her fabricated story. Or, what it's going to mean to me.

Suddenly Red's voice bellows out, stopping our progress. "Nearly took your patch once, Petty. Kind of regretting I didn't now."

He's going to take my patch?

Bemused, befuddled, pain throbbing through me, I don't resist as Hammer and Cobra drag me to the basement. Without speaking, they zip tie my hands and my feet to the chair, and then, with dual looks of disgust, they leave me.

It's not the first time in my life I've been in this exact position, but this time I've got the feeling that Zeke won't be freeing me.

Only the truth is going to save me. That's if they believe anything that I say. And is it worse if they do? Real men don't let their wives beat on them.

Maybe I'll just let them do their worst without ever knowing the truth.

That disappointment in Red's eyes, in Roller's eyes, fuck, in everyone's, was so hard to see.

I can't even imagine how they'd react if they knew the truth.

That I'm a pussy.

I'm weak.

I should never have been patched in to ride by their side.

A groan reaches my ears. *What the fuck?*

I look up and see a man who's in even a worse state than me. He's strung up by his arms, blood pooling on the floor beneath him.

He looks more dead than alive, and I realise who he must be.

It's Saul. RoseLyn's ex who abused her, tortured her and stalked her.

If I wasn't in so much pain, I'd laugh at the situation. The club must think they've put two abusers together.

Fact is though, only one of us is guilty, and it sure isn't me.

CHAPTER TWENTY

RoseLyn

I try to tell myself I'm glad to be back in my own home, but I fail. The factors against me feeling comfortable add up. Foremost is my fear that there's still a snake lying waiting for me, and my ears are attuned for the slightest rattle. I'm tiptoeing around the house, watching where I put my feet, gently removing the couch cushions before replacing them and sitting. I can't get rid of that pricking feeling that somewhere, unfound and unseen, one of the slithery monsters is lurking.

I've returned to an utter mess.

In their efforts to locate and remove any and hopefully all of the snakes, every drawer has been opened and its contents upended. All my kitchen cupboards have had their contents emptied out, the beds have been stripped, and my wardrobes have been cleared.

It's no wonder I can't settle surrounded by everything not in its place.

The task is so big it's overwhelming. But I've got to start somewhere. First, I unpack the few things I'd taken to Texas, putting my toiletries back in the bathroom and straightening everything in there, and then starting a load of laundry. I've only begun to make a slight dent in tidying up when I can't stop yawning.

I'm feeling sorry for myself. I've just returned from my parents, and am missing their company. It's normal for me to feel discombobulated once I'm home after a visit.

Then there's the fact that for the last few weeks I've never been alone, and the silence feels oppressive and heavy. Even though I know Saul's no longer a threat, it's not easy to shake the feeling of having to always look behind me.

I'm also trying to deal with my mixed-up feelings about Petty. I've gone from hating the man, to tentatively liking the side of him he showed in Texas, to developing a fondness for him when he exposed his flaws in our middle-of-the-night conversation. That fondness started to turn into something more. Then, like a switch being thrown, I'd lost the man I was becoming to know, and he turned into a complete asshole again.

That kiss though. That was up there as one of the best I've ever experienced.

I yawn again. *God, I'm tired.*

It's not surprising. I had next to no sleep last night, and then there was the stress of the flight *and* dealing with Petty. It's no wonder I'm tired. I see absolutely no reason why I shouldn't indulge in a little nap. The mess isn't going anywhere and maybe won't be so daunting when I wake up.

So after remaking the bed, checking underneath and lifting the mattress, then gingerly sorting through the clothes still on the floor just in case there are any residual visits of the legless kind, I shut the door firmly, lie on the bed, and close my eyes.

But as so often when you're feeling sleepy, my mind won't switch off. Instead, I find myself analysing what went on between myself and Petty, and trying to solve the conundrum of which manifestation of the man is the real one.

I'm mostly convinced it was the man who'd woken from the nightmare and shared the details of his abusive relationship with his wife. I know had I not caught him in that moment of weakness, he'd never have enlightened me about what had gone on in his life.

Rolling on my back, I can't get him out of my mind. He seems to be a victim of a sort of toxic masculinity. Probably shaped by his experiences in the Army and then in the MC, maybe even from the way he was brought up, Petty seems to have a vision of what a man should be. Having a weakness, admitting he'd let his wife get the better of him and not just once, but on numerous occasions, is something he can't face up to.

It probably doesn't help that I'm admired as I walked out at the first sign of abuse, while he stayed and took it. Who knows though? If I'd married Saul, maybe I'd have been more inclined to see if we could mend our relationship and make it work.

Having been in his situation, my anger is directed solely toward his wife who was abusive from the start. He's a good man for staying, and no blame attaches to him, other than his blindness that he was fighting a lost cause.

His saving grace was that she'd gotten arrested. Distance had brought him to his senses and given him freedom for a few years until she turned up again and he was straight back into that trap.

I hope he escapes this time. Abusers don't mend their behaviour, they get worse. I know. I mean, just look what happened with Saul.

I wonder why she hadn't had contact with him while she was inside. While she might have told him she loved him, she doesn't sound like a very loving wife. I haven't met her, but I hate her.

And if I'm honest, some of that hate isn't on Petty's behalf, but on mine. I could definitely fall for the man who'd been with me at my parents' house, and who'd spilled his all to me in the middle of the night.

I drift on the verge between sleep and consciousness with

things getting twisted in my mind. Thoughts that I can't quite hold onto, but never descending into the sleep that my body requires.

The loud roar of two motorcycles arriving wakes me fully. Not having undressed, I go to the window, and looking out, see two bikes, but not ones I recognise.

They've got Saul, I remind myself. However, I still can't help being a little unnerved as I go to the door and leaving the chain attached, crack it open.

Two men are standing there with their backs turned toward me. I see they both wear cuts, but the backs are bare apart from the word *Prospect.*

One hears the door opening and turns around. He offers an easy grin. "Hi, I'm Owl." As he speaks, he adjusts his glasses to sit more firmly on his nose.

"Meat," says the other. It takes me a moment to realise it must be his name and not an attempt to say "pleased to meet you."

"And you're here…?" I assume they're Satan's Devils but the sense of danger I've carried since Saul reared his head has made me cautious.

"Ah, well, Red expected you'd stay at the hotel for a while. We were going to get your house straightened up before you came back," the one called Owl says breezily. "The Devils made a mess when they caught the snakes. Red sent us here to help you get sorted."

"We're yours to command, ma'am," Meat says, with a small bow. His grin almost splits his face in two.

"I'm sorry, I don't know you." I'm still being careful. While I don't think I'm in danger anymore, I don't want to just let strangers into my house.

"'Course you don't," Owl agrees amicably. "Why don't you call the clubhouse and confirm it?"

As that seems a good idea, I give them a nod, then close the door. I take my phone out of my purse and call Red. It's only seconds before he's corroborated who they are and what they're here for.

"I'm sorry I didn't send a face you'd recognise," he says, regretfully. "But I need all the patched members here."

There's a seriousness in his tone that leads me to suspect something's happened that's important. But I achieved my objective, and apart from sorting out my undie drawer, am relieved to have some help straightening my house.

Ending the call, I return to the door, and this time, open it fully.

"Sorry about that—"

"No need, ma'am," Meat butts in. "Good to see you're being careful."

Waving them in, I don't understand if Red needs all-hands-on-deck, then why they are here. As I point the way to the kitchen that despite my earlier efforts still looks much like a bomb's hit it, I ask them, "Red sounded busy. Are you not needed?"

Owl grins as he shakes his head. "Not yet, as we're just prospects. The meetings are only for patched members."

I suddenly remember some of the things that Sarge had told me. "Ah, recruits. You do all the shit jobs until you prove your-selves loyal to the club."

"Yeah." He snorts and looks around him. "Shit jobs sums it up." He grins and waves at scattered pots and pans and contents of the cupboards stacked haphazardly. Then he must wrongly read the expression on my face. "Oh fuck," he says fast. "I didn't mean…"

I chuckle. "It's alright. It is a shit job. Bet you would rather be at the club and in on whatever they're doing."

Now Owl removes his glasses and polishes them on a rag he's taken from his pocket. After he's replaced them, he shakes his head. "Not sure about that. I think we're best out of it." He sighs. "Petty's gone and fucked up again, and this time I'm not sure he'll be getting away with it."

"Owl," Meat growls, with a pointed jerk of his chin in my direction.

Owl's eyes widen much like his namesake's. He shoots a worried look toward me. "Forget I said anything."

But I can't. My brain whirls. I liked getting to know the man Petty was in Texas. Okay, he came back to his grizzly self on the journey home, but how could he have *fucked up* as Owl had put it, and in only a few short hours?

Meat looks like he's going to make a start on getting some order into this mayhem. He bends and begins picking up items off the floor, then glances up, and I automatically point to the correct cupboard. It seems like he, at least, has finished with the conversation. Taking his cue, Owl crouches beside him.

But I'm far from done with it. It might be irrational, but I've a burning urge to find out what's happening to the man who seems to have multiple personalities. One of which, I admit, I really started to like.

"Hey, wait up. What's Petty done?" Two faces turn to me, both with lips firmly shut. I'm not particularly proud of what I do next. "If you don't tell me, I'll ring Red and ask him."

I don't need to add that will let their prez know that they've said something they presumably shouldn't.

Owl almost squeals. "You can't do that. We'll lose our chance at getting a patch."

"You will." Meat glares at him. "I said nothing."

My gaze goes from one to the other, then I roll my eyes and take out my phone. When they see what I'm doing, Owl jumps up. The motion makes his glasses slip and his forefinger rights them again.

He stands in front of me, his hands clasped as he pleads, "Please don't."

It may be nothing. It might not concern me at all, but I *need* to know, even though that makes no sense. With my fingers hovering threateningly over the keypad, I repeat, "Tell me."

"Oh for fuck's sake." Meat joins us. "Look, I don't know why you've got yourself all twisted about what's happened to that man, but don't waste any sympathy on him. Petty's wife turned up, her fuckin' face all bashed in and covered with blood."

As if I was in any doubt, Owl confirms, "Yeah, fuckin' Petty beat her up."

Now they've started, they go for broke. "She's in the hospital."

I don't believe it. I *can't* believe it. Has Petty finally snapped? Has everything suddenly gotten too much for him? Personally, knowing his story, I wouldn't blame him if it has. I know men shouldn't hit women, but given what she's done to him, I might condone him this once. *But she's gone to the hospital which means it's serious.*

This time I do hit the keys.

"Oh fuck," Meat groans, his fingers splayed over his eyes.

"I'm not ringing Red," I snap. "I'm calling Petty." But when the call connects, there's no answer.

What can I do? Or rather, should I do anything? Petty's business is none of mine, and I've certainly no part to play in their marriage even if I have doubts it's going to last. *And I've no aspirations on the man if they part.* Though, if I'm honest, I wouldn't have minded getting to know better the version of the man who was at my parents.

But now? If Petty's hit a woman, even if in justified anger, that should make me run a mile.

On this, he and I are on the same page. Men have superior strength and they shouldn't use it against a female. Abuse is abuse, and there are far better ways to handle things, like walking away from the situation.

Unless she went crazy and he had to fight back.

Oh, for heaven's sake. I can't pretend to know what is

happening, or validate my interest in what's going on with a man I hardly know. I should leave well alone.

Owl and Meat have been watching me carefully, and seem to relax when I put down my phone. When I move into the kitchen, out of the side of my eye, I see Meat slapping Owl's back as they again try to bring the discarded items into some sort of order.

My role is relegated to just one of supervisor, but while I try to concentrate on what goes where, I can't get thoughts of Petty out of my head.

In Texas, he'd impressed my parents and gained their obvious approval, and that had surprised me. They wanted to adopt him for goodness' sake. When Petty said it would be him accompanying me, I never thought we'd pull it off and they'd actually believe we were together, but something they saw made them think we fit, and they were convinced we were in a relationship. Of course that was only as he showed he had more to offer than being an ass.

How's he feeling now? Is he regretting hitting his wife? The man I'd known in Texas would be horrified he'd hurt her, but perhaps that wasn't who Petty really is. Perhaps he deceived me and is now back to the man he is inside. Though in that late night discussion, he'd seemed pretty adamant that men should never hit women, whatever the provocation.

Had she insulted him in front of his brothers? Left him in a position where he had no choice? Where it was either retaliate or face the censure he expected would follow when they learned, what he'd tried so hard to keep hidden, that he was a man bullied by his wife?

Making an excuse I'm going to make a start on my bedroom, I leave the prospects to their work, and alone try Petty's phone for a second time but again it just rings out. I bite my lip trying to answer the question as to why I care what happens to the man I'd thought I'd disliked but when it came to it, I liked a little too much. Oh why not admit it. I'm tied up in knots not knowing what's going on.

My throat feels dry so I return to the kitchen to get a glass of water, and stop in my tracks, pulling back behind the door, as I hear Owl talking to Meat.

"Red wants to take Petty's patch. They've voting on it."

"Prez doesn't condone unprovoked violence toward women," Meat tells him. "And who'd hit Britney? She's really nice."

"She's nice, yeah, but there's an edge about her. I wouldn't like to get on her wrong side."

"She's been in jail. That would harden anyone," Meat defends her.

"Why would Red take his patch? Surely whatever's happened between them is between a man and his wife."

Again it's Meat. "Britney said he hit her without warning. Just walked in and knocked her down. That's what's worrying Prez."

Owl seems swayed by that argument. "Petty's a bit of a loose cannon. Rumour was Red doesn't trust him, not after what happened with Zeke. He was already walking a thin line. Now if Petty's got an uncontrollable temper, then he might be worried about when he'd flare up."

Again Owl seems to agree. "Thank fuck his temper didn't show itself when he was guarding RoseLyn. Red should never have put him on this job."

"Not this job or any job. Petty will be out of the club."

"With a fuckin' beatdown." I can't see Owl's face but I'd place money he's just grimaced.

I stay eavesdropping though there's now silence. When a few seconds pass, I reckon they've given me all I'm going to get.

But that's enough to horrify me. Retaliation maybe I could understand, but Petty wouldn't have hit Britney out of the blue. Something must have made him snap. Even if she didn't lay a finger on him first, perhaps he was defending himself, knowing the signs she was going to blow from the past.

I haven't met the woman so I only know one side of the story, but I'm certain, after his nightmare, Petty wasn't in any state to lie last night, and why make something like that up? Something he was so scared about his brothers getting to know.

Then there's the fact she was locked up for causing grievous bodily harm which surely attests to her tendency for violence.

One thing I'm pretty certain of is that Petty doesn't have anyone to advocate on his behalf. The man's so damn stubborn he'll keep quiet and won't defend himself. He'd rather maintain his man card than risk losing the respect of his brothers, and his club.

But it sounds like he might lose everything anyway if he keeps quiet, just as much as he thinks he might for speaking up.

While it's good to know the Satan's Devils clearly don't condone spousal abuse when it's done by a man, I'd like to think they also wouldn't support it in reverse, either tacitly or actively. And without the facts, they might end up doing that without realising it.

If Britney has framed him, she's got to be stopped.

And if she hasn't? Well, knowing that might end my stupid infatuation with the man who'd let his mask drop.

I've got to go to him.

"Hey." I stride back into the kitchen. "I've got to go get something from the store. You reckon you can continue without me for a while?"

"Sure." Meat straightens as he reassures me. "We can get everything straightened up. Can't guarantee it will be in its right place though."

Fair enough. I nod.

Well, that was easy. Excuse made and accepted, I go to my car, appreciating now Saul's out of my hair I won't need to keep getting new rentals. It's a sign of how much better my life is going to be without him in the picture.

I haven't asked what's happened to him as I really don't want to know, as long as I can be assured he's out of my way for good.

And knowing that, it's with a new sense of confidence that I get into the driver's seat and head down the road.

While I've never been invited to the clubhouse, when one my bodyguards once needed to collect something, I waited in the car outside.

At least I know where it is, and won't be driving around in circles trying to find it.

CHAPTER TWENTY-ONE

Petty

Being tied to this chair is agony as I'm unable to move in any way to make myself more comfortable. My arms are stretched behind me, the strain on my muscles adding to everything else. I've no way to tell what's happening in the clubhouse above—this cellar is soundproofed for good reason—or to judge how much time has passed since I've been abandoned down here.

I may not be alone, but I ignore the groans from the man hanging behind me. I've too much to concern myself to think about him. There's some comfort from knowing that RoseLyn's problems are over, and that the man responsible is in as much, if not more, pain than me.

However uncomfortable that I am, however much my head and other parts of me throb, I suspect waiting is better than what's to come. I've probably an upfront-and-personal meeting with Twister in his role as the enforcer, on my horizon. What worries me most is how much punishment I can take on top of my current injuries without wanting to beg for the punishment to stop. But I'm a man. I'll just have to fucking take it. I'd rather go to my grave silent than give my brothers any cause to think that I'm pathetic and weak.

I'll use the truth as my defence, that I didn't intentionally lay a finger on Britney, that I only pushed her and that it was her misfortune she hit her head. But if that doesn't satisfy them, then I'll keep my mouth shut. I won't say I acted to save myself.

How could a man admit he's being beaten up by his wife? I think their mockery alone would kill me. I'd rather see disappointment in their eyes and leave them believing I lost my temper and hurt Brit than admit she's been the one torturing me.

How could my brothers trust me to have their back if they knew how pitiable I truly am?

Whatever punishment they dole out, I'll take it.

There's another drawn-out groan from behind me.

"Shut the fuck up," I growl. Out of the two of us, only he deserves the punishment. He should keep quiet and take it. His soundtrack only adds to my own misery.

Why have they been so quick to take Britney's side without waiting to hear mine? How have they judged me and found me guilty without learning all the facts? Do they think that little of me that they think I'd beat up a woman for no reason? Can't they see how manipulative that bitch is? But, of course, they can't. She managed to suck me in and get my ring on her finger without me ever suspecting how violent she was. *She made me love her.* Now I hate her. And I especially hate that she's come back and that she's ruined my life.

If Red takes my patch, he'll leave me nothing to live for.

I shouldn't have allowed her to come to Vegas. I shouldn't have taken that apartment let alone admitted that she was my wife. Fuck, but I'm the pathetic creature who took her back. I should have refused to have anything more to do with her. But shoulds, ifs and buts are no help right now. I could have done many things better in hindsight, such as not marrying in haste and repenting at leisure.

But why had Britney set me up? Does she not know how dangerous it is to play with the Devils? Does she want me out of the club? Is that the future she sees for me? But she's got no fucking idea how serious this is. Not only may I not be a Devil for much longer, I might not even be breathing at the end of whatever I've got to come. I've pushed Red's buttons before, and already walk a tightrope with him. This might be enough to push him over the edge.

What's Britney got to gain from all this? A civilian husband with no way of supporting her? If I live, does she think there's a chance I'd forgive her?

Well not this time. This lie and its consequences are too big to be brushed under the carpet and there will be no coming back from this for us. If I am left alive, the only time she'll have contact with me is to sign those divorce papers. Fuck her parole officer and what's expected of her. I couldn't give a damn if she goes back inside.

Britney can be crazy, but insane she isn't. She's got to know the likely results of her running to the club with this bullshit.

I come back to the question, what does she think she'll be getting out of it? Apart from getting her kicks seeing somebody else beating me up?

It's getting harder and harder to think straight. Even the moans from behind me seem to be fading out. My throat is dry as it's far too warm down here. My head throbs and my vision seems blurry. Everything aches and as stiffness sets in to top it all off, I'm wishing for an end to my suffering, and almost start to hope for a quick bullet to the brain.

It's starting to seem impossible that even Twister could add to the level of pain I'm currently experiencing.

Time passes. I think I drift in and out of consciousness, but eventually I hear the door open, and multiple footsteps come down the stairs.

Struggling to come back to my senses, I blink my eyes as I glance up to see Red leading what looks like the whole club. The basement gets crowded with everyone in it but thank fuck someone has the forethought to turn on the air-conditioning. Yeah, they'll want comfort for themselves if not for me, but I relish the small relief as cool air washes across my overheated skin.

Saul chooses to emit a howl which is quickly cut off as Twister steps forward with duct tape in hand. "You'll get your fuckin' chance later," he growls.

Once he's dealt with me, he means.

When Saul's silenced, all eyes turn back to me. Red pulls up a chair, straddles it backward, puts his chin on his hands and examines me like a specimen in the zoo. Displeasure oozes off him, and as often when he's irate, his freckles are more pronounced. If my balls weren't swollen, I think they'd be trying to shrink back into my body.

Shifting my gaze as it's hard to meet his stare, I analyse the faces of the men who've come down with him. When my eyes meet Roller's, he turns away, waves of disappointment coming off him.

Crash is staring at me with hard eyes, and Twister's got a slight grin on his face as if anticipating the pain he's going to cause. Indian, our sergeant-at-arms, wears no expression at all, but try as I might, I can't find a glimmer of sympathy.

Shadow and Fox are talking quietly among themselves, their quick glances my way show I'm the topic of conversation. Titch has his arms folded and looks completely disgusted.

Keys, too, looks like he's examining some kind of exhibit. Rope, Cuff, Cobra, Sarge and Hammer look like they'd rather be anywhere but here.

Not one of my brothers looks like they'll be on my side, and none look like they can be appealed to.

Maybe this is what I set myself up for, what I wanted all along. For my brothers to see me as a man who doesn't give a damn, who'll stride through life making his own way without a care for anyone. A man who's not going to be cowed or beaten down, and who won't tolerate weakness in anyone.

Maybe I'm going to reap the rewards for becoming exactly

the person I wanted to become. The man with no compassion or tolerance.

I could admit since Britney my life's been a sham.

Or I could take my punishment for becoming the man I portray.

If I show how pathetic I really am, they won't want me anyway.

Whatever I do, I'm damned.

Red clears his throat, loudly drawing my attention back. "I've given you warnings before, Petty."

Yeah, but that was about his child Zeke and how I reacted to them before I got to know them. I'd never have been violent toward a kid, male or female or anything in between. Obnoxious, wounding with words, maybe, but never have I raised my fist unless it was against another man. I stare stoically back and don't defend myself.

"We," Prez continues waving his hand around in the air, "appreciate we don't get up in personal business when a man and his woman are involved, except when it might mean the club has a problem. And, because of the business we're getting into, we've definitely got a problem when you hit a woman totally unprovoked."

I'd never hit RoseLyn if that's what he means. I'm not some unpredictable abusive dick. And I didn't hit Britney, she fell. As for not being provoked. I was fighting for my fuckin' life.

But I keep my lips sealed. I won't be making any excuses. If I think the brothers are looking at me with disappointment now, it's going to be a hundred times worse when they know how feeble I am.

I shouldn't be riding with the Satan's Devils. I don't have it in me to give what they're looking for.

Red's lips purse. "You going to offer a defence?"

My lips thin as I press them tightly together. In any event, I've obviously already been judged and found guilty, and I doubt anything I could say would change that.

Shaking his head that I haven't stood up for myself, or maybe there's a touch of respect that I haven't tried to defend the indefensible, Red closes his eyes briefly. When he opens them, lines crease his face. It's an indication he's about to take action that he doesn't much like.

I swallow a couple of times, trying to prepare myself, knowing there was no fucking way I could ever be ready to hear the next words out of Red's mouth.

"We're taking your patch. You're out of the club."

Now it's my turn to shutter my eyes and squeeze them tight so I don't let any tears escape. I'm trying not to show any emotion. I don't have it in me to beg, wanting their last memory of me to be that of a strong man.

"Take his cut, Twister. Then we'll teach him a fuckin' lesson about what it's like to be on the receiving end of someone's fists." Having pronounced his sentence, Red gets to his feet, and kicks the chair away.

The enforcer's not gentle when he pulls at my cut. With my hands bound, the only way for him to remove it without freeing me is to cut it off.

I feel sick. I want to vomit. I want to scream out against the injustice. But I'd rather go out strong then prove just how weak and pitiable I really am.

As Twister gets out his blade, it flashes in the overhead light. I'd rather he thrust the blade right into my heart than slice through the leather that I'd worked so hard to earn, the cut that I still deserve whatever they think.

Why the fuck have you done this to me, Britney? What fuckin' game are you playing?

Turning my head, knowing that I'll feel everything Twister does but would prefer not to see, my eyes fall on one person I hadn't noticed as she'd been hiding behind the others. It's Britney. And hell, if any of my brothers turned around and could see her face now, it would make the truth drop into place. Even the dressing over her nose can't hide she's fucking elated. She looks like she's getting off on my pain.

I want to know how I hurt her so badly. I gave her a place to stay when she needed it. Was it because I turned the sex down? Surely that's not worth destroying a man's life.

Then, fuck me, Roller goes to her and puts his arm around her. Her expression changes in a flash, and even from here I can see her bottom lip tremble. I watch Roller mouth something that I think I can work out as him reassuring her I'll never hurt her again. *Fucking cunt.*

Twister's in no hurry, he's milking every bit of torture from the situation, making a show out of what he's about to do. He's holding onto one side of my cut, pulling it out from my body.

"Fuckin' hate destroying leather," he states, almost conversationally. "But what's fuckin' worse is seeing a piece of shit like you wearing it."

His knife flashes again—

"Stop!"

The forceful, but undeniably feminine voice is followed by lightweight steps racing down the stairs.

"Stop! You've got this all wrong."

Shocked, I see it's RoseLyn who's arrived, and she's using the power of the lungs that I've witnessed her utilise on stage. I only get a glimpse before Crash and Indian block her, but fuck, the way she's entered in a warrior stance makes her look fucking magnificent.

Despite everything that's happening and is yet to come, warmth fills my heart. Fuck knows how she knows what's going on, but I can tell RoseLyn is on my side. That's the kind of woman I should have had all along—someone in my corner, someone at my side.

But my brief warming lasts only a second before I grow cold. What the hell can she do? Is she about to break the promise she made? How can I tell her I'd rather die than have my brothers look at me knowing what a foolish and sorry excuse for a man I really am?

I'll bask in that she cares enough to intervene, but try to signal her to just leave me.

The new arrival has diverted Twister's attention, and instead of continuing to slash through my cut, he swings around, watching Red pushing his way through the crowd to greet the newcomer. I can't make out any actual words, but from the tones that reach me, I grasp they're having a heated conversation.

Then Red's voice comes clearly. "No."

Again, using those lungs which serve her singing so well, RoseLyn's dulcet tones reach me. "I want to talk to Petty. I'm not leaving without that."

A few more indistinct words, then a loud *fuck this* from Red, and the crowd's parting again. Prez pulls RoseLyn through, planting her in front of me, but before she can do much more than let her eyes reflect her sorrow seeing me restrained, Crash has also brought Britney forward.

"Look," Red demands, pointing to the woman who's unfortunately my wife. "This is what Petty did to her. Do you see a fuckin' scratch on him? Oh, ignore the nose. I did that to him. But other than that, he's unmarked." Rather than waiting for her to answer, he continues with only a slight pause for breath, "A completely unprovoked attack. You might think differently, RoseLyn, but Petty's an unpredictable violent man who I can't have in my club."

RoseLyn looks at me, then her attention is caught by the man behind me. Her eyes widen and her hand covers her mouth. Red swears loudly as though he'd forgotten he was still in here with us.

"Saul?" RoseLyn says, half question, half statement. And what she does next surprises all of us. She steps around me and I twist to see what she's doing, and see her spitting on her ex. Then she waggles her finger at Red. "That, there, is a violent, abusive man. The one tied to the chair is not."

Red closes the gap between them and turns her around, but she pulls away and steps toward Brit. She takes a menacing step forward. "What did you do to him?" Her tone sends chills down even my spine.

"She did nothing," Red answers for her and I don't miss the fleeting look of triumph cross Britney's face.

Oh yeah, she's got the prez right where she wants him. I don't blame him. Back in the day, she'd had me fooled too.

But RoseLyn is made of different stuff. Maybe it's what I said to her, or maybe it's because she's female and doesn't harbour illusions about her gender. She moves closer to Britney, forcing her to step back. "What did you do?" she repeats, her finger jabbing at Brit's chest.

"I-I… did nothing." Brit even manages to get her voice to tremble. "He hit me." Her eyes flick around, trying to find sympathy from my brothers, which she, of course, gets. "He didn't even take me to the hospital."

Because I was unconscious you stupid bitch.

"RoseLyn, just leave." Red pinches the bridge of his nose and says tiredly, "This is club business and nothing to do with you."

RoseLyn sets a stance that shows she won't be moving of her own volition. "I'll go on one condition." As Red sighs heavily and raises an eyebrow, she continues, "Untie Petty and get him to remove his shirt. *If* he's uninjured, I'll accept her," she sneers the word out, "story."

"This is club business," Red warns her again.

But RoseLyn gives a half-smile. "If that's the way you want it. But I know the reason you were providing your protection services to me at a reasonable cost is that you want to expand the business. You throw me out and you can forget any decent reference. I'll be sure to let everyone know you're unfair and unreliable."

"Don't." I enter the conversation and say sharply, "Don't RoseLyn. Red's right. I hit Britney unprovoked. I deserve everything that's coming to me." *Don't out me,* I beg silently, pleading with my eyes.

"I can't step aside, Petty." RoseLyn comes closer to me. "You don't deserve this."

"See?" Brit screeches in that nasal tone I've grown to dislike. "He wants to be with her and not me. He was trying to kill me."

RoseLyn rounds on her. "There is nothing between Petty and me, only that I want to see justice."

Red steps between the two of them. He looks like he'd prefer to be anywhere but here, and in that I have sympathy for him. His nostrils had flared at the suggestion RoseLyn would take her business away, and the threat to our reputation. That must be the reason why he says what he next does.

"Roselyn," he begins sharply. "If Petty takes off his shirt will you be satisfied and leave quietly? And leave us to get on with our own shit?" When she nods, he indicates to Twister. "Untie him and let him stand and strip."

Twister tenses, obviously not happy with the change in proceedings.

I'm feeling about as happy with it myself, and can only hope the bruises are too new to show. "There's no need for this, Prez. I hit Britney. I admit it."

"You don't get a fuckin' say in it," Red retorts. "Now get this over with."

Twister steps behind me and slices through the zip ties. He then does the same to the ones binding my feet. Then he takes hold of my elbow and pulls me, none too gently, into a standing position. I work hard to swallow a cry.

My injuries have stiffened due to me being in the same position for so long, and the jarring starts my balls throbbing once more. My head spins and I have to breathe deeply to remain standing once I'm released. I sway, the deep breath causing my ribs to scream. Gritting my teeth, I force myself to find some equilibrium.

I can do no more then shrug and stretch out my arms, letting my cut fall to the floor, ignoring the shocked gasp at my callous treatment as I've no choice to do anything more. My arm aches as I reach over my head to grab the neck of my shirt, the movement stiff and slow. My ribs feeling like jagged edges piercing me as I try to pull it off, I bite my tongue hard to stop the exclamation.

While I fight to get out of my shirt, Prez eyes me thoughtfully. RoseLyn runs up to look at me and then moves around to my back. I try to pull back my shoulders, but it hurts too much. I'm feeling lightheaded and nauseous and it takes too much effort just to stay standing up.

I hear a sharp intake of breath from behind me, but I'm unable to examine it as I again start to sway and then I lose my fight to stay conscious.

CHAPTER TWENTY-TWO
RoseLyn

"I told you he'd be injured," I shout at Red, and then at the men who've crowded us. "Get away, give him some space. Can't someone help him?" I drop to my knees but am loath to touch him. I'm no nurse.

"Injured?" A huge biker but one who's older than the rest speaks up. "He's fuckin' scared of what we're going to do to him."

"Just look at the way he threw down his cut. He knows he's not a Devil any longer," someone else roars.

I'm usually a patient person but I'm rapidly losing control. "Did you not see the contusions on his back and his ribs? And God knows where else she hurt him." On the word "she," I point an accusing finger at Britney.

"I didn't touch him," Britney objects, but her eyes scanning left and right looking for sympathy tells me something different.

It's obvious that she's still got these men in her camp. She's the one with a dressing on her face and blood still staining her clothes. But I for one don't believe her. I analyse the faces of those and try to find someone on Petty's side. My eyes land on Red.

"We need to know what she did to him. And get a doctor here—"

"Don't tell me what to do in my own fuckin' club," Red snarls, but instead of his ire being directed at me, he turns his flaring eyes on Petty's wife.

Britney starts backing away, but two of the bikers prevent her progress. Ignoring the prone man for now, the Satan's Devils' prez approaches her.

"Where do you think you're going?"

Britney touches her face and wails. "I've a headache and I need to lie down."

"I'll give you more than a headache, you fucking bitch." Feeling helpless that I can do nothing for Petty, I stand and move to Red's side. "You abused him before, and it seems you haven't stopped now."

"If that's what he's told you, he's lying. It was him who abused me." She indicates herself. "How could I possibly overpower him? He lost his temper because he doesn't want the baby."

Red raises his eyebrows toward me as if wondering how I'm going to counteract that point, while I hear male gasps at her voicing the possibility that Petty hit a pregnant woman.

But I'm ready for her. "A baby? You've only been back with him for a few days and had sex the once. You're speaking to another woman here, Britney, and I know the score. Petty doesn't have it in him to hurt you. He just took what you doled out, then believed you when you apologised and said it would never happen again."

Her face blazes. "That's a lie." Glancing around, she plays to her audience, placing her hands on her stomach for emphasis. "I could be pregnant, and… and… just look at me. I'd have to be crazy to anger a man such as him. Who are you going to believe here? The whole idea is ridiculous. He was the one who was violent to me. She's just making everything up—"

"Am I?" My voice is now deadly calm. "Petty's got the hospital records to prove how you hurt him. Have you?"

"I can check," another man speaks.

To which Red responds, "Yeah, check it out, Keys." He casts a look over his shoulder at the man who's still passed out. "I suppose we best get him to Doc."

"Let him fuckin' suffer," the older man remarks. "That woman wouldn't hurt a fly."

"I agree, Titch, it's unlikely."

I toss a glare at Hammer whose name I do know. "He needs a hospital," I tell Red.

Red looks between me and Britney.

Britney seems to realise while the camp is divided, it's the leader she has to convince. Her bottom lip quivers. "I-I love him. I'd never hurt him."

Red glances at me, and I see there's at least some doubt in his mind, and he's not completely swayed by her. His brow furrows, then his eyes sharpen as he turns back to Petty's wife. "Why, after all this time, did you come back? Especially when you say he was violent toward you."

She raises her chin defiantly. "I just told you I love him."

Now Red approaches her, his head tilted to one side. "So why didn't you contact him while you were inside?"

"He's coming round!" Cobra's voice comes over clearly.

Everyone's attention turns back to Petty, except for Red who points his fingers to his eyes and then to Britney. "I'm watching you. Crash? Make sure she stays around." Then he, too, walks over to Petty who's managed to get himself into a seated position, though his head is dropped into his hands.

Red drops down to his haunches and raises Petty's chin with his hand. "One chance, Petty. One chance to tell me the truth. Lying to me is as much a crime as anything else, and if you're dishonest, you'll lose your patch anyway. Do you fuckin' understand?"

Petty's eyes are watering when he meets those of his prez,

though quickly he looks away. "You'll have my patch anyway," he says, his tone that of a man without hope.

Red draws back, his puzzled eyes meeting mine for a moment. He shrugs. "That's for me to decide. Now I want the truth and I want to hear all of it."

Petty shakes his head then places a hand to his temple. He grimaces in pain. I move toward him but Red's arm shoots out and holds me back.

"Brother," Red says, this time more gently. "From where I stand," he snorts, "or from my knees on the ground, you've got a girlfriend who cares about you and a wife who couldn't give a damn."

Three people speak at once. Both me and Petty refuting the fact that I'm anything of the sort to him, and Britney who screeches, "I knew you were cheating."

"I didn't cheat." Petty raises his eyes and manages a glare at his wife. Then he slumps forward into his hands again. When he speaks next, his words come out as a mumble, but clear enough. "I got back from Texas, Brit was waiting for me. She accused me of cheating which I didn't. I was doing my job, Red." He doesn't even glance up to clarify that his prez will back him up. "She didn't believe me and kicked me hard in the balls. Then, when I was on the ground, she kicked me in the kidneys, and the chest. I think she broke a rib, ribs." If possible, his head sinks further into his hands. "I stood and she was going to come at me again, this time with a skillet, so I took it from her and pushed her away. She slipped and fell, hit her face on the edge of the counter-top. I think I saw her going for the skillet again... I don't remember anymore."

"That's all lies!" Britney screeches. When I turn to look at her, she's pointing to herself. "How could I take a man like him down?"

I round on her. "Just like you did in the past."

"I never hit him!"

"Prez?" The man Red had called Keys re-enters the room.

He's carrying a laptop in his hand. "Either Petty went through a period of being the clumsiest asshole around, or he was indeed being abused. His hospital records are numerous, all from the time he was married. I'm surprised the emergency room didn't reserve him a seat."

Red's eyes narrow to focus when he looks at the screen Keys' holds in front of him, then they open wide, and he again turns his attention to the man in front of him.

Petty swallows hard, and I swear tears comes into his eyes as he looks away from his prez. "I'm so fuckin' sorry," he murmurs.

"Brother," Red starts. "You were beat as fuck. Britney do this?"

But Petty won't answer, so I step in and reply instead. "Yeah. His *loving* wife abused him all their marriage."

Two sounds happen simultaneously. One a defiant squawk and denial from Britney who tries to get away but the men holding her don't release her. The second is an agonised wail but it comes from a man this time. Roller pushes his way forward and drops down beside his friend, gently turning him into his body.

"Why didn't you tell me?" Roller cries out. "Why didn't you fuckin' tell me, Brother?"

Petty raises his eyes and briefly meets those of Roller before he can't meet his gaze any longer. "Because I'm so fuckin' weak. I knew you'd never trust me if you knew."

"Shit," Red says with feeling and then stands. He brushes back his hair with both hands. He stares at the man now enveloped in the arms of his friend. Petty's now openly crying, but the prez shows nothing but compassion, and as he glances my way, I think understanding is dawning.

"I think we've got a great fuckin' deal to unpack here." Red catches my eye and gives me a raise of his chin. "Seems I owe you my thanks, RoseLyn. If you hadn't stepped in…" He doesn't have to complete the sentence. I can do so myself.

I shrug. I'm just happy I've prevented an injustice. While I've got no horse in this race, there's one way Red can show me his gratitude. "You're wrong about me and Petty," I tell Red. "We're just friends, nothing else. But will you please make sure Britney never goes near him again?"

Red grimaces, but it's his VP who reminds me.

"She's his wife," Crash says. "It's up to them what goes on. Can't get in between a man and his woman."

Again my temper flares and it's him who gets it full force. "So what exactly were you doing here? Getting ready to punish Petty and throw him out of the club because you thought he hit his wife? And when she came to you with a sob story you believed her without giving him a chance?" As I speak I get even more riled up. "Talk about double standards. You'd be getting Britney away from him if you believed her story. Yet you're just going to step aside and let her go back to him?"

Red's now looking at me with admiration. "She's got a point, Brother."

"He's mine and I love him. And I might be—"

Now it's her I direct my anger on. "He's not even mine and I respect him more than you do. Love? What do you know of love when you hurt him then stood back and condoned what his club was going to do to him? You nearly lost him his reason for living. And don't you dare mention a fucking baby. If you're pregnant, it's on you, not him." As she flinches, I say pointedly, "He told me everything." But I leave it there. Only she, I, and Petty know the word I'm not saying is rape.

"She's won," Petty mumbles, his voice breaking on a sob. "The Devils won't want me now they know the truth."

"What?" Red steps back to Petty, his eyes wide and nostrils flared. "You think I'm going to throw you out?" When Petty doesn't answer, Red makes it clear. "Not going to take your fuckin' patch. Twister, give him his cut back."

Whether it's relief or whether Petty's just at the end of his tether, he's openly crying now. Tears roll down his face, and Roller hugs him again, letting him cry into his shirt.

"Fucking weakling." Britney's voice drips with scorn.

Red swings around fast and for a second just stares at her, then he snaps his fingers. "Hammer, Cobra, get our *brother* up to his room. Contact Doc and get him to make a house call."

"Cheaper to take him to Doc," Fox, who I've met before as he's their treasurer, observes.

"And I think we owe Petty a lot for how we've misjudged him," Red retorts. He continues as if he hasn't been interrupted, "Twister? I want to know why Britney came back." When she squeals and repeats she loves her husband, Red shakes his head. "There's more to it than that. I want to know why she's making Petty's life a misery. At the fuckin' least, she's using him to put a roof over her head."

"I-I don't love her. Haven't for a long time." The defeated words are said quietly, but loudly enough that everyone hears him.

One of his brothers snorts. "And that's one thing I have no hardship believing."

My attention is quickly caught elsewhere. "Carefully," I admonish when Cobra starts to help Petty to his feet.

But Petty tries to brush them off, stumbling when they release him. In the end, he has to give up and allow them to both take an arm and support him.

Pent-up tension releases as I see that he's being taken care of. But I've no idea where I currently stand with the man. His worries about how his brothers will treat him if they ever found out the truth are so deeply rooted, I'm not sure he'll ever forgive me for not doing what he wanted and keeping quiet.

As I stand, watching him disappear at the top of the steps, Red says quietly to me, "Always knew Petty had serious baggage, just didn't know what."

"Treat him gently, please?" I nod as I turn to Red. "He's not the man you think he is. He puts on a front to the world. Now this has come out, I don't know how it's going to affect him."

"But you'll be sticking around to help him?" It's a question and statement all at once.

Moving my head side to side, I reply, "I doubt that he wants me to."

"He's my husband. That bitch isn't going to look after him. That's my job." Britney's annoying nasally tones grate on my nerves, but I don't have a chance to respond to her.

"I think you've fucking done enough," Red roars, then waves me and his men toward the stairs. "Let's leave Twister to get the truth out of her."

Britney starts loudly protesting that she's done nothing wrong. That she wasn't the one to instigate that fight, nor any fight between them. Is it wrong that seeing the pain Petty is in, I have no desire to save Britney from whatever she's got facing her? I don't miss Britney's worried glance at the strung-up man with duct tape over his mouth. It seems a fitting punishment for abusers, and I wouldn't give a damn if she ended up like him.

It's at that point she starts screaming, but I have no problems walking away from either of them. Saul deserves all he's going to get, and so does Britney.

And Red? Well, he's holding onto the wrong end of the stick. Petty and I are nothing to each other. Sure I was attracted to the man who I think he is, but I'm not to the ass he insists on playing. Even with Britney out of the way, he might still continue the act.

Will the revelations be Petty's come-to-Jesus moment when he knows he can leave his fake persona behind as people will still accept him? Or is it so deeply ingrained that he won't be able to be anything other than the misogynistic, chauvinistic, arrogant, obnoxious dick that I first thought him?

CHAPTER TWENTY-THREE

Petty

I'm lying in a bed that isn't even my own as I'd taken that to the apartment. I feel like my whole body is flaming.

I fucking cried in my best friend's arms. Could there be anything more shameful or embarrassing? Could I have torn up my man card in any worse way, other than admitting I'd let my own wife abuse me? And unlike RoseLyn, I hadn't walked away. I'd stayed.

With no fight in me, I'm compliant when the doctor, to whom we pay a huge retention fee, arrives and examines me. He's concerned about my kidneys and suggests further investigation if the blood still appears after a few days. He agrees I've cracked a couple of ribs but they'll heal on their own if I take it easy. My head? Well, that lump and the fact I lost consciousness is apparently cause for concern, and he thinks I've got a concussion. He gives strict instructions that should I start getting worse, they get me to the emergency room immediately. My nose, while swollen and hurting, isn't actually broken. Other than that, he calmly observes the number of bruises littering my body, but doesn't think any have done permanent harm. He states the obvious, that I'll be sore and stiff for a while, but should make a full recovery.

Doc's a professional. He's got his own well-equipped clinic—a lot of said equipment bought with our retainer—which is why we use him. He usually turns a blind eye even to a gunshot injury and treats us without commenting. Today, however, he seems to find amusement in my predicament. When he asks what Britney used on my head, he doubles over when he hears it was a skillet. Apparently, I'm a walking cliché now. His mirth was not something I needed.

Nor did I appreciate when I heard Red, who'd insisted to stay during the examination despite my protestations, chuckling along with him. Luckily, he didn't insist on examining my swollen balls in front of him, just commiserated to that injury with an empathic wince.

When he doses me up with painkillers—the good stuff not that shit you get over the counter—he leaves. I'm left feeling physically more comfortable, but it's the inside of my head that's a mess.

I try to sit up, but Red puts his hand on my shoulder and prevents me.

"Rest for fuck's sake, Petty."

My head is still woozy and I'm not entirely sure what happened down in the basement. I know RoseLyn outed me, but I can't find it in me to be angry as having the truth out there lifts some of the burden, though I still believe I'd rather they'd killed me. I feel so ashamed, and turn away, unable to face my prez.

I was a normal man before I met Britney. Before her, I'd never questioned my masculinity, nor the lessons my dad had instilled in me. Before her, I'd never understood abuse, never comprehended why a woman didn't leave the man who hurt her. Now I know it's all twisted up with the denial that there's any fault with the person you've picked as a life partner, and it's all too easy to put the blame on yourself.

Sure, I left the toilet seat up, and she admitted she'd overreacted when she'd punched me for it. I'd accepted the apology and the excuse she'd been having a bad day. Then I turned a blind eye and tried not to link the other isolated, but regular, incidents together. I never owned the title of a man who was abused.

Men didn't put themselves in that situation. And any who had, and hadn't immediately walked away, was surely not someone anyone could respect.

I can't see how Red and my brothers could condone my behaviour. But they'd brought me up to a room which isn't mine, a room I now recognise as Roller's. And over his chair, I see someone has hung my cut. Someone, my friend perhaps, had brought it up from the basement. Swallowing hard, I remember how close it had come to Twister slicing it off, and know I have RoseLyn to thank for saving it. But I still can't believe I'll ever again be wearing it.

Red leaves the room, presumably to see the doctor out and assure him the bill for his house call will be paid. Tears prick at my eyes once I'm left alone, but I'm not allowed long to enjoy my solitude. Red quickly returns.

"What the fuck's going through your head?" He draws up a chair and places it by the side of the bed.

Summoning my strength, I turn to face my prez. "You want me out of the club." I phrase it as a statement, not a question. Who'd want a man like me at their back?

Red snorts. "I thought I already told you we won't be kicking you out though we might be kicking your ass." He pinches his nose. "You've been keeping far too many secrets from us."

Swallowing a couple of times, I make my apology. "I'm sorry."

"Damn right you should apologise." Red moves closer to the bed and looms over me. "Why the fuck didn't you tell me the truth about Britney? You had enough chances. Oh, I knew all wasn't roses in paradise, but this?" He shakes his head. "This is beyond my imaginings."

"Didn't want you to see me as a coward and fuckup, Prez."

"You're no coward," he retorts. "But fuckup? Yeah, I think we can safely say you are that." There's a smile in his voice as he turns the chair and straddles it. He grows serious. "Twister got Britney to talk, and he didn't need long to do it. She's a coward at heart, just like all bullies. They can dish it out, but they can't take it." He huffs. "Apparently, Twister only had to point to Saul as an example of what we do to abusers. I think she quickly caught on that Twister isn't a pushover."

Like you, I finish his statement in my head. *Nah, I'm the only one Britney can push around.*

I don't even care how he got her to talk. I might not be able to physically hurt her intentionally, but if someone else wants to do the job, it won't hang heavy on my conscience.

"I want her to sign the divorce papers."

"I think you can take that as done." Prez eyes me carefully. "Do you want to know the real reason she came back?"

Although I grimace after the effort, I shrug. "Because I was the mug who'd support her while she got her life straight."

"Nah, Brother." *How fucking good does that word sound coming from his mouth?* "She was far more devious than that. She wanted revenge." He grimaces, sighs deeply, and his mouth twists in disgust, but this time it appears to be at himself. "And if it wasn't for RoseLyn defending your ass, she probably would have gotten it."

"Revenge?" I move my head to the side so I can see him better.

Red sighs. "She's out to destroy your life, Petty. She knew you'd have no choice but to take her back, because that's the kind of man you are."

I don't want to get into what kind of man he thinks I am, so I just repeat, "Revenge for what?"

He stares straight into my eyes. "Because you didn't appear to give a character witness at her trial."

What? "I couldn't perjure myself." I'd been asked to testify that Britney's behaviour was out of character for her, that she hadn't a violent bone in her body. Whether a husband's word would have stood for much, I have no idea. But it seems she apparently blamed her incarceration on my lack of support. There had been no way I could have stood in front of a judge and sworn that Britney was innocent. The jury hadn't been the only ones believing the store owner's side of the story.

Red's eyes soften as he looks at me. "When she came back, she didn't know you were in an MC. She just wanted to destroy your life anyway she could. When she saw how much the club meant to you, she set out to take it from you. It wasn't even her suspicions about you and RoseLyn, she just used that as an excuse. She went on the attack, hoping you'd eventually retaliate. And when you didn't, she fell purposefully."

That's not right. "Fell? I pushed her."

"Nah. That's what she wanted you to think." Red pushes his hair back from his face. "She's crazy, Brother. When she knew you wouldn't hit her, she was insane enough to hurt herself."

"She needs help." Red's right, she's got more than one screw loose.

He sighs. "Which comes to the question, what do you want us to do with her? Twister's holding her downstairs waiting on your decision."

I swallow a couple of times. "I can't hurt her. And… what if she is pregnant?"

"There's a chance?" His eyes focus in on me. "I thought you were sleeping on the couch."

I can't look at him. "There's a chance," I confirm, leaving it at that. I'm not going to compound everything by telling him how Britney took advantage of me.

He winces, but doesn't look critical. He eyes me carefully for a moment. "We got it so fuckin' wrong, jumped to the conclusion that you were the abuser, but instead it had been her taking advantage of you. Fuck knows, none of us like hurting women, but in her case, she could have done with a punch or two."

"Just couldn't do it, Prez."

He sighs. "There's probably a story behind why you couldn't. But hell, Brother, it surprises me. Seem to recall there was an incident in the Tucson clubhouse that you took a beatdown for."

He's right. There was. And it all goes back to how unsettled I was about Joker. In my screwed-up head I had to prove I still had my man card. "I wouldn't have hurt Becca," I tell him, my mouth twisting in shame. "I didn't hurt her, just tore her t-shirt. Thought she was a whore trying to get out of doing her work." Biting my lip, I give him the truth. "I was putting on a show for Roller, or maybe it was trying to prove something to myself."

Another bout of exhaled air leaves his lungs, then, standing, he rests his hand on my shoulder. "I think there's a fuckload of baggage you're carrying around, and maybe someday you'll share it. But getting back to the present, we've got a bitch downstairs and it's up to you to decide what to do with her, Brother. Won't hurt none to keep her on ice a little bit longer, at least until we find out whether she's baking something or not." He starts to turn away, then looks back. "Got a lot to talk about when you're feeling better. Like why the fuck you didn't warn me how unpredictable she can be when we mentioned setting her up with a job with Erika?"

I flinch. Yeah, I should have said something. "I'm sorry—"

"Not now," Red says fast. "But I've certainly got questions I want answered."

I just bet he has.

"Now, you've got a queue of visitors wanting to talk to you. You feel up to seeing them?"

"Who?"

"Well, there's RoseLyn, though she's not quite sure of her welcome." He pauses and looks like he's examining the expression on my face. "Then there's Roller, and," he snorts, "Zeke."

Zeke. I almost smile at the last name. Although I wouldn't admit this to Red, I've come to admire his kid. Zeke has no problem presenting the world with their real face, while I? I'm a fucking coward who's had to hide.

"I should be angry at RoseLyn," I admit. "She broke my confidence." I swallow and realise it's the complete opposite. While I'm still uncertain how this will play out, and whether or not I'll end up the better for it, she's forced me to face up to something that's ruled my life. If she hadn't come to the clubhouse, if she hadn't had stepped up and taken my side, I'd have lost my patch, my club, and if not my life, all that I live for.

"Want me to send her in?" Red stares at me for a moment, then snorts again. "At least I know she won't be in any danger."

I, too, attempt a chuckle, though it hurts my ribs to laugh. Yeah, that's one thing Red can be certain of. I'm not physically nor mentally capable of hurting her.

When Red exits and leaves the door open, RoseLyn's face appears. Tentatively, she hovers in the doorway as if not sure of her welcome. I lift my hand and beckon her to come in.

She grimaces when she sees me, then bites her lip. Her hands twist together. "I'm sorry. I betrayed your confidence."

"Sit." I motion again with my hand to the chair Red just vacated. She seems reluctant, her steps dragging as she crosses the room.

She turns the chair around to face the right way, but instead of sitting, she places her hand on the back and hesitates. "I'm sorry," she repeats.

She knows full well she's abused my trust. But it's because she'd spoken up that I, apparently, still have my place in the club. Whether it's tenable remains to be seen. I'd say there were extenuating circumstances for her betraying me.

I like her hesitancy, like the lack of confidence she has. It's a pleasant change from Brit who'd always been brash and brave in any situation. And aching balls be damned, but I also note her angular, graceful looks, and her lithe athletic body, are really starting to appeal to me. Soft and luscious, it seems, no longer do it for me.

I've no doubt in Red's promise that Britney will have no option other than to give me that divorce, so soon I'll be legally, as well as morally, free. Seeing RoseLyn so unsure of herself makes me want to take her in my arms and show her just how much her caring means. That I'm not currently capable of doing anything physical is maybe a blessing. She'd responded to my kiss, but I have no idea what she really thinks of me. Or, whether she'd want to pursue a relationship.

But she came for me.

Dragging my mind away from thoughts of a future that's wrapped in unknowns, I focus on something concrete.

My eyes narrow in confusion. "Why are you here?" And, more puzzling, "How did you know?"

Finally, she drops her ass into the seat. "I overheard Owl and Meat talking. I couldn't *not* come, Petty. I knew you wouldn't have hurt Britney and suspected she'd been up to her old tricks again. And," she puffs out her cheeks, "I knew you'd have taken the fall for her."

"Maybe that was what I wanted." It had been. I'm still undecided whether it would have been better that way. I might still have my patch. But have I lost the respect of my brothers?

"That would have been wrong," she cries. "You don't deserve anything that bitch did to you."

I turn my head away from her. I'm still trying to process the words Red had said, the reason Britney had given for returning to me and making my life hell. It's as though she can't take any responsibility for herself, always blaming someone else for her actions. I may not have stood up for her in court, but I wasn't the one who took out my frustrations on the poor innocent soul that she hurt.

There's no saying whether a husband's words would have counted for much anyway, and a robust prosecutor might have managed to get a hold of my hospital records. Like Keys, it probably wouldn't have taken long for them to put the pieces together.

Britney was fucked from the start and all because of her own actions.

As if she can read my mind, RoseLyn asks, "What's going to happen to Britney now?"

Grimacing, I move my head from side to side. "I just want her out of my life, but I suppose I've got to wait to find out whether she's adding anything to it."

I notice her chewing her lip, then watch as she tentatively leans forward. "It would be bad freaking luck if she fell pregnant after just one time. She's taunting you with the possibility."

"Of course she is." A blind man could see that, but that doesn't have any bearing on the sorry fact that there might be some truth in it.

"What if you let her parole officer know she attacked you?"

My brow creases as I think about it, then remember she's the one who went to the hospital with a clearly visible injury. "She'd say I was the abuser, and would probably get away with it."

She taps her fingers against her lips. "I know you don't want to physically hurt her, Petty, but there must be some way to set her up. If she breaks her parole, she'd be back inside and not able to bother you anymore."

"I need to know the situation before any decisions are made." RoseLyn's expression knows what I'm alluding to. Anything done to her might harm the theoretical baby.

My head starts hurting again as the painkillers begin wearing off. RoseLyn notices when I rub my temples.

"I'll leave you alone."

I don't want her to go. Even with the topics we're discussing, her presence is somehow soothing. I'd like nothing more than for her to slide next to me in this bed, not for sex, but just for comfort.

But while I owe my life to her, she owes me nothing. And how could she, a strong woman like her, want a weakling like me?

So I just raise my chin as she gets up to go, seeing her hesitate at the door to offer a small finger wave, and then she's gone.

Not for the first time. I admire her. If only I'd met her before Britney. RoseLyn's brave enough to face up to a club of bikers, and to take my wife—hopefully soon-to-be ex—head on.

I'm not man enough for her. I was right to let her go.

CHAPTER TWENTY-FOUR

RoseLyn

On leaving Petty's room, I pause outside his door, relishing the quiet of the hallway for a moment as I try to work out whether I've fucked up by coming here. If I hadn't... I shudder. Petty might not fully appreciate his escape just yet, but hopefully he will in time. I have no doubt his brothers will accept him, and what he thinks is his weakness, they won't see as a crime.

But I betrayed him. I'm not sure we'll ever get past that. How could he trust me again? My hands clench. I'd wanted nothing more than to go to him, hold him, comfort him, but he wouldn't want me to do that. I'm probably lucky he allowed me to see him.

I sigh, pushing away from the wall and the man who a big part of me wishes I wasn't leaving. With a heavy heart, I descend the stairs. At the bottom, I find Red waiting.

"Come into my office."

It's an instruction not a request, so I can do nothing more than follow him. From the stiffness of his posture, I feel like a schoolgirl about to be chastised, and I'm not far wrong, as I find out only moments later, when I'm seated one side of his big desk with him on the other.

He steeples his fingers under his chin, and his green eyes

stare into me. It's at that moment I see why he's the prez of the MC. He's got the intimidating look down just fine. In the brief ensuing silence, I find it hard to stop myself from fidgeting.

When he does speak, it almost takes me by surprise. "I don't appreciate being threatened."

"I…" I clear my throat and inject some strength into it. "I don't like issuing threats, but I couldn't allow Britney to get away with what she had done."

He continues to focus on me, and I try to stop my hands twisting together. While I make every attempt to meet his eyes steadily, I'm the first to look away.

"We liked having your business, RoseLyn, but we don't need your recommendation, whether you want to give us one or not. I do, however, hope you wouldn't lie when we resolved your problem for you."

That puts me in my place. "I'm sorry." I realise I owe him that apology. "I didn't know what else to do." Wincing, I look down at my hands. "I am grateful to you." The memory of Saul down in their basement fills my mind. "You've got Saul, and freed me. I'll give you a good reference, Red." Then I add, lamely, "I would have done anyway. It was the heat of the moment as Britney seemed so plausible."

Slowly Red's face relaxes, and he sits back, brushing his hand over his beard. "She was, which was how I presume she got him to marry her."

"Petty spoke to me in confidence," I point out, hopefully letting him know I won't give anything else away.

One of his eyebrows rises. "Which you broke."

"To save him!"

He leans forward again, clasping his hands. "Why the fuck does Petty think he doesn't deserve to be in the club?" Again his eyes fixate on mine. "Telling me might be another way of saving him, this time from himself."

I shake my head, but before Red can think I'm refusing to answer him, I speak again. "I don't know the answer, but it's deep rooted." Red's right, I've already spilled enough of Petty's secrets, that probably telling the rest that I know won't cause any more damage than I have already. "Petty showed me a different side of him in Texas." I've perked his interest, as that eyebrow rises again. "He was relaxed, fun. It was as if he'd slipped out of character and into the person he'd been all along."

When I pause for breath, Red gestures for me to continue.

"I'm no psychologist, but if you want my thoughts, Petty's got an idea of what each of the sexes should be. A man is dependable and strong, and never shows weakness. A woman is frail and needs a man's protection." I frown. I don't consider myself weak, but even with how I keep myself fit, so many men could overpower me simply because they're bigger and stronger than I am. Maybe that's the key? "Petty's aware that being a man means he can overpower a woman easily. So," I grimace, "if you're asking me, I think that's at the root of everything. And I think Britney taking advantage of him turned his view of the world upside down."

Red's brow creases as if he doesn't comprehend the point I'm making. I don't blame him. I don't understand it myself.

So again I sit forward and now it's my joined hands resting on the table. "Let's say, Britney met the same version of Petty that I saw in Texas. A man who enjoyed life, who was relaxed and kind. The one thing he'd never do is hurt a woman." I glance up to see Red raising his chin. "When Britney hit him, he couldn't hit back. You've seen her, Red. He'd have laid her out flat. So he was helpless."

"Why didn't he leave?"

Again I betray Petty's confidence. "Because he thought he loved her. He was shouldering some of the guilt that it was him who caused her behaviour. And like almost every abused person from the beginning of time, he accepted her apologies that it wouldn't happen again."

"But Britney didn't stop."

I nod. "Petty couldn't understand the woman he married.

She didn't fit into his idea of the feminine role." I try to add more twos together. "And Britney can act the vulnerable female part." I'd seen that for myself in the basement where she'd been playing up to her audience.

At this Red dips his chin and raises it. "She certainly can." He adds, scoffingly, "She had us all fooled."

"Something ingrained in Petty meant he couldn't physically stop her, and her," I use my fingers to put the next words in quotes, "nice times confused him. If she hadn't been locked up, God knows how long he'd have tried to make their marriage work."

Red drums his fingers on the desk and rolls his eyes. "She could have fuckin' killed him."

I continue my amateur psychoanalysis. "When they were forced apart, he gradually came to his senses. He vowed never to be in the same position again. He came to despise the weak man who'd been taken advantage of."

"And became someone else." Red frowns. "A man who'd never be exploited again."

"He became an ass." I huff a brief mirthless laugh.

"Fuck." Red drops his head into his hands and rubs at his temples.

There's a knock at the door. When Red calls out for the visitor to enter, Twister steps inside. His eyes flick to me, then to his prez, and they seem to have some unspoken conversation over my head. After a series of grunts and chin lifts, Red turns to me.

"I've been reminded that you've seen something I didn't mean for you to see." When I query with a tilt of my head, he explains, "Your ex, Saul. You weren't meant to see him like that."

"I can imagine." I give a small smile. "But I suppose you're pushed for prisoner space."

Twister snorts and Red shakes his head.

I remember who else was there. "You didn't seem to have any problem with Britney seeing him."

Now Twister looks abashed, and Red's eyes roll. "She wasn't

supposed to be there either. She must have snuck down. With the prospects at your house, there was no one standing guard."

"Fuckin' women," Twister growls.

"Fuckin' prospects," Red retorts. He raises an eyebrow. "I suppose they've been running their mouths which is how you found out what was happening to Petty?"

Wary of getting the two men in trouble, I choose my words carefully. "They let something drop, and I asked questions." Wincing, I admit, "I didn't give them much choice. I, er, maybe suggested I'd drop them in it with you if they didn't tell me everything."

"You threatened them?" Red's voice rises. "Seems you like making threats."

Blanching, I try to defend myself. "It's not my normal modus operandi, but I was desperate, Red. As soon as I got an inkling Petty was in trouble, I had to come." My voice rises. "If I hadn't, where would Petty be now? With the injuries he already had, you might have killed him."

My words ring in the air long after I've said them.

Twister looks like he doesn't quite know what to say to me, so changes the subject. "The prospects are here now. They came back with their tails between their legs. Thought you'd want a word with them."

Red waves his hand dismissively. "They can wait for now. First, we've got other fish to fry. Like Saul in the basement." He eyes me carefully. "You going to threaten to go to the cops and say we're holding him prisoner?"

Knowing Red may have doubts about me, I gather all the sincerity I can. "No. I won't. I'll be making no threats, but I'd really like to talk to him."

"For fuck's sake, why?" Both men look perplexed.

I haven't an immediate answer. I already misjudged the man, then when he went to jail, I expected he'd stay far away. Instead he stalked me, made me afraid for my life, and those snakes... I shudder. They were the final straw. I'd like to see him face-to-face and get the question answered, why me? Why does he hate me so much?

"What do you want to happen to him?" Red asks me directly, seeming to ignore my request. "And don't ask us to let him free. He might be sensible enough to avoid you in the future, but what about some other woman? Leopards like him don't change their spots."

I can't argue with Red's suggestion. "He's damaged in the head."

"You think he needs therapy?" Twister snorts derisively.

Even I know he's probably far too gone for that to help. "I want to speak to him," I state again. "I just want him to tell me why he targeted me, why he wouldn't let me go. Unlike Petty, we weren't married, there was no real commitment."

"And after you've talked?"

"I don't care what you do with him as long as I never see him again." If I don't know, my hands will be clean.

Red gives me a long hard look and taps his fingers against his desk. After a few seconds, he sighs. "Okay. I'll let you see him and get the answers you need. That's if he has any to give."

"Britney's down there, Prez."

His mouth twists at the reminder. "Take her out and get the prospects to watch over her. Make sure they know she's a lying snake and to make her ass stay put."

The short delay is only for Twister to find the prospects, give them their new instructions, and get Britney moved. I'm pleased that I won't be faced with her. Then, almost before I'm ready, I'm face-to-face with the man who put me in the hospital, and who's been making my life a misery. When I'd seen him before, I'd been more focused on Petty. Now I'm no longer distracted, I examine him more carefully.

He's clearly been worked over. One eye is completely shut and his face and bare-chested torso are a mass of bruises, and I don't have it in me to feel any sympathy.

Saul regards me with a look of hatred as Twister removes the duct tape that's been keeping him quiet.

"Bitch!" Saul shouts out as soon as he's capable of speaking.

Twister's fist lands in his stomach so his next sound is an oomph instead of words.

Ignoring it, I step forward. "Why, Saul? Why?"

"I loved you. You should never have left me."

My jaw drops. "You've a strange way of showing your love. You hit me."

"All I wanted was you. If you hadn't run, I wouldn't have had to follow you and teach you a lesson. But instead of realising how much you meant to me, you went to the cops instead. You got me locked up and put away. And now you've got me trapped again." His eyes find Twister and he flinches.

"So the blame is all on me?" I can't understand the garbage he's spouting.

"Of course. I moved you into my house, gave you everything you wanted…"

I could explain what I didn't want was for him to take his frustrations out on me for having a bad day, but don't waste my breath, as apparently that was one of a partner's duties.

"You injured me enough that you were arrested. What I can't understand is why you came after me, having served your time. Why did you follow me to Vegas? Why didn't you just move on?"

Now I get a sly look. "Let me go now and I'll move on as you suggest." His open eye looks me up and down. "Now you're here, I don't really know what I saw in you. You're not worth the trouble. Let me go and I'll disappear."

"Just like that?" Red queries in disbelief.

Saul turns to his new audience. "Yeah. She used to be soft, pretty. But look at her. She's gone skinny and has more lines on her face. I don't even fancy her anymore. I'll leave Vegas and go somewhere else."

Red touches my arm and leads me out of earshot. "It's your call. What do you want, RoseLyn?."

I wasn't born yesterday. There's no way in hell I believe him or trust him. But if I don't do anything, the Devils will kill him. Maybe I was wrong to confront him. I haven't gotten any satisfaction. Saul shows no regrets and has offered no apology, instead all he's given are excuses, putting the blame on me.

Saul's not going to change, as Red had said earlier. His lack of remorse shows in his eyes at least, he did nothing wrong.

I originally called the Devils in because there had been an attempt to kill me.

I'm in a quandary. I don't want to be the reason a man dies, whatever he's done to me. If I had more faith in the legal system, I'd leave it to them, but I've no confidence in the help I'd get from the cops. They didn't take the fact I'd had a stalker seriously, and I'm not hopeful of him getting more than a slap on the wrist. Even if he did more jail time, it probably wouldn't be for long. Then he'd be released and maybe twice as angry when he comes after me again.

I fear whatever disparaging comments he uttered, he's still fixated on me.

Red's staring at me, sympathy in his eyes. "You want to leave it to us?"

The Devil's reputation had me thinking seriously when I first gave the security contract to them, but their references had all said they were law abiding. Now, looking around me and witnessing how they've already treated Saul, I know there had to at least been some truth in the original rumours I'd heard.

I thought I'd be okay signing his death warrant, but that was before I was faced with the man. But even I don't see any other alternative.

"I can't kill him in cold blood," I whisper, hating myself at that moment.

"Not asking you to hold the gun." Red's mouth turns up before he grows serious again. "How about we test him?"

Test him? "How?"

Red's brow creases as if he's thinking, then he beckons Twister to come and join him. They bend their heads together for a moment and have another conversation where all I can distinguish are grunts.

When they finally part, Twister touches my shoulder, then steps forward. He looks Saul straight in the eye.

"You've got one chance, buddy. One chance and that's it. We'll let you go now, escort you out of Vegas, and you promise to never return or go anywhere near where RoseLyn is. If you do, you won't like the consequences. Do you understand?"

With part relief, part horror, I listen to Twister revoking the death sentence. My mouth opens. I did not expect this. But Saul, grinning as well as he's able with his damaged mouth, swiftly agrees.

With a glance toward Red, and receiving a nod in response, Twister goes behind Saul and unties his bindings, letting him drop to the ground and none to gently.

Saul quickly gets steady on his feet, but instead of doing what any sane person would do and racing to the stairs and the freedom that's within reach, he launches himself toward me and puts his hands around my throat.

But the pressure's immediately eased as a close-up gunshot makes my ears ring, and now Saul's dead at my feet.

I sway. Red catches me and twists me away from the man on the floor. I've never seen a dead body before and couldn't have anticipated the shock. One moment, Saul was living and breathing, and now, he's not.

I couldn't have predicted my reaction. It's one thing to wish a man dead, quite another to see it. For a moment, I'm angry that the Devils had put me on the spot. They'd read Saul better than me, and could see he was driven by such a desire to hurt me, that he'd sacrifice the offer of freedom. Or maybe it had been a test, which he'd certainly failed.

Red's speaking to me, but I still can't hear properly. Still half-deafened, I'm shaking and listening instead to my inner voice.

I'm not proud of myself. I'd caused a man's death.

"He was a mad dog who deserved to be put down." Now the initial ringing is fading, I can make out Red's words.

"I'm alright." I push away from him. "I'm alright," I repeat, mostly to reassure myself. I try to focus on the fact that Saul tried to strangle me, and in the end, it was him or me. At least I now know that he's no longer able to make my life a misery.

But I just saw a man shot dead.

CHAPTER TWENTY-FIVE

RoseLyn

"Let's get you out of here." Red puts his arm around my shoulders and leads me away, making sure to keep my back toward the body so I don't need to see him again.

But even without the evidence of my eyes, the room is tainted with the odours of cordite and blood.

At the top of the stairs, Red pushes me in the direction of his office.

"I'm sorry," he says earnestly as soon as we enter. "But Saul was never going to leave. You needed to see how there was no other way." He peers at my neck, moving away my hair. "Did he hurt you?"

As he removes his hand, I finger where Saul's hands had tightened on me. I'm a bit tender, but I'll live.

Red continues, "He would have killed you, RoseLyn. He was sick in the head."

I'm incapable of saying anything. I just mutely go to the seat when he points it out.

He sits in his own chair and steeples his hands together with his eyes expectantly on the door. Seconds later it opens and Twister walks in. He's carrying something wrapped in a cloth. When he opens it, I see it's a gun.

Twister holds it out to me.

My brow creases and I look at Red. "Insurance," he explains. "Take the gun, RoseLyn."

I tense as what he means falls into place. "I'm not going to say anything."

"Humour me." Green eyes pierce me.

I doubt I have any choice. Hoping I never have cause to regret what I'm about to do, I take the gun from the cloth and clasp it firmly in my right hand, then I lay it back down. Twister wraps it in the cloth again and hands it to Red who opens a safe located behind him, and places it inside.

Frowning, not best pleased at this development, I tell them both, "Trust works both ways."

He raises his chin acknowledging he now has my fingerprints on a weapon that could be used for anything.

A cold shiver suddenly comes over me. A moment ago, I was thinking of the bikers as friends. Now I'm not certain they're any easier to handle than the snakes that I'm so afraid of.

My trials are over. Saul will not be coming for me again. Thankfully, I no longer need the services of these men.

It's ironic that I helped Petty stay a part of this club which makes him just as dangerous to me. Whatever embryonic feelings I have for him need to come to an end.

I need to get out. My lungs feel starved for some fresh, untainted air. Standing, my voice isn't quite steady, even though I pull back my shoulders and try to summon my backbone. "Send Bart the final invoice. Our paths won't cross again."

The prez of the Satan's Devils MC raises his chin. With a quirk to his mouth, he tells me, "It was nice doing business with you."

Twister opens the door and escorts me into the clubroom. He pauses. "You want to see Petty before you leave?"

Yes, my heart screams. *No,* shouts my brain. My head wins out. "Petty belongs here, and I don't."

He grimaces. "Yeah, I kind of got that."

Standing back, he unnecessarily waves his hand toward the door. As I take a step forward, my eyes fall on Britney who's seated at the side of the bar, looking quite at home. She sneers at me, and I turn away.

The sight of her sickens me. Upstairs is the man who she not only beat up, she tried to get evicted from his club. Downstairs is the body of an abuser who's met his just desserts. And here she sits, looking like she hasn't a care in the world.

Not my problem, I tell myself even while my hands clench and my stomach roils. *It's just the way of this patriarchal world.*

Her apparent lack of retribution emphasises I have to leave. I don't want any part of this domain that thinks life is sacred for one sex, and cheap for the other.

I take one step and then another as I head for the door, having to halt to allow a very scantily clad woman to pass. She's carrying a tray that, if I'm not mistaken, looks destined for the invalid in his room above.

A pang goes through me and I try to convince myself I've no reason to feel jealous.

It's not as easy to walk away from Petty as I thought.

But instead of wavering, I resume my walk toward the door, and once outside, head straight for my car.

I start it, take one look behind at the clubhouse full of bikers I doubt I'll ever cross paths with again, then reverse out of my parking spot and drive through the gates.

When I reach a place I can pull over, I stop and let the tears fall. Although he doesn't deserve them, some are shed for Saul. Some for myself at the shock of seeing him killed, but most, well, most are for the man I was with in Texas.

I could easily have fallen in love with Clark. With Petty, I'm not so sure. And he's so much part of the club that I don't feel I can be associated with anymore. Maybe in time I'll accept that there could have been no other end for Saul. The ease at which they'd taken his life had left me shocked to the core.

I dab at my tears and will them to stop, trying to focus that I don't have Saul stalking me anymore. I need no longer be afraid of what he'll do next, or worry about returning to find more snakes in my house.

Perhaps his death can be laid at my door. I insisted on talking to him, though I doubt the Devils would have allowed him to go free, whether or not I saw. But if I hadn't, I could have remained in ignorance about the sort of men that they are, and probably accepted their assurance they'd run him off.

He'd still be dead. Would it really be better if I suspected but didn't know? At the least I wouldn't have a weapon kept in a safe with my fingerprints on it.

Do I trust the Devils to use it simply as insurance, or do I go through life worried they might implicate me in a crime?

I know why they did it. They shot a man right in front of me.

One thing's for certain. I can never afford to get mixed up with the Devils again. I'll get their final invoice paid, give them a truthful reference—they kept me safe and removed the threat from my life—and hope that in future our paths won't cross.

I'll miss Sarge. I'll miss Roller. They've become like brothers to me. As I pull into my driveway and park outside my house, I realise how long it's been since I felt truly alone.

A trickle of unease goes through me as I walk in my front door. The house is quiet, and, thanks to Owl and Meat, relatively tidy, though I suspect I'll be putting stuff back into its right place for days. I pause, listen, but I hear no rattling.

Though there's no evidence that the bikers hadn't done what they said, and had cleared the house of all reptiles, goosebumps arise on my skin at the memory of them being there, and what might have been.

It's then I determine, there are too many memories in this house. I'm going to sell it and move. This time it won't be to hopefully somewhere Saul can't find me, as that won't happen again. *Because he's dead.*

I head straight for the shower, feeling I've got Saul's blood splatter on me, even though I'm pretty sure I don't. My clothes go straight into the garbage, and I stand under the spray for far too long. Even when I'm clean, I feel like the stains still cling to me. I rub my hands up and down my arms, and try to remind myself it was him or me.

It's late, but I haven't eaten all day. I enter the kitchen and pull some chili out of the freezer to reheat, getting rice ready to go with it. I pour myself a glass of wine, thinking I deserve that at least. Maybe I'll down the whole bottle.

It will feel odd sleeping without Sarge in the next room, without hearing the comforting sound of his feet as he tries to pace quietly over the floor. *But he's one of them.* It could easily have been him who'd taken that shot. That's the kind of men they all are, otherwise, they wouldn't be in an MC.

As I force the food down, I wonder how Petty is, and what's happening to Britney. I'm going to miss him, the asshole part and all. He'd been a fixture in my life for the past few weeks. Going to the casino without him is going to be strange.

Spurred by my third glass of wine, I wonder what Kylie and I will have to moan about without him being there.

After rinsing my plate and putting in it the dishwasher, I drink the last dregs of wine rather than putting the bottle away. In the morning, I'll need to contact Bart and tell him the danger to me has gone. He'll be pleased that we can stop the money drain that providing my security has been.

I can move on.

Feeling decidedly lonely, I go to my bed. I thrash, toss and turn for what seems like forever, but just when I give up on sleep, my thoughts becoming jumbled, mercifully, I'm overcome by sleep.

When I wake, my head is pounding, and I down the glass of water I left by the bed. I take another shower, again not feeling clean, and dress for the day. I've just thrown on an old t-shirt and shorts, as I don't plan on going anywhere until I leave for the casino. I've enough chores to keep me busy.

It had been the early hours before I'd eventually dropped off, so I'm yawning as I enter the kitchen. Hand over my mouth and jaw locked open, it takes me a moment to process there's a strange man waiting for me.

"Who the fuck are you?" Strangely my first reaction is indignation rather than fear. I'm annoyed he's standing between me and my coffee.

"You might not know me, but I know you." He looks at me in a disturbingly assessing way. "I've been waiting a long time to meet you, RoseLyn."

Is he a crazed fan? "Well now you've met me, please leave my house." I'm wondering how the hell he got in, then realise in the emotional state I'd been in when I'd returned last night, I don't think I set the alarm.

"Oh, I'll be leaving. But you'll be coming with me."

A flicker of fear rises. "I'm not going anywhere with you. Now please leave before I call the cops."

He raises his hand, showing me he's in possession of my purse. The purse which contains my lifeline otherwise known as my phone. I swallow hard when I realise I won't be calling anyone.

I don't know what he wants, or why he's here, and don't waste time asking him. Instead, knowing the keys to my car will be where I left them, on the table in the hall, I sprint and run in that direction.

But he's as fast, faster than me, and rather than getting the jump on him, he must have expected my reaction. He lands against my back, making me fall to the floor, badly bruising my knees, and slamming my cheek into the ground.

Taking advantage of the fight literally being knocked out of me, he wrenches my hands behind my back, and ties them with something.

I roll, taking him by surprise, and kick with all my might, but he's much bigger and easily overpowers me.

"I don't care if I hurt you. Don't even care if I don't keep you alive. But I prefer to take you. Your choice. Am I going to leave your body in this house, or are you coming with me?"

His eyes are so dark there's almost no white, and he doesn't seem completely sane. It's quite clear he knows that I'm hurting, yet has no pity for me. Unlike Petty, he has no problem using his extra bulk and weight to overpower a woman.

It's a Hobson's choice. I'm damned whether I do or don't. But the only sensible option would be the one that keeps me alive with a promise of a future escape.

"I'll come with you."

"Good girl."

How I hate that phrase. It's so damn condescending. And the last thing on my mind is to be a good girl for him.

I've no idea what he wants, but doubt it's to rape me. Otherwise why not do that here, when he's got me at his mercy?

I'm not given much time for thought as he drags me to my feet and bundles me out through the door. There's a strange vehicle on my drive parked behind my car. He leads me to it, but stops by the door and forces a scarf or something around my mouth. Effectively gagging me, he opens the trunk.

I'm not going in there. While my phobia of snakes is greater than my fear of enclosed spaces, being in there lessens my chance of escape. Especially with my hands bound behind me.

But he proves again how easy it is for him to overpower me, and my delaying tactics only get me a bump to my head which make me see stars, and then I'm lying, curled in the fetal position as the trunk's shut on me.

Darkness descends and fear hits in full force.

My privacy, which I so fiercely guarded, meant I was happy having no neighbours living close. That now comes back to bite me, as there's no one to see me being kidnapped and stolen away.

As the car vibrates when the engine starts and we start to pull off, I begin to have serious doubts about surviving the day.

There's no one who'll come looking for me. Bart won't sound the alarm until I don't appear later tonight.

Will I still be alive then?

Who is this man and what does he want from me?

CHAPTER TWENTY-SIX

Petty

"I didn't like your wife." Angel puts down the tray she's carrying as she sees me struggling to sit up. Putting her arm around me, she expertly supports me at the same time as she plumps the pillows up.

Ignoring the ignominy of needing her help, I don't bother asking how she knows my wife or anything about her. It was pretty obvious when I'd earlier arrived at the clubhouse that Britney had been mouthing off. It was also a certainty that once blame was put in the right place, brothers would have been talking about it. It's a well-known fact the club girls are experts at listening.

"Did you decide that before or after you found out about her?" I indicate she can now place the tray on my lap.

Angel props herself delicately on the bed. "She seemed a bit fake when I met her." Snorting softly, she adds, "She certainly didn't like us."

In itself that's far from unusual. Citizens don't normally understand the symbiosis of bikers and club whores, finding the idea that we've got women who are here just to service us disgusting. For those who are invested in a particular member, they've got good reason. Britney might not care much for me, but she's possessive enough to want me for herself.

Angel watches as I take a sip of the coffee, and then pick up the sandwich. I hadn't realised how hungry I was until I started eating, and don't stop until I've polished it all off. When I've finished, Angel takes the tray and moves it to the bedside table. Then she comes back to the bed.

"You helped us catch RoseLyn's ex." I remember the part she played. While my problem is alive and breathing, I've been told RoseLyn's is now dead. "Gotta thank you for that."

"It wasn't a problem." She shrugs as she minimises the part she played. "All I needed to do was wear a wig."

It was, nonetheless, a brave thing for her to have done, to have put herself at risk, above and beyond the duties of a club girl. Angel's been here a long time and has proved herself loyal to the club.

But when her hand rests on my leg and she asks suggestively whether she can do anything else for me, I can't personally reward her. Even if my balls weren't still swollen from where Britney kicked them, and right now I'm not sure my dick will ever start working again, it's not her who I want.

Red's already spoken to me, has told me what went down in the basement, and how they've ensured that RoseLyn will keep her mouth shut. While I appreciate the reason why Red had done what he had, I worry about the effect it will have on RoseLyn.

She'd known she'd been protected by bikers, known my love for the club. But until last night, she'd never stepped foot in the clubhouse, and we'd kept our lives and hers very much apart.

If it hadn't been one of my brothers, it would have been me taking that shot, and RoseLyn would have been very aware of that. I suppose death comes cheap to us. We serve justice our own way, but knowing it is different to seeing it, and I worry that to RoseLyn the violence must have come as a shock.

RoseLyn had left the clubhouse without coming to say goodbye.

That hurts more than I thought that it would.

Angel sees her work here, for now, is done, and departs with promises that if I change my mind, she'll come right back. As the door closes behind her, I rest my head back against the pillows.

Yet again I've had Red's reassurance that I'm still part of this club. Although I'm worried how my brothers are going to treat me now they know of my cowardice, and am concerned whether they'll still trust me to have their backs, or that they'll think I'll turn and run at the first sign of danger, I still have my patch. I should be elated—I couldn't begin to imagine being happy out in the civilian world—but there's a niggling feeling inside me that being a Devil isn't enough.

Despite what's happened since, or maybe because of it, I look back on that evening spent with RoseLyn and her parents as an oasis of peace. It's been a good few years since I was able to relax and just be myself. And it wasn't being in the heart of a family, it was RoseLyn herself.

RoseLyn outed me, but she'd had no choice. Had I shown that I forgive her? While all I'd ever wanted to do was keep the secrets about myself under wraps, there's a weight off my shoulders knowing I can head into the future being whatever kind of man I want. Petty, the ass, or a new improved version that doesn't need to pretend anymore.

With RoseLyn by my side, metamorphosing from ass to a man worthy of her would be easier. If I lost her as well— goddamn it, I don't want to think about it. I've a chance to be free, but freedom's worth shit if I lose my chance with the one woman I want. The woman who's proved to me that not all females are like Britney.

Britney. Well, I'm going to be rid of her completely one way or another. I'm definitely going to be getting that divorce, and if she causes trouble, I've no doubt my brothers would help me. If she's pregnant, well I'll deal with that too. I never thought of being a single father, but I'll step up if I have to. Britney isn't fit to be a mother.

Britney's reappearance has freed me from the prison I'd built around myself. I don't have to put a fake front on for the world anymore. I don't have to force myself to act the asshole. For perhaps the first time, I understand why Joker and Lady's relationship bothered me so much. It wasn't that they kept their sexual preferences to themselves, it's how they're far happier men now it's out in the open. I didn't resent them for being gay, but that they could live with no secrets between them and the club.

Likewise with Rope and Cuff, I really don't care what they get up to, but it's their confidence that they don't give a fuck I envied. If they want each other as sexual partners, they won't see a reason for hiding that.

My thoughts return to RoseLyn. That fucking kiss was meant to knock the pent-up attraction between us on the head, but it did the opposite. It showed me how much I wanted her, and the old Petty hated that. Now, though, I no longer need to keep her at arm's length. I'd told her secrets that could destroy me, what I told her in confidence is known to everybody. It's down to her there's no longer a need to keep the person I really am locked up. I can be myself. And the new Petty wants RoseLyn.

But that takes me back to that I'm a member of the Satan's Devils MC, and I'm never willingly going to give that up. And RoseLyn's had a recent example of why she should stay far away from me and my club.

What's that expression? You can't have your cake and eat it too. I'm afraid that applies a little too much.

I miss her. I'd spent so much time with her over the last few weeks, I feel there's a part of me missing. But while I've got a chance of remaining a Devil, I'm not going to give that up.

I move to a different position to try to get more comfortable, hating that I've been restricted to bed rest while Doc thinks I could be concussed. I want to be out there, facing RoseLyn, trying to make everything between us right.

I'm not left alone to brood for long. Roller comes in for a while and keeps me company, followed by Titch who seems to think he's got something to apologise for, though I assure him I don't blame him for being taken in by Britney. Cher puts her head around the door to see if I want anything, and then Zeke comes to sit with me. They bring a book in with them and seem content to sit and read while I doze. I admire their sensitivity for realising I appreciate company, even if I don't want to talk.

After they leave, I'm again left alone with my thoughts, and RoseLyn re-enters them. I close my eyes, imagining I'm watching her sing. Hell, what a voice on her. And the way she moves—

"Petty! We need you in church," Crash roars as he slams my door open, but pauses and looks at me dubiously. "You gonna be able to move, Brother?"

What a question. It will hurt, but when's that ever stopped me. The painkillers have done their job and I'm a master at being able to get around with bruises and broken ribs. I wouldn't be summoned if it wasn't important. While earlier I might have worried such a demand for my presence was to be a discussion about taking my patch, from the concern on the VP's face, I quickly dismiss that notion.

"I can be there," I confirm to the VP, while taking my time and moving carefully. I manage to get my legs onto the floor and pull up the pants he's thoughtfully handed to me. Unable to completely swallow the groan, I manage to bend and get my socks and boots on next, then the tee, which Crash helps me feed my hands through the armholes, and finally the cut that he nabs off the chair and slides onto my back. I pause, willing the dizziness away, and belatedly ask, "What's up?"

"RoseLyn's missing."

Missing? I move faster than I should and a bolt of pain goes through my head. Reaching out a hand, I steady myself on the doorjamb.

"Careful, Brother," Crash growls, his hand resting on my arm. "Take it slowly now."

"What the fuck happened?" I rasp, angry at myself for being so fucking helpless and furious at Britney for making me this way.

"She didn't turn up at the casino," he says tersely. "Bart couldn't raise her on the phone so went out to check on her. Her car's in the driveway, front door wide open, and her purse and phone are in the house. There was no sign of her."

I have to concentrate on getting down the stairs as my head is woozy, whether from the painkillers or the blow I'd taken I couldn't say, so I don't ask for more information until I reach the bottom, then I swallow my words as I hear the commotion. The door to church must be open as I can hear the loud voices from here. Crash hastens me forward.

Red's eyes flick to me as I enter, clearly assessing my state. Roller leaps to his feet and pulls a chair out for me. I ease myself down, looking around and noticing the expressions on my brothers' faces. I see Hammer and Cobra both looking flushed while others are angry, or in Titch's case, he looks downright disgusted.

Prez bangs the gavel and the shouting dies down. I just want them to get on with explaining what the fuck Crash meant when he said RoseLyn was gone, but luckily, he's on the same wavelength.

"Where the fuck is RoseLyn?" I ask, as I take my seat and gingerly sit down. "Saul's dead. There's no one after her anymore."

Red shakes his head, and rubs at his temples. "Fuck. Petty, I'll repeat it for your benefit." His eyes flick to mine, and then back to the table again. "RoseLyn's missing. She's not in her house, and hasn't taken anything with her."

"So what the fuck are we doing about it?"

My voice is too sharp, but as Red's eyes again meet mine, I can see some sympathy in them so know he's giving me a pass.

"Keys has pulled the security footage, and this is what we've found." He nods to our computer guy.

Keys passes his laptop to me. From the reactions of the others, I'm the last one to see it. It shows the view from the front door. RoseLyn is being pushed out, her hands tied behind her back. She's taken to the rear of a car parked behind hers, then she's gagged and though she puts up a good fight, is bundled into the trunk of the car which then departs the scene with wheels spinning. I notice two things. One, the car has no plates, and the second, her abductor is wearing a baseball cap and his face has been turned away from the camera the whole time, except for the short moment when RoseLyn was struggling. But that brief glimpse only showed he has a beard.

"You let her go back home alone?" I turn accusing eyes on my prez.

Red doesn't look happy about it. "Saul's dead. There didn't seem to be a risk." He turns the tables on me. "What would you have done different?"

Nothing. My hands clench as that's the rub of it. Prez did nothing wrong.

"Saul was working with someone. That fucker we think is in the cops," Indian states. "Could be him."

"We any closer to finding him?" I was out of the loop when it all went down.

Crash sighs heavily. "No. We pressed him on it, but he kept his mouth shut. Then RoseLyn insisted on seeing him, and you know how that went down."

I know how it ended, with a bullet in his head, and with RoseLyn seeing the club for exactly what it is. Unfortunately, her view can't be rectified, and as for him, dead men tell no tales.

I cry out, my voice anguished. "They've taken her, Prez. There must have been someone else stalking her." I hate to admit I was right when I thought it wasn't Saul.

"Saul admitted it was him," Red points out. "We had no

reason to believe there was someone else. But there obviously was. Who the fuck's taken her now?"

"And why?" Twister says grimly. "We don't know what they're going to be doing to her."

She could already be dead.

Suddenly the thought that I might never see her again, never hear her sing, never talk to her, never have the chance to tell her how I feel or start something with her, slams into me, making it hard to breathe and causing an ache in my chest worse than that caused by the ribs that are broken.

"Well, that's our personal security services thrown out with the trash," Fox states.

Seeing red, I round on him. "Is money and business all you fuckin' think about? What about RoseLyn who trusted us to keep her safe?"

"From Saul." Fox reels back. His face reddens showing I've got to him.

"From whoever was after her, and we knew Saul was getting help." My annoyance isn't helping my throbbing head, and I'm trying to hear over the ringing in my ears. But that could just be the blood racing as I'm fucking terrified for RoseLyn. No woman deserves to be hurt, kidnapped and fuck knows what else, especially her.

"Petty?" The irate tone in which my name is called leads me to suspect Red's been trying to get my attention for a while.

"Prez?" I focus my eyes on him.

"You spent time with her and her family. You and she shared some personal shit." His narrowed eyes warn me to keep quiet. "She tell you anything about this Saul fucker which suggests who else could be around?"

I shake my head in answer to his question while grimacing, knowing if RoseLyn isn't immediately found, there's no way we'll be able to keep this from Rufus and Martina. They'll lose their shit. And I'll have to fess up that I knew she was in danger the entire time and kept that from them, along with the deceit that I'm not boyfriend material at all.

But thinking of that visit brings something to mind. It seemed odd at the time. "That pastor." I raise my head and look directly at Keys. "Did you find anything on him?"

Keys shrugs. "Didn't look into him. By then we had Saul buttoned down and were focused on the operation to take him."

Red's fingers drum on the table. "What's this?"

"Probably nothing." I frown. "Just some pastor randomly showed up at RoseLyn's parents' home and seemed pretty interested in looking through old photos and learning everything about her."

"They religious types?" Shadow asks.

"Not in particular," I reply.

"Get onto it, Keys," Red instructs sharply.

But Keys is already scrambling at his laptop and tapping away, presumably calling up the info I sent him. "Got a Walt Johnson registered at the United Church. They say anything much about him." He queries me with a raise of his eyebrow.

Thinking back, I roll my eyes. "Only that her mom had the idea of setting him up with RoseLyn."

Keys lifts his head. "You're fuckin' kidding me, Brother." He turns his laptop to face me. The screen shows a picture of a grey-haired man, big jowls and by no stretch of the imagination attractive. He's leaning heavily on a stick and looks to be at least a hundred years old.

"That's not him." I think back to their description of the pastor. "They either said or hinted he was about RoseLyn's age." And Rufus had accused Martina of flirting with him. Surely even a middle-aged woman wouldn't try her hand at the old fucker in the picture?

"Her parents security—they got a camera at the front of the house?" Keys demands.

Ignoring the throbbing in my head, I try to think back. "Yes. I saw it." I rub my temples, and raise my eyes apologetically.

Damn, I wish trying to get my brain to work didn't feel so much like sifting through mud. "You need me to contact them?"

"Seeing as RoseLyn was so concerned about keeping her parents out of what was going on, I think we need to hang back for a moment until we've got more info." Red's brows are drawn down. "Keys, you reckon you can hack into their security feed?"

"If I can't, I know people who can." Keys grins as he refers to our brothers from Utah.

Red slaps his hand on the table. "Go check it out, Brother. If the pastor's a fake, he could have something to do with Saul and could have been checking background shit out. Maybe a long shot, but it's the only fuckin' lead we've got."

Keys wastes no time following his prez's instruction and immediately gets up and leaves.

Though I hate to voice it, with a grimace I say, "We've gotta tell her folks sometime, Prez."

He glances at me. "I'm well aware, Petty. You want to be the bearer of the news that their daughter, the person we've been protecting, has been snatched right under our noses? That we fucked up, thinking the danger was gone. Oh, and that you visited them under false pretences—"

"I got it," I reply fast. "We'll hold off."

"We can hold off, as Petty puts it, but for how fuckin' long?" Indian stares straight at Prez. "How the fuck do we get her back?"

Red sighs heavily. "I'm fuckin' stumped, Brothers. We don't even know the motive. Saul's case was plain. He was a fucker who couldn't leave well enough alone. He wanted vengeance." He scrubs at his forehead again. "I fucked up. I assumed the danger was over and it was safe for her to go home."

"It's got to be this cop fucker who was helping him." I raise my chin toward Crash, grateful others are doing the thinking for me. Just trying to get my brain to work makes me feel nauseous. "Utah said they were close to identifying him."

"They haven't gotten back with anything new," Twister admits.

There are shakes of heads all around, and Red actually looks beaten. Once we had our hands on Saul, his accomplice had been ignored. Like them, I think that's the most likely person who's taken RoseLyn. I can't see her having another stalker, or one that would go to such lengths of kidnapping her.

I swallow hard as bile rises. *What's happening to her right now?* Without knowing why she was taken, there's no way to tell.

"The fucker can't know Saul is dead," Indian muses aloud. "He might have taken her for him. As long as he thinks Saul's in the wind, maybe he'll keep her alive."

"Or," Crash grimaces, "maybe as he's lost contact with Saul, he thinks RoseLyn might have information to help find him."

I grit my teeth. In that circumstance, it's imperative RoseLyn lies her head off and denies knowing what happened to Saul. From the brief period of silence and the grimaced expressions on my brothers' faces, I'm not the only one thinking those thoughts.

"I'll question Bart and Kylie again," Crash offers. "Her manager or stylist might know more than they're telling."

I doubt it. Bart's likely to go ape we have no leads to follow. He was the one who brought us in to keep her safe. He trusted us. I don't relish Crash that conversation, and for once am pleased that my injuries give me an excuse to stay out of it.

"We should go to the cops." Twister's grimace shows what he thinks of his own suggestion. "This time they can't dismiss it as a prank someone's playing."

"They'll get no further forward than us," Rope states. "They weren't interested from the beginning."

"And they'll blame it on Saul and waste resources trying to find a dead man," Red points out, looking carefully at us all. We won't be able to tell the cops that that's a literal dead end.

"Involve Utah?" Cuffs suggests. "Not just for info, but actual help. It's right up their street."

Red sighs heavily at that suggestion. "Much as it pains me, I don't see we've got much choice. They've got more expertise. I'll call Snatcher after this meeting."

Utah's business is preventing or rescuing kidnappees, but we've so little to go on, I think even they would be hard pressed. We don't know why she was taken, which puts a thought in my head. "Do you think there'll be a ransom demand?"

Red shrugs. "Maybe. But it won't be to us." Again he sighs heavily. "It will either be to her manager or her parents. Fuck, maybe we're going to have to get in touch with them sooner rather than later. I'm going to leave that to you, Petty."

Oh, fuck. I liked Martina and Rufus. I'm not relishing admitting I was acting a part when I went to meet them. That instead of her boyfriend, I was one of her ineffective bodyguards.

"And before any ransom demand," Crash suggests.

I lurch to my feet, swaying and using the chair to hold me up.

It all comes back to Britney who forced me into this lie. If fucking Britney hadn't played her tricks, I wouldn't have been lying in my bed half-dead. I'd have been with RoseLyn, or at least gone after her when she'd left. And maybe, I would have been able to protect her.

"We've got to find her," I hear myself wail. I can't bear to think of the alternative, that she's gone from my life. Though her initiation into what the Devils can do may mean she'd never be a part of it, I can't bear the thought that I've let her down and she might not be alive. "Where's fuckin' Britney?" My injured body holds a wrath full of anger, and she's my target. I might not have been able to hit a woman before, but I sure can now. I blame her for me not being there to prevent RoseLyn being taken.

"Sit, Brother." Twister walks around and puts his hand on my shoulder. "You leave her to us."

"She had nothing to do with it." Hammer grimaces.

"Her machinations kept me from her side," I cry out. "She—"

"Petty," Red snaps. "Get your ass back on the seat. I know you're frustrated, but taking it out on Britney won't help. One thing for certain, she's got nothing to do with this."

CHAPTER TWENTY-SEVEN

RoseLyn

The car drives for some time, with me bumping and rolling in the trunk. I try to wedge myself in to stop being hurt. The traffic sounds around us increase then fade, and after an unknown time has passed, the car pulls up.

I'm released from the trunk, but that's the extent of my freedom. I notice we appear to be miles from anywhere when he gestures with the gun that I should get into the back seat.

I can't outrun a bullet, so reluctantly, do as he says. Thankfully, he removes the gag from my mouth.

He stares at me intently, then makes that strange statement again. "I'm so fuckin' pleased to meet you."

I'm at a complete loss as to how to respond. With the gun pointed in my direction, I'm not sure it would be tactful to say I wish I'd never come face-to-face with him at all. Once I'm in the back seat, I'm physically more comfortable. Mentally, however, that's a whole different ball game.

He's staring back from the passenger seat as if trying to take in my features, while after my first sneak peek at him, I try to keep my eyes averted. My glance had shown me a man that's probably in the same age bracket as myself, blond hair the colour of mine falling just below his shoulders. If I passed him on the street, I'd probably say he was quite attractive. Certainly not the kind of man who'd need to stalk a woman and kidnap her to get attention.

As his companion starts the car and drives off, his continual staring at me makes me feel very uneasy. Part of me is angry that my bodyguards have abandoned me, while the other accepts that I, too, believed, with Saul gone, there was no longer a threat. Now I'm bewildered and worried. What could this man want with me?

Saul was definitely responsible for the incidents that had made me call in security. So is this completely unconnected? Have I, RoseLyn, singer-not-so-very-extraordinaire, have managed to get two men after me? If it wasn't so disturbing and upsetting, the situation would make me laugh.

"Not going to say anything?" he prompts after I've been silent for a while.

"Will me talking get me out of whatever you've got planned?" I'd rather save my energy and plan to make an escape. I neither know him nor trust him, and won't be able to tell if he's telling the truth even if I ask questions.

I feel a bit like I'm presented with a genie who's going to only grant three wishes. I do need information, but what's more pertinent to ask, and whether he'll give anything away, is going to have to be considered carefully.

"Not even going to beg for me to let you go?"

"Would it do any good?"

He snorts and nudges the driver. "She's a feisty one, isn't she?"

I may be projecting the persona of a confident woman, but I'm trembling inside. After those snakes were left in my house, I know just how dangerous stalkers, and presumably kidnappers can be.

Having turned my head away, I sneak another peek at my kidnapper out of the corner of my eye, wondering again why someone like him would need to take any woman by force.

While I personally don't find him particularly attractive—I prefer my men muscular like Petty—I'm sure there would be any number of women falling over themselves to get a part of him. Which begs the question, why has he taken me?

I thought it ended with Saul, and Saul won't be causing me, or anyone else any more misery. Even though I can't come to terms with the way that he went, some part of me is glad it's over. It seems, though, my troubles hadn't ended with him.

"If you think I've got money, you're wrong." It's the only reason I can think of why he's taken me. "And my family isn't rich. No one would pay to have me back." They'd want to, but the few measly thousands of dollars my parents could pull together still wouldn't be much, and certainly not worth this charade he's playing.

He snorts. "I don't want money."

Inwardly I shiver. *What does he want?* Is he some crazed fan who wants a personal performance? I really don't want to consider the follow on conclusion to that, and exactly how much he's likely to take.

But knowledge is power. So, taking a breath, I pluck up the courage and ask him directly. "What is it you want?" I face him once more, and notice a tic in his jaw.

"What do I want?" He chuckles as if I've told a joke rather than just asked a question. "Let's have this conversation once we get somewhere more comfortable."

As I'm wondering where 'more comfortable' is and what his definition of that might be, the driver flicks the indicator and takes a turn to the right. The building is an old rundown motel that has clearly seen better times and has a *For Sale* board out front. On a rotted sign, I can just make out the words, *Desert Retreat.* The location and name probably indicate the reason for its demise. Who'd want to stay in the middle of nowhere?

The car is driven around the back out of sight from the road, and then parks in the empty parking lot and the engine is switched off.

As though he's been tutored on what to do, the driver gets out, comes around the back and opens my door.

"Out," the man with the gun says.

I do, scanning the surroundings for any chance to escape, but there's nothing but desert and scrub, and I'm not yet that desperate to chance death by a bullet or exposure instead of finding out whatever fate this man has got planned.

When the door is opened to a musty smelling room, reluctantly I have no option but to step inside. While I'm terrified, I won't give them the pleasure of knowing it.

The man with the gun passes an envelope over to the driver who's not entered the door. He takes out the cash, counts it, then with a mock salute turns and walks off. A few seconds later, I hear the sound of an engine start, and then fade as the car drives off.

"Sit." He gestures with the gun toward the bed.

Have my chances improved now I'm up against only one man? I think that they have. If I act compliant and string him along, then maybe I'll be able to surprise him and get the upper hand.

He stands with his back against the door and folds his arms while I gingerly sit on the bare mattress, trying not to think about the origins of some of the stains. While his gun is no longer pointed my way, he's still holding it tight. He's examining me again, his eyes soaking me in, but not in any lascivious way. If I grow more uncomfortable, it's the intensity of his focus that's worrying me.

Silence isn't getting me anywhere. "Who are you and what do you want?"

Instead of a direct answer, he sighs heavily and shakes his head. When I've almost given up on getting a response, he clears his throat. If I was pushed to describe his tone, I'd say it was emotional as he says, "What I want is what I'm never going to get. It's what you've had that I missed out on. Nothing..." he breaks off, and now his mouth twists. "Nothing will ever make up for that." I was never very good at puzzles, and my lack of comprehension must show in his face as he continues, "We were once as close as it was possible for two people to get."

That gets my voice working. "You must have the wrong person. I've never met you before," I object.

He snorts. "Yeah, you have. We spent a lot of time together."

Now my examination is more thorough, but if we have, I just can't place him. *Someone from school?* No, I would remember. And unless he's changed considerably since those days, he'd have been one of the popular jocks and not someone you could forget. Unless back then he was a nerd who wore glasses and kept to himself.

Finally it's me who's now making a negative motion with my head. "If we've met, I'm sorry, but I can't remember. Are you sure you're not muddling me up with someone else?" What a joke it would be if this nightmare was down to mistaken identity.

He barks a laugh. "Oh, you'll wish it was that. But no, I've got the right person. Rose Blakeney."

Well, that's another mystery in that he knows my real name and not the one I sing under. Not that it's hard to find out if you do a bit of digging. But I thought I was being stalked for who'd I'd become, not who I actually am, which adds another level of intrigue to the situation.

I'm fed up with being in the dark, and by him having information which I haven't got. Until I know what he wants, I can't formulate a plan on how best to deal with him.

I stand, and the gun comes out to threaten me again. "Don't try anything. Believe me, I'll feel no remorse at killing you, and I'll still get what I want."

"What do you want?" I spit at him. "Why am I here? What the hell have I ever done to you?"

A change comes over him. Spots of red appear on his cheeks and he clenches his free hand into a fist. Lines appear as his eyes crease. "What have you done to me? You left me alone. That's what you did. You left me to be abused and molested in ways no human should ever be, not least a little kid."

My mouth drops open at the bizarre explanation that comes out of his mouth. I'm certain I've never met him before and though my heart breaks at the dreadful past he's alluding to, I can't see that in any way it can be my fault. *Was he some kid I met in kindergarten?*

"What's your name?" If I knew his identity, maybe that would trigger some long forgotten recollection from the past.

"Thorne," he answers with a wry twist to his mouth. "Rose and Thorne. Someone had a warped sense of humour."

But the name means nothing.

My obvious lack of response has annoyed him. He lurches forward and grasps my arm, pulling me over to the mirror hanging on the wall. He points at his face, and then at mine.

"Same fucking nose, same creases around the eyes. Same fucking dimple."

I screw up my eyes, trying to see what he means. Now he points it out, there is some similarity between us. Differences too, but before I can point them out, he spins me around, pushes me hard so I fall back on the bed, then his larger body comes down on top of me.

He's going to rape me.

But any fear of being molested disappears when he says, "You're my fucking twin. We shared a womb for nine months." There were some things that compared, but we're not that much alike. I shake my head to refute his declaration, but he anticipates my rejection. "Not identical, but siblings just the same. You were actually born first, so technically you're the older, by fifteen minutes."

I was right all along. This is a case of mistaken identity. He must have picked me because of my looks and some stupid notion I was his long-lost sister.

"You're wrong," I tell him. "I'm an only child. I'm not your sister." I wonder whether there's some way I can now get out of this. "But I could help you find her, if you want?"

There's another of his unattractive snorts. "I've found her. She's you. And don't expect brotherly love from me as I fucking hate you."

"You don't know me!"

"No? I know you're a spoiled brat who always had everything handed to her. You're living the dream, and left me to live the nightmare."

"You're wrong." I try to calm my tone, remembering he's still got the gun, and apparently no reason to think kindly of me. "I was born to Rufus and Martina Blakeney. I'm there only child. Anything else is just coincidence."

"The fucking Blakeneys." He says the name as though it's a swear word. "They ruined my life, and now I'm going to ruin theirs."

CHAPTER TWENTY-EIGHT
Petty

My pains disappear into insignificance, my physical limitations an annoyance, but as in the past, I can, and will, ignore them. Even Britney and the dire result of her machinations is of no consequence. Red is right. Taking my anger out on her wouldn't help. And if this fucker wanted to take RoseLyn, he probably would have gotten her, whether Britney had taken me out of action or not.

What matters is finding RoseLyn. Everything else can wait.

While conversations are continuing around me, I put my head into my hands. *Think, man. Think.* I run back over every conversation with RoseLyn in my head, the wording of all the notes she received, and that visit to her parents. But try as I might, nothing sticks out.

Prez gets a prospect to bring in coffees for all of us, and Roller forces some painkillers into my hand. Around me conversations are going on much like the analysis I've just done in my mind. We've fuck all to go on. All our hopes are pinned on our brothers in Utah. It's so damn frustrating. If I had a direction, even hurt as I am, I'd be out searching on my bike.

I fight off the waves of despair that threaten to overwhelm me with the thought that the one woman who ever fought on my side has been stolen from me. Even if there could never be anything between us, more on her part now than mine, my blinders have come off. I can't cope with the thought of her suffering. She doesn't deserve that.

Time seems to slow. It could be just minutes though it feels like hours before Keys exclaims, "Fuck, those Utah boys are hot. Here's the man, brothers." Turning his laptop screen around, men stand and lean forward blocking my view.

I growl, showing my annoyance, and taking pity on me, Roller pushes the laptop across. Feeling men crowding around me, I view the cleaned-up picture from the Blakeney's security camera.

He's pleasant looking, enough so I can see what got Martina giddy. He's got dark hair, and is wearing gold-rimmed glasses. His cheeks are on the side of chubby. He's standing straight, shoulders back, an aura of confidence about him.

"Anyone seen him before?" Red asks.

I look around, but like me, everyone's shaking their heads.

Keys retrieves his laptop and stabs at a few keys. "Whoa." His eyebrows rise, and he peers closely at his screen again. "Honor's just pointed out this man's in disguise. He's wearing a wig, and he suspects there's prosthetics in his cheeks."

"How the fuck does he know?"

Keys furiously taps for a moment again, waits and reads a reply, then he snorts. "Apparently the wig is because the colouring doesn't match his complexion, and as for his cheeks, the skin looks stretched." He stares at his screen in consternation as though trying to see what Honor's pointed out. Shrugging, he says, "Well, let's try this one, Brothers." Now he's turning his laptop around again. "Honor's mocked up the image, thinning out the cheeks, removing the glasses, and there's a variety of hair colourings."

Impatiently I wait for the screen to face me once more, then lean forward and look at the half dozen connotations of the revised image now visible to me. My eyes home in on the blond version for some reason, a niggling at the back of my mind.

"He looks familiar." I'm only half-conscious I'm speaking aloud.

"Same, Bro," Cobra confirms. He creases his eyes as if to see better. "Though fuck knows where I've seen him."

"In the audience, maybe?"

I think it's a certainty he's been watching her shows. I probably just haven't noticed anything suspicious about him.

Keys retrieves his laptop and checks his messages. "Honor's getting hits on the facial recognition. Because he's had to make some guesses, he's checking through them."

"Can we get some security footage of the casino?" Red asks. "See if there's anyone in the audience that resembles this fucker?"

"On it, Prez." Keys fingers start to fly once again. When he gets the file he wants, he comes around my side of the table, waves Roller out of his seat, and plants himself beside me. "You were there most often, Petty. Recognise anyone?"

Remembering the guy could be in disguise, I look very carefully, focusing on height and build rather than hair colour. It's hard to tell, but he could have been there. There are a few people that are likely, though no clear facial shots that would help Honor locate him.

More refreshments are brought in. Though there are sandwiches, my stomach rebels at the thought of eating them. With every minute that passes with no further clues, I'm more and more worried about RoseLyn, and what the fucker might be doing to her.

Raping her? Fuck no, how could she live with that? Being violated is something I have some experience of, and I wouldn't wish that on anyone.

Why else would he want her? It was Saul who's been stalking her these past months, not anyone else.

My hands fist.

"Honor's got a couple of likely looking suspects," Keys says excitedly, his words stopping all other conversation. "There are a few he was able to rule out. One's in New York, and one's in Chicago, but there are two whose last known locations were in Vegas. A man called Phil Catoroise, and one named Thorne Baker."

"Pics?" Prez demands.

"Sure." Keys turns the laptop around.

From the glimpse I manage to see, both men look fairly similar, and both could be equally likely.

"Any more details? Addresses?"

"Phil Catoroise is recently married. Works on a construction site." Keys grimaces. "Must admit he doesn't sound likely. Not likely he'd forget his marriage vows so quickly."

"We don't know the reason he's taken her, Brother," I remind him. "Could be for anything. Can't rule him out on the basis he's got a ball and chain."

"Agreed." Red raises his chin. "But what about Thorne?"

Instead of answering, Keys looks down at his laptop, and checks something. He shakes his head. "Can't find much out about him. Duty and Honor are trying to dig deeper than I can."

"Fake name?" I suggest, sitting as forward as my ribs will allow. If so, this could sound promising.

Keys has his eyes glued to his screen, but Red catches my eye. If the glint in his eyes resembles mine, then he thinks this is a lead as well.

"Why don't we just go pay the fucker a visit?" Twister demands, rubbing his hands together as though in anticipation. "I can think of ways to rule him out or in, wherever he stands." The enforcer's suggestion sounds like a way forward.

"And if he's an innocent civilian?" Prez raises a brow. "Or what if we head off hunting a wild goose and miss the person we should be chasing?"

That brings me to my senses. We've got to find RoseLyn and before whoever's got her has time to do whatever he plans with her. Chills rack my body as I think of her in his overpowering arms.

Suddenly Prez's brow furrows and he takes out his phone which is buzzing in his hand. He's the only one allowed to bring such a device into church, so the interruption isn't normal. He glances at the screen, then answers.

"Snatcher?... Uh-huh... I'll put him on speaker." He glances at me, then places the phone down. "Floor's all yours, Honor."

The voice of the member from Utah fills the room. "Once we managed to find sealed juvie records for Thorne Baker, thought it was best to talk you through what we found. Could be something or nothing, Brothers."

"Go ahead," Red says tersely, while the rest of us stay silent.

Honor doesn't keep us waiting. "Thorne Baker was adopted as a baby. Seems like his wasn't a particularly loving home. Hospital visits suggest he was abused as fuck."

"He was left in an abusive home?" Rope's brow is furrowed.

"His family moved around. Looks like no one connected the dots, or could be bothered to." Honor takes a breath. "His family were carnies, never stayed in one place for long. When he was ten, he pickpocketed the wrong man, ended up in juvie for a few months."

"Any known connection to RoseLyn?" The man's history is something I'm not particularly bothered about, though it certainly doesn't give me a good feeling. He's probably not had a good life, and has been exposed to violence since he was a child.

I don't know what I'm expecting, but I don't expect what Honor says next. "Certainly is. Well, not known, but possible to find if you dig deep enough. Thorne was born a twin, but they were adopted by different homes."

For a moment I can't compute what he's saying, then a light bulb goes off in my mind. "Thorne's RoseLyn's twin? Show me that picture again, Keys."

As Keys taps at his laptop to comply, Honor continues,

"That's what I'm saying, Brother. RoseLyn was born fifteen minutes before him."

"And they were separated?" Cuffs eyes open wide. "Why the fuck not keep them together?"

But for this Honor only has a suggestion. "Maybe the families only wanted one child."

"That's sick," Shadow states. "Twins have a bond and should stay together."

Sarge's eyebrows draw down into a V. "I had a twin," he starts. "Lost him to leukaemia when I was a child. Non-identical." He nods toward the phone. "I drew the lucky straw, but always felt part of me was missing."

"So you're saying Thorne wants to reconnect with his missing part? Could it have been him, and not Saul, leaving some of those notes for RoseLyn?"

"You mean the *I hate you, bitch* ones or the others?" Shadow raises his chin. "Didn't much gel with those that said he wanted her back so they could always be together. Just thought the fucker was schizophrenic if I'm honest."

"It's possible." Red frowns. "Could they have been working together?"

"But what's his connection to Saul?" Twister asks.

"Haven't found that out yet, or if there is one," Honor states. I'd forgotten for a moment we were on a call. "But here's my ten cents. I reckon Thorne got the worse end of the deal. RoseLyn's parents adored her. Thorne's not so much."

"You're saying he's fuckin' jealous of her?" Crash asks, then looks around.

"How the fuck does he benefit from kidnapping her?" I don't understand. If it was money he was after, then RoseLyn might well have been sympathetic to a long-lost brother approaching her. She's not rich, but I know enough about her to know she'd have shared what she could, which leads me to ask. "Why didn't he just approach her?"

"We read data, not fuckin' minds," Honor points out.

"Whatever the fuckin' reason, we now know who we're after. Got any info on where he might be?" Prez stares at the device on the table.

"Duty's looking into that, as I suspect is Keys." Keys nods quickly. "Hang on. Stormy's got something."

Another voice comes on the line. "Checked out the Vegas address for Thorne. He lives in a house along with a fuckin' cop. A guy called Elton Payton. He's a detective."

"He's also the cop we liked for passing info onto Saul. We're checking it out before giving it to you as a solid lead." Honor sounds triumphant.

And right there's the fuckin' connection.

"Give us an address," Red snaps.

Stormy does.

"Okay." Snatcher's voice sounds. "We'll leave you to track down Elton. While in the best of worlds you'll find RoseLyn at the cop's address, getting to know her new family, I reckon we'll work on the worst-case scenario and try to find locations where Thorne could have taken her."

Prez nods and retrieves his phone. With a "thanks, Brother", he ends the call. "Twister, Crash, you want to go check this fucker out?"

"I'm going," Hammer says.

"Me too," Cobra states.

"I'm—"

Red's finger points straight at me. "You're going fuckin' nowhere. You're in no state to ride. You're staying here."

"But—"

"When we've got a lead on RoseLyn, that's where you come in, Brother."

Crash backs up the prez. "Petty, you'd only slow us down."

While everything in me wants to deny it, it's the fucking truth. I'm as likely to lay down my bike as be able to keep up with them, but it irks that I'm going to be left sitting twiddling my thumbs.

"Let me know." I turn pleading eyes on them. "As soon as you—"

"As soon as we've got this Elton bastard singing, we'll let you know."

If I had any remaining doubts that I was no longer accepted by my club, Hammer's look of compassion and his touch to my shoulder on passing would remove any doubt.

It suddenly hits me. Finding RoseLyn *is* more important than wearing my cut. I'd rather have both, but if I had to make a choice, there's only one I'd give up.

CHAPTER TWENTY-NINE

RoseLyn

I eye Thorne much like I'd watch a wild animal, with great caution. I have no idea where he's gotten the idea that we've got any relationship. If he was my twin, surely I'd feel something for him? But looking at him, I feel no more than anger that he, or Saul, or maybe both, have tormented me for months, and now he has kidnapped me.

I try to remain calm, not wanting to anger him. Sitting again, I gather my thoughts. "I know you're mistaken. I was born to Rufus and Martina Blakeney. They'd tried for years to have a child, and I was their only baby. Whatever you think is wrong."

"You weren't their child. You were adopted."

He sneers as I shake my head. "I assure you I'm not."

"I assure you, you are," he retorts, cockily. He studies me. "Let me tell you what your *darling parents* did, shall I?" Without giving me a chance to answer, he continues, "You're right in that they weren't successful in starting a family, so they went the adoption route. But by then they were considered too old to have a baby, so it was a private arrangement." I'm shaking my head as I know the truth. There was no adoption. "Our dear mom, our birth mother, was a fuckin' crack whore. She didn't go to her hospital appointments. Her boyfriend, who didn't want a kid, saw a way to make some money, so arranged an adoption."

I'm intrigued with this story, even though I don't believe for a second it has anything to do with me, so I just shrug and continue to listen.

"When the time came, your parents were at the hospital waiting for news on their baby, when lo-and-behold, you were born first, and then I came along. Well, our sperm donor was delighted, thought he'd double up on the return. But, there you were, pink, happy and healthy, and there I was, small, jaundiced and suffering withdrawal."

"And you want me to believe they took me, the healthy baby, and left you?" Even if I accepted there was any truth in this story, I couldn't believe that. My parents would never separate twins, nor turn their back on a baby that needed them.

He gives a sharp nod and a look of approval as if I've correctly answered a question. "That's exactly what they did. They said they only wanted one baby, that they couldn't afford a second. That they wanted a girl and not a boy—which was stupid as they'd have taken the single baby whatever problems it had or its version of genitals."

"No." I stand again, my finger pointing toward him. "While it's clear you believe this story, and I suspect the basis is true. I'm not your sister, and my parents weren't the ones who took me and left you. It's not something they would do."

And if there was any truth in it, all my life it would mean they'd been lying to me. There had never been a hint that I wasn't their blood daughter. *Could I have been adopted?* I shake my head. Impossible. People are always commenting how much I look like my mother.

Perhaps I should pretend to go along with his ridiculous suggestion just to get me out of here. Even if we're related, I don't know what he wants. But from the way he's spoken, he's jealous that I got the loving parents and a good life, far and removed from where he ended up. Even if he isn't blood related, my heart would go out to him. Except that he's taken it out on me who had nothing to say in the matter at all.

"Just say I accept what you're saying, what do you want from me?" I ask. "If you are my brother, why didn't you introduce yourself? You knew where to find me." I lower my head, thinking I'm missing something. "And what the fuck does all this have to do with Saul?"

He grins. "Seems you and I, sister, have the same taste in men." My eyes crease as I don't understand him. He enlightens me. "Saul's straight as they come and didn't have eyes for me. Doesn't mean I didn't still want him." It's on the tip of my tongue to say he had a happy escape, when he continues, "I bumped into Saul when I was first researching you. Found out he was doing the same thing. I offered to help him." He breaks off and frowns. "I don't know where Saul is. He's going to be so pleased that I've got you. We'd feared you'd never ditch those fuckin' bikers, but I got lucky. He's not answering his phone, though." He looks concerned. "No matter, I'm sure he'll be in touch shortly." He chuckles. "It will be good to reunite you. You see, I know now Saul holds no sentimental feelings for you at all. Why should he, after what you did to him?"

I did nothing but not keep quiet about who had so viciously attacked me. As for Saul getting in touch, it would only be possible via an Ouija board. I'm sensible enough to keep that knowledge to myself. As if our conversation has reminded him, he takes out his phone. But after calling up a number and listening for a few moments, he shakes his head.

His eyes narrow as he mumbles, "Still no fuckin' answer. Not like Saul to be out of touch." His eyes fix on me. "You don't happen to know anything about this?"

I give him the most innocent look that I can. "No." I don't waste words as saying too much could implicate me.

He turns and starts to pace.

"Why are you doing this?" I ask again, wanting to keep him distracted from thinking too hard about Saul.

He stops, glances my way, then says, "I wanted your parents to suffer in just the same way as I suffered all my life."

"But it hasn't been them who's been suffering. It's been me."

He suddenly looms closer and snarls, "Because you didn't fuckin' tell them, did you?"

"I didn't want to worry them!"

He snorts. "Well, they'll be worried soon enough when they find out you're missing. And when I start sending parts of you to them, they'll be out of their minds." He brushes his hands back through hair that's admittedly the same shade as mine. "Saul and I are going to keep you for a very long time, but I don't promise you'll enjoy it."

Not if I have any say in the matter they won't. And, on Saul's part at least, he can't. But the idea makes me shudder. Though I doubt this man would sexually assault me, not when he believes I'm his sister, and on top of that, he's gay, I don't much relish having pieces chopped off me. As for my parents, knowing I couldn't be found would have Dad's heart giving out again, and as for them receiving a finger...

"They're old," I shout. "They don't deserve this."

"They don't?" Twin spots of red appear on his face. "They should have taken me with you. Or taken me instead. I was adopted by abusive fucks who didn't want a kid. They wanted someone to work on their rig, oh, and a toy to play with as well. I was ten when I first tried to run *away* from the carnival, except I was caught trying to steal the money to leave, and was locked up."

I swear he's unhinged. Sure, with a past like that he's got something to complain about, but this is a complete injustice as I'm not adopted, and I don't have a twin.

"I'm sorry for what happened to you." Again, I try to calm my voice. "No one deserves to have a childhood like that. But you're mistaken. If you have got a twin, it's not me."

Is it just the coincidence of the colour of our hair and eyes that's led him to believe it's me? Suddenly I realise he could have been searching for his twin, seen my picture, and decided as my name was Rose, that it had to be me?

"I'm not your twin," I tell him again. "But how about I help you find her?" Not that I want someone else to be tortured instead of me, but maybe I'd be able to leave and get him the help that he surely needs. Neither punishing me nor my parents would right any of the wrongs in his life.

He chuckles but the sound brings me no pleasure. "You're my twin," he states, as though there's no argument.

"Then let's do a DNA test."

He baulks at my practical suggestion. "Don't need no fuckin' test to prove it. I know who I am and who you are." He takes a phone from his pocket and holds it out. "Ring your parents if you don't believe me. And tell them I send my love while you're at it."

I'm obviously doing no such thing, but I'm also at a loss on how to get out of here. Any chance that arises, I'll take it.

Thorne gets back to pacing, and muttering to himself. The words I can make out, chill me.

"Where the fuck are you Saul? I've got the bitch for you." He pauses his step, then starts marching again. "It was easy, there was no one guarding her. First fuckin' time in weeks…" He stops suddenly. "Wait a fuckin' moment. Have they got you, Saul? Is that why they removed her protection? Because they think they've got the person who's after her?" He starts cackling, laughing, bent double, then suddenly freezes.

He changes quickly, going from mirthful to serious. His face contorts with rage as he approaches me.

"Is that it? Have the Devils hurt Saul? Have they got him? Is that why you were alone and I could take you?" When I don't speak, he backhands me across my face.

"Where's Saul?" he shouts again, and this time spittle lands on my cheek.

I wish to God I could wipe it away.

If I tell him Saul's dead, he'll kill me.

He stares intently into my eyes as though trying to read my very soul.

Although I'm a singer, I'm also an actor on stage. Not only can I appear bright and breezy when I'm feeling like shit, but I also portray appropriate emotions for each piece of music we play. A sad song? I sing like my heart is breaking. Upbeat? I dance with a smile. While I doubt I'd ever win an Oscar, knowing this might possibly be the most important performance of my life, I bring forth all my acting skills, and keep my expression impassive.

"I don't know where Saul is." In a way, it's the truth. I have no idea where his body is now.

His mouth twists, his eyes narrow, but he shoves me back and resumes his pacing again, as I breathe a sigh of relief I haven't given anything away.

Thorne seems content not to have a conversation, and that's quite okay with me. It's easier not to lie when you don't have to talk. Instead I use the time, eyeing the room and checking for weapons if, and when, he unties me. Would I be able to get that gun out of his hand?

My face throbs from where he hit me so I've no illusions even if I accept there's a relationship between us that he'll show me any brotherly love. He knows Saul meant to hurt me, and that appears not to bother him at all. I shudder, knowing his lack of compassion means he's likely to follow out on his threats. Sue me if I prefer to keep all my appendages firmly attached.

I try to work out when I'll be missed, and when Bart will send out a search party. I doubt it will before I'm due at the casino tonight. I swallow back tears at the fear Kylie and Bart will feel for me.

They'll report me missing to the police, but all the cops can do is go chasing a man who's already dead. They'll never connect the dots to a twin I didn't know existed. My parents will be distraught, and the Devils? Well, even if Bart goes to them, even if they wanted to help, they'll be just as lost too. They'd done their job, caught my ex, and I'm a witness to how he'll never be talking again.

They won't know about Thorne. Like anyone else, they'd have no reason to.

Would they even try to find me? I didn't say goodbye to Petty, and he's intelligent enough to join the dots. He'll know what happened in the basement and suspect I left not wanting anything more to do with him or anyone who wears a Devils' cut. They're men who'd condone killing, being judge and jury all at once.

Here, now? I wish I could take it all back.

The devil right in front of me is ten times worse than any of the men who took drastic action for good reason. It chills me that if Saul were here now, he wouldn't have stopped at a simple smack to the face. He'd probably have raped me—at least Thorne's belief in our familial relationship protects me from that.

I revise my thoughts on applying swift retribution, knowing now if I had my chance to get hold of that gun, I'd kill Thorne without a second thought. Not only to save myself, but to prevent my parents going through the shock and worry of me never coming home, let alone if he carries out his threat and sends me back piece by piece.

I'm no different to a Devil at heart, and that organ clenches at the thought of never seeing Petty again, never admitting I was wrong. It might have taken a drastic situation, but I understand him better now.

He was going to be free of Britney, and I had a chance to be with him, but Thorne's put an end to that.

Will he ever know what's happened to me? Deep down, I hope that he'd care.

There's nothing I wouldn't give to see Devils busting through the door. Hammer, Cobra, Sarge and Petty himself—oh, how safe I'd felt with them. But they won't be giving any further thought to me. Their contract has ended, and not on good terms. I've annoyed Red.

The Devils will have moved on. They kept me safe from Saul, and that was all they were employed to do. I know too much about them but can't tell a soul. That gun in their safe would incriminate me.

If Thorne kills me today, next week, next month, what I'll regret most is not getting a chance with Petty. I've never met a man who more intrigued me, and I want to learn more about who's actually under the mask.

I want him, and never exploring what was tentatively growing between us is the biggest regret I'll take to my grave.

The silence continues. I presume Thorne is waiting for Saul, but that wait will go on forever. I observe him, now staring out of the window into the deserted parking lot, while checking the screen of his phone from time to time.

He's my brother? It doesn't seem real. I can dredge up no familial feelings for him. Only a moment ago I was wishing him dead, as I know in the end, it will be either me or him.

Of course I'm sorry for the way he was brought up, and if his story is true, have many questions for my parents.

I've been deceived all my life. But hell, I even look like my mom. Thorne's story doesn't seem credible or real.

I could have lived out the rest of my days without hearing the truth.

But now he's told me, I don't know how to deal.

CHAPTER THIRTY

Petty

"I'm a cop!" the man screams as soon as Twister removes his gag.

Unsympathetic, I sit on the seat that someone had thoughtfully set up for me. While the gesture was good, without the additional painkillers Roller again takes it upon himself to give me, sitting, standing or lying now, nothing much eases the aches within me.

Worst of them all is the pain in my heart. The feeling that I've lost my chance. *RoseLyn could be dead already.*

The only thing keeping me taking breath going into my lungs is that the man who's taken her is technically her family. *Her fucking twin.* Blood means more than vengeance, doesn't it?

Family is who you choose, not what you're born into.

"You want in on this?" Twister, his back to Elton, asks me quietly.

I fucking wish. "I can't." I hate that my voice is so weak. While I'd love to be exacting some punishment on the man who aided Saul and Thorne in making RoseLyn's life a misery, I'll save what little energy I have for finding her when the enforcer's beaten the information out of him.

Dead or alive, I'm coming for you, RoseLyn.

Twister grimaces, gives me a knowing nod, then turns his attention to the man Owl and Meat have strung up.

"I'm a cop," Elton repeats.

"Yeah, yeah, I got that," Twister tells him in a bored tone, while turning to the array of implements Owl's just laid out for him. He picks up a cordless drill, tests it, puts it back down, then studiously studies a pair of pliers, before settling on an evil-looking knife.

"You can't touch me!" Elton again yells, his voice panicked as a dark patch appears on the crotch of his jeans.

Red walks past his enforcer, and stands in front of the cop. "Might have more respect for your badge if you hadn't used your resources to terrorise a young woman."

"I don't know anything about that!" Elton's voice rises. "I don't, honestly."

"So you haven't been searching for information on Rose Blakeney?"

His eyes glance to the side. "Never heard that name."

Red shakes his head sadly, and steps back. "All yours, Twister."

"No!" Elton screams as Twister steps up, proving some cops aren't very brave men. They hide behind the badge most of the time, and here is one place that won't work. "My partner is Rose's twin. I was just helping him find her."

Red turns back. "You were giving what you found to her abuser asshole of an ex, Saul."

Elton's eyes widen. "I wasn't. I only told Thorne."

Giving him an incredulous side-eye, Red presses for more. "And why was a police officer using police databases to help anyone at all?"

Elton looks frantic, his eyes wild. "I love Thorne. He said Rose was a missing part of him and he wanted to find her."

If Thorne is indeed looking for his missing sister, then maybe I'm wrong to be worried about her. But in that case, why take her at all? Why not just introduce himself to her? Why wait months and allow Saul to torture her?

"What's the link between Thorne and Saul Ranger?" My voice is so weak and croaky, for a moment I'm worried no one will hear.

But Red turns, raises his chin toward me, then turns back to Elton. "Well?" He doesn't repeat the question so maybe I was louder than I thought.

"Fucking Saul," Elton rasps. "That bastard had Thorne twisted up in knots. Thorne wanted him, but Saul is as straight as they come."

Unrequited love. But it seems instead of making Thorne angry, perhaps he thought the way to Saul's heart was to help him. That means RoseLyn is being used as a pawn, he probably doesn't care for her at all. *What if he finds out Saul's dead? Would RoseLyn mean anything to him?* My hands tremble and it's not from physical weakness.

"Where would Thorne take RoseLyn?" Twister asks, moving that evil-looking knife from hand to hand.

The action's not lost on Elton. He pales. "I don't know. And that's the God's honest truth." He visibly fumbles for words to offer us. "Perhaps to dinner or something to get acquainted?"

I don't think he knows much about the man he's supposed to love. If it wasn't for Saul's involvement, I'd wonder whether Elton was right, but what Thorne and Saul have done to RoseLyn screams she's in danger now.

I can see Red's tension in his body and it's obvious he's quickly losing patience. He jerks his chin toward the enforcer, and I realise it's at that moment all bets are off.

As Twister approaches Elton, his screaming and pleading before having a finger placed on him makes me wonder what selection criteria is used by the cops. A man like him wouldn't have lasted two seconds in my Army unit. I can spot a coward from a mile off.

As it is, Twister barely has to touch him before he starts running his mouth. Apparently Thorne had shown a particular interest in a disused hotel that he'd told Elton he'd like to buy as a project and do up. Elton said he'd thought he was crazy, but humoured him and turned a blind eye when he broke in to explore it.

When pressed, he describes where it is, and the words are hardly out of his mouth before Red's organising brothers to go check it out. He assigns Crash, Hammer, Cobra, Rope, Cuff and Sarge. When he sees me struggling to get out of my chair, he instructs Owl to follow the bikes in the truck, and take me along for the ride.

"Might be nothing," he warns me, with a flick of his eyes toward Elton. "I don't think he's lying, but he might not be right."

But doing something is better than doing nothing, and I can't hurt more sitting in the passenger seat than I do here in the basement.

Actually, I hurt less. Adrenaline starts to course through my body as my brothers quickly wheel their bikes into formation. The traffic is heavy in Vegas, and while the bikes can split lanes and get through it, the truck has to wait its turn in the queue. It seems every set of lights is against us, and by the time we turn up close to the desert location, my brothers have already arrived, parked discreetly a few hundred yards down the road.

When I ease myself down from the truck, Hammer appears to update Crash.

"There's nothing here. Not even a car. I listened but heard nothing."

Dead people don't make any sound. While the VP shoots me a look of sympathy, I plant my feet firmly. "I ain't leaving until we check it all out."

"We're going in," he says firmly. "But you wait here."

"I'm coming."

"You'll slow us the fuck down, Brother."

"Don't wait for me. Just go ahead." I wave them forward.

"Alright, Brothers. Sooner we can cross this place off the list, the quicker we can look in some more productive places."

It's my turn to look to the heavens for inspiration. There's no fucking list, or if there is, this is the only place on it. If this turns out to be a bust, we'll have no clue where to start looking for her unless Twister's got more out of Elton.

Unwilling to give up on any optimism, I push myself forward after the others. For a moment or two my steps falter, but as I get into my pace, I begin to speed up. Bruises and sore muscles start to feel the benefit of being exercised, and while my ribs mean I can take no deep breaths, I've almost caught up to my brothers by the time they reach the entrance.

"Sarge?" Crash beckons him forward.

Sarge gets a tool out of his pocket and approaches the door. Within seconds, he's opened the lock and is gesturing us inside. We're standing in a reception area that looks as old-fashioned as fuck.

I draw Crash's attention to the footsteps in the dust. "Someone's been here recently."

His eyes homing in like lasers, he follows the steps and the clearly made track that leads behind the reception desk. For a second he disappears from sight, then emerges with a drawer full of keys. I can't remember when I last had anything other than a key card in a hotel, but then this place is probably as dated as the Ark.

Crash grins widely. "The keys are numbered." He tips the contents of the drawer out.

Rope and Cuffs help him start sorting them out.

"Thirty-two is missing," Rope, after what seems forever, announces with a triumphant bark. "Well that's made our job fuckin' easier."

Sarge is examining a faded plan on the wall. "Thirty-two is out back."

"Okay, let's check that first."

I'm glad that's what the VP decided as nothing's going to

hold me back. Well, except a little case of probable concussion and broken ribs of course.

"Keep your fuckin' eyes open," Crash warns as we make our way through the gloomy and spooky hotel. "Just because there's a key missing doesn't mean that's where they are."

"Might not fuckin' be here at all," Rope remarks, nudging Cuff in his side. Cuff grimaces but gives a nod to show he agrees with him.

She has to be. I don't think my heart can take much more. It's already thumping hard in anticipation of finding her here. If this is a dead end, it might give out altogether.

I want to shout, to let her hear my voice, to let her know I'm close and coming for her. But just because there's no vehicle doesn't mean she's here alone. And that's if this is even the right place.

Gritting my teeth against the pain, my muscles having again seized in the brief lull, I follow Crash, keeping up as best I can. We approach carefully, sidling along the walls and ducking beneath windows, making utter fools of ourselves if there isn't anyone here.

But at last we come to the right door, and Crash raises his hand, a signal to wait and listen.

It's then I hear the most wonderful sound in the world.

"I need to pee," RoseLyn says loudly and forcefully as if not for the first time.

"I fuckin' told you, there's no electricity or running water."

"Jeez, right now I don't care about washing my hands. I need to pee, Thorne."

Crash turns, but without having to be told, Sarge and Hammer are already moving fast, going around the back of the rooms to see what the bathroom access is like. Leaving Rope and Cuff with Crash, I follow them, slower because I have to concentrate hard as my balance and ability to walk silently have been compromised.

Around the back, we count the rooms until we come to the

right one, finding a sealed window comprising of frosted glass. The only part that opens is the top, impossible for anyone to get out of, but it doesn't faze Sarge. He removes some kind of cutting tool from his well-stocked pack which slices through the glass like a knife through butter. He attaches a sucker onto it, then waits.

"Fucker will probably want to check it out," he murmurs under his breath.

And he's right.

"You satisfied?" RoseLyn's voice comes over clearly, and is answered by a masculine grunt.

"Just do your business quickly."

"I can't pee with you watching me." I grin at the indignance in her tone. It shows me he hasn't hurt her too badly or broken her spirit, thank fuck. "Get out and close the door."

"Don't try to fucking escape."

"How?" I can picture her with her hands on her hips. "I might be skinny, but not so much I can get out of that." I assume she's pointing to the top of the window.

"Just don't try anything," he growls. "And don't lock the door."

Sarge holds up three fingers then puts them down one at a time. When the countdown has finished, he pulls on the glass which comes away from the frame making no sound.

Unfortunately we've caught RoseLyn literally with her pants down, but Hammer reaches in and covers her mouth with his hand before she can do anything but give a startled squeak.

Recognising him, she quickly pulls her pants up, raises her arms and lets Hammer pull her up. She uses the rim of the toilet to bolster herself, and in two short seconds, I've got a shocked, but grinning woman standing beside me.

"You came!" She throws herself into my arms, backing off immediately at my muffled exclamation.

"Get her out of here," Hammer growls.

Without having to be told twice, I pull her away, keeping

again to the side of the building. It was just in time as an angry shout quickly sounds.

"Where the fuck are you, bitch?" That's followed by a loud oomph and the sound of a gun hitting the ground.

Stopping our progress, I turn to see a man, uncannily resembling RoseLyn, struggling in the clutches of Hammer and Sarge. As I watch, they've quickly got him restrained and his hands zip-tied behind him.

As they march him around to where Crash will be waiting, I hold RoseLyn back.

"That was no happy family reunion, I take it?" I doubt it from what I heard, but I need to check.

Her eyes widen. "You know he's told me he's my brother?"

I shrug. "We found out a lot of things as we pulled out all the stops to find you."

Her eyebrows reach her hairline. "Why? I never expected... We didn't leave on good terms..."

"Devils never leave anyone behind, darlin'. Or leave a job undone. You might have walked out on us, but we were still there for you."

"I don't understand why."

My eyes shutter. Was RoseLyn really sitting in that room with no fucking thought of rescue? Did she really believe we'd abandon her? The thought tugs at my heart.

I turn her to face me, hoping she reads the intensity in my eyes. "You're important to us." When doubt shows, I clarify, "To me." I raise my hand and brush hair from her face. "I think Red saw it before I even came to my senses. I want you in my life, RoseLyn. I want you as my old lady and that makes you club."

It's impossible to read whether she reciprocates my feelings or not, but her next words give me some hope.

"What about Britney?"

Ah. The elephant in the room. "We'll divorce. She won't be able to refuse this time."

"What, what if she's pregnant?"

"Babe, we'll face that when and if it happens. If you want to be with me, that's not going to keep us apart."

She looks almost eager as she makes a suggestion. "A blood test reveals results the quickest and might be easier than forcing her to pee on a stick."

Now those words must be a positive sign, unless I'm grasping at straws. I let my excitement show in my eyes. "We have a doc on speed dial."

RoseLyn places her hand on my arm. "It was just once, Petty. Chances are there's nothing to worry about. And," she glances up, making sure I'm looking at her when she adds, "for the record, I like you too. I'd like to hear more about being your old lady."

I could no more stop my lips reaching down to hers than I could prevent myself taking my next breath. It's only when she gasps and not in a good way, that I reel back and take a good look at her face.

"He hit you?"

Ruefully she touches her swollen mouth. "Yeah. That's brotherly love for you."

Brotherly fucking love.

I want to know all that's gone on in that hotel room. Does Thorne care for her at all? His voice, his actions, the way he was all but frothing at the mouth when my brothers restrained him, not forgetting he hit her suggests to me that he doesn't care anything for her at all.

But he's her blood, her twin. While I'd put a bullet in his head for putting his hands on her, their relationship complicates things.

Her reaction to Saul's execution makes me more cautious than I'd otherwise be. She's got to have some say in the outcome.

"What do you want us to do with him?" I ask.

CHAPTER THIRTY-ONE

RoseLyn

What do you want us to do with him?

Now that's the million dollar question, isn't it?

I don't think I'm capable of feeling any love for the man with whom I'm supposed to have shared a womb. Even if we'd met under normal, pleasanter, circumstances, I don't think we would have clicked. Never once in the intervening years have I had a feeling that something was missing. On meeting Thorne, I'd felt no connection at all.

Like many only children, I felt the lack of a sibling growing up. Thorne, though, I'm not so sure we'd have got on. Maybe nurture would have turned him out different, but we'll never know.

"Is he really my twin?" I ask, hoping there's some doubt in the matter. That the unpleasant man I met isn't related to me after all.

"He is."

The quiet confirmation makes it harder for me to think what to do. Suddenly, all the fake bravado that had kept me going in front of Thorne dissipates, and I feel myself start to decompress. Mindful of his injuries, I lean against Petty, needing his support.

"I've got you," he murmurs, softly stroking my hair as I let out a sob into his chest. "I got you, babe. You're safe."

Surprisingly, I feel his body trembling, explained, perhaps, when he says, "Fuck, I thought I might never see you again. Thought I might have lost the chance to hold you in my arms. You know, I'm never fuckin' going to let you out of my sight again."

I, too, want to stay close. All my misgivings about the Devils have disappeared. How could I hold onto them as they'd been the ones to find me? I still don't know how, but I'll never be able to thank them enough.

"He said he was going to send bits of me back to my parents." I shudder. "He wanted to punish them." The implications of the last few hours suddenly hit me. "Who are my parents, Petty?" I wail. "What kind of people must they be to take me and not him? How could they have been lying all these years when they never told me I was adopted?"

"Shush." He strokes my hair again, and I wonder whether he knows how much it calms me. "The only way to find out the truth is going to be if you ask them."

"I don't want to see them right now. It's too much to process." Am I really not who I thought I was all these years? Even now I love them and want to protect them and can't believe they've been lying to me. I'm scrambling to find another reason for all this, some explanation that would show Thorne's story was just a ghastly mistake.

Footsteps sound, and still holding me close to him, Petty turns.

"Owl's taken Thorne back to the clubhouse in the truck. Meat's already on his way to get you with the SUV."

As Crash speaks, suddenly I remember all my obligations. "What time is it? I should be on stage." It's only then I notice how dark it's gotten around us. "I've got to call Bart. He's going to be so worried—"

"Taken care of," Crash states. "Red's updated him already.

There's a substitute act gone on in your stead. Honey, even if you could make it on time, you've gone through too much to sing tonight."

I've been kidnapped, had the fact I'm a twin dropped on me, said twin admitting he'd torture me and probably kill me, and now I'm faced with Petty, and my emotions are all in a turmoil over his pronouncement he'd like us to be a thing, and my reciprocal yearning for him. Each of those is a reason for me not being able to give my all to a crowd of strangers tonight.

I hate to let anyone down, but trust Bart to have it covered.

In the distance I hear the sound of a vehicle turning up.

"Come back to the clubhouse." Petty pulls slightly away so he can take hold of my hand.

Shuddering as I remember what happened when I went off on my own, my fingers grasp his as though he's a lifeline. There's no way I want to go home. Seems I always find snakes there.

I thought I'd be safe once Saul was killed, but then Thorne took me instead. I'm starting to wonder whether there's anyone else waiting in the wings. Petty might not want me out of his sight, but unless I'm forced away, I've no desire to leave.

As we walk around the front of the dilapidated building, the SUV pulls up. Watching Petty gingerly pull himself inside, I remember how injured he is, and feel dreadful I've not asked.

"Oh my God, Petty," I start, as I, too, ease myself inside. "How the hell are you even walking around?"

He chuckles softly. "The adrenaline from knowing you were missing helped for a start, as well as the painkillers I've been using." He winks at me. "Let's just say it's safest that I don't drive."

The SUV hits a bump eliciting a swear word from him. I realise now the adrenaline's wearing off, Petty's level for pain tolerance is probably crashing as well.

Meat's obviously heard and takes it as carefully as he can while we continue to the clubhouse. Once we've arrived, Petty looks like a clock that's run down as he exits the car, walking stiffly and holding one arm over his ribs to protect himself.

"I'm going to take you straight to bed," I announce. I can only imagine the pain he's in. Thorne's fist to my face had hurt me enough. Petty's got bruises all over his body.

He snorts and pauses his step. "Bit forward there, babe, aren't you?"

I'd elbow him in the ribs if he wasn't injured. "I don't mean that way."

His pupils darken. "Babe, if you want your wicked way with me, go right ahead."

His voice, his suggestion, make my toes curl, and does unspeakable things to my lady parts. Instead of admitting anything, I laugh.

I've been attracted to Petty from the moment I met him, physically attracted when I knew he was an ass. Now? It's hard for me to resist him. If he wasn't hurting so much, it probably wouldn't take much persuasion to jump into his bed.

"Want a hand, Petty?" Twister yells, seeing him pause at the bottom of the stairs, eyeing the way up as though he was being asked to summit a mountain.

"I'm okay," he snarls, and I'm pretty sure any animosity is toward himself, worried about showing weakness in front of his brothers.

"I can give you a fireman's lift," Titch calls out. I reckon that's probably unlikely. The old man looks like he'd be more likely to fall down.

"Yeah, like that would help." Petty touches his ribs carefully, then leaving his arm there to support him, starts to carefully walk up the stairs.

I hover behind him, though hell knows what I'd do if he were to fall back down. He'd crush me in an instant, but mentally it makes me feel like I'm doing something to help.

He reaches the top step, pausing to breathe heavily, then

continues on, avoiding the room I last saw him in, and stopping with his hand on the door to another.

"Shit," he breathes out. "Fuckin' forgot."

"You can go in, Brother." Twister, who seems to be concerned about him, has followed us up.

With a puzzled look behind, Petty at last opens the door, then almost staggers. I bump into him, having expected him to walk in.

As if reading his mind, Twister explains, "Couple of the boys went to bring your stuff back from the apartment. We kind of guessed you wouldn't want to go back there again." He winks down at me. "And if either of you two are wondering, the girls changed the sheets."

As if he's in a trance, Petty walks to the closet and opens it, touching some of his clothes he sees hanging there. He pulls open a draw and sees his t-shirts laid out.

When he turns, his eyes are glistening. "Can't fuckin' thank you enough."

Twister shrugs off his gratitude. "We misjudged you, Brother. Can't do much to apologise for that, but thought bringing you home would help."

"Sure does," Petty replies, his voice sounding choked. Then a pained sound comes from his mouth which puts me on my toes, wondering what's hurting him most. But it seems it's not physical. He looks down at me, puts his hand on my shoulder, and turns to Twister. "This is me, Brother. You sure you want me in the club? Ain't going back to the Petty you know and hate any longer."

I realise just how much it's taken for him to say that.

Twister, in turn, speaks in a voice that isn't quite even. "Fuck, Bro. You're no coward if that's what you're thinking. You were a man in love. And hell, it's not hard to see what lured you in. You and Britney have one thing in common, you're good fuckin' actors, you let us see what you want us to. I, for one, am looking forward to getting to know the real man who's dropped the act. And you've already proved you're no fuckin' weakling." He holds out his hand, and when Petty takes it, he adds, "I for one am fuckin' glad you're still here." He looks at Petty carefully, then barks a laugh. "Hey, don't cry, fucker."

"Not fuckin' crying," Petty snarls back.

Twister laughs again, and then turns away, saying over his shoulder, "I'll leave you two lovebirds alone."

Lovebirds? I glare after him. "Is that what they think of us?"

Petty turns me back to face him. "Pretty sure they're on the right track, and I don't think there's anything wrong with that." His face twists. "Just fuckin' sorry I can't do anything about it." He stares at me for a moment, then shakes his head as he gets onto a safer subject. "I need a fuckin' shower."

He eyes his bathroom much in the same way as he regarded the stairs, like it's a problem to be overcome.

"I'll help." The decision's easy.

"Not sure the first time I want to get naked in front of you is when I'm black and blue."

"You've nothing to prove to me," I assure him. "Petty, a weak man would have stayed resting in bed, not struggled out with his brothers to rescue me. A weak man wouldn't have cared." I swallow hard and my voice cracks as I realise the magnitude of what he's done, even if he can't see it. "You came for me."

"I'll always fuckin' come," he assures me. "Always, babe. You got me?" Then a sly look comes into his eyes. "As it happens, I might need help in the shower. And you can't do that in clothes."

"Nice one, Petty," I mock complain.

Is there something wrong with me that I can't actually wait to see the man I've been admiring for ages in all his glory? Never mind it might be discoloured right now. If getting him out of his clothes means me getting out of mine, well, that doesn't much bother me.

So I take the plunge, whipping my shirt over my head. His

eyes dilate as they feast on my bra-covered breasts. Then I slide my shorts down, leaving me in my panties.

"No fuckin' fair," he complains. "Not when I can't do anything about it."

"Your turn." Knowing he'll find it hard undressing himself, I take the bottom of his t-shirt in both my hands.

He bends to help and raises his arms as much as he's able to so I can slide it off. I then give him a moment to steady his breathing, only continuing when his fists unclench. I use those seconds to admire his physique. While discoloured, his abs are defined and he's got one of those delicious Vs that makes my mouth water. Unwittingly, I lick my lips as he stares over my head when I reach for the button on his jeans.

Carefully sliding down the zipper, I start to push the denim over his hips, pausing as he hisses in air, then continuing when he gives me a nod.

I go to my knees to remove his boots. He balances by putting a hand on my shoulder, and helps by lifting his feet one at a time, then repeats the actions so I can remove his pants.

He's now in his boxers, and as I watch, what's underneath gives a twitch.

Suddenly, I'm nervous. Not that he'd hurt or take advantage of me, but Petty's become important to me, and like any woman, I'm worried about being found wanting. Though the evidence is growing in front of me that he likes what he sees, I'm reluctant to expose everything.

I'm not like Britney. Some men like curves, and I'm almost as muscular as him. My boobs aren't large, my stomach is firm, and my ass isn't the handful you so often read that men prefer.

Businesslike, I leave him and go to the bathroom, then take a second to work out how the shower works before turning it on.

"You've got to get naked before we get in." His voice right behind me makes me jump.

I can't help my hesitant response. "What if you don't like what you see?"

He snorts. "Babe, you've got to be fuckin' kidding me." He moves in front of me and his hands expertly unclasp my bra. As the garment drops to the floor, the hiss through his teeth is not from pain this time. It's clear that he likes what he sees. He slowly slides his fingers over the front of my panties, the touch making my stomach muscles clench. "You've got to remove these for me. If I get to my knees, I don't think I'm going to be getting up anytime soon."

I'm slightly breathless when I respond. "Only if you remove yours too."

"Together?" He grins, and places his thumbs in the elastic.

Quickly, before I have second thoughts, I whip off my panties, and help him by pushing his boxers down. He leans against the wall and kicks them off his feet. His now fully erect cock bobs up as if to greet me.

When he sees my eyes fixed on that particular part of him, he looks down himself, and palms his dick. "Thank Christ it's working. After what Britney did to me, I wasn't sure it would ever rise to the occasion again."

Suddenly the door to his room bursts open. I squeal.

"Oh God. My eyes!" At the open bathroom door stands Roller with his hand covering his face. "I brought your painkillers, but I think you've got a much better anaesthetic in front of you."

"Get out of here, Roller," Petty growls.

To my horror, Roller's peeking through splayed fingers. "Must say you've upgraded. I much prefer this model."

"Get the fuck out!" the man naked in front of me roars.

Roller chuckles and takes a step back. He holds something out alongside the pain bottle. "Just thought you might like to have this, Bro. Kind of makes what you're about to do legal."

"What the fuck?" While I'm standing with one hand over my groin and the other arm over my breasts, Petty steps forward without a care that his dick is swinging in the wind. He reaches for the papers Roller is holding out, and reads them for a second. "How the fuck?"

Roller taps his nose. "Ain't gonna give away my methods of persuasion, Bro. But just accept Britney realises your marriage is over." He peers around Petty who's blocking his view of me, and winks broadly, and chuckles. "Okay, then. As you were." He swiftly moves to the door, and pauses. "If I were you, I'd lock it after me. Honestly, Brother, we thought you'd be lying flat out and groaning." He slaps his hand over his mouth. "But you haven't got that far—"

"Get out!" Petty again roars, his voice rattling the rafters.

The door slams. I run past Petty and lock it myself.

"I'm divorced," Petty says disbelievingly, a wide grin appearing. "Fuckin' divorced. Or will be, when I file these papers."

"So I won't be encouraging you to commit adultery." I smile at him.

"Babe, I think you could encourage me to do anything."

I raise an eyebrow. "Like get in the shower before the water runs cold?"

CHAPTER THIRTY-TWO

Petty

"**M**ustn't waste water." I smirk, fully on board with what RoseLyn's suggesting. While my initial thought had only been to get clean, I'm now determined to make the most of the situation. While she's helping me, I'll get my hands on her amazing body.

I just wish I could do more than look. My dick, which thankfully Brit hadn't put permanently out of action, is clearly ignoring that the rest of me has the flexibility of a hundred-year-old man, or probably less at this moment.

My heart though, well that feels lighter as a huge weight's been lifted off me. Britney will never be a part of my life again. *Unless she's pregnant.* But I put aside that little voice that has the ability to make my dick deflate by bringing back the memories of how she might have got that way.

For now, I've got to concentrate on the lithe woman in front of me.

When we get into the shower, for a moment, we just stand under the spray, me letting the warm water massage my sore body. It's awkward as fuck. It's far from the first time I've been naked with a woman, but normally there's been some foreplay first.

I want to touch her. I want my hands on her small, but perfectly formed breasts. I want to wrap my lips around her pert nipples. But while my cock is waving the flag, my sore ribs won't allow me to follow through on any promise.

"Turn around," RoseLyn says softly, having put a good portion of soap on her hands. I do, leaning my forearms against the shower wall. As she strokes the lather gently across my bruised back, over my buttocks, and down my legs, I can't help the hiss coming out of my mouth. Fuck, but that feels so good. Arousal is warring with pain within me. *If she starts washing my front, I might not be able to control myself…*

When she stands after washing my feet, I swing around and take the soap in my hands. Squirting out a generous portion, I warn her, "My turn."

As she starts to give me her back, I pull her toward me, and with her spine gently resting against my ribs, I enjoy her breasts by pure feel. They fit perfectly into my hands, making me realise I don't need larger. And that gasp she makes when I toy with her nipples? Pure magic to my ears.

Her skin is smooth and silky, and I can't prevent my fingers moving lower, exploring her stomach, and then drifting further down.

I have a moment of indecision, wondering whether she'll stop me, but she gently pushes her ass against my erect dick, letting me know she's not complaining about the liberties I'm taking.

"Petty," she gasps, when my finger brushes over her clit. And then she repeats my name as my fingers separate her labia and I broach her entrance with a finger.

She writhes against me, stilling when I take in a sharp breath. "Sorry." But when she goes to move away, I clamp her to me.

I can always take the painkillers Roller brought up for me during his rather indiscreet entrance. Right now, I want nothing more than to feel RoseLyn let go while I'm holding her in my arms, any penance I'll happily pay later. The only thing better would be if my cock were inside her, but that would put too much strain on my ribs.

"Petty," she moans as I start making lazy circles around her clit, while pushing two fingers inside her.

I start curling them around and yeah, that's it. I find that special spot and she starts tensing.

"Petty!" My name on her lips emerges as a scream, as her whole body tightens and she convulses against me.

I bite back my exclamation of pain and try to concentrate on the pleasure she's taking.

Fuck. Had I ever had a genuine response from Britney? RoseLyn gives herself over to the sensation completely. When she slumps against me, I give her a moment, and then allow her to turn and face me. Her hands come to my cheeks and she draws my head down, and then our lips meet.

Neither of us care about the slight pain from our injuries. She takes control, her tongue sweeping inside. But this is no sign of dominance, it's the merging of equals. Our kiss goes on, getting more urgent, and my hips move against her as my cock seeks relief. Just when I think I can stand no more before saying *fuck it*, and getting my dick inside her even if it's going to cause me permanent injury, she pulls away.

Leaving a line of kisses down my chest, she sinks to her knees.

She's going to blow my fucking mind if she puts those lips around me. *I'm going to die if she doesn't.* I lean my head back against the wall of the shower, hoping and praying that she's going to put her mouth where I want it.

And it's my lucky day as I'm not disappointed. First she grasps my dick in her hands, and I have a moment thinking if that's as far as she's going to take it, it will be more than sufficient and I wouldn't last long, when, *fuck me*, she engulfs me in the warmth of her mouth, expertly hollowing her cheeks as she sucks me in.

I've had whores aplenty suck me off, women who've

perfected their skills, but RoseLyn's experimentation is fast undoing me.

Hell, I've got the woman I've been fantasising about on her knees in front of me. What man could blame me for not lasting long? Familiar tingles start to make their way down my spine and my balls grow heavy.

"I'm going to come," I cry out to warn her.

But she stays where she is, and when I blow, she takes every damn drop that I give her. I'm drained dry when the pulses fade, and my fucking legs feel like they're going to give way. I breathe in deep in post-orgasmic pleasure, only to buckle as I'd forgotten the state of my ribs, and that I really must breathe shallowly.

"Oh fuck," I exclaim.

She realises what's wrong immediately, turning off the shower and placing a towel around me. I should feel emasculated as she dries me off and leads me to the bed where I collapse on the sheets. But because it's her, because she's staring at me with such soft emotion on her face, I realise she's getting pleasure from caring for me. Britney would have jumped on any sign of weakness and mocked me.

There's no way in which these two women are the same.

I watch avidly as she dries herself, then, when she comes to the bed naked and aligns her body with mine, I manage to get my arm around her and draw her into me.

"You used to intimidate me," I admit.

"Me?" She snorts.

"Britney did a real number on me." I nuzzle my lips against her neck. "I saw you, an independent woman, and it scared the fuck out of me. I thought you were the type to take a man's balls, and carry them in your purse."

"Ew." She chuckles. "I assure you I don't want to emasculate you and carry that particular part around." Before I have the chance to laugh, her voice becomes serious. "I know Britney fucked you up, but she's one of a kind. Oh, I know there are others like her, and men, like you, who stay silent because they think because they're a man, they can't be abused." She pauses. "What's going to happen to her? And to Elton and Thorne?"

I roll onto my back, ignoring the question of my soon-to-be ex-wife, as I really have no idea what I'd be able to do. Even though she hurt me, and tried to get me kicked out of the club, ignoring the possibility she could've gotten me killed, the thought of hurting her makes my stomach roil. So I turn the tables. "What about Thorne?"

If my intention had been to switch off our post-orgasmic glow, I'd done so by bringing that fucker into our bed.

She's quiet for a while, considering the issue for herself, and it's a few minutes before she imparts, "I want to know the truth. And for that I've got to speak to my parents. Even the thought I'm adopted means they've been lying to me all my life." Her hand comes into mine, holding tight as though she needs an anchor. "I don't know who I am anymore."

"You feel anything for Thorne?"

She huffs. "I can't believe I've got a twin. Surely there should be some connection between us? Don't studies show twins who are raised apart go on to live similar lives?"

While that of hers and that prick couldn't be further apart. She's made something of herself, while he let his resentment fester. Then, she had the benefit of a loving family to support her, which, by all accounts, is very far from what he had.

When she yawns, I remember the fuckup of the day that she's had, all the information piled upon her, along with the fear of being kidnapped. I tense as I recall the horror that I'd felt when I heard she'd been taken, and thank whatever deity exists that somehow she's been brought back to me. Having pulled my head out of my ass, I now have her in my arms. Arms, which, if I have my way, will hold her forever.

There's a fuckload of deep things we need to talk about, but now's not the time. She needs to recuperate mentally, and fuck knows I've stretched my body beyond tolerance today.

"Petty…"

"Shush," I admonish her. "Try to sleep, darlin'."

"Can I just ask one thing? Would you like me to call you Clark?"

The idea makes me recoil inwardly. "I was Clark to Britney."

She squeezes my hand, letting me know she understands. Then, as she turns and lays her head on my chest, I start to stroke her hair rhythmically, and gradually her breathing evens out. Before too long, she's sleeping.

It's not unexpected when a nightmare wakes her up in the small hours. To be honest, she'd woken me from one of my own. But I hold her as tight as she holds me, and we allow sleep to again take us under.

Sometime early in the morning, I fall into a deep sleep, only to be woken by a banging on the door.

Glancing at my phone, I see it's only just gone on seven. *What the fuck?* "Go the fuck away," I call out.

"Petty, get your ass up. There's someone here to see Rose-Lyn." Owl, the prospect, yells.

At this time in the morning? But the noise has woken the woman at my side. "Who is it?"

I'm no clairvoyant, and won't know until I ask. "Who the fuck is it, Owl?" I shout.

"It's her parents. They flew in on the red-eye."

"My parents?" RoseLyn's eyes open wide and she leaps up. Probably too fast as she sways, then puts her hand to her head and pauses a second. She recovers fast. "I'll be there as soon as I'm dressed."

While she's speaking, she's already picking through the clothes on the floor, picking up her panties she discarded last night, and wrinkling her nose in disgust.

"Can't help with those," I say, pulling myself up, more slowly than her and favouring my ribs. "But I can lend you a tee and some sweats."

"A tee would be great, but these will have to do." She pulls her jeans on as I ignore the protestations of muscles which have stiffened during the night, and go to one of my drawers. I pull out a Satan's Devils' tee, knowing I'll love seeing her wear an emblem of my club.

She hesitates for just a moment. "I should really have a shower."

"Where's my daughter?" a loud voice shouts.

Rolling her eyes, RoseLyn pulls the shirt on. Not wanting her to face her parents alone, I slowly get dressed. I'm just about finished when RoseLyn's tamed her hair. A fleeting thought crosses my mind. At least I won't have to pretend I'm her boyfriend. I'm that for real. Although I've stated I want her as my old lady and we haven't had that discussion about how long term will work for us, I know I don't want to see her walk out of my life and will do everything I can to prevent it.

"Ready?" I hold out my hand, and she takes it.

But when I go to move forward, she holds back. "I don't know what to say to them." She glances up, and I don't think I've ever seen her so unsure.

Her parents have been lying to her all her life. She wasn't born to her mother. Though blood doesn't matter, the perpetuation of a lie does, and I can understand how hard it is for her to accept it. She'll have to re-evaluate everything she's ever known as truth, and that's leaving aside that her parents had apparently chosen her, and callously left her twin behind.

One way or another, whatever happens today is assured to change their relationship.

Even as the harried voice shouts again, and the slamming of doors tells me we're not the only ones to have been woken, I turn her around to face me.

"RoseLyn, I know we've had no time to talk about this, and I know I've given you no real reason to trust me. But I know in here," I thump my heart, "how important you are to me. You've got me. Whatever happens in the world outside this door, I'll be there for you." *Just as you were for me*, I silently add.

Her eyes stare into mine as though trying to read my sincerity, then she tightens her fingers against my hand and takes a step forward. "Nothing will be made better by waiting," she says.

The sound of voices arguing downstairs reaches my ears as we move to the staircase. Still holding her hand, I use my other to grip the bannister so I can navigate the steps carefully.

As soon as we start to descend, a shrill voice cries, "Rose." Martina comes running forward, quickly followed by Rufus. "Rose, are you alright?" Her mother's eyes are peering at her closely, seeming to study the way that she moves in case someone's hurt her.

Rose comes to a halt. Though the room is filling with men roused from their beds, she seems oblivious to anyone other than her parents being in the room. Apparently she's reluctant to take one step toward them before asking the burning question that trumps even the one about why they're here this early.

In a quavering voice, she bursts out, "Am I adopted?"

CHAPTER THIRTY-THREE

Petty

Perhaps her outright approach was the best one. It certainly knocks them off the offensive. While Rufus stammers out a denial, Martina's hand goes to her mouth, and she lets one too many seconds pass before she cries, "What on earth would make you ask such a thing?"

RoseLyn's fingers curl around mine so tightly they almost cut off the blood supply, but I make no protest or sound.

"I think we should take this to my office." I hadn't notice Red was around, but he seems to have been woken by the commotion like everyone else.

It's a good suggestion. I know RoseLyn would prefer to wash this particularly dirty linen in relative privacy.

While Rufus looks at Red as if wondering who he is, Red's obvious authority cuts through, and he automatically follows in the direction that's been pointed out. Once inside, I see him eye the large Satan's Devils flag hanging behind Prez's desk with more than a touch of unease. I don't blame him. At first glance, the large rendition of the grim reaper looming over three demons with red glowing eyes can be intimidating. Not for the first time, I read it as an interpretation of Red ruling over his tribe of Devils, all willing to do his bidding.

Red barks for a prospect to bring in another chair. That makes four in total in front of the desk. I hide my smile, no one, except him, would dare sit behind it.

"I'll leave you to it." Prez begins to back out of the door.

"Stay." I find the word coming out of my mouth. I'm not quite sure why I want him here. Some things are going to be said in here that some of us might come to regret, but he makes a good arbitrator.

"RoseLyn?" Red defers to her, instead of her parents.

I see by Rufus's glare that he'd rather not have an audience for what's about to be said, but RoseLyn seems relieved that I asked. "Please, Red."

He shrugs and takes his chair, leaning his elbows on the desk and sitting forward. Now he's staying, he seems determined to be an active participant.

Rufus is equally set on taking the initiative. "I want to know what you're doing with an outlaw gang," he starts, his cheeks glowing red. "Why the hell did Bart send me here to find you? And you, sir, why are you wearing a cut with that same damn image on it?" His eyes flick to the oversized insignia behind Red.

Red, as I expected and welcome, takes charge. "First, we're a club, not a gang. And I'd prefer you to leave your misconceptions aside until you get to know us, with particular reference to our part in RoseLyn's life." He does that prez stare that he's perfected, and surprisingly, Rufus stays quiet.

Martina, sitting alongside RoseLyn, reaches out her hand and touches hers. "Honey, you had us so worried. When we couldn't contact you, and Bart was being evasive, we came to Vegas…"

RoseLyn pulls her hand away. "I didn't want to worry my *parents*," she starts with a sneer on her emphasis. Red catches her eye and raises his chin slightly, a gesture she correctly interprets. She sighs and joins her hands in her lap. "I've been having trouble for months. When Saul got out of jail, he made it his mission to make my life a misery. He stalked me, left notes, then escalated his threats." As her mom gasps, RoseLyn continues her soliloquy, "He wanted me back, and obviously I wasn't going near him. So, he decided if he couldn't have me, no one else would. He…" her voice catches, "he, well it looked like he was trying to kill me. Bart decided I needed protection, so employed security for me."

"You should have come home immediately." While she's been talking, Rufus's eyes have widened. "Why the hell are we only just hearing about this? You say it's been going on for months?" he snaps.

"Because that's what you'd have done. Called me home," RoseLyn explains. Her eyes, opposite to his, become slits. "He could have gotten to me just as easily in Texas. I'm a grown woman. I made the decision to handle this myself, and not cause my *parents*," there's that sneering emphasis again, "worry."

"And where does he…" Rufus points my way, all his previous geniality toward me missing from his voice, "come in?"

Red steps in, as though seeing RoseLyn's floundering. "The Satan's Devils run a security business. Her manager approached us to provide bodyguards for her."

"I can imagine what your security service is. Isn't it normally called a protection racket?"

Red snorts, his eyes flare, but that's the only outward sign he's taken umbrage. "Quite the opposite, in fact. I'd be grateful if you could suspend your suspicions and hear the facts."

"Dad, they run a casino. They're legit," RoseLyn cries out. Her gaze flicks to me and then to Red as if shocked at her father's disrespect. "You don't get to judge them."

"And you?" Rufus turns on me. "You're part of this crew. You really her boyfriend?"

I clear my throat and prepare to face up to my confession. "Not when we were in Texas. I was there as her bodyguard, but since—"

Rufus's hands clench as he interrupts, "You're a legit business?" He snorts. "Legit bodyguards don't sleep with their clients."

"It's not like that, Dad." RoseLyn sits forward and faces her father. "Red's men needed me out of the way so they could draw Saul out. Petty—Clark—came with me so I was still protected. We thought introducing him as my boyfriend would explain his presence best. We were pretending. We didn't have sex."

"I put you in the same bed." Martina looks horrified.

"Told you they were fucking," Rufus says disgustedly, then glances at Red as if to ask him how to explain that.

"We weren't." RoseLyn shakes her long hair over her shoulder. "Not then. But being away did help us get close." She leans away from her mother and into me. "There's been a lot of things to sort through, but yeah, now we are together. And," she throws a glare at her father, "believe it or not, as you so delicately put it, we haven't yet fucked."

I hide my grin. She's splitting hairs. We've come close, but no cigar as yet due to my injuries caused by my wife. I don't think Rufus would appreciate that explanation, so I keep my mouth shut.

Martina shifts awkwardly, obviously uncomfortable with the words for the sex act that her husband and daughter are using, but Rufus is all glares. He examines RoseLyn's face carefully, as though trying to catch her out in a lie. She holds her head up and returns his stare steadily.

After a moment, he turns his attention to Red. "And did the ruse work? Did you get Saul?"

Red lets no emotion show as he raises his chin. "We did."

"And has he been arrested?"

"He's been dealt with," Red states. "You won't need to worry about him anymore."

"He dead?" Rufus's expression manages to convey his disgust at the option.

"He tried to kill me, Dad," RoseLyn reminds him. "He got out of prison once before and immediately came after me."

"So I'm right?" he addresses his daughter.

RoseLyn, showing how good an old lady she'll make if she

has me, shakes her head. "Red says he won't be coming after me again. I don't need to know more than that."

"You'd condone killing?" Martina asks, having remained silent for a while.

"You'd like to see me dead?" RoseLyn challenges, then uses her mother's question as a launching board to address the subject that's burning at her. "Well, what do I know how you think? You're not even my real mother."

Martina's hand covers her mouth, and Rufus takes her other and holds it tightly. It's him who answers. "She's been a mom to you all your life. We've given you everything, Rose, how could you ever doubt that?"

"But she's not my mom, and you're not my dad."

Red leans back and folds his arms. He drawls lazily, "The problem with secrets is that they have a habit of coming out. RoseLyn knows the truth." He states that so they know they have no room to argue. "It was easy enough to find out. You're just lucky RoseLyn never thought to ask or have a reason to investigate earlier. And unlucky you never told her the truth."

"You're my child." Martina's eyes brim with tears, realising Red's right and there's no point denying it. "I didn't give birth to you, but I held you before you were a day old. You've never been anyone else's, only ours."

"We couldn't have loved you more if your mom had birthed you," Rufus states, his voice not as firm as it was before. "You can't hold this against us, Rose."

RoseLyn leans further into me, and I put my arm around her, ignoring that her position means she's putting pressure on my sore ribs.

"If it was just that I was adopted, I'd be stunned, but wouldn't think the worst of you. But..." Words seem to fail her.

I speak for the first time in ages. "We couldn't figure out how Saul kept managing to find her. It seemed likely that he had help from someone, and it turned out he did. From a cop. Long story short, while it wasn't the cop who was actively harming her, it was another man acting out of unrequited love, and the over-whelming desire for revenge."

"Revenge?" Rufus looks confused. "Hold up a bit. You're losing me here. Saul…" he shakes his head. "I always thought he was a decent sort, but realised he was capable of anything once he put my daughter in the hospital. It's a stretch, but maybe I can accept he was obsessed and wouldn't move on. But who are these other people? A cop who was giving Saul information and another man… I'm lost. Who was he, and what did he want with her?"

"Saul was as much of a pawn as RoseLyn," Red butts in, and I give him a grateful nod. "Saul was an instrument." Prez brushes his hand over his beard. "Could be Saul just wanted RoseLyn to go back to him, but another seed got planted in his head, maybe about how much she'd wronged him. He was used by the other side to this triangle. A man who was out for vengeance."

"Why should anyone else want revenge against Rose?" Deep creases appear on Rufus's forehead. "What have you gotten yourself into, baby?"

"He didn't want revenge against her, well, not entirely." It's me who tells him, "He wanted to hurt you, for what you did, or maybe more accurately, didn't do, for him."

Rufus stands and leans his hands on the table. "Will you start making some sense?" He looks at me, then Red. "We've never caused harm to anyone."

"But you did," RoseLyn says, deceptively calm, and it's only because I can feel her hand shaking that I know she's not as steady as she's trying to portray. "Mom, why did you take me and leave my twin? You could have raised us together. Instead, he was left to suffer a life of abuse. And the other difference?" she huffs, "was that he knew the people who raised him weren't related by blood."

Rufus looks mystified. Martina looks to him for guidance, but he appears stumped for words, so it's her who answers. Her back seems to straighten. "Honey, you have no twin." She holds up her hand as RoseLyn goes to refute her. "We couldn't have kids of our own, and were getting on in years. We tried to adopt, knowing we had so much love to give to a child, but kept missing out. Your dad," knowing by the look on RoseLyn's face that this is no time to use that title, she corrects with a distasteful grimace, "Rufus found we could get a baby if we paid."

"So my adoption wasn't even legal." RoseLyn rolls her eyes.

Martina's face hardens. "Oh, it was legal. All the paperwork is there. But it was a private arrangement. We knew the reasons your birth mother couldn't keep you. She didn't want a baby in her life, and had… problems."

"We met your birth mother before the birth." Rufus removes his hands from the desk and straightens, his eyes glazing slightly as though remembering back. "She was in a dire situation. She'd had problems with drugs, and couldn't afford prenatal care. She didn't even know what sex she was having, but we didn't care. There was a man there handling the adoption. We'd pay for you, and the birth mother would get some of the payment, enough to get her life straightened out." Red snorts loudly, but Rufus continues, "I don't know where this idea of a twin comes from. We saw you shortly after you were born, but you needed some care due to your mother's addiction and were whisked straight away to get postnatal care."

"I was worried out of my mind," Martina takes over. "I spent all my time in the nursery."

Rufus grimaces. "There was another baby there, a boy. He was apparently born around the same time as RoseLyn, but he was much smaller. Like Rose, his mom had had a drug problem. He was weak and jaundiced, and they weren't even sure he'd make it."

"The same man was handling his adoption," Martina says, her eyes glazing as though thinking back. "I remember asking about him. He said, if he lived, he was wanted by a good family.

I was worried as it looked like he might have problems throughout his life.

"You were everything to me, Rose. Right from the beginning." Her voice drops to a whisper. "If I had birthed you myself, I couldn't have had more love for you. You were mine from that moment."

RoseLyn doesn't seem convinced by the story. "So why is Thorne so convinced he's my twin?"

"I have no idea," Martina replies.

Red draws his hands over his face. "Another way for his adoptive parents to taunt him, perhaps?"

Rufus sits down, his ass meeting the chair with a heavy thump. "And he's resented Rose all his life because he thinks he should have been living her life?"

"He resents you more," Red states. "For not adopting him, and leaving him to suffer a lifetime of abuse." He raises his hand. "For the record, there was no other mother. Thorne was Rose's twin."

There's silence, and it's broken by Martina. "Oh my," she wails, and starts openly crying now. "If I'd known—"

"You didn't know," Rufus interrupts her. "And neither did I. It's too late to know what we would have done. We were hard pushed pulling together the money for one baby, let alone two."

"I couldn't have left him." Martina grabs Rose's hand. "You've got to believe me. I never knew."

CHAPTER THIRTY-FOUR

RoseLyn

It's a hell of a lot for me to process. My parents, no, or perhaps as I should be calling them, Martina and Rufus Blakeney, have been lying to me all my life, or at least, not telling me the truth and letting me believe I was a blood relative. They'd emphasised the similarities between me and my mom, perhaps to give credence to their story.

I've had a good life. There's nothing I could regret about my childhood. But it still doesn't stop me being hurt. Maybe I wouldn't want to trace my birth mother if she was, as they said, a junkie who basically sold her baby for her next fix. She might not even be alive. The odds are probably against it. But I should have been given the choice. It should have been for me to decide whether I might want to search for other family.

I do believe they didn't know about me having a twin, but maybe I'd have found him if I'd gone looking. But then, at the age of eighteen, the damage would probably have been done. It could have already been too late to fix him.

They bought me. More than that, they picked me, like some piece of furniture they'd chosen from a store.

I wonder what it would have been like if they hadn't been the ones to adopt me. With no checks and the adoption arranged without the blessing of social services, I could have ended up in a family like Thorne's. I shudder. I'd had a lucky escape. Although I don't like him, it doesn't stop my heart going out to Thorne, and while there are no excuses for his behaviour, his jealously is understandable. Then again, maybe it is a kind of justification for the way he treated me. I know the statistics. A child brought up in an abusive house is more likely to turn out abusive themselves.

Red seems to be giving me a moment as he takes over the conversation. "You've met Thorne." His gaze goes first to Martina, and then to Rufus who look shocked. "He came to your house. He wore a disguise, thinking you might see the resemblance if you met him. He does look uncannily like RoseLyn." Red's eyes stare at them, but they look more incredulous than awkward at being caught out in the truth.

"I hear what you say, but I still don't believe you. We'd have known if they were twins." My dad, Rufus, looks down his nose at his hands. "Surely we would have realised? Any resemblance has to be coincidental," he states. "Someone's sold the kid a pack of lies." He thinks and then latches on to the important part. "What do you mean, he came to our house?"

Petty goes to speak but Red stops him with a raise of a hand. "We've got the records from the clinic. There's no doubt there were twins, and that there was only one woman who gave birth." He drills them with his piercing gaze. "I don't attach any blame to you for not knowing, but the facts stand as they are."

"He came to our house?" Martina seems to be fixated on that part. "Why didn't he say anything? And why was he there? When?"

This time Petty is allowed to speak. "The pastor you found so endearing," he retorts, and even upset as I am, I hear the sting in his voice, and link it to their statement that Mom, at least, had liked him for me. "That was when you met Thorne."

"But why?" Mom cries. "Why would he come to us?"

Again, it's Petty who answers. "He was interested in Rose-

Lyn's life. Unfortunately, you confirmed she'd been brought up in a loving, decent home. She got to live in comfort, surrounded by love, while he was brought up knowing nothing but physical and sexual abuse."

A sideways glance at the woman who I've called Mom all my life shows that she's sobbing. Guilt? Or just compassion for an unknown child? When her hand shoots out and grabs mine, holding it so tight I can't pull it away, I turn and meet her glistening eyes.

"That could have been you, Rose." Her voice falters, and she's openly crying now.

Petty's arm tightens around me, showing he's thinking the unthinkable too.

But it's Rufus who surprises me, and perhaps re-earns the title of Dad. "What can we do now? Not saying there's anything to make up for, we weren't to know. But if there's some way of showing this boy, man, some love and affection that he surely deserves, maybe it's not too late to bring him into the fold."

"I'm afraid it is." Red moves his head slowly side to side. "I think he's far too gone for redemption. Inviting him into your family will be like inviting a snake into your house." He grimaces when he sees my shudder. "I wouldn't trust him. He might say the right words, but what if the cuckoo decides there's only room for one chick in the house?"

I wouldn't put it past Thorne to make sure of it. I hate to say I agree with the Satan's Devils' prez, but I do.

"Perhaps we could speak to him?" Mom seems to have picked up on Dad's idea. "Explain we had no idea?" But then they're innocent in the horrors of life.

Petty and Red seem to have one of their manly conversations which don't include words.

It's left to me to answer. "I don't think that's a good idea. He's not exactly stable." Maybe he hadn't been from the damage done by the drugs his birth mom had taken. Maybe his lifestyle had only made whatever was already there worse. "His mind's twisted with bitterness and resentment. He's as likely to question why you abandoned a sickly child anyway, and just took the healthy one." I give a little shake of my head when she goes to argue. "Anything you say is likely to be twisted to fit the narrative in his head."

"You've spoken to him?"

"He kidnapped me, remember?" They seem to have glossed over that. They need to know everything, so I continue to answer my dad. "He wanted to make you suffer and knew hurting me was a way to get to you. His plan was to cut pieces off of me and send them to you."

"What the...?" Dad's on his feet now.

Mom also stands but places a hand on his arm. "Maybe we can get him help?"

"You heard what she said, Martina." Dad's obviously having difficulty processing what Thorne had done.

"Everyone deserves a second chance."

"We did him wrong in the past," Dad states, backing up his wife. "Do you know where he is? We'd like to talk to him."

"He has to be in police custody if he kidnapped our daughter," Mom retorts.

I know, however, that's not the way the Devils roll. Worriedly, I cast a glance at Petty, to see how he's going to handle their erroneous assumption.

But Red stands and beckons Petty to go outside with him. Petty stands awkwardly, bending to lessen the pressure on his ribs, and stiffly follows him outside.

"What's wrong with him?" Mom asks, obviously just noticing for the first time.

I suspect it would go down like a lead balloon if I told them his wife had beaten him. That she's a soon-to-be ex probably wouldn't sweeten the deal. So I shrug as if I don't know, or can't be bothered to answer.

It's only a minute later that Red re-enters. "Rufus," he starts. "If you want to meet Thorne, I'll give you that chance. But I don't think it's a good idea for your wife to be present. And I'll be in control of the situation." He pointedly looks at me, making me shiver as I recall what happened to Saul.

Mom starts to bristle, but Dad seems to grow in stature. "He's here?" At Red's confirmatory rise and dip of his head, he turns to Mom. "Let me go check it out first."

First and last if I have any say in the matter. There's no way Mom's going to be confronted with the man who wanted to take his revenge on her. I don't think he's going to believe their story for a start. Maybe it's because I've a vested interest, but on my part, I believe them. It doesn't absolve them from the crime of keeping it a secret that I was adopted all this time. I should have known, should have been eased into the situation, but at least they didn't compound that by knowingly leaving my twin behind.

I might be a grown woman but knowing I'm not who I thought I was has unsettled me.

When Red beckons Dad to follow him, I stand.

"You stay here, RoseLyn."

"I'm coming." I glare forcefully at Red, letting him know I'm not going to be moved. I am concerned about Dad, and whether his weak heart will stand what he sees in the basement. I know Thorne's demeanour had shocked me, and once faced with who he sees as his number one enemy, who knows what bile and hatred will spill from his mouth?

Red stares at me, but even his glacial look doesn't have me backing down. With a shake of his head and a quick grin, he states, "Let me see if Cher's around. She can keep your mom company."

He taps at his phone, and only seconds later, his wife pops her head in. We leave the two women introducing themselves, but Mom shoots a worried glance after me.

I had wondered where Petty had gotten to, but it all becomes clear as we descend into the basement. Instead of being strung up as Saul had been, both Elton and Thorne are sitting on chairs, their hands cuffed behind them. Cobra and Hammer are standing guard, while Petty's leaning against a wall for support. His pained expression shows me he's in dire need of a top up of painkillers.

"What the hell kind of place is this?" Dad blusters as he reaches the bottom of the stairs. I'm only glad they seem to have tidied up and there are no instruments of torture in sight. There is a curtained-off area, where I suspect they've been hidden. "Who are these men?"

Red lazily waves his hand toward the one on the right. "This is Elton. He's a crooked cop who was feeding information to your daughter's stalker, and to Thorne, who you can see seated to his left."

"I'm a cop," Elton says, eyeing myself and my dad, as if hoping to see some compassion. He puffs up his chest. "You people could get into trouble if you don't release me now."

Red chuckles. "And with the information we've got on your crooked practices, we could end your career for good. I'd be careful about making threats if I were you."

Elton's mouth snaps shut.

Dad doesn't seem to have any sympathy for him. "You were giving Saul information so he could stalk and hurt my daughter?" His question is answered when Elton looks to one side, his guilt apparent without any need for him to open his mouth.

But surprisingly he has second thoughts and starts to speak. "I was doing it for him, not for Saul." He jerks his head toward the man at his side. "I thought I was helping Thorne find his sister. I wouldn't have done fuck for Saul."

"See?" Petty comments from his position where I'm certain he's using the wall to help keep him upright. "It's a bit complicated. Elton here is in love with Thorne, while Thorne was in love with Saul. One-sided, unfortunately, Saul was straight. But he wasn't beyond using Thorne and his connections to get what he wanted."

Dad looks bemused. He takes a step that places him in front

of Thorne. "I've been informed you've been acting on some misunderstandings, son. My wife and I had no idea that you were Rose's brother when you were born. We were led to believe otherwise."

Thorne spits on the ground. "Of course you'd say that."

"It's probably hard for you to believe me, but neither my wife nor I would have separated twins."

"You're lying." Thorne scoffs.

"Thorne?" Elton addresses him directly. "You've found her now. It's not too late for you to have a relationship with your sister, even if you can't forgive her parents, or believe what they're telling you."

It's then I realise he truly thought he was helping his lover right a wrong. I hope the Devils show mercy on him, and from the slight shift in Red's stance, think that he has come to the same conclusion.

"I don't need no fuckin' relationship with my sister. She deserves to experience the life that I've known." He stamps his feet so hard the chair rocks back. "She's been living my life. She fuckin' stole it. She deserves to die for that, or better still, become someone's sex slave." He grins evilly at that thought, then his face reddens again. "And as for what she did to Saul—"

"Saul got sent down for assault," Elton says calmly, "You know this."

"Little Miss Perfect set him up." Thorne isn't having any of it. "It's all her fault. Everything is her fault, including being fuckin' born first else I'd have had her life. Just get me out of here and I'll fuckin' kill her."

My dad is standing wide-eyed while Elton's paled. "You told me you just wanted to befriend her. That she was your sister who you wanted to get to know. You were trying to find the best way to approach her. You lied to me. I knew you were still chasing Saul, but knew he'd never look twice at you." The cop's eyes glisten. "But I didn't know you were plotting with him to hurt RoseLyn. I'd never have helped you."

"You stupid ugly fuck. You think I'd have let you touch me if I hadn't wanted something from you?" Thorne looks at the cop in disgust. "I nearly vomited every time we had sex."

Elton, if possible, has lost even more colour from his face. "I risked my career for you."

"Your career?" Thorne sneers. "You can't even do that right. You didn't see what I was doing right under your fuckin' nose. You were just so pleased to have a dick in your ass that you didn't look further. You're so fuckin' weak."

Elton hangs his head, and I hear a choked sob.

"What did you do for him?" Red steps up to Elton, and raises his chin with his hand. The cop's eyes are brimming with tears, a few escaping down his cheeks. "I need you to tell me, Elton. Did you use the police databases to find information on RoseLyn's whereabouts? Used your badge to get into the hired car records?"

Elton nods.

"Words, I need words."

"Yes, yes. I did all that. I thought he was finding his long-lost twin. I…" he breaks off as another sob escapes. "I thought I was helping him."

Red produces his phone and shows it to Elton. "I've recorded this conversation. As far as I'm concerned, you were abusing your position, and if RoseLyn had been harmed, this would have ended very differently. But I'm willing to let you go, as long as you understand that one word out of place, I can ruin your career. And, just promise, next time you need a hole to sink your dick into, you choose more carefully."

Elton turns wide eyes up toward Red. "You're letting me go?" His incredulous gaze turns calculating. "I suppose you're looking for a dirty cop to have on your payroll."

Red snorts. "Not at all. If I want information, I've far better ways of getting it, and better contacts than you have. And as what we do is all legal, we don't need anyone in the law to look the other way."

They killed someone in front of me, but I suspect Red's got confidence he's got everything handled. I wonder if he'd be so lenient if it wasn't for my father bearing witness to what they are doing.

But Elton doesn't believe him. "I'll just be waiting for the hammer to drop."

Red shrugs. "At least you'll still have your job in the meantime."

"Why?" Elton's still not buying it. "Why would you let me go free? With your reputation—"

"What fuckin' reputation?" Red yells. "You got us pinpointed for anything?" He waits for Elton to shake his head, then he puts away his phone and folds his arms. "You were a man taken in by someone who used your emotions against you." His eyes rise and land on Petty for a moment. "You're not the first and won't be the last to be taken in."

Personally, I suspect if there's ever a need, Red won't waste the chance to use what he's got on him. But I'm pleased that he's giving the man another chance. There are similarities between him and what's happened to Petty. Maybe there's a way out for Elton, and like Petty, he'll be more careful next time who he gives his heart to.

"Untie him," Red instructs Hammer.

Within moments, a bemused cop is shaking out his hands, and standing. When Hammer indicates the stairs, he starts to walk, turning his head as if unable to believe he's going to be allowed to go free.

But his progress isn't impeded. As he comes level with my dad, Dad shoots out his hand and grasps his arm. "You could have gotten my daughter killed." His growl is a tone I've never heard from him. "One step out of line, and it won't just be these men gunning for you. I heard your confession, and my word won't be discounted, I assure you."

Elton staggers slightly as he's released, then he takes the stairs two at a time as if all the demons of hell were after him.

"You going to let me go now?" Thorne asks, sneakily. "I mean, I can't help who I am. It's not my fault, I was abused."

"I hope to God setting you free is not in these men's minds," Dad states, sounding bloodthirsty. "You were going to chop up my daughter and send me the pieces. I hope the Devils have plans for you."

"It was all Saul," Thorne says quickly. "Find him and he'll tell you. He encouraged me. He told me what I should do to get revenge on Rose."

"There was nothing to seek vengeance for," Red tells him. "Sure, your life could have worked out differently, but we all have to deal with the cards as they fall."

"Saul egged me on. Talk to Saul." He sounds sly and only a stupid person would be fooled.

"Oh, Saul won't be talking to anyone," Red informs him.

Thorne stills, and looks at the Satan's Devils' prez' face. "What do you mean?" He doesn't sound quite so sure of himself.

Red says nothing.

Thorne's starts to cotton on, and as he does, he begins to tremble. "You killed him?"

Again Red stays quiet so as not to incriminate himself, but Thorne reads the truth in his silence.

"Nooooo!" he wails. "Not Saul. No." He looks at me with a twisted expression on his face, part sadness and part fury. Then he launches himself forward, the chair he's attached to coming with him, and roars, "It's all your fuckin' fault—"

But my dad gets in his way, and Thorne headbutts him instead of me, the sound of the two skulls meeting seeming overloud.

"Dad!" I scream as my father crashes to the floor. He's passed out, or, was knocked out.

Thorne's quickly restrained as I drop to my knees. "Dad, wake up," I implore.

Red drops down beside me. He glances at Petty and demands sharply, "Call for an ambulance." As Petty doesn't delay and takes out his phone, Red gives me a look full of sympathy. "I don't like that grey in his face, RoseLyn. You said he had a weak heart…"

Oh my God. No.

"Daddy," I wail. "Stay with me."

CHAPTER THIRTY-FIVE

Petty

There are no words that can console RoseLyn as her dad is gently carried upstairs to wait for the ambulance. He seems to be getting greyer by the second, and Red's call was confirmed when the medics appear. They, too, diagnose a heart attack and whisk him and her mother off in the ambulance.

RoseLyn, beside herself as all she's done up to now is try to protect her dad from this very circumstance, isn't going to stay behind. So I instruct Owl to take her to the hospital with promises I'll be there as soon as I can.

As I stand watching them leave, I hate letting her go by herself, but Red's indicated we've unfinished business.

If I believed in a god, I'd pray Rufus survives. I might not have known him long, but believe he's one of the good ones. I worry that RoseLyn might never forgive herself if he dies. She might only have recently discovered that she's not related by blood, but that means fuck all in this world where sometimes it's blood who can hurt you the most. Case in point, the fucker we've got in the basement.

"I need to be with her." My fingernails dig into my palm. It's not usual that I'm willing to duck out on club business, but Rose-Lyn's needs trump those of the club, or at least, in this instance.

"And you will be." Red puts his hand on my shoulder. "For now, she's with her mom, and there's nothing you can do, Brother. We'll get you to her as soon as we can, but I think she'd feel better if we bring this chapter to a close before you next see her. Owl will keep us updated with her dad's progress."

I hate thinking of RoseLyn coping with her mom's distress when she's got no one there to support her. I'm her man, whether she accepts it or not, and it's my right to be with her. Yet Red's got a point. Some things are best to be brought to a conclusion sooner rather than later.

Irate that I'm being kept away from my woman, and by the very man who's responsible for putting her father on the brink of death, I growl my response, "Let's get this the fuck over with. Thorne's got to die."

Red chuckles softly, showing he's not going to argue. "Then let's get this show on the road."

Roller appears as if he's my own personal medic. "I got your tablets here." Grimly, his face showing that he can see how much pain I'm in, he passes them to me with a bottle of water.

Hoping the tablets soon start to work their magic, I carefully descend the stairs. In my mind, the events of the last half-hour roll back in my head, and I can still see Rufus's body lying there.

Ignoring my injuries, I launch myself forward, reaching my victim in just a few strides. Placing my hands around his neck, I squeeze and shake him.

"You murdering little thug." His face is going red and he's struggling to breathe, but restrained as he is, there's no way for him to protect himself. But while I'm throttling the life out of him, there's a mad glint in his eyes that shows he's amused.

Hands grasp my biceps and pull me away, the sharp pain in my ribs loosening my grip on Thorne's throat.

"Reckon that death is too quick and easy on him, Brother," Twister rasps into my ear.

Right now I don't care. I just want him dead. Then I can go to my woman.

Thorne's choking and coughing, but he's laughing as well. Twister turns his attention from me to the man in the chair. "What the fuck have you got to laugh about?"

In between chortles, Thorne spits out the words, "I got my revenge. That bastard who left me is dead."

Not yet, or so I hope, but it's touch and go, and no thanks to him. This time it's Red who holds me back.

Thorne's insane eyes settle on me. "And you can't kill me." He looks sly as he adds, "I'm RoseLyn's twin. She'd never forgive you."

"You might be her blood but you're nothing to her." I hate to think anything of his is running through her veins. She's an example of how nurture can win out over nature. RoseLyn hasn't a bad bone in her body, and certainly not his black heart.

A rattling alerts me that Twister is wheeling out his tray of implements that had been tactfully hidden from Rufus.

Red steps forward. "We've got things to do and places to be. Let's move this along. Thorne, you're a rabid animal and deserve to be put down."

Thorne rears back, well as far as he can being so tightly restrained. "You can't!" he screams.

Oh, I think that he'll soon find we can.

"Give me one good reason to spare you." Red raises an eyebrow.

"I'm owed," Thorne yells. "I'm fuckin' owed. RoseLyn had my life, my parents. This is my fuckin' time."

"When the cards fall, it's up to you to make the most of it," Red says evenly. "There were a million different ways to handle this situation. Once you knew you were related to RoseLyn, you could have contacted her, introduced yourself, and maybe even had a relationship with her. Instead, you tried to take everything she's got." He shakes his head. "Your actions weren't those of a sane man, Thorne." He half turns, addressing himself to Twister. "Get it done."

The enforcer's eyes move between Prez, me and finally land

on our captive. He raises his chin as he announces, "Seems we should take a page out of his own book. Thorne was going to deliver RoseLyn to her family in pieces. I say we deliver him to Satan the same way."

And there's the point it's easier to dispose of a body when it's in many parts. I have no problem at all with Twister's plan.

Neither does Red who replies, "Let's start with his hands."

Hammer and Cobra loosen his bindings but keep him firmly secured as Twister places a short plank of wood beneath his arm.

"No. You can't do this. You can't touch me," Thorne shouts, spittle running from his mouth and tears from his eyes as he starts to realise he's lost. "You can't fuckin' do this."

"I don't think I'll bother with fingers, takes too much time," Twister drawls, ignoring the condemned man. "After all, you've got places to be, Petty." Before Thorne can process what Twister's about to do, a small axe appears and his hand is severed from his wrist.

An animal scream rises into the air as well as the smell of shit. But before Thorne stops screaming, his other hand joins the first on the ground.

Blood spurts out, a veritable fountain from the severed arteries, staining the plastic sheeting that's already been laid down.

Knowing I've not got long if I want to add to his pain, and that I certainly do from the torture he put RoseLyn through, I push away from the bench I'd been leaning against, feeling the painkillers kicking in and doing their work, giving me the strength to break his nose with my fist.

Twister steps back and lets me have at him. I let loose on his ribs, and for good measure, sink my fist into his dick.

His screams start to weaken as his lifeblood drains out of him.

When he slumps over and his chest barely moves, I step back, allowing satisfaction to seep through me that both RoseLyn's stalkers have now gone. She's safe. She can go back to normality, well, her new one with me by her side.

"He didn't deserve a quick death," Red murmurs from beside me. "But you've got places to be, Brother. Now you can assure RoseLyn that she doesn't need our professional services anymore." He catches my eye and winks. "You're free to provide all of your personal ones."

"Except for Britney." My brow creases. "Where is she, anyway?"

"Rope and Cuff are keeping her entertained in one of the bedrooms upstairs." He pinches the brow of his nose. "Up to you to decide what you want to do with her. If you want her to go the same way as Thorne, the decision is yours. You deserve some payback, Brother." His hand indicates the state of my body.

My gut roils. I want her out of my life forever, but despite what she's done to me, the lessons ingrained so long ago are keeping me back from seeing her hurt.

There's only one way I can go. "When the papers are filed, I'll be free of her." Unless she's pregnant. But I'll deal with that when, if, it happens.

He looks at me sharply. "Doesn't seem right to let her walk away."

The painkillers are clearing the throbbing from my head, enough for me to get my brain to work. "I may have an idea, Prez."

"Well tell me about it on the way to the hospital." Red gestures toward the stairs.

"You coming with me?" I'd assumed I'd hitch a ride with Meat.

His face screws up. "Feel I failed our client in some ways. RoseLyn wanted her parents kept out of it for the very reason Rufus is now lying in a hospital bed. I'm partly responsible. Perhaps we should never have brought him down to the basement."

"He wanted to see Thorne," I remind him. "And it may not have been Thorne's attack that caused his heart to give out. It was stressful enough, him finding out that his daughter had been in danger, and then discovering she knew she wasn't really theirs."

He raises a brow. "She is, in all that matters."

She is, and I know she'll come to see that in time.

Red grabs the keys to one of the SUVs and opens the passenger door so I can ease myself inside. With every twinge going through me, I think more on the plan I've come up with to deal with Britney. As he drives us to the hospital, I fill him in on the details.

It's got obvious flaws which he's quick to point out. "It's not a permanent answer."

"Nah, but it gives me a few years. By then, hopefully, she'll be sensible enough not to fuck with me again."

Red dips his head. "At least she won't have the benefit of using your marriage against you, as you'll be divorced, that's for sure. I still think it would be better to dispose of her for good."

Grimacing, I admit, "I can't have that on my conscience, Prez. Even if I wasn't the one pulling the trigger."

He shakes his head, but even without the weight of a father's influence, I'm not certain it would be easy for him either. Men are fair game. They fuck up, they end up underground. It goes against the grain for us all to bury a woman, even if they've hurt one of us. And RoseLyn was cut up enough about what happened to Saul. I'll never tell her the details about Thorne, but she'll suspect, and that by itself will be hard for her to deal with. I don't think she'd ever forgive me if Britney, too, met her demise. For her, it will be enough that Brit is gone from our lives.

Red manages to park, then chuckles as I carefully get out. "Want me to get a wheelchair?"

I growl at him and try my best to stand straight without wincing, then pace myself as we steadily approach the door. Red's already texted Owl who's waiting for us, and who leads us up to the floor where those who need critical care are taken. I take that as meaning Rufus is still hanging on, and hope that he stays that way.

In the waiting room, RoseLyn is seated by her mother. It's hard to read anything on their faces as I approach, so I have to ask to get any answers.

"How's he doing?"

Standing, RoseLyn takes my arm and leads me to the quieter corner. Her face twists as she tells me, "It was touch and go in the ambulance. His heart stopped but they managed to get it restarted. They're doing bypass surgery now. If that's successful, the prognosis looks positive."

Red's by my side. "If you need any help with the bills, let me know."

"His insurance should cover most of it, and Red, it wasn't your fault." She grimaces. "If I hadn't gotten myself kidnapped, then he'd never have had the worry that I had gone missing. And," she swallows a sob, "maybe I'd have calmed down before talking about the adoption. If I hadn't given him reason to come here, he'd never have met Thorne."

"Hey, this isn't down to you," I tell, her reading between the lines. "Your dad probably needed the surgery for some time. Anything could have pushed him over, and at least we were fast getting him treatment."

"If you want to blame anyone, blame Saul and Thorne. Hell, blame the Devils as we should have protected you better." Red's eyes narrow at her.

"I ran because I couldn't handle what you did to Saul." She bites her lip. "It was down to me."

"Not you," Red interjects. "We thought the danger ended with Saul. We took our eye off the ball too, sweetheart."

There had been so many clues that there wasn't one schizophrenic person after her, but two different people, and we'd ignored them all. Had we given more thought to it, then even if I wasn't capable, someone would have had eyes on her after she'd left the club.

Would it have been better if she'd never met Thorne and had had the ugly truth of his life laid out for her? The idea that they could easily have lived each other's lives must be disturbing for her.

"I hate Thorne," she spits out. "I hate what he'd done to Daddy."

"You don't have to worry about him anymore." When she sends me a sharp look, I know she's joining the dots, but the confirmation and truth I'll always keep from her. "He was beyond redemption. He'd had everything stacked against him from the start. Fuck knows how his brain was screwed from how he reacted to the drugs your birth mom imbibed while she was pregnant. Then there's his abusive and twisted upbringing." Wincing, I admit to her, "I know how hard it is to shake off the shackles of your past life, and in his case, Thorne had no hopes to recover. He was an angry, sick-in-the-brain man."

"Was," she picks up. "Past tense." She bites her lip and shoots a look toward her distraught mother. Then says, half to herself, "But he was my brother." Then to me she adds, "Why aren't I more upset?"

"Because he wasn't your brother," Red states firmly, still hanging around close enough to overhear. "Technically, perhaps yes, but you've nothing in common with him, and nothing to regret."

But she looks down to the ground before saying quietly, "I could have been him."

Red puts his finger under her chin and lifts it. "Sweetheart, there's nothing to say even with the same hand dealt, that you wouldn't have been different. Sure, you shared a womb and a mother, but what makes you, you, is in here." He lays his hand briefly over her heart, then removes it fast before I do it for him. "No one's going to deny he lived a bad life, but other people do, and move on from it."

For a moment, I wonder where I'd be if I'd had a different dad, or if mine had lived longer. Nurture had led me, not in making the initial mistake in taking Britney as my wife, but in staying with her. Violence doesn't solve anything, but if I hadn't been so wary of hurting her, maybe I could have kept her in line. Or, if violence isn't an answer to violence, I'd have absolved myself of my responsibilities for her. *Women are to be protected, cherished and loved.* But not all women, perhaps.

But then I wouldn't be here today, with a woman who's as much right for me as Britney was wrong.

Pulling her to me, ignoring how the action jars my ribs, I place a kiss to her forehead. "You're going to be okay," I tell her, vowing I'll be there to ensure it. "And, your dad's going to come through, I feel it." I do, if only because the universe couldn't be so cruel as to send more troubles her way.

She clings onto me, and instead of dismissing my positivity, seems to hold onto it.

While I had no way of guaranteeing his survival, someone, somewhere, must have been listening to me today.

In all, Rufus is in surgery for almost six hours. When the doctor finally appears to say the operation was a success, and that he can have visitors after he's come around, the atmosphere lightens.

Martina, who'd spent most of the wait playing with the gold cross that hangs around her neck, visibly relaxes and slumps as if a weight's been lifted off of her. Tears fall again, but this time from relief. RoseLyn again is there to comfort her, but gradually their mood becomes more upbeat.

When RoseLyn disappears to answer a call from nature, Martina comes and sits beside me.

"I liked the man you were in Texas," she starts.

"I'm still the same man," I respond, knowing it's true. RoseLyn has made me drop my mask, and I have no desire to wear it again. "I'm the same man," I repeat, "All that's different is that I'm wearing my cut."

"Rufus didn't like that." Allowing her a liberty not often granted, I sit stiffly as she fingers the leather. "But he'll come around, I know it, if you've got good intentions toward our daughter." She breaks off, and directly enquires, "Can I ask what they are?"

"To never let her go? To protect her? To love her and cherish her forever if she'll have me? If those are your questions, then my answer is yes."

"Will you marry her?"

Being of the citizen world, she wouldn't understand that in my life a claim is more important. "Yes, Martina, I'll marry her. As soon as my divorce is finalised."

"What?" Her eyes become slits and her mouth a thin line. "You're married?"

She should know exactly what kind of man is going to be shacking up with her daughter. I close my eyes briefly, then having gathered the strength to admit my crimes, start to speak. "I married eight years ago. My ex was abusive and violent, but I stayed with her." I don't give her a chance to interrupt when she opens her mouth but just carry straight on. "She was sent down a few months into our marriage on abuse charges—not on me, but an innocent bystander who got the worst of her temper. While she was locked up, she refused all contact with me. I was screwed up in my head. I'd vowed to love and cherish her, yet the violent woman I lived with was not what I expected. I didn't intend to go back on my promises to her, but she'd made certain that there was nothing to sustain my feelings toward her. Eventually, I realised how emasculated I'd been while I was with her, came to my senses, and issued divorce papers."

"And it took you meeting my daughter to do that?"

Emphatically, I shake my head. "I sent them six years back. She never signed or returned them, but in my head, I believed I was no longer married." I put my head in my hands and rub at my temples, and then feel a soothing hand at my back.

"Britney's a bitch, Mom. Clark rightly couldn't testify in her trial that violence was unusual for her, and she held his lack of perjuring himself against him. When she got out a month or so back, she played on the fact that he was technically still married to her. Clark," RoseLyn's voice softens, and now her fingers squeeze my shoulder, "is a good man, and believed he owed that debt to her. But happy families did not play out, and Britney left the penitentiary just as violent as she was when she went in. She wanted revenge, and as you can see, she hurt Clark pretty badly."

"That's how you got hurt? She hit you?"

"Broke ribs, and bruised him all over." RoseLyn continues to speak for me, as now she starts rubbing my back. "And before you ask, Clark stood back and let her. He didn't retaliate in any way."

I raise my head and look at Martina. "You need to know the man who wants to marry your daughter. I'm fuckin' weak. I let Brit walk all over me and took everything she dished out."

"Weak?" Martina squawks. "Oh, honey, I think that shows fortitude of character. At least I have no concerns about you being abusive to Rose."

"He's one of the strongest men I've ever met," RoseLyn speaks over my head. Then I hear the smile in her voice. "But maybe not the brightest. He kind of has forgotten that if he wants to marry me, he's got to ask me."

Her words make me smile as she's completely wrong. I haven't forgotten at all. But now is not the time nor place to tell her my plans for that.

CHAPTER THIRTY-SIX

RoseLyn

When I go to see my dad after he comes out of recovery, I'm ashamed to think I stopped referring to him as that, even if only in my mind and for a short time. The emotion that flooded through me when I saw him so fragile and pale made me realise while he wasn't my sperm donor, I couldn't love him more.

While Mom openly cried, clasping his hand as though needing to assure herself he was alive, and hopefully now, out of danger, I stood back and watched them.

As parents, I had certainly lucked out.

On the second day after his surgery, Dad's encouraged by the nurses to get out of bed, start moving around and sit in a chair. I see the spark of who he was returning as he gives them shit about their bullying. That is, of course, in between him trying to flirt. His joking around has the effect of drying Mom's tears and instead, on the many times I see her rolling her eyes, I hear, "Oh, *Rufus*," in an exasperated tone on repeat. I smile, knowing things are returning to normal.

On the third day, he comes out of ICU, and I, finally, get Mom to leave the hospital, come back to my house and have a shower and a few hours of decent sleep. It's then she tentatively broaches the subject of whether I wanted to contact my birth parents, feeling guilty that, by keeping that information from me, I may have missed out on family.

It isn't a hard call. As Mom and I talk, I discover while I hadn't been in such a poor state as Thorne, I, too, had been suffering from withdrawals when I came out of the womb. Did I want to see the woman who bore me, only to sell me the moment I was born? Who had no care for my health while she carried me?

No, I have absolutely no desire to see her at all. It had been a tossup whether I'd gotten amazing parents like mine, or abusive ones like Thorne. While I think I'll always live with some semblance of guilt, I can't help but be thankful that I got the best part of the deal.

Petty is a regular visitor while my dad is in the hospital, but stays in the background, quietly offering his support. He gives his time equally to Mom and me, and even stays behind reading to Dad when I take Mom to get a coffee to give her a break.

I appreciate him being around, more than I would have thought.

Any doubts I have about him staying in the character I'd grown to love slowly ebbs. This is the real Petty, not the man Britney had made him become. He fits it as though he's discovered an old pair of comfortable shoes.

I'm lucky to have solid people around me. Bart's told me not to worry and that there's no need to rush back to the casino. While I'm missed, the stand-in band taking my spot are happy to continue for as long as it takes. He's also, though quick to reassure me, they can't compete with me, and I won't be replaced.

After a week, Dad is allowed to come home. My parents have decided to stay in Vegas for now, partly as there is nothing urgent for them to return to in Texas, but mainly they want him to continue the same medical support. Dad will need care for a while, and it will be months before he can get back to all his normal activities. Being here, as Mom says, at least stops him trying to return to the golf course too soon.

I breathe a sigh of relief when Dad arrives at my house. Mom fusses, of course, and takes the earliest opportunity to get him resting in bed, going up to be with him. I don't blame her. I know the luxurious feeling of sleeping with someone by my side and understand how she must have missed that while he'd been in the hospital—a cot in his room didn't really count.

Their early retreat means Petty and I are left alone for the first time since Dad had collapsed, and from the gleam in his eye, I just know he's going to take advantage.

His ribs are still healing, but his other bruises have faded and he moves easier now, as proven when he prowls toward me.

"I've missed you," he growls in that tone that sends shivers through me.

Teasing him, I reply, "You've been with me every day."

He takes another step. "I haven't been able to kiss you."

There's been numerous pecks on my lips, of the type acceptable in front of your parents, so I refute with a glint in my eye, "Yes, you have."

"Not the way I want to," he grumbles, another panty-wetting rumbling sound.

And then he's on me, his hand dominantly sliding around my neck and pulling me to him. I have no intention of resisting as our mouths meet and meld, tongues sliding together. I respond ardently, my enthusiasm matching his own, my hands roaming just as much as his.

When we're both gasping for breath, he pulls away. "I fuckin' need you, babe."

And heaven help me, I need him too. "Your ribs—"

"Fuck my ribs."

Brazenly, I reach down my hand and palm his rock-hard cock. "I'd rather fuck this."

Air whistles through his teeth, then he grins widely before taking my hand, tugging me behind him until we reach my bedroom. I'm giggling like a teenage girl by the time we get there.

As soon as the door's closed behind us, he's kissing me again, devouring me as if he'd starve without his mouth on mine. I'm consumed by him, his scent in my nostrils, his taste on my tongue, his face a feast for my eyes as I flick them open. The appreciative growls coming out of his mouth ramp up my own desire, and all this is punctuated by constant caresses of his lips.

Unbidden, my hips thrust against his, my arousal wanting an urgent response. It's been like the last week has been foreplay, leading us to this point.

The point where for the first time, he takes me. My whole body trembles in anticipation as he pulls his mouth away and starts removing my shirt. I let him pull it over my head, and impatiently unfasten my bra for him. Although he's seen my naked body before, it doesn't stop him inhaling a sharp breath and his eyes flaring as his hands reverently come out to trace my breasts.

I see his intention as he starts lowering his mouth, but I want to drink him in with my eyes too. Reaching out, I take hold of his tee, taking advantage of his bent position to pull it over his head. Last time, his skin was marred with purple bruising. Today, it's clearer and the fading yellow allows his tattoos to shine through.

Under my gaze, his muscles involuntarily flex. Before he can start on me, I lean forward, gently taking one of his pert nipples between my lips, my attention making him suck in air.

"I gotta taste you." His voice sounds hoarse. "Babe, get naked, please."

Oh, I don't mind obeying that instruction. Taking a step back, I seductively undo the buttons on my shirt, taking my time, revealing more and more glimpses of tantalising skin.

His breath hitches, his eyes darken, and his hands clench as though he's having difficulty holding himself back and giving into his desire to take over. As I slide my shirt off my shoulders, and slowly, very slowly, slip out of my bra, I hear a muffled curse under his breath.

His hand reaches down to cup himself as if he's in pain, and he grimaces.

Next come my shorts. I undo the snap, then pull down the zipper, then pause. He draws in air and his mouth tightens.

Then, backing away toward the bed, I inch down the material and leave myself wearing only lace panties that don't hide much of anything.

His control snaps. He launches forward, pushing me so I land flat on my back then rips away that last vestige of covering.

At first his impatience makes me grin until he pushes my legs apart and dives in. Then I no longer find anything amusing. This is wonderfully, pleasurably, serious.

Oh my God. His fingers, I already know, are talented, but his tongue? Has he read a manual or something? However he's gained his knowledge, or maybe it's instinctive, he knows exactly what to do as he assaults my clit in the nicest possible way.

I feel myself getting wetter by the second, and when he slides a finger into my slit, it glides in easily.

I thought I already knew what to expect, but somehow he's taking me to new levels. I catch my breath as my muscles ripple then clench, and far before I was expecting it, waves of pleasure sweep over me. Remembering my parents are close by, I stuff my fist into my mouth at the last minute.

It's so intense I think I pass out for a moment. I see planets and stars, then just as I'm starting to come down, he begins feasting again.

By the time he's finished with me, I'm limp and drained, and feel I've nothing left in reserve. Moving up with a satisfied grin on his face, his lips cover my mouth and I taste myself on him. I clasp my hands to his head, holding him to me. For a moment, he lets me enjoy the caress, then he carefully lifts himself, a wry grimace showing he's trying to ignore his sore ribs. At that moment, I remember how much I hate Britney.

Then all thoughts of anyone else leave my head as he begins to get payback, torturing me in the same way I'd taunted him. First, he makes a show of removing his boots and his socks, and then he straightens and pauses with his hand on his fly.

When he cocks an eyebrow at me, I wave my hand impatiently.

Chuckling, he flicks the top button, then the next, then, *damn him*, he pauses.

"Petty," I moan.

Giving a soft laugh, he takes pity on me, and the last two are opened as well. Then, moving his hips like a male stripper, he flaunts his still-covered manhood as he lowers then kicks off his jeans.

I've touched it, held it in my hand and had my mouth around it, but now I want to take time to examine that part of him that will soon be inside me. I moan as he delays removing his boxers, knowing the bastard is completely aware of the effect he's having.

Then, *finally*, the material is gone.

His cock is impressive, thick and long, vein covered with a bulbous head. Knowing how talented he is giving head, I grow wetter still at the thought of how much pleasure he's going to be giving me. I doubt he's going to disappoint. I'm slightly disappointed when he slides down a condom hiding the sight.

He tries to bravely hide how his face contorts as he starts to move over me, and I suffer a moment's guilt, knowing he's not healed, but I'm too damn impatient and a little bit selfish to suggest he stop, trusting he knows how to treat his own body. *I'll die if I don't have him inside me.*

He's more cautious than he'd normally be, I'm certain of that, but that feeling of slowly being filled, as he starts to move in, gaining ground with each gentle thrust, has me putting my fist to my mouth again.

Pausing when he's fully in, he meets my eyes and checks in. He's at that perfect place, near enough my cervix to make me feel great, but not bumping painfully against it. Then, satisfied I can take him, he pulls out and pushes in, starting to punctuate his movements with a swivel of his hips.

I know of necessity due to his injuries he's being gentle, but this is more than that. We're not fucking, we're making love. Resisting the urge to wrap my arms around him, I place my hands above my head, using my body to match his thrusts.

I may have already had multiple orgasms, but my body doesn't care. I moan as I feel the telltale signs once again sweep through me. Opening my eyes, I watch his face. It's contorted in effort as he continues his slow onslaught. As the feelings rise in me and again my muscles tense, I'm on the brink of not knowing whether I'll be able to survive the release that's coming, and being aware that I'll die if he doesn't take me over the top.

"That's it," he grunts. "Babe, you've gotta come for me. You feel so fuckin' good. You're squeezing my dick. Babe, you've got to come all over it."

He thrusts again. "Babe, you close?" His voice has dropped an octave, and it sounds like he's struggling to form words. "Oh, fuck, doll."

He needn't worry, I'm right there with him. I swear I can feel his cock inside me swell and that tiny movement is enough for me to let go. At that precise moment, his mouth covers mine, swallowing my scream.

This time, I'm shot right into another universe and down a darn black hole, or so my senses would have me believe. For a moment, I can't even breathe. His cock twitches inside me as he fills the condom, the small movements extending my pleasure.

Then, with one final push, leaving him in as far as he can go, a huge sigh comes from him. He lowers his forehead and rests it against mine.

"I fuckin' knew you were going to be perfect for me."

That's funny, as I had the same feelings about him.

We stay like that, emotions flowing between us. I've never felt such a connection with a man before, as if our bodies and minds are totally aligned.

So when he says quietly, "I fuckin' love you, RoseLyn," I don't have to think for a moment before I say it back.

"I love you, too, Petty."

CHAPTER THIRTY-SEVEN

Petty

For a prisoner, Britney's been treated pretty well. She has her own room, one of the few with an attached bathroom. She has a television for entertainment, and I know Cher set her up with a kindle and books for her to read. She's had three meals a day delivered, and has a fridge full of water and snacks.

As it's a vast improvement from where she spent the last seven years, I feel no guilt at her being kept captive.

The plan that Red had agreed with that day, driving me to the hospital, necessitated Britney remaining our guest for a while. I felt choked when he took it on himself and his wife to make sure she was looked after, seeing as I couldn't bear to be in the same room. I hadn't even been to see her, as I'd been spending all my time with RoseLyn and her folks.

Today, though, I have to enter. I steel myself before going in, taking a moment to remind myself that my brothers don't see me as weak or less of a man, even though I'd been taken in by this woman and had let myself be abused. From now on, I'll refuse to allow Britney to belittle me.

Britney hadn't bothered to keep up the sweet act with Cher or my brothers, so they knew what a cunt she really is. She'd tried to attack Owl when he brought her a meal, and since then, they'd only visited in pairs. Cher was always escorted, but despite having no regard for the woman, continued to visit in case Brit needed women's stuff.

I take one final deep breath, then turn the key in the lock. As soon as she sees who's entered, she starts.

"I wondered when you were finally going to show your face. Fucking coward," she sneers.

I try to let the words flow off me like water off a duck's back, but it's hard. Immediately seeing her, part of me wants to appease her and make amends. But I jam that minute part of me back down, remembering RoseLyn loves me for the man I am. Now I'm free to be me and have the woman I want, I wouldn't change anything about myself. And definitely not for Britney.

"Are you letting me go?" she asks, and waves her hand around. "I've done my time in prison."

She's not done nearly enough, as I hope she'll soon find out.

Ignoring her question, I get a piece of paper out of my pocket, and throw it at her. "Uncontested divorce, it's been finalised." It's been three weeks. Three weeks which have both been the longest and best of my life. The longest because the time I was still tied to Britney has dragged, the best, because I've spent most of it with RoseLyn.

"I was forced to sign those papers. I'm going to challenge it—"

I growl. I'd get up into her face, but I'm wise enough to stay out of range of those fists. Roller had suggested he tie her up before I entered, or at least, come in with me, but it's time that I face her as the man I really am.

"Let it go, Brit. You don't stand a fuckin' chance. You've not got a leg to stand on. Admit it, why don't you? You don't even want to be married to me."

"You're fuckin' right there. But what about the tie between us?" Her voice has become deceptively soft. "You can't turn your back on the baby."

I snort and take the second piece of paper out of my cut.

She'd refused to do a pregnancy test, but Twister wasn't averse to using force on a woman, and took some of her blood a few days ago. The doc we use expedited the results, and surprise, surprise, there is no child.

"You're not pregnant." I toss her the proof.

She doesn't look the least bit surprised, and lets the paper drop to the floor without looking at it. "Of course there isn't," she sneers. "I got the shot before coming anywhere near you. I knew I'd have to fuck you, but didn't want your spawn. Devil spawn, got it?" She cackles as if she's made a joke, but I'm not in the least amused, or surprised that she'd used just one more way to torture me. I wish though I'd known she was protected, I'd been on edge until I'd seen those results. Though in her case, sterilisation would probably be a better option.

She stares at the divorce papers she still holds in her hands, then raises her eyes to me. "So, we're divorced, and you know there's no baby. What happens now?" There's a slight uncertainty in her voice as if she knows I hold all the cards.

After our brief marriage and her reappearance in my life, it's a heady feeling to know I'm now the one in charge.

"Now, you leave. The club, Vegas, Nevada if you know what's good for you. No one wants you here." As she starts to redden, I warn her, "I may not be able to hurt a woman, but not all my brothers feel the same way. You keep showing your face or trying to cause trouble, and you'll be six feet underground before you realise it."

"Are you threatening me?"

I shrug. "Just telling you how it is."

Her mouth opens and shuts. Her eyes widen then narrow. It's as if the wheels are turning in her head as she tries to work out how to come out on top. She pulls on all the tricks in her book as finally her bottom lip trembles, and she asks timidly, "What do you expect me to do? Are you giving me money?"

I'm not weakening, not even an inch. "You even read that

divorce settlement you signed? You agreed to take nothing from me."

"I'll go to court."

"Then so will I. With your record, the hospital evidence and my brothers' testimony, who do you think will acquit you of yet another charge of abuse?"

Her hands fist, and my body tenses. "You always were a sorry excuse for a man. You'd do that? Admit in court how pathetic you are?"

"Not hitting back isn't a sign of weakness." I tiredly explain the truth I've come to accept. "And I assure you it doesn't suck to be me. Just look at what I have. A home, a family, brothers around me. A soon-to-be wife."

"You what?" she shrieks, this time throwing herself forward, but I'm prepared.

Ready for her attack, I swing her around me, holding her back to my front and clamping her arms. There's nothing inside me that wants to appease her or reduce to her level of rage.

The opposite, I want to intensify it.

"Oh yeah, I was just waiting for the divorce to be finalised before asking RoseLyn to marry me."

She struggles to get loose but she's no match for me, though her foot does hit my shin. I suppress the oomph so as not to give her satisfaction.

Realising she can't get free, she stills, but her voice is filled with hate and ire. "And how are you going to propose, soldier boy? Like you did to me?" Spittle lands on my hands which are still wrapped around her.

I proposed to her in a restaurant, flowers and a perfect dinner all arranged, and yes, I'd gotten down on one knee. I won't be doing it the same way this time.

I chuckle softly. "I'm going to do it in front of our friends, family and even her fans."

"What the fuck do you mean?"

I wasn't sure I'd be able to lead her there, but now I've got her just where I want her. "On stage. When she's performing." I pause, then add, "And I'm not wasting time. Tonight, *she'll* have my ring on her finger." My brothers had taken Britney's when they forced her to put her signature to the divorce papers.

Bart had managed to find a stand-in for a couple of weeks, but for the last few nights, she'd been singing again. Briefly, my mind gets lost in the emotion I felt knowing I was free and able to admire her, no longer a client, but my woman, as she wiggled that sexy ass and used that gravelly voice that always turned me insane.

Taking advantage of my momentary loss of concentration, Britney almost gets away from me, but I take the initiative and push her away.

"You fuckin' stay away from me and my woman," I roar, in a voice I'd never used on her. She reels back at the unexpected force in my tone. "Just get out of Vegas, and forget I existed." I start to retreat, making sure not to show her my back. "I've already wiped you from my mind like dog shit from a shoe."

I close the door on her final scream.

"Done?" Roller's standing, his back against the wall, waiting for me.

I fill my lungs with air that's no longer tainted by her presence. "Done," I confirm.

He slaps me on the back and walks beside me as we descend the stairs. "All we've got to do now is see if she takes the bait."

"Knowing her, she won't be able to resist, Brother." And even if I'm proved wrong, she'll be leaving Vegas. Without being trapped in matrimony, she'll have no call on me.

I give Owl and Meat the confirmatory nod they need as I pass, and they start to climb the stairs I just descended. Their instructions are to get Britney packed up and taken directly to the airport. If she gets on a plane and flies out of my life, well, so be it. At least she'll be gone.

I've good reason, though, to think she won't surprise me. But never let it be said I didn't give her the chance.

I go to my bike and head back to RoseLyn's house.

I greet my woman with a mouth-to-mouth kiss, then give a peck on the cheek to her mom. Rufus is lying in a lounger and makes no effort to get up. If he did, his two personal nurses would be straight on that. But he waves me over to him.

"How did it go?"

"With Brit?"

When he gives a cautious nod, I know that he's worried. He knows Thorne will no longer be a problem, and being that it was his life or his daughter's, he had no difficulty with that. Not when he'd had such a close call with death himself.

"You're still in one piece, I see," he teases me.

I snort. "Last I saw, she was heading for the airport."

Again his head dips up and down, and his exhaled breath now is one of relief. "So she's got a choice." He, too, has been briefed over the plans for the evening. "What if she does take the chance to get out of your life? Will you still go ahead?"

It's my turn to nod, and I do so emphatically. "My only regret is that you won't be there." I've already arranged for Owl to come sit and keep him company. Meat will be FaceTiming so Rufus will see what's going on.

"I worry she's dangerous, son."

He'd taken to calling me son ever since he's been out of the hospital and seen RoseLyn and I together, and probably after Martina had brought him up to date with my intentions. It's been a goddamn long time since anyone had claimed me in that way, and I have to admit, I'm fine with it.

Placing my hand over his, I reassure him, "I won't allow anyone to hurt her."

He might be weak, but I've no doubt he'd find some way to exact revenge on my body as he threatens, "She better not harm one hair on her head."

I raise my chin to show I understand.

I leave him and go to speak to RoseLyn. "How was your rehearsal?" I know she's enjoyed getting back with her band.

"Good. I'm still getting used to not having a Devil following me around." She grins, then sobers. "How did Britney take that she's not having your baby?" The revelation had come as a relief to us both.

I roll my eyes. "She'd had the shot. It was just one more way she was torturing me."

RoseLyn gasps, then doesn't hesitate, just throws her arms around me. "You can trust me," she says, fervently. "I would never, ever, do anything like that."

I know she wouldn't. "You want kids?"

My out-of-the-blue question has shocked her. "Maybe, some-day." She shrugs. "When and if we're ready."

Whether we do or not is fine with me. Deep down, I'm shit scared that I could fuck up a kid like my father unwittingly fucked up me. Not that he wanted to or meant to. He didn't expect to die before he saw me again.

Noting the time, I see she's got a couple of hours before she has to leave. I pull her into my arms, and lower my mouth to her ear. "What about we get in some practice, just in case?"

"I like how you think." Grinning, she grabs my hand and leads me straight into her room.

I'll take my time with her later, make love to her in the way she deserves. But for now, I give her some biker loving in the time-honoured way, fast and furious after, of course, making sure she comes first.

CHAPTER THIRTY-EIGHT

RoseLyn

"He does know he doesn't have to do that anymore, doesn't he?" Kylie asks as she re-enters my dressing room, carrying some stuff she'd left in her car.

It doesn't take a genius to know she's referring to Petty, who's resumed his role waiting for me, standing in the corridor on sentry duty.

Since I've been back, when Petty's come with me to the casino, which is more often than not, he's been in the dressing room, watching with interest while Kylie transforms me or when he gets bored, sinking his nose into a book. I don't enlighten my stylist that it's because we're expecting trouble today, in the form of an ex-wife who didn't take a flight out from the airport.

Petty wants to be on guard and not get distracted. Even though the casino's swarming with Devils, he'd rather be looking out for me himself. On my part, there's no one I trust better.

I'm part excited and part full of dread about how the evening is going to play out. It's supposed to be spontaneous, but we've rehearsed our roles. The only player who's not had the chance to learn their part will be in the starring role.

I'm not convinced Britney will be stupid enough to turn up,

but Petty seems pretty convinced that she will, that she'll be unable to resist at the very least spoiling my special moment.

Little does she know Petty's already proposed, and while some people might not think it romantic, I was overjoyed and felt it was right when he was deep inside me, just having made me come on his dick.

Mom's in the audience, escorted personally by Red, Cher and their kid, Zeke. I'm upset my father can't make it, but pleased Petty thought of that and set it up so he'd be able to watch.

"Which dress are you wearing?" Kylie goes to my wardrobe and starts moving hangers. "Oooh, that's pretty, I've not seen it before."

She wouldn't have, I only just bought it—a shimmering gown with a deep V at the front and bares my back almost down to my ass. It's in peacock colours, the material changing from a dark blue to green depending on how the light falls on it. Petty's going to shit himself when he sees it.

Kylie's still lovingly fingering the material. "Say this one, please."

"That one." I grin as I watch her bring it out, holding it up against herself and doing a twirl. "You're going to look amazing."

Well, that's what I hope. Now I see it again, I have doubts. "Just make sure you glue it to my tits."

As she sniggers, a voice comes from the other side of the closed door, "She fuckin' better."

Both Kylie and I laugh loudly. When she approaches me sitting in front of the mirror, knowing the walls are paper thin, she says loudly, "You got any other hot biker brothers for a girl like myself?"

"You hear that, RoseLyn? She thinks I'm hot," Petty calls back.

I snort. I think he's pretty hot myself, and he knows it.

What Kylie doesn't know is that I'm going to ask her to do my makeup on my special day. But I'm sure she'll be all over that later once the evening's conclusion is reached. Like everyone else, she doesn't yet know I'm engaged.

She does miracles with my hair, somehow digging in her voluminous bag and coming up with a fastener the same colour as the dress which she proceeds to fix to my hair. As she gradually transforms me, I begin to feel like the performer I'll need to be soon.

Finally, it's time for me to throw aside all modesty as she applies the stick-on bra cups, manoeuvring my boobs until they're in just the right place. Then I wriggle into the dress and she ensures the bra's attached firmly to the material. When finished, I do a little shimmy to make sure everything stays in the right place.

With high-heeled, dark-blue satin shoes to complete the ensemble, I feel like a rock goddess in the flesh.

Petty gulps and swallows hard when he sees me, and not so discreetly reaches down to adjust himself.

"I'm going to have to kill a few brothers tonight," he warns me. "I don't want anyone else looking at you."

"Then you're going to have to kill a whole audience," I respond with a dry laugh. Inside I'm chuffed that my costume is having the effect that I hoped.

He growls. "If I have my way, you're not even going to make the performance looking like that. I want to kidnap you and take you somewhere where only I can look at you. Then, I'm slowly going to peel you out of that dress—"

I bat his arm. "Well, you're not going to have your way. I only pay Kylie to do my makeup once."

"You don't need makeup," he informs me softly. "Naked, exposed, flushed, that's when I like you best. You're fuckin' beautiful, RoseLyn. Far too good for the likes of me."

I stop, turn and cup my hands around his face. "You've got that the wrong way around."

We stand for a moment, just staring into each other's eyes. He licks his lips as he makes no move to kiss me, having received the lecture from Kylie before about redoing my makeup.

"Time, RoseLyn," comes Bart's voice. "Come on, girl, time to show Vegas what you got."

"Not everything." Petty pulls me close and cups his hand to my bra. It's non-sexual, and I know it's only to check my dress is fixed tight.

Laughing, I pull away and slap his hand.

Then we're behind the curtains, Petty slipping into his space backstage, throwing me a kiss which I pretend to catch with both hands.

The band strikes up the beat, the introduction is done, and I burst out.

"Good evening, Vegas!"

The crowd seems louder tonight, but then it would, all his brothers—except for the prospect, Owl—are there. Sweet butts have been invited—maybe to see proof Petty's off the market—along with the old ladies and Zeke. I swear their voices and cheers carry over the rest. When the spotlight shifts from me, it gives me a chance to see my mom's face. She's glowing with pride and the sight warms me, and along with Petty quietly supporting me from behind, gives me the impetus to give it my all tonight.

I catch a glimpse of Meat, his phone held toward me as he FaceTimes my dad. Despite how much I look though, I can't see the person I expect to find. I'm not sure whether I'm disappointed or not. The evening's going to end the same way.

The first set down, a ten-minute break to rush to the bathroom, down a drink, then it's back on stage. We turn it up a notch and launch into our favourites. The claps and shouts become thunderous, well, at least from one part of the room.

Then we're down to the final song, and I pause.

Petty doesn't miss his cue. As the drumbeat starts, he pushes through the curtain and onto the stage. As he steps into the spotlight, my heart speeds up. He looks so good in his clean jeans, white shirt, and of course, his cut.

I put my hand to my mouth as if surprised, and the drumbeat slows and then stops.

Petty raises a microphone to his lips as he falls to one knee on the boards.

"RoseLyn, when I found you, I found the love of my life. I want you—"

"No!" The loud shriek needs no help from amplification, and all heads turn to swivel Britney's way.

She tears off the wig she's used very effectively to disguise herself and is pushing through the crowd, winding her way around tables. Tears, real or more likely fake, stream from her eyes.

Petty gets to his feet as she climbs up onto the stage.

"You don't get to disrespect me," she screams, throwing a punch into his face. I wince at the blood streaming from the side of his mouth. Britney's arms flail as he moves back, his hands held up defensively.

But she doesn't stop with him, turning and throwing herself toward me, her fingernails heading right for my skin and I brace…

She's torn away from me and is held tight by Twister and Cuff. She's screaming and shouting obscenities at us, clearly out of her mind with rage.

Another man, escorted by Red, comes to stand in front of the stage. He looks disgusted. "Call the cops," he demands.

Oh, I might not have seen him before, but I know exactly who he is. He and his wife had been eager to accept an invite to a free night out tonight. He's Britney's parole officer and has seen for himself that she definitely isn't obeying the rules.

The cops don't take long to arrive. Bart had managed to get the casino to offer free tickets to law enforcement tonight, so the parole officer didn't think it odd that he received one for himself. Though dressed up in their suits and off duty, they've come prepared for whatever the night might bring. Quickly, badges come out as well as handcuffs.

"I want her charged," Petty says, but softly so as not to upset the paying guests.

"We'll need your statement."

Petty nods. "I'll come to the precinct tomorrow."

"You bastard! You set me up! You fuckin' deserve to be in a box. I'm going to fuckin' kill you—"

"Ma'am, I suggest you shut up," one of the cops struggling with her advises. "You're making it worse with these threats."

Ignoring him, Britney screams, "You're fuckin' dead!"

It takes a moment to get her off the stage, and once she's gone, the auditorium is so silent you could hear a pin drop.

"Ladies, gentleman, theys and them." Bart takes the microphone. "I'd like to apologise for the interruption and get back to business. While Petty and RoseLyn get back to what was so rudely interrupted, the waitstaff will be coming around with free glasses of champagne for everyone."

Just like that, the mood turns and becomes expectant.

A drum roll sounds, and Petty resumes his position on the floor. He doesn't bother repeating what he already said, instead heading straight for, "Will you ride with me through life? Become my old lady and be my wife?"

The beat stops, and I let a theatrical pause linger, before putting him out of his misery and replying, "Yes."

I'd had it planned in my head. I was going to jump into his arms. But despite Britney trying her best to ruin this moment, the earnest look on his face, the hope in his eyes, glues me to the spot.

He takes advantage, standing, taking my hand, and placing a gorgeous diamond ring on my finger. Then, reaches his free hand behind him, in an obviously rehearsed move, and takes what one of his brothers—I think it was Roller but couldn't be certain as I've only eyes for my man—hands him. When he holds out a cut bearing the words *Property of Petty,* I thread my arms into it.

Then we kiss to the sound of cheers and foot stamps, and that drumbeat starts all over again.

"And now I'd like to present the finale for tonight," Bart shouts to be heard over the din. "Petty and RoseLyn."

We take our cue. Still holding his hand, I wait for the right note then begin to sing. When his turn nears, Petty's throat works, betraying his nerves, but his gravelly voice is firm as he takes over for his part. Together we sing *"Love Lift Us Up Where We Belong."*

Oh, it was in rehearsals when I'd heard Petty quietly singing along that I discovered he could carry a tune. It was Bart's suggestion that we try a duet. Petty had doubts, but for me he was prepared to give it a try.

The audience is stunned. When the song ends, there's a moment of silence before all hell breaks out.

The cries of encore go unheeded, as we'd only practiced one song. But I've a sneaking suspicion from the stunned pleasure on Petty's face, as his brothers surround him, congratulating us, and asking him why he kept that ability under wraps, that one day soon, we'll be singing together again.

And hopefully it's a sure sign that for the rest of our lives, we'll be in harmony.

EPILOGUE

I'd enjoyed singing with RoseLyn, though wouldn't want to make it a career. My nerves when I waited for my cue had been worse than when facing insurgents. But for her, I'd pulled up my big-man pants, and hadn't fucked up, or not too bad. I'd gone off key once, but hoped no one noticed.

As it was, that night ended with all outcomes as planned. RoseLyn had an engagement ring on her finger, and my cut on her back. She was mine, or will be, in every way I want her.

Britney, to no one's surprise, was sent back to serve the rest of her ten years with another good few added on. She had only herself to blame, possessive to a fault. While she didn't want me, she couldn't stand the thought of me being happy in another woman's arms, or perhaps being happy at all. Her predictable attack had proved how well I knew her.

After spending six weeks with us, Rufus and Martina had returned home to Texas, but not before seeing RoseLyn agree to become Mrs Petty, in one of the chapels in Vegas. RoseLyn had said she was too used to adulation on stage to want a big audience for her wedding day and was more than content to get married with just her parents and the club in attendance.

Since the night of my proposal, I've suffered the teasing of my brothers who were surprised to find out I could sing. I'd actually being quite shocked myself, not realising I had it in me. But while Bart tried to persuade me to sing more duets with the woman of my dreams, I told him in no uncertain terms, I was more than happy to stay on the sidelines and let the expert do that work. That's not to say we never sing together. If, often, when we're preparing a meal, I pick up on a song my *wife* is singing and join in for a few notes, who's to know but us?

My ribs are fully healed, and all the physical signs Britney had left have disappeared. Mentally though, I still wake from the odd nightmare, reliving that night when she took consent from me. But RoseLyn holds me close, reminding me that my second is nothing like my first wife. Likewise, I comfort her during her nightmares when those fuckers Saul or Thorne, or both, get into her head.

"Well that's me out." Roller throws down his cards with a look of disgust on his face.

Alternatively, I grin, pulling my winnings toward me. As RoseLyn leans over from behind and presses a kiss to my cheek, I realise she's more of a prize than any of the dollars in my hand.

Not for the first time, I wonder how I got so lucky.

"Ready?" Cher, Red's woman, walks up.

RoseLyn turns to her with a grin, saying, "Sure am. What about you, Zeke?"

As Zeke nods, I turn and give them a fist bump, then watch as the three of them go out the door. I don't believe in any deity, so it must just have been fate who delivered me someone like her. I still question how I deserve it, but she's more than made up for my experience with my first wife.

She's fitted in with the club as though she was born to be here. She's gained the respect of all my brothers and women. Today's a shopping trip for clothes which I'm more than happy to help her get out of.

Rope comes over and takes Roller's recently vacated chair.

Titch picks up the cards and expertly shuffles them, dealing me in.

The old man stares at me as I'm keeping a strict poker face, examining the hand I've been dealt. It's a bummer but maybe enough to fool them. When I see I remain the target of his intense gaze, I shift awkwardly in my seat.

"What's up?" I brush my hand over my mouth in case I left some food there.

"I never particularly liked you, Petty."

I shrug, it's no news to me. But then it's part of being in the club. You're prepared to give your life for your brothers, for the greater good, doesn't mean you need to be bosom pals with them all. But still I raise an eyebrow wondering where he's going with this.

He winks at me. "But hell, I like you now. Wondered whether you were going to revert to your former self, but RoseLyn is keeping you on the straight and narrow."

"This is me, Brother," I tell him, no umbrage taken at all. "And a lot's down to RoseLyn, but it's down to you too. I dropped the act I thought I had to put on. No man likes to admit he's been abused."

"Not all abuse is bad." Rope winks at me.

I snort. "Don't want to know about Cuff whipping you."

"Ain't Cuff," he refutes, but doesn't seem particularly bothered by any connotations we may make. But then, Rope and Cuff are a strange pair. Fuck knows we tend to avoid them when they head down to the basement with their latest victim or two.

Titch rolls his eyes and at last removes his gaze from me. For a moment, we're all focused on the cards. I throw one in and draw another which doesn't particularly help matters, but I let my mouth twitch to trick them.

Looking up from examining his own cards, Crash places some money on the table. "It's fuckin' strange how we'd all be against any man who was abusive toward a woman, but when it's the other way around, it's harder to know what to do. I'm fuckin' glad that bitch of yours is facing a long sentence, but in the ground is what she really deserves."

"I'd have taken her out for you," Titch states. When I give him a sharp look, he shrugs. "Abuse is abuse."

"What are you old ladies talking about?" Red's voice booms.

"About how abusive women are given a pass not allotted to me," Titch, with narrowed eyes answers. "I fuckin' hate I believed her and not him." Again he meets my eyes in apology.

"Way of the world, Brother." Red pulls up a chair and sits down, placing his beer in front of him. When he's offered to be dealt in, he shakes his head. After he's watched us play a few hands, I notice he's been staring at me.

Automatically brushing my hand over my face, I check to see if I've anything on it. When I'm satisfied I don't, I challenge him head on. "What?"

He shrugs. "Got something to tell you, Brother. Britney crossed the wrong bitch in jail. She's dead."

His calm words wash over me. To understand, I need to repeat them in my head. *Britney crossed the wrong bitch in jail. She's dead.* I frown, then try again. *Britney's dead.*

Women are to be loved, cherished and protected.

While around me brothers are saying it couldn't happen to a better person, and giving each other high fives, I feel sick to my stomach, stand and rush to the heads as I start to retch.

In my most ignominious moment, my prez is standing behind me. When I finish, he clears his throat.

"Whatever you're thinking, this isn't on you, Brother. Your only fuckin' crime was not leaving her earlier."

"I sent her back, Prez."

"You gave her the choice. She could have taken that flight out of Vegas." Red reaches down, grabs my arm and pulls me to my feet. "Now I suggest you get back in the clubroom, share a drink with your brothers and never look back. I know, though you haven't told me, there's some shit in the past that's at the bottom of all this." He pauses. "Titch was fuckin' right, we do give women a pass they sometimes shouldn't have. If Britney had been a man, she'd have met her demise a long time ago. You've got your future, Petty, and it's looking like a damn good one. Don't let Britney fuck it up."

I let his words sink in, think on them for a moment, then realise he's right. When I tell him so, he grins.

"Of course I'm right. I'm the fuckin' prez." He cocks his head to one side. "From the sound of it, the women have returned. Think you need to walk out there and see your old lady, and leave the past where it belongs."

He leaves me alone. I splash water on my face, take a moment to steady myself, then walk into the clubroom.

I stand for a moment observing.

Zeke's obviously been trialling some new makeup. Their eyes are laden thick with shadow and eyeliner, and their lashes are too long to be real. They're modelling some tunic thing they've bought. Their exuberance makes me grin. With the Devils behind them, Zeke can be anything.

RoseLyn is heavily laden with packages. I rush across to relieve her of her burden, realising as I do, how just the sight of her relieves me of mine.

I hold her for a moment, just taking her in, as always hardly daring to believe she's mine.

But for some reason she is. And as Red reminded me, the past has been left behind. RoseLyn is my future.

I did the crime, and I've done my time.

COMING SOON

Pre-order: Amazon
   StoryTeller's Tale: Wretched Soulz MC
   Release date: February 4 2023

Being a nomad, I spend all my time travelling the road. Moving from place to place, with little or nothing pulling me back to what could be considered home.

That is, until I get a call from my prez, demanding I return.

I make my way back to the clubhouse, traversing hundreds of miles and making use of rest stops on the way. At one, I find a discarded book, brand new, with a date, a dedication, and the signature of the author inside.

I took it as the owner wasn't around.

Then I was schooled that a book so recently purchased, and direct from the author, was likely to be a prized possession, and only accidentally left behind.

Not usually one to feel guilty, I had this crazy idea to reunite book and owner.

I didn't realise that, for a woman I didn't even know, I'd end up putting my life on the line.

ACKNOWLEDGEMENTS AND AUTHOR'S NOTE

Usually, I write a note of how the story of the book came about. In this case, there's not much to say.

If you're one of my regular readers, you know I like to explore the depths of the human psyche, putting my characters into situations and watching them get out. Such as it was with Petty.

Whether it's the more likely male against female, or, as in this case, the woman who's at fault, abuse, is unfortunately a way of the world. Too many people stay in relationships that are toxic for them.

Petty's Crime simply explores how a man who presents a *"you can't touch me"* front to the world can be brought down.

It wasn't an easy story to write story. It took me far longer than I at first hoped. I wasn't sure I was portraying motives and reactions in a believable way, that is, until I let my beta readers and editor have the draft.

Luckily, they reassured me, which leads to you having Petty's Crime in your hands today.

It's not really unusual, I agonise over every story I write.

So a very grateful thanks to the beta readers who encouraged me, Sheri, Jo, Tami, Tera, Alex and Zoe, and, of course, to my long-suffering editor, Maggie Kern.

Darlene Tallman, thank you for proofreading this book, and for the comments you send me while reading it.

Once again, Dar of Wicked Smart Designs has produced a cover that I hope you love as much as I do.

Finally, last as always, but definitely not least, thanks to all of you, my wonderful readers who've taken a chance on this book. If it wasn't for your encouragement, I wouldn't keep writing. I have recently received messages and emails telling me how much you like my books, and I love reading everyone. A positive message inspires me to write more.

This book, like all of my works, has been to beta readers, through editing twice, to a proofreader and then to ARC readers, but there could still be the odd typo that's crept through. Please message me if you've found anything, so I have a chance to correct the book. I love to hear from readers, even if you're pointing out something I've got wrong.

If you've enjoyed this book, please consider writing a review. Reviews are essential to us authors, and I appreciate and read them all.

I will be writing another Satan's Devils' book shortly, but I'm first getting a project out of the way. Keep your eye on my newsletter or join my group for information about StoryTeller's Tale. It will release in February, but at the moment, that's all I can say.

StoryTeller's Tale is the first in a new series featuring the Wretched Soulz MC. Avid readers will know how that club is the dominant club in the southern states of the US. Some of the characters you will have met already in other books. I've long been asked to write about them. I hope you'll love them as much as the Devils.

Love and peace be with you all.
Manda

OTHER WORKS BY MANDA MELLETT

<u>Blood Brothers – A series about sexy dominant sheikhs and their bodyguards</u>

Stolen Lives (#1) Nijad and Cara

Close Protection (#2) Jon and Mia

Second Chances (#3) Kadar and Zoe

Identity Crisis (#4) Sean and Vanessa

Dark Horses (#5) Jasim and Janna

Hard Choices (#6) Aiza

Satan's Devils MC - Arizona Chapter

Turning Wheels (Blood Brothers #3.5, Satan's Devils #1) Wraith and Sophie

Drummer's Beat (#2) Drummer and Sam

Slick Running (#3) Slick and Ella

Targeting Dart (#4) Dart and Alex

Heart Broken (#5) Heart and Marc

Peg's Stand (#6) Peg and Darcy

Rock Bottom (#7) Rock and Becca

Joker's Fool (#8) Joker and Lady

Mouse Trapped (#9) Mouse and Mariana

Blade's Edge (#10) Blade and Tash

Heart Mended: A Satan's Devils MC Novella

Truck Stopped (#11) Truck & Allie

Satan's Devils MC Boxset 1 Books 1-5

Satan's Devils MC Boxset 2 Books 6-8

Satan's Devils MC Boxset 3 Books 9-11

Satan's Devils MC - Colorado Chapter

Paladin's Hell (#1) Paladin and Jayden

Demon's Angel (#2) Demon and Violet

Devil's Due (#3) Beef and Steph

Devil's Dilemma (#4) Pyro and Mel

Ink's Devil (#5) Ink and Beth

Devil's Spawn (#6)

Satan's Devils MC - Next Generation

Amy's Santa (#1) Wizard and Amy

Hawk's Cry (#2) Hawk and Olivia

Twisted Throttle (#3) Throttle and Gwen

Satan's Devils MC - San Diego Chapter

Being Lost (#1)

Grumbler's Ride (#2)

Avenging Devil Part 1 (#3)

Avenging Devil Part 2 (#4)

Satan's Devils MC - Utah Chapter

Road Tripped (#1)

Stormy's Thunder (#2)

Satan's Devils MC - Las Vegas Chapter

Red's Peril - Part 1

Red's Peril - Part 2

Wicked Warriors MC - Arizona Chapter

Warts an' All

Tickety Tock

ABOUT THE AUTHOR

Manda's life's always seemed a bit weird, starting with a childhood that even today she's still trying to make sense of, then losing her parents in the late teens. Going from the tragic to the bizarre, who else could be unlucky enough to have had two car accidents, neither her fault, one involving a nun, and another involving a police woman?

There isn't enough space to list everything that's happened to Manda, or what she's learned from it. But by using the rich fabric of her personal life, psychology degree, varied work experiences, and amazing characters she's met, Manda is able to populate her books with believable in-depth characters and enjoys pitting them against situations which challenge them. Her books are full of suspense, twists and turns and the unexpected.

Manda lives in the beautiful countryside of Essex in the UK, the area's claim to fame being the Wilkin's Jam Factory at nearby Tiptree. She can usually find jars of jam which remind her of home wherever she goes. As well as writing books and reading, Manda loves walking her dogs and keeping fit. She lives with her husband of over 30 years, who, along with her son, is her greatest fan and supporter.

Manda is thankful that one of the more unusual, and at the time unpleasant, turns her life took, now enables her to spend her time writing. Confirming, in her view, every cloud has a silver lining.

Photo by Carmel Jane Photography